DARKWOLF

RESURRECTION

E. Don Harpe

Flint River Press

Ellijay, GA

E. Don Harpe

Flint River Press - Ellijay, GA 35040
ISBN-13: 978-0692625910 (Flint River Press)
ISBN-10: 0692625917

This book is dedicated to my wife Helen, and to my chidren, Shelly, Jason, Nikki, and Derek, all of whom have never wavered in their faith in me and my writing.

It is dedicated to Keith Vinsonhaler, who saw promise in the early work I was doing on the Harpe books, and encouraged me to follow the dream.

It is dedicated Alexandria Altman, who has never wavered in her support of me and my work, and who has been there at every turn to back me up and to do all she could to muster interest in the finished Harpe books.

First last and always, it is dedicated to my father, Birtle Odell Harp, who was the Harpe before me, and to my mother, Lena Walker Harp, who gave me the gift of loving to read and write. I think of them daily, and miss their wisdom and guidance.

I told the fictionalized account of the Harpes in my first book, *born wolf, Die Wolf,* and when I managed to secure my publishing back, I re-edited it, and re-released it as *DarkWolf Unleashed.*

DarkWolf Unleashed took place in the years between 1780 and 1799, and is the retelling of the Harpe brothers store. They have been called *America's First Serial Killers,* and their story is one of history's most fascinating action stories. In researching and finally writing the book, I came to like the characters, and I began to wonder what might happen if two brutal men such as the Harpes were turned loose on today's society. What might happen if they were traveling through the same part of the country as they did back then, killing with the rage and abandon they did in 1799.

This is a tale of two of histories most prolific killers brought back to life today through supernatural means, and set upon a path of destruction that leaves bodies strewn along the way like firewood. The mystical fury of the DarkWolf is driving the brothers to seek out the Harpe Amulet, and to kill anyone who dares to stand in their way.

DarkWolf: Resurrection is a wild ride down through Kentucky from the spot on Green River where Micajah was killed in 1799, and up through Mississippi, from the gallows in Greenville where Wiley was hanged in 1804. The Wolf is loose, rampaging again, and it's a hit or miss proposition as to whether or not the combined powers of Jake Trabue, Daniel Hawk, and Andrew Stegall will be enough to stop them.

The Harpes are coming.

Again!

PROLOGUE

In 1804, some five years after the death of Micajah Harpe, Wiley Harpe was recognized and arrested in Greenville, Mississippi, where he stood trial for his crimes. He was quickly found guilty and sentenced to be hanged, but simply hanging him wasn't enough. Not only did the good gentry of Greenville hang Little Harpe, after a day on the gallows the body was taken down and the head cut off. They nailed the head to a stout pole in a field at the edge of town, where it remained for many years.

A few miles outside Greenville, Kentucky, in the forks of a tree rested the grinning skull of Big Harpe, and a few miles from Greenville, Mississippi, on the pole in a killing field rested the head of Little Harpe. A sigh of relief went up in the settlements as the people learned the reign of terror of two of the most violent killers in the history of the country had finally ended.

So everyone thought.

In the shadows of the cave in the spirit world, the Wolf slumbered, waiting only for a call from the Harpe to awaken.

In August of 1799, when Micajah was run to ground and killed, the cry rang throughout the settlements.

"The Big Harpe is dead. Tis true I say. They've killed the Wolf, and his head is nailed up in a tree. I've seen it myself. Have ye heard the news, the Big Harpe is dead."

All along the frontier the settlers passed the word. The most feared killer of all had been caught and killed, and his head had been nailed in the forks of a sturdy oak tree for the world to see.

Relieved faces were abundant as each new person learned the Harpe was dead. The men knew they no longer had to worry about a monster such as the Harpe coming to their cabin and killing their women and children. The women were happy that once again their men could walk the forest trails in relative safety, and would reach their destination without running into the vicious wild wolves called the Terrible Harpes.

Throughout much of Kentucky and Tennessee, it was as though a violent storm had passed. The Wilderness Road was passable again, without fear of the vicious rage of the Harpes.

The brothers left behind a torn and twisted legacy of terror and bloodshed, but with the 1799 death of Micajah and the 1804 hanging of Wiley Harpe, at last the storm was over. The Harpes were a force of nature that had touched the lives of every man, woman and child in the territory. And now they were gone.

As the word spread, the lives of the settlers began to return to normal, and many of the more courageous traveled to the cross roads to view the head of the man they had once feared so much.

The small community near the crossroads eventually came to be called "Harpshead," and the road called "Harpshead Road." There were few in the country that could not tell a stranger how to find Harpshead, and most were more than happy to spend a moment of two relating the gruesome tale of the outlaws and their women to any travelers who didn't already know the story.

In the days following his death, to those who came to view the head, there was no doubt Micajah Harpe was truly dead. There was no mistaking that awful countenance. The spike that held the head had already begun to rust, but for years there remained faint traces of a reddish substance on it, and many thought it was the blood of the outlaw that stained the iron. Eventually the hair fell out and the flesh rotted away, as the birds and the elements took their toll.

Still, deep in the vacant eye sockets, it appeared as if the skull were watching, waiting for something, keeping vigilance over the crossroads and the people who visited there. More than one traveler swore he felt a burning gaze from the skull as he rode beneath the tree.

Even in broad daylight, strong men felt the bumps rise on their necks as they walked the trail, and almost everyone avoided the crossroads when night had fallen.

The men who took part in the killing of Micajah Harpe stayed clear of the spot. They remembered all too well the promise made by the Harpe to return.

"Yer a damned rough butcher, but cut on and be damned," the Harpe had said, as Moses Stegall drew the knife around his neck. "I am the Harpe, the Wolf, and I can't be killed. I'll return, for I am yer death and destruction."

These words haunted John Leiper. They kept him awake at night, and he heard them rustling through the leaves in the trees as he rode in the forest. He collected his gold, but he would never go near the crossroads again.

The words came stealing into the cabin of Matthew Christian in the middle of the night, waking him in a cold sweat, and causing him to arm himself and sit at the door of his cabin staring out into the darkness.

Most of all the last words of the Harpe forever after whispered in the mind of Moses Stegall. Stegall knew much more than the others about the Harpe, and about the Wolf. He knew it was not a question of if the Harpe was coming back, but when. Stegall knew the Wolf could not die, that it was an evil spirit and was only waiting for the time to be right to return.

Stegall took Harpe's long knife home with him, and spent countless hours sitting at his tiny kitchen table, staring at the knife and reflecting on the ghastly deeds of his past. He whiled away the hours sharpening the knife, keeping it as keen as a razor. The blade gleamed and shimmered in the light of the oil lamp that Stegall kept burning at all times, night and day.

From seasoned oak he fashioned a case for the knife, and lined it with two thicknesses of blood red velvet. He locked the case with a sturdy padlock, and placed the key on a leather thong he wore around his neck until the day he died.

Stegall passed the story of the Harpes down to his son, along with the key to the case, and bade him to pass it along to his first-born son. He recited the admonition over and over that the Harpe would return, until his son was caught up in the same terror that lived in Moses' heart.

"Listen," he told his son. "Listen well to this story for there may come a day when these words will save your life. Till this day I recall the words of the Harpe, and I recall the sound the nail made as I pounded it into his dead and bloody skull. Thud. Thud. Thud. Thud. The nail sounded as I struck it with the hammer and drove it through flesh and bone. Remember well that sound, for when ye hear it onct again, t'will mean the monster has come back. Remember the sound, and understand that one day it will sound in yer mind even as it now sounds in mine. On the fateful day when ye hear the sound, the Wolf will be back, and will onct again be hunting men to feed upon. No man will be safe, and certainly not one that bears the name Stegall."

Moses Stegall could be seen at times riding about the tree where the skull still rested, staring at the head and mumbling to himself. All too well he knew the Harpe, and all too much he feared the Wolf.

During the time when the DarkWolf and Micajah Harpe were one and the same, the Wolf realized the day would come when Harpe would lose his life doing battle with one or another of his enemies. Not even the power of the spirit world could hold off the power of Fate. No matter how strongly the spark of life burned, in the end, the grim angel of Death won every battle. The body of the Harpe would die, and the Wolf would have to retreat back into his own world. Knowing this, the Wolf laid his plans well.

The Wolf knew the power of the Amulet could awaken him, and all that had to be done was for the Amulet to be placed about the neck of a first-born Harpe son. Once this happened, the doorway

10

between the two worlds would open, and the Wolf would be free to hunt once again.

However, being the most cunning of the forest spirits, the Wolf devised a secondary plan. He sent a bit of energy into the great knives the Harpe carried, and caused Micajah to hide one of them in a crevice deep inside Cave In Rock. Should a Harpe child find that knife, the spiritual energy of Micajah Harpe and the DarkWolf would be released into that child, and that energy would once again unite the forces of the two worlds.

The plan of the Wolf was twofold, and was well prepared. When the time came that Micajah fought his final battle, the Wolf was ready. The day the Harpe fell, the Wolf gathered the energy of the dying man and enclosed it within a circle of the scared blue flame.

So it was that even as the body of Micajah Harpe died, the energy of the being known as The Harpe lived on. With a final curse at the murderers of Micajah Harpe, the Wolf withdrew into the spirit world; there to remain until one or the other of his well laid plans come to fruition.

For countless years the Wolf slumbered deep inside the spirit world's chilly cavern. He slept the deep peaceful sleep of an innocent child, restful and unencumbered by dreams. Time meant nothing to the Wolf, and only the growing hunger within told him that years were passing by in the world of man.

Occasionally some small thing would bridge the gap between the human world and the place where the Wolf slept, and at those times one eye would open slightly and a blue flame would flicker for a few moments. But there never came a call from the Harpe, and the Wolf never fully awakened.

In 1849, Micajah's first grandson was born. James named him Thornton, and when the midwife slapped him on the behind and he uttered his first cry, the eyes of the Wolf slowly opened. He looked around the cave and saw only darkness, and let his vision shift to the eyes in Micajah's skull. Though the physical skull had long since disappeared, the spiritual presense of the skull still rested in the forks of the tree, keeping vigilance over the crossroad as it had since the day it was nailed there. The Wolf looked out across the road and saw nothing of interest, not even one single traveler. He listened for a few moments but when the Harpe child did not call out to him, he once again closed his eyes and continued with his sleep.

More and more settlers came down into Kentucky and Tennessee, and the land changed. Trees gave way to houses, and more and more roads began to crisscross the wilderness.

In 1861 the Wolf's eyes suddenly snapped open. Even deep within the confines of the spirit world, he could feel the awful tension that wracked the world of men. Yet, even though the next few years were the worst the young country had ever seen, not once did the Harpe call upon the Wolf.

Thornton had three daughters, but his firstborn male child came in 1901, and was named James after his father. Once again the Wolf waited, and again was not summoned. The blue flames flickered briefly and the hunger grew.

Odell Harp was born in 1940, and with his first cry the Wolf felt more intensity than he had felt in a generation. He yawned, opened his eyes, and once again peered through the eyes of the skull. He was not prepared for what he saw. There were houses and people everywhere, and strange machines roared along paved roads. With a low growl, the Wolf prepared himself for one more short nap.

In 1988, two hundred and twenty years to the day from the day Micajah Harpe was born, another firstborn Harpe child drew his first breath. He was Odell's child, and they named him James William Harp, and called him Billy. When he was born the eyes of the Wolf snapped wide open. The blue flame danced in all its wild fury, and the hunger inside his belly grew to gigantic proportions. The Wolf had no doubts. This child was the one. He was the Harpe, the chosen, and he had finally returned. Soon would the boy know the hunger, even as the Wolf had known it for the past two hundred years.

As Billy grew, now and then the Wolf would open his eyes and watch for a moment or so. He watched for any sign of weakness in the boy, ready to breach the line between the two worlds and send part of his spirit to reinforce the boy's resolve, but not once did he find a single chink in the boy's armor. Occasionally, when Billy would injure himself, the Wolf would send the energy through the gate to aid in his healing, and more than once he sent tiny fingerlings of wildness slithering through the darkness between the two worlds and into the boys mind.

The boy grew strong and brave, ready to face anything life threw at him, never once suspecting the presence of the Wolf, never knowing of the coming battle.

Billy was eleven the first time the Wolf touched him with the rage.

Billy had a brand new pocketknife his father had given him just a few weeks before. He had sharpened in until he could shave the soft hair on his arm with it, and had practiced getting it out of his pocket and opening it as quickly as possible. He was very fast with it, never knowing it was a talent he was born to.

It was Halloween, and Billy had collected a large bag of candy on his trick or treat rounds of the neighborhood. He had told the last of his friends' goodnight and continued home alone, never once thinking to be afraid of the bigger kids that lived nearby.

As Billy passed the last street light before he reached his own home, he heard a voice softly call to him from the darkness.

"Hey, Harp," the voice said, "come over here for a minute."

Billy walked over to the tall hedge where the words had come from.

"Who's there?" he asked.

"It's just me and Tommy," he heard a rough voice say, and recognized it as belonging to Buck Hendricks, one of the biggest bullies in school.

"What do you want, Buck," Billy asked, his own voice sounding loud in his ears. He realized the two of them were probably going to try and beat him up, and though he wasn't afraid of them, he'd really just as soon pass on fighting them both.

The two of them stepped out from behind the hedge and stood in the pale yellow glow of the small streetlight, staring at Billy with open hostility.

"Don't worry, Harp, we just want to talk to you. And maybe eat a little bit of that trick or treat candy you got in the bag. We ain't going to hurt you."

Stepping back a step, Billy slowly eased his hand into his pocket where the knife rested.

The knife was warm from being in Billy's pocket, and at the same time that Billy's hand touched the steel of the blade, deep in the cave on the sprit world, the eyes of the wolf snapped open. The wolf peered through Billy's eyes and saw the two bigger boys, and without a thought he sent a small hunger pang through the gate and into Billy's mind.

Yeah, I know, Billy whispered, in response to the thought of the DarkWolf. Billy took a deep breath, and his voice was quieter now. For some reason he had suddenly become very calm.

The steel of the knife felt familiar as Billy drew it from his pocket and opened it. As the blade unfolded, something strange happened. A feeling came over Billy that he had never felt before, and a tiny blue flame began to flicker deep in his eyes.

"No, I know you're not going to hurt me," Billy said, whipping the knife open and holding it in front of him. The blade caught a tiny ray of light from the overhead street light and gleamed yellow in the darkness. A wolf's tooth made of old ivory may have gleamed in much the same way.

14

"I've got a sharp knife and a short temper, boys, and I'll cut you if I have to. And I'll only tell you the one time."

Perhaps it was the knife in Billy's hand, or perhaps they heard something in his voice that told them he was deadly serious. They may have even seen the faint glow in his eyes and recognized something that struck fear in their hearts, but whatever it was, it was enough to convince them to leave him alone. Turning away from Billy, the two bullies began to step back through the hedge.

"Just a minute," Billy said. "You'll be wanting to know the next time I hear of you two bullies beating up one of the little kids, you'll have to answer to me. And I won't be playing any games with you." Without another word, Billy left the two boys standing by the hedge and walked on down the street toward his house.

He was almost home before he noticed he still held the open knife in his hand, and only then was the urge in his heart to use it beginning to fade.

The wolf smiled and closed his eyes.

Yesss, the Harpe is back. Soon will we hunt. Hurry Harpe, I hungggerrrrrrrr

During the next few years the Wolf visited Billy Harp several times, each time bringing Billy closer to the day when he would be ready to become as one with the Wolf. Ready to take up the mantle of the Harpe and resume the hunt.

The Wolf knew it was only a matter of time before Billy found either the Amulet or the Blade. Either would do. There was no doubt in the mind of the Wolf that the Harpe had returned, and the world would once again tremble. The Wolf is dead! Long live the Wolf!

####

BILLY HARP
CAVE IN ROCK, ILLINOIS - FRIDAY - LAST WEEK

Dexter Morgan and his brother Ronnie were sitting at a corner table with Jimmy Ellis when Billy Harp walked into the café in cave In Rock. The three of them had been laid off from the factory for over a month, and they'd taken to having lunch together in the Main Street Cafe a couple of times a week. They could come in, get a good plate lunch at a good price, and talk about how rough times were and try to figure out how they might make a little money to help stretch their unemployment checks.

Work was scarce around the area, and the small unemployment checks they drew weren't enough to pay their bills and keep gas in their trucks and their boats. All three men had been known to rustle up a few dollars anyway they could once in awhile.

Just last weekend they'd driven over to Owensboro and held up a small convenience market, and the week before that they'd hit a Quick Stop in Evansville. In both robberies combined they'd only managed to steal a little over five hundred dollars, and that was already gone. Now they sat in the Main Street Cafe eating their late lunch and trying to figure out another way to score.

"It's just getting a little more risky than I like," Jimmy said, when Dexter brought up the question of robbing yet another store. "They're watching for us on both sides of the river, and if that damned girl you shot in Evansville dies, they'll be hotter than ever."

"Damnit, you don't have to keep on remindin' me about that," Dexter exclaimed. "It wasn't my fault. I told her not to holler, but did she listen? Oh no. She had to start screamin' her damned ugly head off. I didn't mean to really pull the trigger, but I got so damned rattled that it just happened. So shut up about it. I don't give a damn if she dies or not. Now are you going with me and Ronnie to hit that little gas station we talked about, or are you just going to sit up here like a little girl?"

"Dex, you know I'm in, I...oops, hang on, take a look at what just walked in." Jimmy motioned with his head at Billy Harp as he walked over and sat down at a side booth.

Dexter and Ronnie slowly turned and looked over at Billy, trying to be as casual as possible. "Check 'im out, Ronnie," Dexter said. "Big sumbitch ain't he?"

"Bigger they are, harder their ass hits the ground," Ronnie answered. He had a weighted baseball bat behind the seat of his truck just in case he ran into a big guy who wasn't afraid of them. "I'll knock his brains out if he screws with me.

The three men sat and watched as Billy ordered his meal, and listened as he talked with Helen for a few minutes. They heard him say he was going to the cave this afternoon, and exchanged a few knowing looks between themselves as they got up and left the restaurant.

He might be big, but once the three of them got him alone down by the cave, big wasn't going to be enough. They'd take what money he had, and if he gave them any crap, they'd beat his butt. Or worse.

It was about four-thirty in the afternoon when Billy started down the concrete steps that led to the cave, so he knew there would be plenty of light for a few more hours. Light was important, because Billy wanted to see as much of the cave as he could today.

He stopped about half way down the steps and looked out across the river. Once again he wondered how the river must have looked some two hundred years ago.

For a moment he closed his eyes and let his imagination take him back through the years. He could almost see an old flat-bottomed boat coming down the river, with the men poling along, trying to avoid the rocks and hold the boat on a steady course.

Billy had read how the pirates along the Ohio had plied their trade, and it wasn't hard to imagine the scene.

The mighty Ohio river was known for dealing death and devastation to inexperienced travelers who insisted on making the trip downriver without the aid of a captain who knew the treacherous rapids and sinkholes, not to mention the many other dangerous places where the river ran its wildest. Most of the immigrants knew little about boating, and without help would have lost all they owned to the river. What they didn't know was that when they accepted the help of some of the men who posed as guides, there was a chance they would lose all they owned to the pirates, and, more often than not, they would lose their lives at the same time.

It was a common practice for one of the pirates to ride upstream, offer to guide an unwary party past the dangers on the river, and then lead them directly into an ambush.

When the boat approached the ambush site, the inside man would have the party pull the boat to the river bank, where his comrades lay hidden among the trees. As soon as the boat touched ground, the pirates would swarm out of their hiding places and quickly overcome the men in the party. After that, the pirates unloaded the cargo and the boat went to the bottom of the river, joining the many others already there. The members of the boat's party were either killed, or, if they happened to be a person or persons of some substance, sometimes they were held for ransom. The pirates had adapted the old adage that dead men tell no tales, and usually they left no one alive to identify them, or to testify against them should they ever be caught.

As Billy looked at the profusion of trees and undergrowth that lined the banks of the river, he decided it had probably changed very little in these past two hundred years. Except for the roads and the ferry, and of course the concrete steps leading down to the cave itself, the cave and the river were pretty much unchanged.

Billy wasn't sure how long the town of Cave In Rock had been there, but he guessed it was probably originally settled either by the descendants of the pirates themselves, or by some of their victims, or a combination of both. Of course, he wasn't sure about that. He made a note to ask the waitress if she knew how long the town had been there. Maybe he could find out tomorrow.

Billy had continued down the steps while he was thinking, and all at once he found himself standing in front of the cave. Looking around the mammoth opening, he realized he didn't really have a clue about what he'd come here to find. All at once he found his arms covered with chill bumps. Although it was a typical scorching hot August afternoon, a cool wind blew from the cave and caressed his body, causing him to shiver.

Walking inside the cave was like taking a step back into history. The present was gone, and it was easy to see the huge cavern as it must have been in 1799, when the Harpes rode out of here on their last rampage.

Billy took a deep breath, and began walking deeper into the darkness of the cave. He was startled when he suddenly heard a man's rough voice, low and menacing.

"Hey pal, you got a light?" the voice said.

Billy squinted his eyes and peered into the deeper shadows inside the cave and was surprised to see the three men who'd been in the cafe.

"Yeah, I think so," Billy said, and pulled his lighter out of his pocket and walked over to the men.

"Thanks, buddy," one of them said, "got any money?"

"Wha..." Billy began, when suddenly the larger of the men launched a quick right fist into Billy's face.

Jimmy Ellis's big fist caught Billy high on the side of his cheek and knocked him backward some four or five feet. Before he could recover, the man was on him again, hitting him first in the belly and then again in the face. Billy fell to the floor of the cave and tried to cover his head with his arms. He knew he had to fight back or else the men would kill him right here.

He lurched to his feet and plunged into a headlong dive at Ellis's legs, grabbing the man around the knees and throwing him backward. With all his strength, Billy pushed away from the man and managed to throw one long looping punch that only barely connected, and didn't seem to do much damage. Billy shook his head and was bringing his right arm back preparing to swing again, when Ronnie Morgan got in on the action.

Ronnie had brought along his favorite weapon. A solid ash baseball bat, loaded with almost a half pound of lead. With a grunt he swung the bat in a tight half circle and smashed it into the back of Billy's head with enough force to drive Billy to his knees. With an oath, he swung the bat a second time, this time hitting Billy in the shoulder, and would have hit him a third time had not Dexter stepped in and stopped him.

"Wait a minute, Ronnie, don't kill him. At least, don't kill him yet. I got a better idea. Remember the stories about them old boys that used to hide in the cave? Remember the one where they tied the feller on his horse and blindfolded both of them, then run 'em over the bluffs? What 'd ya say? Want to try? This guy rode in here on a motorcycle. That's kinda like a horse. C'mon, let's take the rest of this fight to the top of the cliffs."

A wild glint flashed in Ronnie Morgan's eyes. The vision of a man astride a horse plunging off the cliffs ran through his mind, and was quickly replaced by a vision of a man on a motorcycle.

"Damnit, Dex, that's a hell of an idea. Let's do it."

He grabbed Billy by the hair and roughly jerked him to his feet. "C'mon feller, get on your feet," he said. "You're too big for us to carry. Haul yourself up them stairs, your motorcycle is waiting for you."

Billy rubbed a hand across his face, then felt the back of his head where the bat had smashed it. His hand was covered with blood when he brought it back down, but he hardly noticed it. He staggered a few feet toward the entrance to the cave, and felt himself violently pushed from behind.

He staggered forward into the cave wall, and then turned to look at his attackers. Jimmy was picking himself from the floor of the cave where Billy's blow had sent him. Ronnie had a huge grin on his face like the cat that swallowed the canary, and was still holding the bloody bat in his right hand, every so often hitting the palm of his left hand with it. His left hand was covered with a smear of Billy's blood.

But it wasn't really the bat that bothered Billy. It was the .38 special Dexter Morgan casually held in his right hand. It was pointed at the floor of the cave, but Billy knew it would only take a moment to be in firing position. He knew what, or rather who, the target would be.

"Get it in gear, city boy," Jimmy half shouted. "I'll kick you all the way up the stairs if I have to." He grabbed Billy and threw him against the side of the cave wall, then kicked him as he stumbled.

"Damnit, I said move it," Jimmy said, and kicked Billy again, as Dexter motioned with the pistol for Billy to start walking.

Billy half stumbled, half fell to the front of the cave and around the small path to the foot of the stairs. He looked up the stairs and didn't think he had the strength to climb them.

He shouldn't have worried about it.

The three men would help him make it, all the way to the top.

With oaths and kicks, and a lot of well placed punches, the trio made its way up concrete stairs. The Morgan Brothers and Jimmy Ellis laughed out loud on more than one occasion as they saw their victim fall into the hard concrete of the stairway.

Blood was streaming from a half dozen or more cuts on Billy's body when they finally reached the top of the stairs.

Ronnie grabbed Billy by one arm and the back of his head and roughly pushed him to the ground. The blow with the ball bat to the back of Billy's head had dazed him, probably given him a concussion, and for all practical purposes had ended Billy's chances of winning the fight. As big as he was, he might have been able to hold his own with the three of them, or else somehow gotten away, had it not been for the smashing blow of the Louisville Slugger. Now it seemed likely he was going to die here in this place where the old Harpe brothers had raised so much hell so many years ago.

As he lay face down on the ground and felt one of the men digging through his pocket and grabbing his motorcycle key and his wallet, he thought how ironic it was. It was the Harpe brothers, maybe his ancestors, who had driven man and horse off the cliffs almost two hundred years ago, and now here he was, about to experience the same thing, only from the other perspective.

He lay there for a moment, gathering his strength for one last effort, determined to fight to the last.

Risking a quick glance, he saw the one named Ronnie walking around about ten feet from where he lay, and Dexter had disappeared behind a tree to take a leak. Billy rolled over and pushed himself up on one elbow and looked around for a stick or a big rock or something he could use for a weapon. There was absolutely nothing within reaching distance.

He had decided to just jump up and attack the two men, when all at once he heard the other one coming back.

"Damnit Ronnie, there was too many people down in the parking lot for me to get the bike. Guess we'll just have to throw him off the cliff."

"Well damn, Jimmy, I wanted to run that bike over the cliff and see how far out it would go before it started down. Sheee-it."

As the last word left Ronnie's lips, Billy took his chance. With a grunt, he pushed himself to his feet and jumped at the nearest man, that happened to be Jimmy. He threw a roundhouse right and grinned as it landed squarely on Jimmy's chin. The man spun around and hit the ground like a felled oak tree. Billy kicked him once in the side, and then felt one of the other men grab him from behind.

Ronnie spun Billy around and shoved him into the man lying on the ground. Billy's legs got tangled up and he tripped and fell, and looked up just in time to see Dexter swing the pistol straight at his head. Then the lights went out.

When Billy next opened his eyes, he was standing on the edge of the highest damned cliff he ever seen. *Damn,* he thought, *we must be close to two hundred feet high.*

"We're way up here, ain't we hoss?" he heard one of the men say.

"Take a good look boy, cause in a minute you're gonna be flyin' right out there with that little bird."

"Go ahead, you dirty sonsobitches," Billy said, "shove me off. And if you're on speaking terms with God, you better make your peace. If the fall don't kill me, I'll see you back in town in a few days. If it does, I'll look you up when you get to hell. Either way, my day is coming. Push me boys, push me and be damned."

The words were barely out of his mouth when he felt a terrific blow to his back and suddenly found himself flying out over the bluff, headed for the dark waters below. The last thing he heard was the wild laughter of the three men as they stood and watched him fall.

He tried to bring his feet together and point them downward, but wasn't sure if he made it or not. He lost consciousness at some point during the fall, and never knew when his hurtling body struck the surface of the river.

Just before he hit the water, Billy's last fleeting thought was; *How did I manage to get myself in this mess?*

BILLY HARP
SATURDAY - TWO WEEKS AGO

James William Harp, Billy to almost everyone who knew him, was visiting with his friends Jack and Kate Wilson in Owensboro, Kentucky.

They spent some time at Jack's farm and made a few trips into nearby Evansville, Indiana, and it had been a good visit. But although Billy always enjoyed the visits with Jack and Kate, he was looking forward to getting back home tomorrow. Billy lived in a small one bedroom apartment a few miles North of Nashville, and while the size of the place sometimes made him feel a little closed in, he felt more comfortable there than almost anywhere else.

The air conditioner hummed softly, holding at bay the heat from the late August evening. Billy was sitting talking with Jack in the large, comfortable living room when the conversation took a turn that was destined to change Billy's life forever.

"Say Billy," Jack said, "did you know there used to be community not far from here named after the Harp family? Might still be there for all I know. It was just a little wide spot in the road. Named Harpshead, as I recall."

"Harpshead?" Billy answered. "Why would anyone name a town something as ridiculous as Harpshead? This is just another of your wild old stories, ain't it?"

"Now Billy," Jack answered, "in the first place I don't tell any 'wild old stories' as you call 'em, and in the second place, I can tell you pretty close to where that old town is, or was, and how it got its name. Of course, if you don't want to know..." Jack let the words fade away.

"Well, if this isn't some kind of joke you're trying to play," Billy said, "then why don't you just tell me about this Harpshead?"

"You got it, son," Jack said. "Now the best I could ever narrow it down, Harpshead was somewhere down in Union County, just outside a town called Dixon. Take Highway 41 South and there should be an old country road that'll take you right to Harpshead. I'm pretty sure the town ain't there no more, but you should be able to find someone who can show you where it used to be."

"So what's the story on that name, Jack?" Billy replied, "You've gotta admit it's pretty strange."

"That it is, my boy, that it is. I know you've read of the old outlaw Harpe brothers who terrorized the country back in the late seventeen hundreds. Well, the story is that when the brother they called the Big Harpe was finally caught and killed, his head was cut off and nailed up in a tree. The little community where that happened became known as Harpshead. Folks from all over came to see the head, and..."

His wife Kate interrupted Jack as she came into the room with a freshly brewed pot of steaming coffee.

"You boys want me to freshen up your cups?" she asked.

"Don't mind if I do, Miss Kate," Billy smiled his answer back at her. "And you might even force me into one more little piece of that apple pie you made this afternoon."

Kate laughed and went back into the kitchen for the pie. She always baked for Billy when he came to visit, and Billy suspected she was trying to make up for the meals she probably thought he wasn't getting at home.

"Now, where was I," Jack said, blowing the steam off the coffee before taking a taste. "Oh yeah. How much have you read about the Harpes, Billy?"

"Not much. After you told me about them, I borrowed the book from the library, but I haven't much more than opened it. I read about them living in Knoxville and killing some people, but that's about all."

"Well, if you really are interested, you might want to see if you can find Harpshead. It shouldn't be too far out of your way when you start home tomorrow. You said you were wanting to break in that new motorcycle of yours a little more anyway."

"I gotta admit the story has me interested," Billy said. "Tell you what. When I leave here, maybe I will see if I can find the place. Hell, there's no telling what I might be able to dig up. You don't think those old boys could be ancestors of mine, do you?"

"Well, I don't know," Jack said. "but if they are, I sure hope none of that homicidal crap got passed down to you. Sometimes you act like you ain't got good sense, but I don't think you're dangerous."

"Dangerous hell," Billy laughed, "I ain't got a dangerous bone in my body, and I'll kill any man that says I have. Well, I think I'll turn in, get me a good nights sleep, and leave early in the morning."

"Goodnight, boy," Jack said, as Billy left the room.

Turning to Kate, Jack had a rare moment of clairvoyance.

"You know Kate, I've got the funniest feeling I shouldn't have told Billy about Harpshead. I don't know why, but I've got a feeling it might not have been the smartest thing I ever did."

"Well," Kate sighed, "you've done a few things in your time that weren't real bright, but for the most part they've always worked out fine. This will too, just wait and see."

"I hope so, Kate, I really hope so."

But Jack didn't get much sleep that night. The feeling just wouldn't let him go.

SUNDAY

Billy's night was not very restful either. He woke up several times during the night and had trouble getting back to sleep. When he did sleep, his dreams were troubled by vague faces with strange voices, whispering words he couldn't understand, and somewhere way in the back of the dream was what sounded like a baby crying.

The third time Billy awoke it was twenty till five, and he decided to stay up.

He lay in bed for about half an hour, smoking cigarettes and thinking. When he heard Kate stirring about in the kitchen, he dressed and went in for his first cup of coffee.

After two or three more cups of coffee, a plate of scrambled eggs and bacon, and some of Kate's home made biscuits, Billy told Jack and Kate his goodbyes and headed his motorcycle out of Owensboro and down toward Dixon. He didn't actually have a lot of faith in finding a community called Harpshead, but he was intrigued by the story, and besides, he was in no hurry to get home. Anyway, Jack was right. Billy did want to ride his new bike a little more.

It wasn't really a new bike , it was just new to Billy. He'd bought it from a friend at work, and this was the first time he'd had the opportunity to get it out on the open road. If there was one thing Billy loved, it was to ride a big, powerful motorcycle out through the open countryside. He felt more alive at those moments than at any other.

He took his time cruising down the two-lane blacktop toward Dixon. It was beautiful country, and even though Billy had never been through there before, he began to notice some of the landmarks seemed hauntingly familiar. It was strange, but now and then he thought he could almost recognize the way the hills lay against the sky. The closer he got to Dixon, the more familiar the country became, and once he even stopped the bike and sat staring down across a little valley, and could almost swear he'd been there before. Been there more than once. Several times in fact.

This is crazy, he thought. I know damn well I've never seen this place before today.

It was the middle of the morning when Billy got to the outskirts of Dixon. He rode around for an hour, but had no idea where to begin looking for Harpshead, so he finally stopped at a little country store and went in to see if there was anyone who might help him.

He had the old man at the counter make him a sandwich of a thick slice of fresh bologna, with a huge slice of home grown tomato on top, then he grabbed an ice cold bottled cola and went out on the front porch of the store to eat his lunch in the shade.

Outside the store, two men who looked as ancient as the Kentucky hills sat hunched over an equally ancient looking checkerboard, moving a faded red or black checker every now and then, and taking turns cackling and cussing at each other.

Billy sat down in an old straight backed chair, tilted it against the wall, and watched the checker game as he ate his lunch, chuckling under his breath at the antics of the two old men. By the time he was finished with the sandwich, he was sure he didn't want to play either of them in a game. They'd beat him with one eye closed.

He looked again at the two men and decided to ask them if they knew anything about Harpshead.

He rocked forward and let the front legs of his chair touch the plank porch, then stood up and walked the few feet to where they were about ready to begin a new game.

"Howdy, fellers," Billy said, "do ya mind if I ask you a question?"

Neither of the men looked up from the checker board, but one of them spat out a long thick stream of ugly brown tobacco juice in the general direction of a an old tin can that sat about six feet away on the ground and replied.

"Damnation, young feller, can't you see we're a'playin' a game here?"

"Yes sir, I see that, and I'd damn sure hate to have to play either of you boys. I just got one quick question. Won't take but a minute of your time."

"Well, now that you've disturbed us, go ahead and ask away. Ain't none too sure neither one of us will have an answer fer you, though. We're just two dumb old country rednecks who spend all their time playing checkers." The two old men looked at each other and each let out a cackle. This wasn't the first time this had happened, and Billy could tell they were putting him on.

"Well, I wanted to know if there used to be, or if there still is, a little community around here named Harpshead. S'posed to have been where they nailed some old outlaws head up in a tree. I heard part of the story, and I was just a little interested."

"You a Harp, boy?" one of the men asked.

"Yes sir, I am," Billy replied, "that's why I'm interested."

"You ain't the first Harp that's come a' smellin' round up here looking for Harpshead, you know," the old man said, finally looking up from the checker board. He fixed Billy with a quizzical stare.

"I'm not?" Billy was a little surprised. He hadn't thought that other Harps might have had the same idea.

"Naw, you're not. Ever few years, now and agin' somebody named Harp will read them old stories and decide to come pokin' round. Ain't none of 'em ever found a damn thing yet. Course, could be you might get lucky." He looked at the other man for a minute, a question on his face.

For the first time the other man also looked up from the board, and stared for a minute at Billy.

The first man now stood up and voiced his question aloud.

"Pete, take a good look at this here young feller's eyes. Ain't they just about the strangest color blue you ever did see?" Turning to Billy he said, "Bend down, young feller, and let Pete see your eyes. You gottta get close, cuz he don't see too good anymore."

The man called Pete took an old pair of wire-rimmed glasses from the bib of his faded overalls and placed them on the end of his nose. "Bend down boy, and let me see them eyes," he echoed.

"What the hell is this," Billy said. "You two old farts want to answer my question, or do you just want to sit around staring into my baby blues?"

"Don't get smart with me, young feller, or I'll knock you on your butt. Them blue eyes of your'n is the only reason you're fixin' to get a damn thing from us. Now hold down here and let me see 'em."

Billy sat down in the chair and stared for a long moment into the bespectacled watery eyes of the old man called Pete.

Pete and the other man exchanged several glances, and finally seemed to come to some kind of silent agreement between themselves.

"Like Clay said," Pete went on, nodding at the other man, "you ain't the first Harp that's come pokin' round here lookin' for Harpshead. We've showed several of 'em where the old town is supposed to be, and they've went out ooin' and ahin' round the field for a while, then went back home just as happy as a pig in slop. But you're the first one, to my knowledge least ways, that's got the Harp eyes. Folks round here heard all the stories bout the Harpes, including the one where Big Harpe told old Stegall he was a'comin' back from the dead one of these days. Now we don't necessarily believe that crap, but we was never folks for taking chances. Anyway, we just decided not to show anybody the true location where that old tree used to stand. The one where they nailed up Harpe's head. Well, by God, with them eyes, maybe you ought to see the real place where the tree used to be. What do you think, Clay, want to take him on out there?"

"Maybe you're right, Pete. His eyes shore do look like the old stories said the Harpe's eyes looked. He might be the one. Hell, yeah. I say let's show him the place. Foller us, boy," Pete said, "hit's just a short drive from here."

The two old men climbed into a half rusted out old Ford pick-up truck, cranked the engine and took off down the road, not waiting to see if Billy followed.

Billy wasted no time in jumping on his bike and roaring off in pursuit of the truck. Pete was driving as if he was racing at Daytona, and Billy was choking on the dust.

That's when he had the wreck.

He remembered turning onto an old dirt road, hardly more than a wide path really, and that was when he first heard the damned pounding in his head.

Thud. Thud. Thud. Thud.

Billy was only doing forty, but the ruts in the old road and the dust from the truck's wheels made it seem twice as fast. By the time they had gone a quarter mile the pounding in his head was so loud it was driving everything else out of his mind.

Thud. Thud. Thud. Thud.

For only a second he took his left hand from the handlebar of the bike to hold his head, and before he knew it he was off the road and flying along in the grass. For an instant the dust cleared and he saw a huge tree, directly in front of him.

He threw the wheel hard left and laid the bike down in a slide to avoid the tree. As he slid along the ground, all he could hear, just before he lost consciousness, was the pounding in his head, even louder than before.

THUD. THUD. THUD. THUD.

When Billy opened his eyes, Pete and Clay were anxiously bending over him.

"Wake up, young feller, wake up," Clay was saying, and Pete was pressing a dirty wet blue checked handerchief against this head.

Billy looked up at the two wrinkled faces. "What the hell happened?"

"Well," Clay said, "we thought you was right behind us, but when we stopped the truck, you was laying over here in the field, out cold. Looks like you hit your breaks for some reason, and slid for a good little piece."

"Damn," Billy said, with part of what had happened beginning to come back to him. "I reckon I did hit the damned brakes. It was either hit the breaks or hit that tree. If I'd hit that big son-of-a-bitch as fast as I was going, it would have probably broken my fool neck."

"What tree is that, Sonny," Pete asked? "They ain't a tree fer fifty yards in any direction."

Billy pointed to a spot just in front of where the cycle lay and said "That big old tree right ther..." His words faded away. All it took was one look for Billy to see the old man was right. There wasn't a tree in sight.

Billy rubbed his eyes with both hands. "Damn it, I know there was a tree. Right there. I would've hit it if I hadn't laid the bike down. And there was some kind of white thing sticking up the forks. I know I saw it. I tell you, I know I did."

"Boy, there ain't been no tree in this field for as long as I can remember," Pete said. "How bout you, Clay?"

"Naw, Pete, they ain't," Clay said, "and I've lived in shoutin' distance of here for more'n eighty years. Now when I was a boy, must have been 1920 or so, they was a big old stump right about where we're standing. Lightning hit the tree, they said, and left nothing but the stump. All the kids herebouts used to play on the stump. Don't reckon I have to tell you what tree it was, do I young feller?"

THUD. THUD. THUD. THUD.

Suddenly the pounding was back in Billy's head, louder than ever, and more persistent.

"Don't tell me you can't hear that damn pounding," Billy shouted at the two men. "What the hell is that?"

Clay and Pete glanced at each other, but made no comment. It was plain they couldn't hear the sound, and had no idea what Billy was talking about.

"Let me take a look at your head," Clay said. "Could be you hit it harder than we thought."

"I heard that damned pounding before I wrecked the bike. That's one of the things that distracted me. There was all that dust from your truck, and then the pounding was trying to split my head open, and then I saw that frigging tree. And now, here I lay, flat on my back in the dust, my bike wrecked God knows how bad, I got Ringo playing Wipeout inside my brain, and there's no damn tree."

Billy was more than a little upset, now he was madder than hell. "Well, I'm getting the hell out of here, right now. If I'd known what trying to find Harpshead would do to this Harp's head, I never would have come up here in the first place."

Billy got to his feet, walked over and picked up his bike.

The bike wasn't hurt very much, except for one nasty scratch on the left side of the gas tank, so Billy climbed on and cranked the engine.

"I want to thank you guys for bringing me out here," Billy said. "It's not your fault I wrecked my bike, and I am glad I found out where Harpshead really is. When I figure out what the hell is going on, I'll be back up this way, you can count on it. I appreciate your help. See ya later." Billy let the clutch out and disappeared in the dust as he headed back along the dirt road toward the main highway.

Clay looked at Pete as they watched the boy and the motorcycle disappear down the road.

"That boy had the dangedest eyes ever I seen, Pete. You reckon he really is the Harpe?"

"I don't know, Clay," Pete answered, spitting tobacco juice in the dust, "I just don't know. I do know there's something damned funny going on. I reckon if that boy really is the Harpe, I sure as hell hope he forgets about coming back up here."

There were still a couple of hours of daylight left when Billy parked his bike in front of his own apartment. He was tired and sore, and a little stiff from the wreck, but the farther he'd driven from Harpshead, the weaker the pounding in his head became. It hadn't disappeared altogether, but it was far enough back in his mind that it didn't hurt all the time. It was now just a dull thump, with none of the power it had had that afternoon.

He'd stopped and picked up a couple of Bar-B-Que sandwiches and a cold six pack of beer, and after eating he'd filled the tub with steaming water and soaked his aching body until the water grew cold, and some of the pain had washed away.

That night was the first night he'd had the dream.

After his bath, Billy stretched out on his bed and closed his eyes, the weariness inside weighing him down. He had just started dozing when....

THUD. THUD. THUD. THUD.

The pounding was back, harder and more insistent than ever. Once again he was standing underneath the big tree at Harpshead, with the same white object stuck in the forks. Billy realized he was dreaming, but he couldn't wake up.

THUD. THUD. THUD. THUD.

With an almost superhuman effort, Billy managed to get his eyes open, and make them stay open. As quickly as it had started, the pounding was gone. He was bathed in sweat, and his heart was beating almost as hard as the pounding had been in his head. He was filled with a terror he hadn't known since he was a little boy.

He quickly reached over and flipped on the lamp beside the bed, welcoming the bright light that washed over the room.

He lit a cigarette, then rolled out of bed and headed for the bathroom. After splashing cold water on his face, he found a half dozen aspirin in the medicine cabinet and popped them into his mouth. Picking up a small glass on the sink he washed the pills down and headed back to the bedroom. He lay back down, but this time he left the light on.

The same dream came to him the next two nights in a row.

There was the tree, with the white thing stuck in the forks, the terrible pounding, and that same God-awful feeling of terror. Both nights he awoke in a cold sweat, his heart racing and his pulse pounding, leaving him feeling scared, helpless and extremely pissed off.

After having the dream for the third night, Billy found that sleep was impossible. He stretched out on the couch, picked up the book, and finished reading the story of the Harpe brothers. The next day he went back to the library and read every thing he could find about them.

He already knew a lot of the story, but the parts he learned at the library were almost unbelievable.

The Harpes were the two most ruthless killers the frontier had ever seen. The books didn't know for sure how many people the brothers had murdered, but most accounts estimated they had killed some 35 - 40 people. A few historians guessed even higher, putting the count at as many as two hundred lives taken, if they counted the Indian dead. What made it worse was that each killing was at close range, most with a knife or a tomahawk, and many for nothing more than just the pleasure of killing another human being.

It was while Billy was studying the old newspapers and census records that he came across a fact that chilled him to the bone.

There was every indication that he, Billy Harp, might be a direct descendant of the eldest Harpe brother, William Micajah Harpe himself.

The one they called the Big Harpe.

Billy remembered his parents speaking of the Harpes, but had never been able to get his Dad to tell the complete story, or about their connection to the family. His Dad was very secretive about his family, and wouldn't even tell Billy the name of his own Grandfather. He'd tried, more than once, to get his Dad to tell him about his ancestors, but he'd never succeeded in learning anything. Once, when Billy had asked a direct question about the old outlaws, his Dad had told him; "Yes Billy, I know all the stories. When I was a little boy, the old folks used to tease me about my hair and eyes. They said I had the curly black hair and the wild blue eyes of old Micajah Harpe. Well, I don't know if that's true or not, Son, but I do know that there was a mean streak running through my family, and I didn't want any part of it after I married your mother. Of course, if I've got the Harpe hair and eyes, so do you. Look in the mirror, Billy. You sure look a lot like your Dad, don't you? I sure as hell could never say you didn't belong to me, now could I?"

His father laughed at his own little joke, and Billy joined in, but when he looked in his Dad's eyes he saw that inside he wasn't laughing. Billy asked a few more questions after that, but never got another answer from his father. From then on, sometimes when Billy looked in a mirror and got a glimpse of his own curly black hair and strange blue eyes, he'd remember what his Dad had said. "Yeah, Pop, you sure as hell could never say I didn't belong to you. And that's a natural fact."

Among the things Billy learned at the library was that the Harpe brothers had used a cave on the Ohio river as a hide out for a while. He did a little checking and found out the cave was not only still there, but the area was now a national park. It was in a little town called Cave-In-Rock, Illinois, and it was open to visitors.

Billy wondered what it would feel like to stand in a place where he knew the old outlaws had actually been. The more he thought about it, the more he liked the idea of taking a ride up to the cave. He'd found Harpshead, hadn't he? Why not visit the cave? He decided to ride up next Friday, and spend the weekend exploring the cave.

Who knows, he might even be able to shed a little light on what had happened to him in Harpshead, and why he'd had the dream, and maybe even find an answer to the pounding in his head.

THURSDAY NIGHT

Thursday night Billy packed a small bag and got into bed early. He wanted to get a fresh start the next morning, and he was hoping he could get through the night without a recurrence of the damned dream.

He should have known better.

thud. thud. thud. thud.

The pounding started small and dull, like it was a long way off in the distance, and sounded a lot like someone in the supermarket thumping a ripe melon.

Thud. Thud. Thud. Thud.

A little louder now, and this time in the blackness Billy could just barely make out twin spots of faintly glowing blue light.

THUD. THUD. THUD. THUD.

The giant hammer was beating inside his head again, and the spots of light had grown so bright he had to turn his eyes away from their brilliance.

THUD. THUD. THUD. THUD.

There was nothing in the world except the sound and the light. Only now Billy could see that it wasn't a light at all, what he saw were two eyes, and they were on fire. They danced with a wild blue flame that burned into Billy's brain, and before he knew it he was consumed by the fire, and lost deep inside the glow.

Billy was not sure where he was. But the space was small and cramped, and filled with darkness. He couldn't move, and he could see nothing save the twin flickers of cold blue flame that danced about him. It was as though his arms and legs were chained. His fingers seemed to be as sharp as knives, and he had never felt such strength, as was coursing through his body, yet still he couldn't move.

As the blue glow grew stronger, Billy looked around, his eyes wondering at the way his fingers and hands seemed almost transparent in the light. For some reason, he looked down at his chest, and there he found the biggest surprise of all.

In the middle of his chest, against a blood red background, was a beautiful shining four pointed silver star, softly gleaming in the illumination of the glowing eyes.

Billy held his breath. The star was fascinating, and it captured his attention, holding it like a magnet. He'd never seen anything like it, yet it was as familiar to him as his own right hand. It seemed to be almost alive, and Billy could feel its energy flowing into his body, giving him the fantastic strength he felt.

Suddenly, from the darkness just beyond the blue flame, came a voice.

Harpe. At last you return. At last. Long and long have I slept Harpe, waiting for this day. I hunger, Harpe, we must hunt, we must hunt soon.

"Who are you," Billy managed to whisper, in a voice so low it could scarcely be heard.

Look in my eyes, Harpe, and look also at the living star on your chest, and you will know who I am. I am your father, and I am also you. I am the Harpe, I am the DarkWolf. I am you.

Suddenly a shudder ran through Billy's soul. What could this demon from hell mean? How could he be my father? How could he be me. Who in the hell is the Harpe? And what in the hell is the DarkWolf?

"What the hell are you," Billy cried, but got no answer as the dream began to fade, leaving him staring directly into the flaming blue eyes, trembling like a baby.

With all of his will he shook himself awake, realizing finally he was still in his own bed, and to his relief, the pounding in his head was easing up. The cold sweat was beginning to dry but he lay still for several minutes, trying to tell himself he was really awake. When he thought he could stand, Billy rolled out of bed and stumbled to the bathroom, still half blinded from the light he'd seen in the nightmare, and with some difficulty managed to turn on the shower and throw himself under the cold water.

Even with the water beating it's tattoo on his face, the vision of the terrible DarkWolf lingered in his mind, and his chest tingled even though there was no evidence of the star itself there.

Climbing out of the shower, Billy slowly walked back to the bedroom. He had a feeling he wouldn't be getting much rest for awhile. As he lay back down, there was the faintest trace of some old familiar song echoing through his mind, but he couldn't place where he'd heard it before. No matter how he tried, he couldn't shut the melody out of his mind.

Billy didn't know what was happening to him, but he was pretty sure he was about to find out.

FRIDAY MORNING

Friday morning found Billy up at six-thirty, in spite of the way the dream had interrupted his night's sleep. He was still caught up in the idea of going to Cave-In-Rock, and nothing was going to make him change his mind.

Especially some damned dream demon called the DarkWolf.

Looking back on the dream, Billy thought how silly it was that a grown man should have a nightmare like a child. Oh well, maybe the weekend trip would make him forget all that nonsense.

After a hot shower, he breakfasted on a couple of strawberry pop tarts and a large glass of milk, finished off with two cups of steaming hot black coffee. Then he picked up the small bag he'd packed and headed out the door. By this afternoon he should be inside the cave.

"Time to rock and roll," he said aloud, as he cranked his motorcycle.

Out of Tennessee and up through Kentucky the powerful motorcycle rolled, the mufflers thundering as the bike ate up the miles. Billy took as many back roads as he could, trying to attune his mind and body to the vibrations he had begun to feel all about him.

He found the closer he got to Dixon the stronger the vibrations became, until finally he pulled the bike off the road, almost forced into stopping by the strange feelings. He parked the bike and sat still for a minute, trying to figure out what the hell was happening. He'd never felt anything like this before.

As the feelings became stronger, he left the bike and walked down through the trees to a small river that rushed alongside the highway.

This must be Pond River, Billy thought, remembering what he'd read. It might be interesting to look around a little.

As he walked along the riverbank, the inner vibrations became even stronger, and by the time he came to a large field, some two hundred yards from the roadside, he was trembling all over.

To his surprise, Billy found the field was as familiar to him as his own backyard. He had the incredible feeling he'd been here many times before, even though he knew for sure this was his first ever visit to this part of the country.

He stood atop a small rise and looked down across the field, and an almost overwhelming feeling of dread passed over his mind. Slowly, he began to walk down off the rise, instinctively headed toward the distant tree line.

He was almost a hundred yards from where he had entered the field when something struck him in the back with incredible force. He dropped to his knees and quickly looked around the field, but saw nothing at all. Except for him the field was empty.

Rising to his feet, he gingerly used his left hand to examine his back where he'd been hit, but found no evidence he'd been struck by anything. There was a small, sharp, stinging pain, low on his spine, but that was all. He noticed the strange vibrations were stronger than ever.

There was no blood, no rock or stick on the ground, nothing that could have caused the blow, and nobody in the clearing that could have done anything. Billy was about to head back to his bike when suddenly it happened again.

He felt another terrific blow, this time higher on his shoulder blade, and with a loud curse, he spun around to look back across the meadow.

Now he wasn't alone.

A man was kneeling in the clearing, a long rifle in his hands still smoking from the shot he had fired at Billy. Out of the woods behind the kneeling man rode a large group of men, ten or twelve strong, each armed with a rifle and all of them yelling curses and shooting at him as fast as they could pull the triggers and reload their weapons.

Though Billy couldn't believe this was real, he quickly dropped into a crouch and started a shambling, ungainly run towards the cover of the nearest trees, some fifty feet away. He knew he'd never make it. The men were on horseback, and they'd be on him well before he reached the woods. In his haste, he failed to notice a fallen branch and suddenly found himself on the ground, rolling head over heels. When his motion stopped, he cautiously raised his head and risked a look toward the riders.

There was no one there. The clearing was empty. The riders as well as the kneeling man had vanished as mysteriously as they'd appeared.

Now Billy was totally confused. He un-buttoned his shirt and felt the spot on his back where he'd been shot. He ran his hands around his back, but once again could find no evidence of any wound. Damn, was he going crazy?

Turning his attention to his right shoulder, he wasn't surprised to find no trace of a wound there either. No bullet hole, no blood, no nothing.

With haltering steps and a watchful eye, Billy slowly retraced his steps, going back across the meadow to where he'd seen the men. For three or four minutes he looked around, but found no trace of the riders, nor anything to indicate they'd ever really been there. There wasn't even a single hoof mark in the soft earth.

Deliberately buttoning his shirt, Billy decided to leave this place as quickly as possible. But when he turned for one last look across the field, to his horror he discovered the men were back, this time across the meadow in the same spot he'd been when he'd felt the blows to his back.

The men were struggling with someone on the ground, and whoever it was, he was putting up a hell of a fight.

Billy saw a knife rise and fall several times, as one of the men repeatedly stabbed the man on the ground. Realizing he was witnessing a murder, Billy tried to run across the field to help, but it was as if the entire scene was in slow motion. The harder he tried to run, the slower his motions became. They were killing the man on the ground, and there was nothing Billy could do to stop them.

All at once, the man with the knife let out a wild cry. He lurched to his feet and lifted his arms above his head. In his right hand was a long, gleaming butcher knife, the sun glinting off the shining blade, and in his left hand...

Oh God, Billy thought.

In his left hand the man held the head of the man he'd just murdered. The dark hair was flying as he waved the head about, and blood was cascading down his arm and spattering over the men on the ground. Worst of all, the eyes of the head were wide open, and seemed to glow with a strange light.

Wide open, and staring directly at Billy.

Once again Billy tried to move, and once again found it impossible. He opened his mouth to yell, but no sound came out. All he could do was stand frozen in his tracks, staring at the group of men who still stood over the headless body.

Then, in a moment that seemed to last an eternity, Billy found himself staring directly into the eyes of the man who held the head in the air...

As their eyes met, Billy felt a shiver run through his body. His arms were covered with chill bumps, his mouth was dry, and the hair stood up on the back of his neck.

Suddenly a grim smile began to play around the corners of Billy's lips.

Deep inside his wild blue eyes, a tiny spark sprang to life. Billy closed his eyes as if to ward off the brightness he felt beginning, and in a subconscious act, he slowly brought his left hand to his neck.

He rubbed the tender skin of his Adams apple, and then ran his hand up to his chin and back down. He closed his eyes and ran his hand around to the back of his neck, carefully feeling first one side and then the other. As he brought his hand back around to the front of his neck, his eyes opened, and the spark had grown to a full, roaring fury, terrible in it's intensity.

Once again Billy met the gaze of the man holding the head aloft, and directed the full power of his stare into the other mans eyes.

"Cut on, and be Damned..." Billy whispered, knowing that even at this distance the killer would hear.

The man dropped his eyes from the intensity of Billy's gaze, and then, as if he had gathered his courage, in a sudden move he once more shook the dripping head in the air, and began to run straight at Billy, shouting curses as he ran.

For the first time, Billy focused his full attention upon the features of the face of the severed head...

And saw himself.

"Oh God, oh God, oh God," Billy whispered. "It's me, oh God, it's me."

Billy sank to his knees, clutching his head with both hands, and then slowly raised his face to the heavens. His eyes were now completely consumed by the blue fire. Billy once again looked at the head he knew to be himself, and screamed, and screamed, and screamed.

The scream tore through the air of the small meadow, and echoed around the fallen body. The men covered their ears and closed their eyes, and still the scream rang. It rang across miles and it rang across time. To the pearly portals of heaven and to the rusty gates of hell, the scream rang.

Deep in the darkness of the cave on the Spirit World the DarkWolf heard the scream, and slowly opened one eye. Casting an unhurried glance about the cave, he opened the other eye, and revealed the blue flame that had been rekindled in their depths. The flame quickly became a furnace, raging out of control in the wild eyes of the DarkWolf. He was hungry. It had been over two hundred years since he last fed.

Suddenly the DarkWolf became aware of a pounding in his head, the same pounding that had been present the day he had withdrawn to this cave. But now the pounding was not as before. Now it seemed to be calling to him to come out of the cave where he had rested for so long.

As the DarkWolf gathered himself and began to creep toward the light, the darkness began to fall away. Inch by inch he pulled himself forward, until at last he was free. The blue eyes focused and once again the DarkWolf looked out upon the world of man.

He was free.

It was time to hunt.

Call my name, Harpe, he whispered, I will come.

ANDREW STEGALL

Belying reality, Billy Harp's savage scream tore across until it echoed off the walls of a small house outside Eddyville, Kentucky. It thundered and cascaded through the mind of Andrew Stegall, and he removed a small key from its leather thong around his neck, and fitted it to the small lock in the wooden chest he held in his lap.

BETHANY ROBERTS

In Lafayette, Tennessee, Bethany Suzanne Roberts had to rush home from work to care for her baby. Something had wakened the child, causing it to cry, and it could not be hushed.

DANIEL HAWK

In Cherokee, North Carolina, the scream roared into the mind of Daniel Hawk, causing him to cry out in pain, and blinding him to everything around him. Through his blindness came a vision of the Eagle, and Hawk knew the prophesied time had come at last.

WILEY

The scream struck the place where the old town of Greenville, Mississippi, had once been. It roared like a tornado out of hell across an old overgrown field outside town, and the world seemed to come to a grinding halt. Though the wind was still, dark black storm clouds rolled across the sky.

Like a knife the scream cut into the mind of a young man driving a blue Pontiac, and he grabbed his head with both hands, causing the car to swerve and leave the road. By it's own volition, the car plunged at breakneck speed down an old abandoned dirt road, then overturned in the middle of the overgrown empty field where the echo of the scream still lingered. A field where once, long ago, a grinning skull had been nailed to a tall post.

As the car came to a grinding stop where once the pole had stood, the scream pierced the very fabric of reality itself, and touched the mind of the long dead Wolf Brother. The Wolf Brother heard, and slowly opened his eyes, raised his head and sniffed the wind.

BILLY

In the field outside Greenville, Kentucky, Billy Harp collapsed upon the ground, and the scream died away. Soon even the echo was gone.

But now the DarkWolf was wide awake, the Wolf Brother was slowly awakening, and once again the countryside sat poised upon the brink of destruction.

ANDREW STEGALL

Andrew Stegall was one mean old son-of-a-bitch. He'd been born mean, he'd lived mean, and he'd die mean. He was a tall man, slim, tough and tanned as whitleather, and in his youth had been hell on wheels. He drank hard and fought hard, asking no quarter and giving none. He was born in 1932, and had been too young to go to war in World War II, but everyone that knew him knew he was a fighting man.

That's why the situation he felt developing bothered him so much. He'd prayed the time would never come when he felt the need to open the box, but the dream and the awful feeling in his gut were telling him different.

When he heard the wild scream in his mind, he knew the rebirth was close at hand. Andrew didn't know if he had enough left in him to handle all the trouble that was coming.

He could remember times when his own father would awaken in the night, take the wooden box from the shelf in the closet, and sit out on the front porch holding the knife, watching the night sky.

For years he didn't understand the look on his father's face as he held the knife. There was a far away look in his eyes, and even though the night air sometimes had a chill to it, there was always a shiny, moist film of sweat on his forehead. It was as if he were seeing something no one else could see, way back in the past, or maybe something he thought would happen a little farther down the road. Andrew remembered sitting on the edge of the porch, watching the sky with the same intensity as his father, afraid to speak, not knowing what might lie out there in the darkness.

The day he turned thirteen, his father sat him down at the table and placed the box in front of him. Without a word, he took the leather thong from around his neck and showed Andrew the small, worn key that was the only thing the leather held.

He had placed the key in the lock on the wooden box, and with a tiny, almost inaudible click, the lock opened. His father reached into the box, and very carefully withdrew the knife.

It was the most beautiful thing Andrew had ever seen. It was long and shiny, and the boy's eyes could see it was razor sharp. It was a big knife, solid and heavy, its bone handle tightly wrapped with leather. The leather was lightly worn, as though it had been recently used, but Andrew knew it hadn't. He had never seen the knife this close before. He wanted to hold it, to feel the steel, and test the balance for himself.

His father gently moved the wooden chest to one side, and laid the knife on the table in front of the boy.

"Touch it," he said. "Pick up the blade and feel its strength. Let your hand become accustomed to its heft. Learn the knife well boy, for one day your very life may depend upon it."

For over an hour his father sat at the table and told Andrew the tale of the Harpe Brothers, and of the legacy that had now been handed down to him.

As soon as he had finished the story, Andrew Stegall's father walked out into the back yard of the house, shoved his pistol into his mouth, and blew away the back of his head.

Andrew could remember that day as though it were yesterday, even though it was over sixty years ago. He had buried his father in the small family plot on the side of the hill, and two or three days later, when he felt up to it, he once again took out the knife.

He sat down at the table again, and unlocked the wooden box. For a long time he sat there staring at the blade, wondering what its power could be that was strong enough to cause his father to take his own life. Then once again he took up the blade.

A shock ran through him. Like a bolt of electricity the knife's energy sprang to life and coursed throughout his body. He could hear the singing within the blade, and taste the blood it had drank. It was a terrible weapon, and even as young as he was, Andrew knew the blade was forged for one reason, and for one reason only. It was made a killer weapon, forged for nothing other than to take the lives of men, and to taste blood. Its balance was perfect, almost a tangible part of the blade, and it was plain the knife was made for throwing as much as for hand to hand combat. Andrew Stegall knew from that first encounter with the knife that one day the blade would either save his life, or take it.

Andrew was shaken by his father's graphic description of the killing of Micajah Harpe, and shaken by the knowledge that the very knife he held in his hands was the knife used to perform that bloody deed. He turned the blade around and around in his hands, watching as it caught the dim light from the 40 watt bulb in the old lamp that sat on the shelf by the table and sent strange, quick flashes of brightness into the shadows of the room. He imagined he could see dark stains on the blade, and wondered if they were traces of Harpe's own lifeblood. It was a strange and wonderful weapon, yet frightening, and it brought a thrill to the boy simply to hold it in his hand.

Yet even then, as a boy, Andrew realized the knife was an evil thing, bringing death and destruction to whoever was foolish enough to use it. Now, as a man wizened well by the course of years, he still thought of the knife in that respect.

Moses Stegall, his ancestor, had become a victim of the blade, even as had Micajah Harpe. Even his own father, though only a keeper of the knife, had met a violent and tragic fate. The knife had only been out of it's hardwood casket a few times since the killing of Harpe, and then only for the purpose of telling the story to each generation of Stegall men, as it was passed from father to son.

That suited Andrew Stegall just fine. He had no wish to use the knife. Since that day he had seen more than his share of bar room brawls and back alley fights, but not once had he been tempted to use the Harpe knife. He didn't know how much of the story his father had told him was true, but he'd never been one for taking unnecessary chances.

I remember the day Daddy gave me the damned blade, Stegall thought. I didn't believe all that crap then, but now I'm not so sure. There's sure as hell something going on. This damned pounding in my head is just like Daddy described it, and I'll be a sumbitch if I can shake this feeling down in my bones. Like somebody was walking across my grave. Might be my old age acting up, but I doubt it.

Tonight again Andrew was sitting in his rocking chair on the front porch, watching the night sky, just as he had almost every evening of his life.

Weather permitting and notwithstanding an emergency, it was a nightly ritual. He'd sit on the porch rocking, holding the wooden box in his lap softly rubbing the wood, thinking about what his old man had said, and wondering if the call would come in his lifetime.

Andrew didn't like any of this crap. He was actually beginning to think a man that had been dead for almost two hundred years might be coming after him.

Not that he was scared. It wasn't that. Andrew Stegall wasn't scared. But Andrew didn't get to be so old by being stupid. If some damn ghost was coming after him, he wanted to be prepared.

For a moment, Andrew let his mind take him back into a past that was probably better forgotten, but one that still flared to life in times such as the last few nights.

Andrew was now in his seventies, and time had not been kind to him.

His six feet four inches was stooped, and his once dark brown hair was almost snow white. His face also showed the ravages of time. Wrinkles and crows feet were abundant, and his bushy eyebrows were the same color as his hair. His skin was the texture of old leather, and the muscles of his youth had lost their elasticity and strength. There wasn't quite as much bounce in his step, and it took him longer to get from place to place. But his green eyes were still as clear as water from a mountain spring, and his old looking hands were still as steady as a rock, especially when he was holding the knife.

Andrew had been married once, when he was about twenty, to a beautiful young girl named Minnie who thought he hung the moon. He often thought about her and always thought his life would have been different if she had lived. But she had died giving birth to their only child. Andrew had never gotten over it, and had never remarried.

He'd raised their son Adam the best he could, but without the hand of Minnie to help shape him, the boy learned little of softness and kindness, and much of Andrew's wild and sometimes violent ways.

Adam was a wild youngster, and more than once Andrew had had to get him out of one kind of scrape or another. He'd finally had to withdraw the boy from school for fighting, and as Adam grew older, Andrew had more than one fight with him himself. Andrew wasn't at all surprised when he'd learned Adam had lied about his age and enlisted in the Army when he was only seventeen.

Adam never saw his twentieth birthday.

He lost his life in a hot, angry jungle country called Vietnam. A country Andrew Stegall didn't know very much about. They shipped his body home, in a casket draped with an American flag, and Andrew buried him on the hillside, not far from he'd laid his father and Minnie to rest. Maybe she'd be able to guide Adam through the after life better than Andrew had managed to guide him through this one.

With a start, Andrew pulled himself from his reverie, and forcibly brought his attention back to the matter at hand.

If this stuff is really true, and Harpe is coming back in the next couple of days, just how in the hell am I supposed to stop him?

Andrew was thinking out loud, as he often did, asking questions and answering them.

He'll be the meanest sumbitch that ever walked, that's for sure, and I ain't the man I used to be. I've got this damn knife, and that's in my favor. It's supposed to be able to kill the Harpe, but not if he kills me fore I get a good swipe at him. Jesus, why'd he wait till now to come back?

Andrew wasn't afraid of anything that walked the earth, and that included a two hundred year old ghost, but just the same he was cautious. He knew he was old, and he knew he didn't have the strength for a prolonged fight. If he intended to take on the Harpe, he'd need all the help he could get. Trouble was, he didn't know where he could get a damn bit of help. Not one single bit.

Why didn't he come back twenty-five or thirty years ago? I'd have kicked his butt good for him then, I would have. I'm an old man now, and not worth a plugged nickel in a fight.

But Andrew knew he really had no choice.

Well, the hell with it, he thought, let him come. I'll get in at least one swing before I go down. Maybe I'll get lucky. It was a Stegall that killed him the first time around, maybe a Stegall can handle the job this time.

Even with all the brave thoughts, still Andrew wasn't fooling himself. If Harpe was even half as bad as he was supposed to be, Andrew Stegall's days were numbered.

Somehow, in the back of Stegall's mind, he was sure Harpe would probably be twice as bad as his Daddy had told him he'd be.

BETHANY ROBERTS

The small town of Lafayette, Tennessee, in Macon County, is some thirty miles north of Nashville, and about two hundred miles as the crow flies from Cave-in-Rock, Illinois. Lafayette is a small, close-knit community, made up of hard working people who mind their own business, and like it just fine when other people do the same. Still, like most small towns, most everybody always knows what's going on, with whom, a large part of the time.

Probably not more than a handful of people in Lafayette had ever heard of Cave-in-Rock, and the ones who had didn't place any particular significance on it. But for one of Lafayette's prettier young women and her seven month old baby, the events that would soon take place in the sleepy little Illinois national park town on the Ohio River would have a devastating effect.

Bethany Suzanne Roberts was one of the ones who hadn't heard of Cave-in-Rock, and neither had her boyfriend, Joshua Harp. Even if they had, they wouldn't have thought the small Illinois town could have anything to do with them.

Bethany and Josh had thought they were in love. In fact, they'd thought so for years. They'd thought so enough to conceive the child they had named Michael. However, even now, this many months after Mike had been born, they still hadn't told anyone who the father was. One or two of Bethany's closest friends may have suspected, but no one ever came right out and said what they thought.

The thing was, Bethany and Joshua both knew it was absolutely forbidden for a Robert's and a Harp to go out together, much less talk about love and marriage. Having a child was completely out of the question.

Nobody ever bothered to say why that was so, but it was hammered into the Roberts and Harp children as soon as they were big enough to begin to understand things. Roberts and Harps didn't marry. Period. No ifs, ands, buts, or maybes. That was it. Not now, not ever. No, no, no, Plain no, Hell no.

So they didn't. They talked about marriage, and about running off down to Georgia or somewhere and tying the knot, but deep in their hearts they knew they'd never do it.

After the baby was born, Josh seemed to take a back seat anyway. They named the child William Michael, and called him Mike, and he was all that mattered. As long as no one found out he was really a Harp child.

Bethany looked at the beautiful child lying in his crib, and couldn't believe he really belonged to her. He was such a perfect baby. Born seven and a half months ago, he weighed almost twelve pounds at birth, and was getting bigger every day. He had a head full of very thick, coal black hair, that was already beginning to get curly.

They marveled at his strength. When he got his tiny little fingers wrapped around something, you almost had to pry them open.

In spite of growing so fast and staying hungry most of the time, Mike almost never cried. He was a good-natured child, and nothing seemed to bother him very much.

That is, until the last couple of days. A few days ago, Mike had started waking up in the middle of the night, screaming his head off. Not normal baby crying either. It was as if something were scaring him half to death. But even that wasn't normal for him. He'd never seemed afraid of anything before. Bethany remembered once when the cat had jumped up in the crib with Mike and started licking him on the face. The baby had just stared at the cat, his strange blue eyes never leaving the cats face, and damned if the cat hadn't jumped out of the crib and ran away. Never came back either. Bethany always said Mike had just plain ole scared the hell clean out of the cat.

Last night and then again this morning had been the worst times Mike had experienced. He awakened Bethany early, crying as hard as he could, again sounding scared to death. He wasn't hungry, or wet, or sick, or anything else. He was just plain scared.

Bethany had picked him up and held him to her breast, and hummed the little song he liked so well. She'd learned the melody from her own mother, before her mother had passed away, and remembered it being sung to her when she was just a baby herself. She knew the song seemed to have the same soothing effect on little Mike as it had on her.

But this morning, even the song didn't completely calm him down. He cried and cried, until Bethany was sure she would be late for work again today. She paced back and forth across the floor, wondering if she should call and wake up her Aunt and tell her about the baby. She decided not to. Aunt Norah hadn't been feeling well lately, and she didn't need to lose any more sleep right now.

But it sure would be nice to have someone to talk to, Bethany thought.

Her Aunt hadn't been very understanding when Bethany became pregnant, and when Bethany refused to tell her who the father was, they had several really bad arguments. Bethany had gone to spend some time with her cousin, at least until after the baby was born, and was still living there. Her cousin meant well, but she wasn't in the best of health either, and couldn't handle the baby when he threw one of his crying fits.

Of course, not being able to call on Joshua for help really pissed Bethany off. Damn it, it took both of them to make the baby, why the hell couldn't Josh help out now and then? Of course, she knew why. But that didn't help much at times like these.

Damnit, she thought. If a good man was to come along today, and ask me, I'd just pack up and leave with him. I'd get me and my baby out of this town, and go somewhere where nobody has never heard my name, and didn't give a damn who the child's father was. Lord, I'm so tired of fighting with everyone. And all this crying is driving me crazy.

After about a half hour, the baby finally stopped crying, and didn't wake up when she laid him down in his crib. She tiptoed to the door, and was ready to leave for work when she remembered she didn't have the necklace. She softly crossed the room to her own bed where she lifted the mattress a few inches and ran her hand under it.

Her hand closed about the old worn leather pouch she touched there, and she withdrew it from its hiding place between the mattress and the bedsprings. She felt the oval shape of the object inside the pouch, and it dawned on her she hadn't looked at the necklace in over a week. The leather was very old, so she was extra careful as she opened it. Pulling the opening apart, she turned the pouch upside down and gently shook it until the object inside slipped out into her hand.

Just like every other time in her life she'd ever touched the necklace, she felt reassured just holding it in her hand. She had a feeling of warmth and safety when she held it, almost as if it were magic. One thing was certain; she needed to feel better today. She turned it over and over in her hands, and sure enough, after a minute, she actually began to feel more like facing the world.

Bethany was only seven when her Mother had passed away, and her Mother had given her the necklace and told her as much of its story as she could only hours before the end. She kept it with her at all times, just as her Mother had told her to do.

It was a family tradition that the oldest girl in the family keep the necklace and the old worn leather pouch. For some reason, they couldn't wear it around their necks, so they always kept it inside their blouse, close to their heart. She wasn't sure why, but she knew she didn't feel right when the necklace wasn't with her.

It's just a plain old necklace, she thought, but it really is pretty, She let her gaze slowly drift across the softly glowing object she held in her hand. With her thumb she traced the outline of the bright, four pointed silver star, and her fingers gently caressed the background of blood red crimson.

DANIEL HAWK

Daniel Hawk couldn't get back to sleep, no matter how he tried. The damn dream had just been too real. Daniel knew you couldn't dismiss any dream in which the animal spirits came to visit. Especially if the visitors were the Eagle and the Wolf.

Not to mention the pounding in his head that accompanied the dream was driving him crazy.

Daniel's father was almost seventy years old, and even though Daniel hadn't lived at home for over five years, he valued his father's opinion highly, and never failed to seek his counsel when faced with something he didn't understand, or something he couldn't work out by himself.

Daniel sure as hell didn't understand all the things that had been happening lately. First, that damn pounding had started, like someone was beating on a big bass drum in his head. It didn't last long, but it had given him one hell of a headache.

That same night was the first night he'd had the dream. The dream was really weird. Daniel knew in the old days the People would go out in the forest and try to have a vision of the animal spirits, to ask for guidance and wisdom.

But this wasn't the old days, and he wasn't in the forest.

This was a new century, he was in his own house, lying in his own bed, and he sure as hell wasn't trying to get in touch with any animal spirits. But obviously the spirits were trying to get in touch with him, and were doing a pretty damn good job of it.

Daniel wasn't surprised to find his father waiting at the door when he reached his house. His dad had a way of knowing when something was going on, and this time he was even more excited than usual.

"Come in, Daniel, I have been waiting for you," his father said, as soon as Daniel had stepped from his parked car.

"I need to talk Dad," Daniel started. "I think I've had a visit from the old animal spirits. I'm not really sure, but I think that's what's going on. Is that possible? Does that stuff still happen?"

"It happens, Daniel, of course it happens. But not as in the old days. These days there are too many young people who do not believe. You were raised to believe the old traditions of the People, and of course your ancestors were among the most powerful of the Cherokee medicine men. You are descended from Dancing Hawk himself, so of course it is possible you have indeed been visited by the animal spirits. Tell me what has happened."

"Well, it all started last weekend, Dad," Daniel began. "But I'm not sure exactly what happened. I was grilling some hamburgers for Linda and myself last Sunday around noon, when all at once I got this terrible pounding in my head. Not only could I feel it, I could almost hear it. It was like a bass drum. Thud. Thud. Thud Thud. After five or six minutes, it just stopped. That night was the first night I dreamed about the Eagle and the Wolf."

"The Eagle and the Wolf. You were visited by the Eagle and the Wolf together?" His father was clearly disturbed.

"Well, not really together," Daniel said. "The Eagle was real cautious, and kept circling overhead. The Wolf didn't speak, he just stood there watching me and the Eagle. I think the Eagle is afraid of the Wolf."

"Not afraid," his father said, "the Eagle is merely cautious. The Eagle is as powerful as the Wolf, and was waiting until the time was right to speak."

"Anyway, the next night I had the same dream. And also the night after that. Last night was the seventh night I've had the dream, and for the first time the Eagle landed and spoke to me."

Daniel closed his eyes in concentration. He wanted to recite the words exactly as the Eagle had spoken them, for he knew each word held a particular significance.

"O.K. Dad, here's what the Eagle said'

Quickly, Hawk, Go Quickly,
 Find the Magic Blade.
 Beware the Wolf, Young Hawk, Beware
Lest You Become His Slave.

"That's exactly what the Eagle said, Dad. Exactly. Not talking, just kinda singing the words. Oh, and the Wolf was there too. He was standing in the background, just watching. It was like he wanted the Eagle to talk to me. I got a real good look at the Wolf this time. He is one mean looking son-of-a-bitch. Oops. Excuse me Dad, I didn't mean to say that." Daniel's father didn't swear, and didn't like it at all when Daniel did.

This time his father didn't seem to notice. "What do you mean, he was mean looking," he asked Daniel?

"Well, the best way I can describe it, that Wolf looked evil. He looked really evil. He was completely black, very big and always stood in the shadows, but I could see his eyes. They were the weirdest shade of blue I've ever seen. It was like they were burning with blue fire."

Daniel could still feel those eyes staring at him, and the look still sent shivers down his spine.

"What. Blue eyes. Why did you not mention this sooner? The Black Wolf with the blue eyes of flame is no ordinary animal spirit." His father was really upset now. He stood up and began to pace the floor.

"I just now thought about it, Dad. The blue eyes, I mean. Sorry. What do you think it means? Big trouble, huh?" Daniel knew anytime his father was this agitated, it meant a much larger than normal problem.

"I'm afraid we're going to find out exactly how big," his father replied, "and it will be the biggest problem any of us will ever face. No wonder the Eagle wouldn't land. Forget what I said about him not being afraid of the Wolf. The Eagle is very afraid of this Wolf. This was no ordinary animal spirit, Daniel. You had a visit from an ancient evil, an immortal, one of the original forces of nature, and he is the most powerful spirit demon of the old ways. Daniel, the Black Wolf with the blue flame eyes is known as the DarkWolf."

"The what?" Daniel said.

He'd never seen his father this upset over anything before. He was pacing the floor, his hands clenched into tight fists, and Daniel could see he was trembling all over.

"Damn, Pop, settle down." He was afraid his father might have a stroke or a heart attack. "You can't let this nightmare get to you like this."

For once his dad didn't call his hand about the cursing. He stopped in the middle of the floor, and stood there silently staring at his son for several minutes. He slowly ran his fingers through his thick hair, and gently rubbed the back of his neck before answering.

"The huge black Wolf with the eyes of blue flame is called the DarkWolf, my son, and he is worse than any nightmare. The legends of the People say he sleeps in a cave in the Spirit World, and has been there for over two hundred years. If the DarkWolf is awake, there may not be anything in the world powerful enough to stop him."

"I don't know what this damned DarkWolf is, Dad, but he can't be all that bad."

"He is even worse, Daniel. The DarkWolf is a demon, and is the most powerful being in the spirit world. When he last walked the earth, he lived inside a man named Harpe, and together they sent hundreds of souls to eternal torment. But Harpe was killed in 1799, and with his death the DarkWolf was cast back into the spirit world, where he has slept for these many years. With Micajah Harpe dead, there was no reason for the DarkWolf to awaken. Something has happened, Daniel. Something has called to the DarkWolf and he has heard, and I'm afraid I know what it is. The legends say the day will come when the Harpe shall once again walk the countryside, seeking revenge on those who killed him. If this has happened, if the Harpe has returned, then the DarkWolf may truly be awake. The Eagle came to you for a reason, Daniel, and we must find out what it is. It will be our only salvation."

Daniel followed his father into a small back room of the house. He had built the room years ago, as a place of meditation. It was here he came when he needed guidance and solitude. It was here they would find the answer to Daniel's dream, if indeed the answer could be found.

The room held all the magical trappings of a great Cherokee medicine man. It was filled with things handed down from father to son over generations, and was probably similar to the inside of one of the old wigwams. Perhaps even the wigwam of Dancing Hawk himself.

The old man settled cross-legged on the floor, and from a small stand he picked up a long, intricately carved pipe. He lit the pipe with a small, green plastic butane lighter, which seemed strangely out of place, but at any rate got the job done, then closed his eyes and began an ancient Cherokee chant. Slowly he inhaled the thick smoke, and after a few silent tendrils began to weave toward the ceiling, he began to call upon the Eagle spirit to appear.

Daniel lost track of time as he sat watching his father, and as the smoke became heavier and heavier in the room, he wondered how many times the men of his family had sat in this fashion, offering prayers to the animal spirits, and awaiting an answer.

Seven times his father called upon the Eagle, and on the seventh the room shook, and the smoke cleared slightly near the ceiling, and suddenly the Eagle was there.

Daniel was aware of his father speaking, and of the Eagle answering, but realized they were speaking in an ancient language only the two of them could understand. For several long moments they spoke, the old medicine man and the Eagle spirit, and then as suddenly as he had appeared, the Eagle was gone.

Daniel watched as his father laid the pipe aside, and slowly got to his feet. He walked over and opened a small window to allow the smoke to escape, and only when the air was almost cleared did he once again speak to Daniel.

"As I feared, Daniel, it was the DarkWolf in your dream. In some way, unknown even to the Eagle, the Harpe has indeed returned, and the DarkWolf is awake." His father was bathed in sweat, and his voice sounded older than it had ever sounded.

"The Eagle came to you with a warning, my son, and perhaps with an answer. The warning was of the coming of the Harpe, and the awakening of the DarkWolf, and the answer lies in the magic blade. You must exercise great care lest you fall under the power of the DarkWolf. His power is great, and his guile unequalled. The blade itself is a great tomahawk fashioned by Dancing Hawk and given to Micajah Harpe. It is a weapon that was blessed by the animal spirits for Harpe to use in his fight to help the People keep their ancestral lands. When Harpe was slain, the tomahawk was never recovered. Even now it lies where Harpe last dropped it, and it is this blade you must seek out. It was our ancestor who crafted the tomahawk, and so it is you who have been chosen to wield it in the coming fight. You must also seek out a man called Stegall, though I know not where he may be, and enlist his aid in your battle. Stegall holds the long knife that was used to slay the Harpe those many years ago, and Stegall himself may prove to be a valiant warrior. The tomahawk and the long knife are your only chance against the forces you are to do battle with, and even the two of them may not be enough. Would that I were younger, son, and could accept this challenge myself. But you have been chosen by the Eagle to carry the fight to the DarkWolf, and so must it be. Give me a minute to finish up here, and we will decide on how best to find the tomahawk."

Daniel left the room without a word. He knew his father had said all he would say, and Daniel was expected to follow his words without question.

The funny thing was, that was exactly what Daniel would do. He believed in the old ways, just as his father did, and if his father said he had to fight some demon DarkWolf, then so be it.

.As he passed the refrigerator, Daniel helped himself to a cold beer, downing it in one long hard swallow. He went into the living room to wait for his father. The needed to figure out what the next move must be. As he stood there, Daniel silently hoped this Stegall character was some kind of superman.

WOLF BROTHER

A FEW MILES FROM THE SITE OF OLD GREENVILLE, MISSISSIPPI

Charlie Myers didn't actually hear the scream, but that didn't stop it from affecting him. Charlie and Debbie had taken Debbie's sister Lisa to the mall in Natchez to shop for a new dress to wear to the big bar-b-cue next weekend, and were on the way back to Washington when Charlie decided to pull in at the Quick Stop for some gas.

It was another of those hot and steamy August days Mississippi is noted for, and Charlie also decided an ice cold brew would be just what the doctor ordered. It was only a little after nine in the morning, but that had never stopped Charlie before. Debbie would be madder'n an old wet hen, but he couldn't help it. He wanted a cold beer, and damnit, he was going to drink one. Hell, maybe he'd drink two. Screw Debbie.

Hey, that wasn't such a bad idea either, Charlie thought, as he paid for the gas and the six-pack.

It had rained the night before, and the ground was still a little wet, which only made the sun that much hotter. Charlie hadn't really wanted to take Lisa shopping, but he sure as hell didn't want to piss Debbie off any more than he already had.

He had used part of the money he had been saving for them to get married on to buy this old car, and Debbie wasn't any too happy about that. So, if it would keep her happy if he ran a few small errands, then he'd run the damn errands. He really did love Debbie, but he also loved the Pontiac Firebird Trans Am he'd bought from his sister's old man. Actually, he'd gotten a really good deal on the car, so what the hell.

Charlie was pumping the gas when Dave Cooper's old pick-up truck pulled in to the market. He recognized Jake Trabue in the truck with Dave, and waved as they got out of the truck. Dave and Jake went in the side door of the market, just as another guy stepped out through the front door. He stood in front of the station for a minute, and then walked over toward Charlie's car.

Charlie took a good look as the guy walked in his direction. Charlie had never seen him before, he knew he'd remember if he had. The guy made quite a first impression. He was an inch or two over six feet tall, and weighed about two hundred and twenty pounds. He had thick dark reddish hair, but Charlie couldn't make out the color of his eyes. He was wearing faded Levi jeans, and well worn, round toed, cowboy boots. His T-shirt had the sleeves cut out, and from the size of his arms it was plain he must have worked out a lot. He was darkly tanned and wore a gold bracelet on his right wrist that gleamed in the sun.

Charlie turned his attention back to the gas pump, but he saw the guy was leaning down and talking to Lisa through the back window. He couldn't hear what they were saying, but she was laughing, and as he slid back under the wheel, Debbie asked it they could give the guy a ride into town.

"He's a friend of Lisa's," Debbie said, "so I thought it'd be okay. It is okay, isn't it Charlie?" Debbie's voice was a mixture of pleading and demanding.

"Course it's okay, hon. Get in, feller," Charlie said.

"Hey, thanks Bubba," the guy said, "'preciate the lift. It's for damn sure too hot to be walking. Hey, Lisa babe, what's happenin'?"

They were rolling North on 61, approaching the turnoff to Highway 553, when all of a sudden Debbie exclaimed.

"Damn guys, look at those clouds. Looks like we're in for one hell of a storm."

The black storm clouds had seemed to come out of nowhere, and were filling the sky. The clouds looked to be moving at an impossible pace across the heavens, but for some strange reason, the air on the ground was almost completely still. Strange, the clouds were coming from the North, which was highly unusual. Normally they would have come whipping up across the Gulf or from the West, out of Texas.

Charlie looked at the storm clouds, and without warning his vision blurred and his mouth became very dry. The world began to turn a little fuzzy as he became more disoriented. He never knew it when he whipped the car onto Highway 553, and had no idea at all where he was. He could hear Debbie saying something, and Lisa and the guy in the back seat talking, but he couldn't make out the words. He shook his head but that didn't seem to help at all, and now it looked as if the road had started moving about under the car, instead of the other way around.

What the hell is going on? Charlie thought.

All at once he had the damnedest pounding in his head. It felt as if his head were going to explode. He glanced down at the beer can in his hand, as if that might explain what was happening, but found he couldn't even focus on the label. The pounding was now a loud *THUD. THUD. THUD.* and was drowning out everything else.

Charlie looked across the seat at Debbie, and saw her staring back at him, but had to quickly turn his eyes back to the highway. The car was gaining speed, weaving crazily across both lanes of the road, and the last thing Charlie remembered was turning the wheel sharply and heading down a long abandoned old dirt road. He could vaguely see Debbie's face twisted in a scream, and could hear the two in the back seat shouting at him, but he could feel himself losing consciousness, and there was nothing he could do about controlling the speeding automobile. He felt the car leave the road and roar out into the middle of a large field, and then it violently lurched to one side, slid for a few seconds before overturning and beginning to roll over and over. After the first roll, Charlie's world turned dark.

PEANUT ROLLINS

HIGHWAY 553 - JEFFERSON COUNTY, MS

Peanut Rollins, on the other hand, did hear Billy Harp's scream.

At least he heard something he thought was a scream. He was headed home, taking a shortcut across the old field, when his mind was suddenly blasted by a sound such as he'd never heard before. The wild keening had no sooner died away than it was replaced by a dull pounding in his head. It was like the grand daddy of all hangovers.

As if the headache weren't enough, the darkest storm clouds Peanut had ever seen had started gathering, and were rolling in from the North at a frightening pace. From all his years of living in Mississippi, Peanut had seen a lot bad storms, but never anything quite like this. There hadn't been a cloud in the sky one minute, and the next it was so dark it was almost like night. Suddenly, everything got so quiet you could have heard a pin drop. Peanut stopped dead in his tracks and looked around the field, and all at once a terrible feeling of dread came over him.

There wasn't a bird singing, or even a squirrel playing in the trees. It was downright strange. Not a leaf on the trees was in motion, and Peanut had the feeling maybe the whole world had stopped moving.

Peanut continued across the field to his own house on the other side. He went inside, but the feeling was so strong he couldn't stay there.

He walked back to the edge of the field and stood for a moment, not sure what he was looking for. The pounding was still a dull ache in his head, and he didn't know what to make of it. As he walked back into the field, the pounding once again became worse.

The field had been overgrown for years. No one used it for anything anymore, though they said it used to be a gathering place for people who were traveling down the old Natchez Trace. There were still traces of an old dirt road running from the main highway to the field, but no one used the road any more either. As far as Peanut knew, nobody ever went into the field for anything. Not even to hunt an occasional rabbit or squirrel.

The story was that once the field was used to exhibit the dead bodies of the outlaws that were captured along the Trace. When one of the old bad boys was caught, they often brought him to Greenville to stand trial, and to be executed. Sometimes they were hanged in the field, and local legends told that one of the most terrible outlaws on the Trace, Wiley Harpe, even had his head cut off and nailed to a post, right here in this very field. Stories like that were probably why the folks of Greenville were still a little skittish about the old field, and seldom visited it. Folks said sometimes you could hear whispers, like somebody talking very quietly, when you were alone in the field.

Nowadays Old Greenville was just a small town, a few scattered houses here and there, not much more than a wide spot in the road, but back then it must have been something else.

Peanut Rollins had lived on the edge of the field for almost thirty years, and today was the first time he'd ever seen anything strange happening here. What with the pounding in his head, and the storm clouds, Peanut wasn't sure what he believed anymore.

He was still standing there staring out across the field, trying to decide what to do, when he heard his telephone ring. With a final glance at the clouds, he hurried inside to answer the phone.

It was Jacob -- calling from the Quick Stop to remind Peanut he was supposed to go fishing with Jake and Dave Cooper tonight. Dave was headed for work right now, and wanted to remind Peanut about the fishing trip.

If Peanut Rollins had a passion in life, it was surely fishing. He forgot all about investigating the old field, and instead walked out to his garage to make sure all his fishing gear was in order. He'd been looking forward to this trip for a week now, and Jake didn't have to worry about Peanut forgetting about it.

He sat down at a workbench he had in the garage and just as he was opening his tackle box all hell broke loose.

The pounding was back in his head with a vengeance.

He stood up so quickly he upset his tackle box, and without even knowing why, he began to run in the direction of the old field.

He reached the edge of the field just in time to see a dark Pontiac Trans Am go careening down the dirt road, kicking up dust as it gathered speed. Peanut thought he could make out four people in the car, but couldn't be sure.

What the hell... Peanut thought, they can't drive down that road. They'll wreck for sure.

The thought had no more than entered Peanut's mind when the car skidded sideways and left the road. It was almost airborne for a minute, then settled back down on its wheels and hit a large rock. The car twisted sideways again, then violently flipped on its side and began to roll.

Peanut ran across the field as fast as he could, and reached the car almost by the time it came to a complete stop. The car had landed on its wheels, and the driver's door had been thrown open from the force of the crash. With a quick look inside Peanut saw there were indeed four people in the car, two boys and two girls, and all of them were unconscious.

Damn it to hell, Peanut thought, there's blood everywhere. It'll be pure luck if any of these kids are alive.

He grabbed the door on the passenger side and tried with all his strength to open it, but it was jammed shut. He left it and hurried around to the other side and saw the driver was half in and half out of the car, held in place only by his seat belt. Working as quickly as he could, Peanut wedged himself inside the car, unfastened the seat belt, and began to drag the driver from the wreckage. Peanut dragged the driver about twenty-five feet from the car, and then ran back to try and help another of the victims.

He'd noticed the girl in the back seat was bleeding badly, and knew he'd have to get her out next. He ran back around to the passenger to try the door again. Peanut was surprised to find the door had been violently wrenched open, and the two girls were lying outside the car on the grass. Peanut saw there were several footprints leading away from the car, but there was no sign of the other boy, the one who'd been in the back seat. Peanut would have to figure that out later, right now he needed to get both girls to safety as quickly as he could. He smelled leaking gasoline, and knew if the gasoline found its way to the blistering engine block, it was gonna get hotter than hell around here in a damn hurry.

Peanut was just laying the second girl on the grass beside the other two when he heard the loud wail of a police siren. He laid the girl down just as the police car came roaring into the field.

He stood up and waved at the policeman to stay back, just as the gas finally reached the engine. The car went off like a bomb, with enough force to knock Peanut flat on his back on the ground. Slivers of glass and sheet metal filled the air, and rained down about Peanut as he lay on the ground, but other than a few minor cuts and bruises he discovered later, Peanut came through without injury.

His ears were ringing and there were spots dancing before his eyes, but at least the damn pounding in his head had stopped. The police car came to a sliding stop and two officers jumped out and ran over to where Peanut sat holding his head.

"Damn, Peanut, what the hell happened here?"

The speaker was Deputy Larry Dodd, and he and Peanut had known each other for years.

"I ain't sure, Dodd," Peanut answered. "I saw the car come roaring down the old dirt road like the driver thought he was out on the interstate, and the next I knew it was rolling all over the field. It happened right after all that damn pounding started, I'm sure about that much. I heard that crap and when I came out in the back yard to see what the hell it was, that was when I saw the car."

"What kind of *pounding* are you talking 'bout Peanut?" the deputy wanted to know.

"Aw, hells bells, Larry. Surely you heard that loud pounding noise. Sounded like someone was beating a big bass drum, and it was loud enough to have been heard in three counties." Peanut looked at the deputy for the first time.

"I ain't heard no kind of loud pounding, Peanut. You already been drinking today? Aw, never mind." Larry Dodd knew it was likely Peanut had had at least one beer today, and maybe more, but he could tell he was far from being drunk.

With a puzzled look, Larry Dodd turned to the second deputy.

"You got any idea what the hell Peanut is talking about, Buddy?" he asked.

Dodd's partner, Buddy Ryan, was a heavy set, balding man, with a ruddy complexion that showed he spent a lot of time in the sun. Without a smile, he answered his partner.

"Naw, Larry, I ain't got the slightest idea. I ain't got no damn pounding in my head." With a scowl, he turned to Peanut, "Peanut, you got anything else to tell us?"

"Hell yeah, Buddy, I have," Peanut said. "When I first got over here to the wreck, there was four kids in the car. I looked in and counted 'em. And the passenger door was wedged shut. I got the driver out of the car first, and pulled him over there on the grass, and when I got back to the car, the door was open and the guy in the back seat was out and gone."

"What do you mean, out and gone? Ain't no way nobody could have walked away from that wreck. I think that pounding in your head has addled your brain just a little. Look Peanut, you've been a big help to these people, and if any of them live, they'll owe it you, but you look like you could use a little rest. Tell you what, we'll go over this field with a fine toothed comb, and if there was another kid in the car, we'll find him. Why don't you go on over to your house, and we'll come by later to get your formal statement. And don't worry. Oh, and Peanut, maybe you oughta take a couple of aspirin for your head."

When he finished talking to Peanut, Buddy turned to see Larry Dodd bending over one of the hurt girls, trying to stem the flow of blood that gushed from a gash on her arm. He walked over and saw Larry had used the first aid box from the patrol car on the girl's wounds. It was plain the other two kids were beyond needing first aid.

"The ambulance is on the way, Larry. Say, did you see anyone else in the wreck? Peanut swears there were four kids in the car when he first got here."

"I didn't see anybody else, but I ain't really looked yet. When the rescue team gets here we'll have time to check out the scene a little better." Larry looked at Buddy Ryan and shook his head. "This girl might make it, but I don't think the other two ever knew what hit 'em."

"It sure doesn't look like it," Ryan agreed.

Peanut had started back toward his house as Ryan had suggested, but had decided to take one more look around the burning car before he left the field. He walked around to the passenger side, thinking he might be able to follow the footprints he'd noticed earlier. But the heat from the car was still too much to allow him to get close enough to find the footprints, and it looked as if all the traces had been wiped away by the flames. The grass had burned in a large circle about the car, and any clues that might have been there were destroyed. He thought about telling the deputies about the footprints, but reconsidered. Hell, they had already asked if he was drinking, and after he'd told them about the pounding, they probably thought he was half crazy.

"Aw, hell," he said, "I might as well go on home. Ain't nothin' more I can do here."

He waved at the two deputies as he began walking across the field, and stopped for a minute and watched the ambulance scream to a stop beside the victims. As he started walking again, he suddenly had the funniest feeling someone was watching him. Quick as a cat he spun around, but except for the police officers and the rescue workers, the field was empty. With a shrug, he decided he'd get on over to his house and have that beer the cop had asked him about.

What the hell, he deserved it.

WOLF BROTHER

Wiley Harpe heard the scream as it tore through the fabric of reality, and with the sound he became aware he was awake again, after so many years.

How could this be

The last thing he remembered, four men were slipping a rough noose around his neck. He'd felt a sharp jerk, a moment of agonizing pain, then nothing.

Now he was awake. Awake!

Aw damn. There was a great big wagon of some kind headed straight at him. It was roaring loudly, and moving as swiftly as the wind. Double damn. There were no horses attached to the wagon. It was moving by its own power.

Suddenly the wagon hit a large rock and flipped onto its side and began to roll over and over. With a screeching sound of tearing metal, the wagon came to a sliding stop directly in front of the tall post where Wiley's head was once nailed.

Where his head had been nailed? How did he know that?

From his position high atop the post, Wiley could see down inside the wagon, and could see the four young people who were trapped inside. Suddenly a man ran up and began to drag the boy from the front seat out of the wagon, and at that same time, the boy in the back seat looked up and stared directly into Wiley's eyes.

Suddenly, Wiley was inside the boy.

He could breathe and taste, and touch, and all at once all of his senses came rushing back to him. With a quick look around, he realized he was in a hell of a lot of danger. This car could blow at any minute. He didn't even know how he knew this was a car, but somehow he did. He also knew he had to get out.

With the strength of the Wolf, Wiley kicked the door open and crawled out onto the grass. For some reason he didn't understand, he quickly pulled both of the girls out of the car. That must have been the last act of the boy whose body Wiley was in, for it was not something he himself would have done.

Wiley looked about the scene for a minute, trying to find the man who had tried to open the door. He saw him on the other side of the car, and before the man could get back from dragging the driver to safety, Wiley had fled into the trees. He needed to stop and think for a while, and already he felt the hunger beginning to gnaw at his insides.

It had been a long time between meals and now the Wolf needed to feed.

Without a sound, he crouched in the trees and watched as the police arrived and the wrecked car blew to kingdom come. He watched as one of the men left, and saw him suddenly turn and stare in his direction.

The man didn't see him. He was sure of that.

He was also sure he must satisfy the terrible hunger, and quickly.

WILEY

Miss Mattie Hastings had never mistreated a single one of God's creatures in her life. Well, she had thrown a couple of rocks at that infernal old tomcat that kept bothering her birds, and once or twice she had chased some dogs away from her garbage cans, but she'd never hurt any of them. Mattie was seventy-eight years old and had lived in Old Greenville all her life. She loved her charming little southern town, and she knew she'd never leave it. Her family was all from Greenville, and though Miss Mattie herself had never married, both of her parents and her two sisters were buried here. "I'll be buried here myself, one of these days," she'd often think to herself.

Miss Mattie had no way of knowing, when she lay down for her afternoon nap this hot August day would be her last day alive. She was dozing as the window was silently opened, and she didn't hear the soft footsteps of the intruder as he walked across the carpet of her small living room. Her bedroom door was open, allowing the air to circulate throughout the house because of the oppressing heat, but there was no noise at all to awaken her as the stranger stole into the room and stopped beside the bed. There was no sound to offer Miss Mattie the slightest hint someone had entered her home, and was standing staring at her as she lay asleep.

But for some reason, Miss Mattie woke up. Some inner voice called to her and she aroused from her sleep. Maybe it was a deep, subconscious sense of danger, or maybe it was the intensity of the man's strange blue eyes as he stood watching her. Whatever it was, Miss Mattie came awake with a start.

"I know there's someone here," Miss Mattie called into the semi-darkness of her bedroom, as she began to try and sit up in her bed. "I'm not scared of you, whoever you are. What do you want? You've got no right to be in my house. Get out of here. Get out before I call Sheriff Rice."

When he saw Miss Mattie's eyes come open, the intruder stepped away from the bed, into the deeper shadows offered by the partially opened door. He stood silently, betrayed only by the strange way his eyes seemed to glow in the half light. Almost like a wild animal, the eyes caught small rays of light and reflected them back toward the bed. They burned with some wild inner fire, which grew stronger with each passing second.

"I said, I know you're in here," Miss Mattie said again. "What do you want?" She slowly moved her hand toward the old fashioned phone that rested on her bedside table.

From the darkness by the door, the stranger spoke for the first time.

"It would please me greatly, Ma'am, if you wouldn't make any noise."

The voice was like a rusty file grating on an old tin washboard.

"And I'll only tell you the one time."

Although rough, the voice was soft and not really threatening, but still Miss Mattie felt an underlying tension, some hint of violence in the stillness, and she suddenly became very afraid.

"Please don't hurt me mister," she pleaded, and at the same time made a quick lunge for the telephone.

The stranger was on her before she even reached the side of the bed. His big fist came down on the back of Miss Mattie's head with such force her face was driven into the bedside table hard enough to break her jaw in three places, and send fragments of her nose bone straight into her brain. Miss Mattie was dead before her body stopped moving. From the time her eyes opened, until they had been closed forever, had taken less than one minute.

As she had supposed, Miss Mattie Hastings would be laid to rest in the small cemetery beside her parents and her sisters.

The stranger took his time looking around Miss Mattie's house.

He needed money, and he needed transportation, and while he was there he decided to have a bite to eat.

"My compliments to you, Ma'am," he spoke aloud, as he took a bite of the left over beef roast he found in the refrigerator, "You sure were a good cook."

Dumping the contents of Miss Mattie's purse on the kitchen table, he found her car keys and slipped them into his pocket. Opening her billfold, he was surprised to find over three hundred dollars in cash.

"Thank you kindly, Ma'am," he offered, and turned to the counter to make a sandwich of the remaining roast beef.

Holding the sandwich in one hand, he walked back into Miss Mattie's bedroom.

"Pardon me, Ma'am," he said, as he rolled her body the rest of the way off the bed, "but I need to look under your mattress, if you don't mind."

Sure enough, he found a medium sized brown envelope tucked under her mattress. But upon examination he found only two paid up insurance policies, totaling a little over forty-six hundred dollars, some old faded pictures of a young, quite pretty Mattie Hastings, and a letter from someone named Charlie, postmarked England, 1944. None of the papers were of any value to the man, so he dropped them on the bed and walked back into the kitchen.

He helped himself to a glass of milk and a handful of fresh baked chocolate chip cookies, and began rummaging through the silverware drawer. Among the shiny forks and spoons in the drawer, he struck pay dirt.

There were only a few small paring knives in the drawer, and four mismatched butter knives, but the treasure was a large, heavy, wooden handled butcher knife, sharp enough to shave with. Smiling broadly, the stranger lightly drew his finger across the edge of the blade, bringing a single drop of blood to the surface of his skin. He brought his finger to his mouth, and his strange eyes glowed once again with the blue fire.

Reaching to the gas cooking range, he turned all four burners on high. As an afterthought, he pulled the old cloth curtains from the window and placed them on the stove, watching as they rapidly caught fire. He waited only long enough to see the wall behind the stove was beginning to burn, then turned and left the kitchen.

As he passed through the house he poked his head back into the bedroom where the body of Miss Mattie lay.

"Ma'am, I want to thank you once again for your kind hospitality," he said. "You were a fine cook, and a fine lady as well. May your soul rest in peace."

Driving away in Miss Mattie's seven year old Dodge, he looked in the rear view mirror and smiled as he saw the flames break through the kitchen window.

BILLY

Billy Harp slowly opened his eyes but continued to lay quiet, not knowing what to expect next. Without moving he looked around the field. The last thing he could remember was some crazy fool running at him, screaming as loud as he could, and waving the severed head in the air.

The head.

Damn! Now he remembered.

Suddenly the whole thing came back to him. All the crazy things that had been happening to him. The motorcycle wreck at a tree that wasn't there, the wild dreams, and that crazy, never ending pounding in his head. And now all the stuff that had happened this morning. The feeling of familiarity he had experienced when he first stepped into the field. The men shooting at him, the riders, and that damned fight. Then those guys killed that man and cut off his head. Then, the strangest thing of all. The head looked just like Billy. It was entirely too much for Billy to take in at one time.

After not seeing any activity in the field for a few moments, Billy sat up and rubbed his eyes. He had a doozy of a headache that wasn't showing any signs of easing up. He slowly got to his feet and brushed off his clothes the best he could. He looked across the meadow to where the men had been fighting, and wasn't surprised at all to find not a soul in sight. There were no signs at all anyone had ever been in the field, besides Billy himself. Hell, he could have sworn there was an old log on the ground where the fight had taken place, but even it wasn't there now. He walked over and stood looking at the spot where he knew the fight had taken place, not understanding one damned bit of what had happened.

In an almost involuntary motion, and one he made without consciously thinking about it, Billy brought his hand to his neck, and softly rubbed it. His mouth was as dry as a cotton ball, and when he tried to swallow, he found it was difficult.

As Billy turned around and started to walk back towards the road, he heard his own voice coarsely whisper;

"Cut on, and be damned."

He shook his head and wondered why in the hell he'd said that.

Reaching his motorcycle, Billy decided it was time to head straight to the cave. He had spent enough time riding around, and there were too many strange things going on. Maybe he would be able to explain things a little better once he had seen what surprises the cave held in store. If it was half as crazy as the rest of the stuff that had been happening, it should be one hell of an interesting visit.

The rest of the ride passed without further incident, and Billy got his first look at the cave about three that afternoon.

The only way across the Ohio River at this point was by ferry, and the boat was about halfway back to this side when Billy stopped his bike. He sat there and looked across the river at the cave, and wondered how it must have looked in the old days. He was still daydreaming when the ferry touched the bank, and the people waiting started to drive on.

Other than Billy there were only five cars waiting to cross the river, so it wasn't long before the boat was slowly headed back toward the Illinois side of the river.

Billy took his time getting off the ferry, standing for a moment and looking at the little town that waited at the top of the hill. He wasn't really in a hurry now that he was close.

CAVE-IN-ROCK, STATE PARK - ILLINOIS

Billy Harpe rode up the hill to the small town called CAVE-IN-ROCK and parked his bike in front of a cafe on the town's main street. He hadn't eaten since breakfast, so he decided to grab a cheeseburger and a coke before he went to look at the cave.

When he entered the cafe, he noticed a small rack of post cards at the door. He paused a minute to look at some of them, and was surprised to find a few that told part of the Harpe's story. He took one with him as he went over to sit down at a table.

An attractive young waitress soon came over to take his order, and Billy held up the post card. "What do you know bout these old Harpe boys," he asked, smiling up at her?

"Well," the girl said, "not really very much. Almost everybody around here has heard the story bout the Harpes. They were supposed to be the worst killers that ever used the cave as a hideout. They said even the other pirates were afraid of them. That's about it. What can I get you?"

"I'll have a cheeseburger and fries," Billy said, "and a coke. And your company if you're not too busy. Maybe you can tell me a little about the old days."

It only took a few minutes to prepare Billy's order, and the waitress brought it over to the table. She sat the plate down and placed the silverware in a rolled up napkin on the table. Sitting the coke in front of Billy's plate, she pulled out a chair and sat down.

There were only three other customers in the cafe at the moment, and they looked to be busy eating their food.

"I'm not very busy right now," she said, "what do you want to talk about?"

"I'm just real interested in what happened way back then, you know. Just anything you may be able to tell me." Billy took a bite of his cheeseburger, and shook the plastic ketchup bottle until the thick red tomato sauce poured over his French fries.

"I don't know all that much that isn't on the post card you're holding Mister Harp," the girl said.

Billy looked at the girl, his surprise showing in his eyes. "And what makes you think my name is Harp," Billy asked?

"Is it?" The girl countered with a smile of her own.

"Well, yeah, it is" Billy said, "but how did you know?"

"Every so often somebody will come up here looking around, and asking about the cave. When somebody asks about the Harpes first, and the cave second we all just kinda assume their name is Harp, or they're related to the Harpes in some way. Been a lot of Harps up here you know. You ain't the first." The girl seemed to be kidding Billy just a little bit but he didn't mind.

"Looks like you got me cold" Billy said. "I'm a Harp, sure enough. I'm gonna go down to the cave and poke around a little I guess, see what's in there."

"You won't find anything," the girl said, "nobody ever has. If the Harpes left anything in there it's long gone by now."

"What do you mean, if they left anything in there?" Billy wanted to know.

"Well, some folks believe they might have hid some money, or gold, or something like that in the cave. The old legends say they did. Some folks say that's why they kept coming back here. But I don't believe it, not for one minute. Way I see it, if they'd left any gold or anything up there them old pirates would of found it." It didn't seem like the girl believed very much of the old tales about the cave, or about the Harpes either, for that matter.

"I didn't know they were supposed to have left anything in the cave," Billy said. "The books I read didn't mention that."

"The people around here have heard that old story for years," the girl said, "but if there had been anything in the cave the pirates missed, you can bet your bottom dollar somebody else would have found it long before now. Nah, there ain't nothin' in there, you're just wastin' your time, Mister Harp."

"Well, it's my time to waste, Miss. Uh, what's your name, if you don't mind me asking," Billy said. He kind of liked the openness of the pretty young waitress, and if she wasn't married or involved with somebody, he'd kind of like to talk to her some more. After he finished looking at the cave of course.

"Helen," she said, "Helen Rogers. And my husband will be in here in an hour or so. Have fun at the cave, and don't be too disappointed if you don't find anything."

The three men sitting at the other table had finished their meal, and were standing at the counter waiting to pay their check, so Helen stood up, "See you later," she said. With another smile Helen walked over to the cash register and picked up the men's check.

"Everything OK, boys," she asked.

"Everything's just fine, honey," Dexter Morgan told Helen. "Who's your friend?"

"Nother guy named Harp, come up to look at the cave. You know how it is."

"Yeah, guess we do. See ya later babe."

Billy watched the three men leave the cafe, but didn't really pay them much attention. He was still thinking about what the girl had told him about the cave.

Billy walked over to the counter with his own check in his hand. He laid the piece of paper on the counter and spoke to Helen.

"Thanks for the story," he said. "I'll look real close, and if I do come up with anything, you'll be the first to know." Billy took his change and decided to give the girl a good tip. The cheeseburger was pretty good and the girl was friendly, and she'd told him something about the cave he hadn't known.

As he handed her the money, she looked at the backs of the three men who had just left as they climbed into a pick up parked outside.

"Let me give you a tip too, Mister Harp. If you run into those three guys who just left, give 'em plenty of room. They're mean as hell and they're always looking for trouble."

Billy glanced at the truck as it pulled away from the curb. "Well, I'm not looking for trouble, so I'll try not to get in their way. Anyway, I'm just gonna be here for a little while. What could happen?"

"You never can tell, buddy, you just never can tell," Helen said.

Billy smiled at Helen and walked out the door, his mind already off the three men and back to wondering if the Harpes really did leave something in the cave, If they did, what in the hell could it have been? Oh well, it was like the girl said, if they left something, it would have been found a long time ago.

Billy headed for the cave, and didn't give another thought to the three men Helen had warned him about.

####

THE DARKWOLF

Billy hit the water feet first and hard, driving downward for long agonizing moments before he finally stopped. The coolness of the water woke him, and he began kicking as hard as he could toward the surface.

He was more dead than alive when his head came sputtering and spitting into the evening air, and he inhaled several large gulps of fresh air that were liberally mixed with Ohio River water.

He looked around to get his bearings, and saw the bank some twenty feet away, and weakly started paddling in that direction.

By the time he made it to the bank, he was barely breathing, and it was all he could do to pull himself upon the ledge and roll the short distance over into the mouth of the cave.

He'd hit the water hard but had somehow managed to miss hitting any of the large rocks that were strewn along the bank. The fall should have killed him, and probably would have had he not been able to get his legs straightened out in time to hit the water at a reasonable angle. Billy had grown up swimming in an old rock quarry on the Kentucky state line, and while he wasn't a great diver, he'd jumped off the cliffs many times. He knew enough to get his body straight, and try to make sure he entered the water feet first, and that was undoubtedly what saved his life.

Even though Billy was alive, he was far from being in good shape. Every breath felt like a knife was being twisted inside his rib cage, and he was pretty sure something was broken. One eye was swelled almost shut, and there was a dim, far off ringing in his ears that might signal a concussion. If he didn't get some help shortly, there was a good chance he might still end up dead.

As the thought of dying ran through his head, Billy found himself for some reason thinking about the old Harpe brothers.

Wonder if either one of them ever lay here in the cave, hurt as bad as I am, he thought. What would the big Harpe do to a man who did something like this to him.

Billy was close to losing consciousness again. The cave walls were spinning around and each minute the light seemed dimmer and farther away.

As he felt the last bit of awareness fading from his mind, he suddenly had the strangest thought.

The DarkWolf, boy, a voice in his head whispered. *Call on the DarkWolf. Call on the Harpe.*

With one last heart stopping effort, Billy sent a call ringing through the cave. He was never sure if he actually screamed the name, or if it was only an echo in his mind, but as he finally blacked out, he knew he had called one name.

Harpe.

Haaaaaarrrrrpe.

Billy didn't know how much time had passed, and wasn't quite sure if he was even awake or not. He could feel things, and he knew where he was, and somehow, although just barely, he could move.

With a superhuman effort he slowly raised himself to his feet. He knew he shouldn't even have been able to stand, let alone walk, but somehow he was moving around in the cave. Once again, everything was in slow, just like when he was back in the meadow.

Billy wasn't quite sure when the vibrations inside his head began, but when he felt them he recognized them.

They were the same vibrations he had experienced in the field outside Greenville, but many times stronger.

Every time Billy blindly touched the walls, the rock seemed to be alive, and almost in perfect tune with his body. He somehow climbed from ledge to ledge, and he could almost feel eyes on his back. More than once he wanted to turn to look behind, but something kept him moving ever deeper into the cave.

As Billy inched his way deeper and deeper into the cave, he began to hear the whispers.

Soft and low, the whispers came, and he could not quite make out what they were saying.

Often he thought he heard his name called, but he wasn't sure.

Deeper into the cave he went, and deeper still.

There was almost no light, and time had melted away.

The whispers became louder, the wild vibrations became stronger, and stronger still.

Louder they grew, ever louder, until Billy felt like his mind was slipping out of his body.

It was too late to run, too late to get out of the cave.

Too late.

The DarkWolf was awake and hungry, and he was answering Billy's call.

Billy found himself pulled ever deeper into the cave, until at last his trembling legs stopped before a huge rock, wedged deeply into a crevice in the wall.

His shaking hands reached out and touched the surface of the rock, and Billy was surprised at its coolness. The rock was much too large for Billy to move, but he wrapped his arms around it anyway, and pressed close against it, and almost passed out again as he stood there.

As Billy pressed his fevered face against the rock, the whispers suddenly became shouts, screaming his name out loud.

Harpe. *Harpe*. The voice called.

The Harpe has returned the voices screamed, and now the vibrations had become almost too much for him to withstand. They were tearing him apart, and there was nothing he could do.

Billy tightened his grip on the huge rock and lifted, and the rock moved.

It was impossible.

The rock was much too large for any one man to move, but move it did.

Billy lifted it higher, as if it were the most natural thing in the world. Slowly, Billy placed the rock on the ground in front of the ledge as easily as if it were a pebble.

Billy's eyes snapped open, clear and strong. The strange blue fire that had started in his eyes when he was lying in the field began to glow even brighter.

Just as though he had done it a thousand times, Billy reached deep inside the crevice. Farther inside he reached, until all at once he touched something that felt like cold steel.

As his hand curled around the object, the steel became warmer, then grew hotter, and hotter still as he withdrew it from its two century year old hiding place.

When the object came into view, Billy saw it was a knife, and such a knife as he had never seen before.

When the knife came slipping out of the crevice, the whispers reached a crescendo and the vibrations threatened to tear Billy's heart from his chest.

The trembling in Billy's hands stopped as he finally brought the blade completely out of the crevice in the rock, and held it in his hand. As suddenly as they had started, the whispers and the vibrations ceased.

The world inside the cave stopped, and Billy collapsed to his knees on the floor, his eyes tightly closed and his fingers still securely grasping the bone and leather handle of the blade, and the fire in his eyes was now burning completely out of control.

For a few moments he lay quiet, letting his body recover from the terrible vibrations it had undergone. Then, somehow, he sensed he was no longer alone.

Opening his eyes Billy tried to get his blurred vision to focus, and after a few seconds he began to see a figure in the darkness. As his vision cleared, Billy opened his eyes wider, and all at once he saw what he was afraid he would see.

Billy saw a demon thing that could only be the DarkWolf.

The voice of the DarkWolf was course, and not much above a whisper.

I said you had but to call and I would answer. I am back, Harpe, and I am hungry. Tis time once again to feast. You must find the Amulet, Harpe, and the child. We must find the babe. I will help you find them and then together once more shall we hunt.

"Who are you?" Billy asked.

Well and well do you know me, Harpe. I am the DarkWolf. I am your Father. I am you. We are the Harpe. And it is time to hunt. Hungry, Harpe, the DarkWolf is hungry...we must killlllll...

Billy Harp knew no more.

SATURDAY MORNING

CAVE - IN - ROCK

His glowing blue eyes slowly came open.

He glanced at his watch and saw it was almost five A.M.

He had been in the cave for almost twelve hours, and remembered none of it. None of it that is, after the three men had pushed him off the cliffs.

Remembering, he gingerly touched the back of his head and found to his surprise there was no damage, no blood, do indication at all he'd been hit with a baseball bat. The small scratches and cuts were gone, and Billy could breathe with ease, showing no sign of the injury to his ribs he was sure he'd sustained. He didn't understand it at all. Something strange was happening, but Billy didn't question it. He was just glad to be alive.

He got to his feet and walked to the mouth of the cave as a blood red sun rose in the sky. Without haste he walked to the concrete steps and began to climb.

Halfway up he paused, looked out across the river and lifted his great head to the morning sky.

He sniffed the wind.

"Are you ready, Stegall?" he asked aloud. "Your destruction has returned."

He could almost smell the fear of his old enemy, and knew the man was not far away. He intended to tear Stegall apart, an inch at a time, with his bare hands or with the long knife in his belt. He could feel the presence of the knife's twin, and knew Stegall waited. Long had he slept, but sweeter would be the vengeance after the passing of two hundred years.

Suddenly the air was filled with the sound of a baby crying.

And not just any baby.

A Harpe child.

He placed his hands over his ears but could not drown out the sobbing sounds. The cry echoed in his mind, and tormented him greatly.

Inside he heard the whisper once again.

The babe, Harpe, we must find the babe.

He turned his face to the southeast, toward Tennessee, and breathed deeply.

He knew he had to do as the Wolf had said. He must find the baby, and this time he would keep it from the Wolf. No more Harpe's would feed the demon. He would find the baby, that was for sure, and the child would be hushed, but the Wolf would not get this one.

It was then that he recalled that he had sent the women to Tennessee, and Wiley to the Trace.

To Tennessee it is then, he decided.

"Stegall, I come for you. I would have my other knife, Stegall, and the Wolf would have your heart. Remember, Stegall, remember how the Wolf feeds?"

Suddenly, Harpe felt the presence of the Harpe Amulet, and knew everything would be all right with the Wolf.

The Amulet was the most important thing in the universe to the Wolf, and so to Harpe. With the Amulet once again around his neck, he would be invincible, and the Wolf would feed until it was satisfied.

Other strange vibrations poured in upon Harpe as he stood there on the steps. He knew he must find their source.

He'd find the Amulet, and he'd find the baby and stop it's crying.

He'd find Stegall. Oh yes, he'd find the man who betrayed him, and his knife would drink deeply of Stegall's blood.

Once again he raised his head to the South and sniffed the wind.

Yes, he thought, South.

Suddenly his head snapped sharply to the right and upward, as if there had come some strange sound or odor blowing down across the hill above the cave.

Again he turned and stared out across the waters of the mighty Ohio, full into the face of the blood red rising sun.

Now, as the sun brushed his face, it was not Billy Harp who stood there. The man standing on the steps staring at the slate gray Ohio River was Micajah Harpe.

Wolf Spirit.

The DarkWolf.

The eerie blue eyes blazed with the Wolf fire, and once again he thought of Stegall. The time was at hand, southward would he go, and the Wolf would have his revenge.

"But first," the Wolf growled, as he turned and began to climb the steps, "I have business in the town."

RECKONING

Dexter Morgan kicked six or seven empty beer cans out of his way as he climbed out of the bed of the pick-up truck. He stretched and yawned, and then half jumped, half fell to the asphalt of the parking lot. He leaned against the truck for a few seconds, rubbing his face with both hands, trying to get his eyes accustomed to the early morning sunshine. He had a worn out old mattress in the bed of the truck and a couple of ragged quilts, but even with them a night spent sleeping in the truck left his bones stiff and sore.

Ronnie and Jimmy were both still sound asleep in the cab of the truck, and Dexter could hear loud snoring coming from both of them. He shook his head and began moving over to the tree line at the edge of the lot. He had to take a piss in the worst way.

As he walked across the lot, his mind went back to the big old boy they'd caught in the cave yesterday. Damn, that had been fun. They just might have to bring somebody else up here and throw them off.

The boy had only had a little over a hundred dollars in his pocket, but they planned on going through the saddlebags on the motorcycle today.

They had intended to go through them last night, but after they started getting drunk they kind of forgot about it. Anyway, they had plenty of time to do that today. After all, it wasn't like the bike was going anywhere.

After they'd thrown the kid over the cliff, they'd gone into town and bought six or seven six packs of beer and had come back out to the parking lot to drink it.

The lot had a few boat trailers parked over night, and it wasn't unusual for a few fishermen to sit in the lot, drink a few beers, and wind up sleeping in their trucks. The law hardly ever checked the lot out, so Dexter wasn't worried about a ticket or getting arrested for public drunkenness, or anything like that.

He scratched both his rear and his front as he stumbled his way across the lot, batting and blinking his eyes, and occasionally rubbing the back of his neck. He had the damnedest headache he'd ever had.

He touched the blue steel of the pistol in his belt as he walked, and remembered the eyes of the boy yesterday when he pointed the gun at him. Damn, what a rush.

Dexter stepped off the asphalt and into the grass and headed for the nearest tree, already unzipping his jeans.

"Hi ya, pal, got a light?" Dexter heard a low voice say.

Dexter had his right hand halfway inside his jeans when the man spoke, and he was concentrating more on taking a leak than he was on whoever was standing there. It should have been the other way round.

"Get the hell out of here," Dexter growled, as he finally finished fumbling with his pants and felt immediate relief as the hot liquid began to splash against the tree.

He glanced over his shoulder and saw a large man had stepped out from behind a tree, and was standing looking at him.

Dexter finished his business and got his jeans zipped back up before he turned to look at whomever it was that had spoken to him.

He got the shock of his life.

It was the guy they'd killed yesterday. Or at least, Dexter thought they'd killed him. But there was something different about him. His face had somehow changed. He looked older and rougher, and Dexter might not have recognized him if he hadn't been wearing the same clothes.

When Dexter looked into the eyes of the man standing before him the fear brought a rush of bile from his stomach, and an almost unbearable bitterness to his mouth.

Dexter's hand began creeping toward the pistol at his waist, but the little grin on the face of the stranger told him there was no way in hell he was ever going to get the pistol out of his pants.

He was right.

Harpe didn't even really hit Dexter. He simply wrapped his right hand around Dexter's face and smashed the back of his head into the tree. Dexter went out like a light, and hit the ground hard, lying face down under the tree where only seconds before he'd relieved himself.

When he woke up it was like a scene out of hell.

He was buck naked, lying on the ground beside the pick-up truck, his hands tightly bound in front of him with his own belt. A quick look around showed him his brother Ronnie and Jimmy Ellis were in a similar state of circumstances.

They weren't in the parking lot anymore.

Dexter looked around, and suddenly realized they were back on top of the cliff. The same place they'd been yesterday. The big guy was sitting on the same log where Dexter had sat yesterday, and he was holding Dexter's pistol.

"Hey. Hey, you dirty sumbitch, you better let us go. When I get up I'm gonna..."

"What'cha gonna do feller, push me off the cliff," the man said, his voice still very soft. "Sorry son, been there, done that. Anyway, I've got a better idea."

The big man stood up and walked over to where the three of them lay. Without a word he reached into the truck and got the baseball bat from behind the seat. He then walked over close to the edge of the cliff and snapped the handle off against a large rock. Without looking at the three men, Harpe casually propped the bat up against the rock, with the fragmented, splintered shaft pointing upward at a slight angle.

Still without speaking, he walked back to where the three men lay and scooped Ronnie up by his hair. He half carried, half dragged the struggling man back over to where the bat was waiting.

"You seem to really like that ball bat, hoss," he said, "I think I'll let you take it to hell with you."

Saying that, he roughly spun Ronnie around and grabbed him by his shoulders. With almost no effort, he lifted Ronnie straight up over his head, shook him for a second till his legs were flying, and then quickly slammed him butt first down on the broken, splintered handle of the bat.

He left him there and then turned and walked back to where Dexter and Jimmy looked on in horror.

He quickly shoved the two of them into the cab of the truck, using Dexter's belt to secure their hands to the steering wheel.

The only thing Dexter noticed was Harpe's eyes. They were balls of blue fire, raging like the flames of hell itself.

Ronnie had gone into shock and passed out, and never knew it when the big man threw him into the bed of the truck. He never heard it when Harpe started the truck motor, wedged a tree limb against the accelerator, jerked it into gear and slammed the door. He didn't hear the motor's whine or see the dust and grass that flew from its wheels as it headed toward the cliff.

The other two weren't so lucky.

Jimmy screamed loud and long, but Dexter found his throat so dry he couldn't make a sound. He couldn't even shout one last curse at the man as the truck began to move. The last thing he remembered was the cold, soft voice of the stranger.

"Take a good look, boys, cause in a minute you're gonna be flying. Just like that little bird out there. Give the devil my regards, boys, and tell him the Big Harpe is back."

Dexter may have wondered what the hell the Big Harpe was, but he didn't wonder long. The pick-up gathered speed as it roared across the grass, and then soared outward for ten or fifteen feet as it became airborne off the edge of the cliff. With the motor still screaming, the truck then took an abrupt nosedive toward the sluggish, early morning waters of the Ohio River. It turned one flip and threw Ronnie out of the truck bed, baseball bat still embedded between his buttocks.

Ronnie was the lucky one. He was already dead. Dexter and Jimmy were tied tightly to the steering wheel of the truck, and would have the entire ride down to the river, and most of the way to the bottom, to wonder how they'd screwed up so badly.

By the time the truck hit the river, Harpe was well on his way to the small diner. He had fed the Wolf, now it was time to feed himself.

DANIEL HAWK

It took Daniel and his father the better part of the day to decide they knew about where Harpe had been slain. The story of Wolf Spirit and his brother had been passed down through his family in its most pristine form, for it was their ancestor Dancing Hawk who had made the tomahawk and had first presented it to Micajah Harpe.

There were several old maps and drawings in an ancient chest that showed the location of the killing, and by carefully comparing those with a recent map of the area, they were reasonably sure the exact spot could be found.

Daniel's father walked into the room just as Daniel finished packing his travel bag. In his hand he carried several small items Daniel did not remember ever having seen before. One look at his fathers face, and Daniel could see just how serious he was taking all of this.

"Daniel," his father said, "in our family have been many powerful medicine men of the People, and in your veins runs their blood. Upon this leather cord are many symbols of that power, which I hope will protect and guide you on your journey. Wear the necklace at all times, it could mean the difference between life and death. Open the small pouch only if there is no other means available to you to stop the demon, and then only if your life itself is in danger."

With these words his father placed the leather thong and its symbols around Daniel's neck.

He then began speaking again.

"In this larger pouch I have placed paint and a feather from the sacred Eagle. When you gain the magic tomahawk, prepare yourself in the traditional manner, and use the feather to aid you in contacting the spirit world. It is only there you may find the knowledge you will need to conquer the DarkWolf. Go now, my Son, and may the Eagle guide and keep you."

Even though it was early fall in some of the most beautiful country in America, still Daniel wasted little time sightseeing on his trip through Tennessee. He felt a terrible sense of urgency, as though time were about to run out.

He crossed into Kentucky around noon, and by two-thirty he was standing in a field just outside Greenville. He had no way of knowing barely twenty-four hours earlier Billy Harp had stood on this same ground, and had experienced the very event Daniel himself was here to try and learn about. The decapitation of Micajah Harpe.

Daniel's father's old maps and their research had brought him to the same place Billy's inner vibrations had brought him, and from this day on neither of them would know peace until the DarkWolf was finally beaten.

Daniel Hawk stood in the center of the field and looked all around. According to the legend, Harpe was shot from his horse and fell to the ground at the bottom of a small rise. There was only one such rise in the field, so it was there Daniel began his search.

He walked to the top of the rise and stood looking down at the tree line. Without thinking, he brought his hand to the pouch and brought out the Eagle feather. Holding the feather in his hand, he began to walk down across the field toward the trees. About half way down he felt himself being drawn to the right, and he gave in to the pull of the ancient feather that seemed to be leading him. When he finally stopped, he was almost to the trees, and was very certain he was near the spot where Harpe had fallen.

The tomahawk should be here, he thought. Harpe used it in his last stand, and no other mention is ever made of it. If no one removed it from this field, I should be able to find it.

Daniel sat cross-legged on the ground, as he had seen his father do many times. He closed his eyes and tried to picture what must have happened here those many years ago.

In his mind he saw much the same scene as Billy had witnessed yesterday, although not nearly so vivid. He saw the men riding out of the trees, heard the gunshots, and saw the outlaw lying on the ground behind a fallen tree, almost at this exact spot. He saw the man's bloody head lifted aloft, and he also saw the tomahawk, lying where Harpe had dropped it.

Without knowing why, Daniel raised his hand and sent the Eagle feather point first into the air, then watched as it spiraled and turned, and finally landed at a spot some twenty feet from where he sat.

Daniel was trembling when he stood up, and his knees were weak when he tried to walk.

He carefully made his way to where the feather lay on the ground and then got down on his hands and knees and began crawling about on the ground, searching every inch of it.

After an hour of searching and finding nothing, Daniel became convinced if the tomahawk were indeed still there, it would be buried under several inches of dirt and fallen leaves and dead grass. He had brought along a small shovel, and after removing his shirt and putting it aside, he began to dig around the area. The ground was not as hard as it might have been, due to recent rains, and was not as hard to dig in as he'd expected.

He'd been digging about an hour when all at once his shovel point struck something hard. He had already dug up a good many rocks, and at first thought this was just another. But as he lifted his shovel, he noticed this particular rock had an unusual shape. Taking it from the shovel, he sat down on the grass and began to clean away the dirt. In a couple of minutes he knew the object was man made, and was about the right size of the blade he was searching for. He walked through the trees to the nearby stream, and squatted down at the edge of the water and began to wash the object.

The crystal clear running water revealed the thing Daniel held in his hands to be the blade of a great tomahawk.

There was no doubt in Daniel's mind this was the magic blade fashioned by Dancing Hawk and won by Harpe in his battle with BearKiller.

Daniel could almost feel the power of the blade as he balanced it in his hand.

The weapon was heavy, much heavier than he'd had imagined, and after all these years it still held an edge. Harpe must have been a very strong man to swing a weapon such as this. With the passage of years, the handle had rotted away, and so had its leather wrappings, but the blade was as perfect as the day it had been made.

O.K., Daniel thought, what did Pop say to do now? Prepare myself in the traditional manner. Just how in the hell do I do that? It's been a long time since I learned that old stuff.

Glancing at his watch, Daniel saw it was only five-thirty. He had plenty of time before dark to get ready.

He gathered up a lot of the driest wood he could find and placed it in a pile on the bank of the stream. He was miles from the nearest farmhouse, so he wasn't worried about anyone seeing him, but still he checked all around the field, and back up toward the road where he'd left his car.

When he was satisfied he was truly alone in the woods, he stripped himself naked and began the process of painting the magical symbols of the Hawk upon his body. As he painted, he chanted to the spirits for guidance and help.

On his chest he painted his families mightiest symbol, the sign of the hunting Hawk.

On his forehead, he painted the sign of the Owl for wisdom.

On his arms he painted the symbols of courage and strength, and the symbol of speed and endurance was painted on each leg.

On each eyelid, he painted the magical symbol of Vision, known only to the Hawk family.

Lastly he prepared the pipe with the tobacco his father had placed in the pouch and placed it upon the ground near the pile of firewood.

When he was finally ready, he lit the fire, and as it began to burn he started his dance around the flickering flames. As he danced, he chanted the People's age-old call to the animal spirits.

Daniel chanted and danced around the fire until he was totally absorbed in the ceremonial rite, and as the fire began to burn down he settled cross-legged upon the ground to meditate. He lifted his father's pipe he had prepared, and lit it with a glowing ember from the fire. He inhaled deeply, and felt the hot acrid smoke fill his lungs. He held the pipe in his left hand, and with his right hand used the Eagle feather to fan the smoke back into his face, even as he exhaled it from himself. He didn't know how long he had sat before the fire in this manner, but at last he saw the air in the darkness shimmer, and out of the fire a figure emerged.

Daniel was sure it was the Eagle or the Hawk, come to guide him and offer wisdom, but when the figure stopped shimmering and became focused in Daniel's eyes, he gasped as the saw the figure of the mighty Wolf standing before him.

It was the same Wolf he had seen in his dream. The Wolf with the blazing blue eyes, the one his father had called the DarkWolf.

The two stared into each other's eyes for a few silent moments, before the DarkWolf finally spoke.

"When you reach into my world, Daniel Hawk," the Wolf said, *"you do not always get what you expect. The Eagle shall come to you in due time, but first, hear the words of the DarkWolf. I bring you a warning most dire, young Hawk. You deal in things you know little of, and in so doing you set yourself against me. Leave the magic blade where you found it, and return to the home of your father. Only by doing this can you spare yourself my wrath. The blade has no power over me in the world of man, and will do you little good should you find yourself face to face with me in battle. Therefore, leave the blade and do not seek out the Harpe. To do so will mean your destruction."*

As suddenly as he appeared, the DarkWolf was gone.

He melted back into the shadows as if he had never been there. As soon as the DarkWolf has disappeared from sight, Daniel felt the air disturbed for a second time. This time he heard the soft beating of wings, and above the fire the Eagle appeared.

"I could not come to you until the DarkWolf was gone, Young Hawk," the Eagle said. *"The DarkWolf is all powerful, and it is possible that even I may not stand against him. The time of our greatest battle is at hand, and we both know it. Even now we seek to line up our warriors. Listen well, Hawk, for time is short."* The Eagle paused, looked even more fiercely at Hawk.

"Your father told you of the DarkWolf and his bond with the Harpe, and so you already know much of what happened so long ago. What you do not know, what no one save Harpe himself knows, is that the power the DarkWolf holds in the world of man lies not in Harpe, nor in the tomahawk, nor even in the twin blades. The DarkWolf power lies dormant inside the Amulet. The Star of the Harpe Clan. The star, when worn by a first born Harpe child holds power far and above any other that resides in either of our worlds. The Amulet has not been worn since Micajah Harpe was slain, and we of the spirit world have not heard its battle cry since then. We hoped it had been lost forever. But such is not the case. The Amulet has once again been found, and there are two new Harpe firstborn sons, either one of which may well be called upon to hold the power. The DarkWolf has been awakened, and so too has the power of the Amulet roused from its slumber. Though the Harpe you seek does not wear the Amulet as of yet, it is only a matter of time. Even as we speak, the Amulet is softly calling to Harpe and leading him to it. He will seek out the Amulet and the new Harpe son, and so will the DarkWolf. If the big Harpe should find the Amulet, all the fury of the DarkWolf will once again be unleashed upon your world, and this time perhaps upon ours as well. This must not happen. What may be worse yet, young Hawk, will be if the new Harpe son is taken by the DarkWolf. This also must not happen. Should the DarkWolf gain both the babe and the Amulet, and bring them both to the spirit world, even the heavens themselves may tumble. By

*himself, the Harpe is a mighty and terrible warrior, and will bring
death wherever he walks. He can feed the Wolf, but until the wears
the Amulet around his neck he cannot call the DarkWolf from our
world into yours. In our world, we can partially contain the evil, for
we have powers of our own which serve to hold the DarkWolf at
bay. But should Harpe regain the Amulet and place it around his
neck the gate between our worlds will open and the DarkWolf shall
be unleashed upon your world. The power he will gain will be too
much for even those of my world to control. Beware, Daniel Hawk,
for the Harpe you must do battle with is one and the same Harpe
who long ago made your world tremble in terror. He has regained
part of the power of the Wolf and lives again to serve that power.
He is the only Harpe to learn the secret and the power that lives
within the Amulet, and because of that he is the most dangerous
man you shall ever meet. He has visited in our world where he
learned much of our ways, and is a most terrible adversary even
without the Amulet. If he regains the full power of the Amulet, both
our world shall be in mortal danger. Your task then, Daniel Hawk,
is plain. You must endeavor to find the Amulet and keep it from
Harpe, or else kill the man by whatever means you may. And you
must under no circumstances allow the DarkWolf to take the babe.
There is a man called Stegall who holds the knife that once killed
Micajah Harpe. Seek him out and enlist his aid. Do not be deceived
by appearances, for there is more to him than meets the eye. Go to
the Nickajack Spirit Cave and call upon me once again. In the cave
is a gate I may temporarily open, and you and Stegall may visit my
world. There is power here that perhaps will aid you in your battle.
The tomahawk and the knife are powerful weapons, but even they
may not stand against the Harpe. Remember, Daniel, the Harpe
alone is as one with the wild Wolf, but with the Amulet around his
neck he gains the power of the DarkWolf himself, and will be nigh
impossible to stop. No one, even myself knows the power that could
be unleashed if the DarkWolf gains both the Amulet and the babe.
Or what might happen should the Harpe seek to take the Amulet and
he and the Wolf battle for its possession. The Harpe will try to keep
the babe from the Wolf, but even his power may not be enough. The*

only chance is for you to find the Amulet, Daniel Hawk, find the Amulet."

With those last words, the Eagle spread its wings and flew into the shadows and disappeared even as the DarkWolf had done, leaving Daniel Hawk alone by the dying fire.

Daniel came out of the trance slowly, and as his vision began to clear he saw he campfire was almost out. Suddenly, he felt an involuntary shiver run down his spine that had nothing whatsoever to do with the dying fire.

As his senses returned, he looked at himself and felt more foolish than anything else. He was naked, with wildly colored paint streaked all over his body, standing in a clearing in the woods in the middle of nowhere, talking to himself. He took a few wipes at the paint with his handkerchief and hastily dressed. Foolish or not, he thought he'd better try to find this Stegall character as quickly as possible.

The blood of the medicine men that ran through him told him a visit from the DarkWolf and the Eagle in one vision was out of the ordinary, and must be acted upon in haste.

He'd have to find Stegall and convince him how serious this matter was, and someway together they'd have to find Harpe and the Amulet.

Then there was the baby! As if things weren't complicated enough, they were going to have to keep the child from the Wolf.

Damn.

Walking back to his car, he found the biggest question he had to answer was just what the hell would he do when he finally came face to face with Harpe. Someway, the man had to be killed and the Amulet destroyed. He wasn't sure if he were up to the task.

I hope this Stegall is badder than the Devil and bigger than two pro wrestlers, Daniel thought. *Something tells me I'm gonna need all the help I can get.*

MICAJAH - CAVE-IN-ROCK

Helen Rogers had been at the cafe since four-thirty that morning. She always opened up a little earlier on Saturday because there were so many more fishermen than there were during the week. A lot of them would stop in for a cup of hot coffee and a cinnamon roll or bacon and eggs before the hit the river.

The coffee was ready, and Helen had the biscuits in the oven when she heard the door open.

"Be right with ya," she called, "help yourself to the coffee."

"Don't mind if I do," Helen heard a man's voice reply, and then the sound of someone rattling the cups and the smell of the steaming coffee.

She walked up to the front of the cafe and saw a lone man sitting at one of the booths. Picking up her ticket book, Helen walked around the counter and over to the booth.

"What'll it be this morning?" she asked. "I've got some fresh country ham that'll be ready in just a minute."

As Helen reached the booth and got her first look at the customers face, she saw it was the Harp man that had stopped in late yesterday afternoon. But he didn't look like the same guy. His face appeared older and harder, and his eyes seemed strange and distant. His clothes were dirty and had spots of something that appeared to be dried blood all over them. But that wasn't the strangest thing about him. Not at all.

For some reason, he looked bigger, more muscular, and something about his eyes had changed. It was apparent he didn't have the same attitude as when he was in the cafe yesterday.

"Jeez, what happened to you? You didn't by chance have a run in with Dexter Morgan and his friends, did you?"

"A run in? You might say it was more like a run off," he laughed. "Anyway, I don't expect they'll be botherin' anyone else in the future."

Once again noting the dried blood on his clothes, Helen tried to change the subject.

"I see you're up bright and early this morning. Going down and check out the cave today?"

"I checked it out yesterday afternoon, Ma'am, and learned all I needed to know. Reckon I'll be heading home today."

"Did you find anything interesting," Helen asked.

"Yes Ma'am, I did," the man replied, looking up at the pretty waitress.

Helen found herself once again looking into the strangest blue eyes she'd ever seen. She didn't remember his eyes being that color when he was in here yesterday.

"I'll have some of that ham, and maybe a few scrambled eggs and some gravy. And five or six biscuits, if you don't mind," he said, never taking his eyes off her face.

"Won't be but a minute, honey," she said. "Here, let me freshen up that coffee for you."

Helen picked up the cup and walked over to the counter. The way he was looking at her made her nervous. She was not quite happy about the way he had changed since yesterday. She suspected he might have had a run-in with the three men, and from the looks of him, he must have won. But what had happened to the others?

She looked out the window and saw Irving Thacker and Morris Hill stopped across the street buying gas for their boat. She gave the two men a small wave neither noticed, but when she looked back toward the booth, she saw the Harp boy had noticed her gesture.

She put four hot biscuits and several pats of butter on a plate and walked back over to the booth.

Neither Irving nor Morris was looking this way yet, so Helen stood by the booth hoping one or the other would finally see her. She knew she had a minute or two while the ham finished cooking, so she decided again to try a little small talk, hoping to stall until the two other fishermen came in.

"Just what did you find in the cave that was so interesting?" she asked, and once again got a glimpse of the boy's wild eyes. "Did the guys that were in here follow you to the cave, is that what happened?"

"Yes Ma'am, they did. And you were right, they were looking for trouble."

"Oh my God. They hurt you didn't they?"

"No Ma'am, they didn't. Least ways, nothin' that didn't heal. Actually, it was the other way round. You might say trouble found them. They wanted to raise a little hell, so I went along with 'em. I let 'em raise their hell, and then I cultivated it for 'em."

Helen looked out the window again, but didn't see either of the fishermen this time. She twisted a strand of hair between her thumb and her index finger as she stood there.

The boy noticed the waitress' nervousness, and had seen her wave at the two me across the street a little while ago.

"Well, I guess I might as well show you what I found, it won't make a hell of a lot of difference anyway."

He leaned down and unzipped the overnight bag that lay at his feet and slowly withdrew a long, gleaming knife. He held it up for Helen to see.

"What do you think of this?" he asked. "I found it hidden in the cave."

With her first glimpse of the knife, she opened her mouth to scream. Maybe the fishermen across the street would hear her.

The scream never materialized.

As soon as she opened her mouth, the man in the booth brought the blunt handle of the blade upward in a savage backhanded blow that caught her high on the forehead. As she lost consciousness, the last thing Helen saw was the fire that was burning in the man's wild blue eyes.

Harpe was moving out of the booth as soon as he'd felt the knife strike the girl. He caught her as she fell and quickly carried her behind the counter, where he softly sat her down in the floor. It wouldn't do for her to be noticed any too soon. He had a nagging doubt about leaving any live witnesses behind, but he kind of liked the girl, and besides he had other fish to fry. Much bigger fish.

Turning around, he grabbed a fork and speared two thick slices of the ham and two more of the golden brown biscuits. Without haste, he walked back over to his booth and sat down.

Using her damp towel, he quickly wiped as many traces of blood from his clothes as he could. Helen had noticed it, so that meant somebody else might pay attention to it also. After a few moments cleaning, he returned to his breakfast, needing the hot black coffee, and relishing the country ham and biscuits. He was finishing his breakfast as the two men from across the street entered the cafe.

"Where's Helen?" one of the men asked. "I need some of her coffee right now."

"She said she needed something she'd left at home, and she'd be right back. But I'll be more than happy to pour you a cup."

"Thanks, Mister," the second man said, "but we just need to fill our thermos and go. We'll drink it once we're on the river. The fish 'er waitin'."

"Y'all been catching a lot?" Harpe asked, taking the steel thermos from the man.

"We been a'gettin' our share of 'em," the man replied, and began to follow Harpe over to the coffee urn. "You ain't from around here, are you young feller?"

"Naw," Billy answered. "I'm from down in Tennessee. Just came up here to see the old cave. It's pretty interesting, ya' know. Say, what d'ya use for bait, seeing as how you're catching so many fish? If you don't mind me asking, that is?" As he spoke, the big man was calmly filling the thermos with the hot coffee. They were standing by the counter, not three feet away from the body of the unconscious.

"Hell naw, son, I don't mind you asking a'tall. Course, that don't mean I'll tell you," the man laughed.

The other man had stopped by the booth where Harpe had been eating and was standing looking at the long knife Harpe had left on the table.

"I'll thank you not to bother the knife," Harpe said. "I'm a little particular about it. It's been in the family a long time."

"Ain't gonna hurt it none, Mister. Just looking, that's all. That's a hell of a knife you got there."

"Yeah it is. Ain't but two like it in the world. And I own 'em both."

He came around the counter and over to the booth, stopping in front of the man who was still looking at the knife. Harpe picked the knife up, and there was the hint of a soft glow rekindling in his eyes as his hand touched the warm steel. He ran his thumb along the razor edge of the blade. For a long second he stared at the two men and then asked; "Anything else I can help you with?" The fire glowed a little brighter.

"Naw, all we wanted was the coffee. We got to be gettin' to the river. I can hear them catfish callin'?"

The men walked over to the cash register and stopped. "Helen charges two bucks to fill up the thermos. I'll just leave it here by the register. Be seein' you."

Harpe watched as they walked out the door and noted they climbed into an old green pick-up truck with a good-looking fishing boat hooked behind it.

Harpe held the door open for a second and called to the men; "That's a fine boat you got there. Good luck on the river."

He barely heard the last words of the sentence as one of the men said; "... good chance we'll run into Constable Beale on the river. We'll tell..."

The men pulled away from the cafe without Harpe hearing anymore, and he went back inside. He drank another cup of coffee, and then wrote a note on a sheet of notebook paper he found behind the counter.

EMERGENCY AT HOME.

BACK LATER. HELEN

Harpe stuck the notice to the inside of the window on the front door with a piece of scotch tape and locked the door as he left the restaurant. He was whistling his mother's nameless little tune as he cranked up his motorcycle and headed down the hill toward the boat dock. He had a little business with a couple of good ole boys in a green pick-up. Letting the waitress live was one thing, but there was no way he was going to leave behind two additional witnesses. Especially if there was a chance they might run into a Constable while they were out fishing.

Irving backed the truck down into the water at the boat dock and set the parking brake while he and Morris put the boat in the water. When the boat was floating free from the truck, with Morris already getting ready to crank the powerful Mercury engine, Irving pulled the truck back up into the parking lot where they'd leave it while they were on the river. Irving stopped for a minute and poured Morris and himself a cup of the hot coffee, and then started back down to where Morris had pulled the boat over to the riverbank.

Irving saw Morris had tied the boat to a small tree on the bank, and couldn't figure out why. They were ready to go, and all Morris should have done was keep the boat steady with the engine until Irving was aboard. Irving couldn't see Morris in the boat, and that was strange too. The boat was drifting in and out, first to the bank, then back into the river, with no one at all at the controls.

Irving got a little closer, and noticed something that looked like Morris' bright yellow "CAT" cap floating in the water beside the boat. He dropped the coffee and ran to the boat as fast as he could.

It was Morris' cap all right, and Morris was still in it.

Irving jumped into the water and grabbed Morris' body under the arms and tried to lift him out of the river. The water was about seven feet deep where the body was, but Irving was standing in water that was only four feet deep. Irving waded out a few more feet, till the water was almost up to his chin, but still couldn't budge Morris' body. He quickly ducked under the water and saw Morris' right foot was wedged tightly between two rocks.

No wonder I can't move him, Irving thought, and with his last breath he pushed himself hard toward the surface.

But his head touched something, and he found he couldn't move upward. He bent his knees and pushed up with all his strength, but whatever was holding him still wouldn't let his head above water. He was quickly running out of air, and used the last of his strength to spin around and try to find out what was holding him. The last thing he saw was the cold blue fire burning in the eyes of the young man they had met in the cafe just a short while ago. The last thought in Irving's mind might have been relief that at least the man hadn't used the knife.

Harpe knew no one had seen him cross the parking lot and go down to the boat dock, and he took his time going back up the riverbank. He picked up the thermos where Irving had dropped it, and found there was still a little coffee left in it. He finished the coffee, and carefully wiped away his prints before he laid the thermos on the seat of the green pick-up. Without stopping, he walked over to the edge of the lot where he'd left the bike, climbed on and cranked the engine to life.

Other than the girl, the two fishermen were the only people who had seen Harpe in the cafe this morning, and he had made sure the two men wouldn't be talking. It had worked in the old days, no reason it wouldn't work now. He didn't think the waitress could give anyone a very good description, as his appearance had changed quite a lot from the first time she saw him to the last. As long as he didn't leave any other witnesses behind, the police would have a hell of a time figuring out what he looked like, where he was going and how he was traveling. There was no one in Cave-In-Rock that could tell anybody anything. He had kept his helmet on when he crossed the river on the ferry yesterday, and would do the same when he crossed back today. All anyone could say was they had seen a man on a motorcycle cross on the ferry, and that sure as hell wasn't unusual. Harpe was a careful man. He believed you lived longer that way.

All in all, Harpe was satisfied with the way the day had started.

Harpe looked at his watch as he mounted his bike and rode toward the ferry. It was seven thirty-four, Saturday morning.

At Lasssst Harrrpe, at lasssstt I feeeeed

BETHANY

It wasn't starting out as such a great day for Bethany Roberts.

She was late for work, just as she'd thought she'd be, and today being a Saturday made it even worse. It was an overtime day, and the boss expected everyone to be there exactly on time. Her foreman was a just a kid who had been promoted mostly because his father was the plant manager, and he didn't know his elbow from a hole in the ground. His head had swelled so big when he was made foreman that nobody liked him anymore. Even the guys who used to be his best friends didn't have much use for him now.

To make matters worse, he'd been after Bethany to sleep with him for several months, and now that he was the boss, he figured he wouldn't have to take no for an answer. Bethany would either screw him, or he'd make life on the job so miserable she wouldn't be able to stand it. He knew she needed the job because of the baby, and thought it was just a matter of time until he got in her pants.

So far though, she was resisting his every move, and he was doing all he could to make her days pure hell.

If she was a minute late, he was standing by the time clock, waiting for her to punch in. Today was no exception.

"Well, Beth baby, this is the third time in two weeks you've been late. I told you the next time meant a write up, didn't I?"

His name was Jeffery Hankins, and he was tall and skinny, with dirty looking dishwater blonde hair and a face pitted with old acne scars. He was ugly as homemade sin, but he thought he was God's gift to women. Now that he was foreman, he thought every woman in the plant should be standing in line, waiting for the chance to peel off her clothes and jump into bed with him.

"Yeah, Jeff, you told me. So write me up, I don't really care. I'm the fastest machine operator you've got, and you know it. That's why you keep scheduling me with Saturday work. So write me up if you think you have to, and give me two days off. Then who'll make the precious production schedule for you. Just how long you think you'll keep your job if you don't make your schedules? Now, either write me up, or get off my case."

Bethany was mad, and she was tired of taking all this crap off the little foreman. She'd been working here for seven years, since she graduated high school, and the only time she'd had off was when the baby had been born. Well, she'd made up her mind she didn't have to take any more of the jerky little foreman's crap. She'd read in the paper about a girl in Nashville who had filed a sexual harassment lawsuit against her boss, and had won. Bethany knew she had more grounds for a lawsuit than that girl had had. If Jeff didn't get off her case, and especially if he ever actually touched her, she was taking him and this whole company to court and suing them for all she could.

"Settle down, Beth, settle down," Jeffery said. "It ain't the end of the world. You have trouble with the baby again last night?"

"Yeah, he's been up again most all night. I'm so tired I can barely keep my eyes open. It's a wonder I got here at all today. Thanks for asking, Jeff, but I meant every word I said. I'm just too tired to argue with you today." Bethany was trying to be civil to her boss. She just wanted to go to work without a hassle, put in her eight hours, and go the hell home. That didn't seem like it was asking too much.

"Aw Beth, don't worry 'bout it. I ain't gonna write you up, you know that. Get on over to your machine and go to work. Oh, and Beth, I really do hope there's not much wrong with the baby." Jeff turned around and walked over toward the break room.

As she watched him walk away, all Bethany could think was, Thank God for small favors. She hurried over to her sewing machine, turned it on, and sat down behind it.

She had just barely started work when all at once she felt the necklace in her blouse growing hot. Alarmed, she quickly reached inside her bra and removed the leather pouch.

Sure enough, when she opened the pouch, the Amulet felt warm to the touch. It had never done that before. For several minutes it continued growing warmer as she held, and then began to cool off.

Strange.

Finally she placed the Amulet back into the pouch and laid it on the table beside her sewing machine. She'd have to ask her aunt if she knew what could cause this to happen.

She looked at her watch and saw it was a little past seven-thirty AM. Seven thirty-four, to be exact. For some reason, she thought the time might be important.

It was almost eleven the next time Bethany thought about the necklace, and this time when she touched it, it had cooled all the way back down to normal. She put it back inside her bra where it belonged, and by the end of the day she had forgotten about the incident.

That afternoon, Mike had one of his hardest crying spells yet. His little body shook with the sobs, and it took Bethany almost hour to quiet him down. She knew she had to do something, but she couldn't figure out what. Whatever she decided to do, it would have to be in a hurry. All of this was about to drive her crazy.

STEGALL AND HAWK

Andrew Stegall could have told you almost to the minute when Micajah Harpe walked out of the cave. He could feel Harpe's return deep down in his bones, and it was an ache he knew damn well aspirin wouldn't relieve.

Andrew went out on his front porch and sat down in his old rocking chair. He let his eyes turn to the Northwest, in the direction of the cave, and then carefully inserted the small key into the lock on the wooden box he held on his lap. He opened the box to reveal the magnificent knife. Stegall removed the knife from its resting place and held it in his right hand for a moment. Again turning his eyes to the Northwest, Stegall held the knife so that the morning sun was reflected from its blade, and after a moment of silent contemplation, Stegall spoke.

"I know you've come back, Harpe, you can't hide from Andrew Stegall. I mean to fight you. If it comes down to me and you, and I expect that's what's bound to happen, then that's just the way its gotta be. I know how to use this knife, and I sure as hell ain't afraid of the likes of you."

Even though the words of the old man were brave, Stegall knew if he were to stand a chance of beating Harpe, he'd need more than just the knife, he was going to have to have quite a bit of physical help from someone.

Yeah, he'd need help all right, and a hell of a lot of it. If he was anything at all, Andrew Stegall was a realistic man. He knew he was unlikely to find anyone who'd believe his story, and even if he did, not many folks would buy into a fight that was probably going to get all of them killed.

Stegall had been awake most of the night, ever since he'd felt the presence of Harpe, and at dawn he'd settled down on his front porch in his rickety old rocking chair to try to decide what to do, and maybe to wait for Harpe to come to him. He knew damn well if he waited, the Harpe would come. After all, that was the promise.

It was now a little past noon, and he still sat there, slowly rocking back and forth and now and then reaching for the clear quart fruit jar that rested on the plank porch beside his chair. The fruit jar had started out the morning filled with potent homemade whiskey, or "white lightning" as folks hereabouts still called it, but was now half empty. Stegall would rock for a few minutes, pick up the knife and rub his fingers along its razor sharp edge, stare off into the distant horizon, and then reach for the fruit jar. With the knife in his right hand and the fruit jar in his left, he'd mumble a few words under his breath, then take a long pull on the jar.

He was working on his second chaw off a homemade plug of good Kentucky tobacco, and every now and then he'd spit a long stream of the brown juice out into the front yard. The tobacco in his mouth made a good sized bump in his jaw, but didn't seem to affect his whiskey drinking in the slightest.

Stegall had just placed the jar back on the porch and laid the knife back into his lap when he heard a car turn into his drive and come to a stop in the gravel. Stegall kept rocking but slightly turned his head to see who his visitor was.

The young man who got out of the car and walked across the grassy front yard and stopped at the edge of the porch was a complete stranger to Stegall. He'd never seen him before, he was sure of that.

The stranger was about six feet tall and had very dark, straight hair. His complexion was also very dark, and his eyes matched the color of his hair, giving Stegall the distinct impression the boy was probably some kind of foreigner. What startled Stegall was the faint streaks of color smeared on the man's face, and the tiny gold earring he wore in his left ear. Stegall didn't know whether to laugh or get mad at the intrusion, and he wondered just what in the hell the boy wanted.

"Mister Stegall," the man asked, "Mister Andrew Stegall? The man down at the filling station said I'd find Mister Andrew Stegall here."

"That's me boy. What the hell do you want?"

Stegall didn't see any point in beating around the bush with the kid. He didn't like strangers in the first place, and it was for damn sure he was none too fond of the face paint nor the earring.

Daniel Hawk didn't have a hell of a lot of time to pussyfoot around with this old man either. If the fruit jar held what Daniel suspected, he didn't know how much good it'd do to talk to him at this time anyway.

"Mister Stegall," Daniel said, "my name is Daniel Hawk, and I've come to talk to you about Micajah Harpe."

The young man's words hit Stegall with about the same effect as if he had popped him between the eyes with a ball-peen hammer. He couldn't believe his ears.

He'd been thinking about Harpe all morning, and out of the blue comes this kid asking about the son of a bitch. It was downright spooky.

Andrew Stegall wasn't one to put a hell of a lot of stock in coincidence. He was suspicious, to say the least.

Stegall took another, much longer, pull on the contents of the fruit jar.

"What're you asking 'bout the Harpe for, boy?" he said, once he got over his initial surprise.

"Well sir, I know this is gonna sound funny, but just please hear me out."

Daniel Hawk still wasn't sure he'd found the right man, and he needed a little more information before he committed himself to telling anyone his story.

"I'm a full blooded Cherokee Indian," Daniel started, "and I come from a long line of powerful medicine men. A few days ago I started having this strange dream, and last night was the seventh night in a row it came to me. With the help of my father, I learned the true meaning of the dream, and that's what has brought me to you. If you are truly the Stegall I seek, you know by now the Harpe has returned. And you know that there are very few things that have any chance of stopping him. The Stegall I seek has a knife, in fact he has the very knife that was used to kill Big Harpe in 1799. I too have a mystical weapon that was owned by Harpe, and may be used against him this time around. Tell me if you are the Stegall I'm looking for, and I'll finish my story. If you're not the right man, I apologize for interrupting your medication and your medication."

Although Stegall was an old man, the combination of whiskey, apprehension, and adrenalin had given him a strength and quickness he didn't know he possessed. Before Daniel had gotten the last words out of his mouth, Stegall had whipped the knife up and brought it to the boy's throat, ready to slash his neck.

"I'm the right Stegall, that's for sure," he said. "And this is the knife. The question is, how do I know you ain't the Harpe yourself, trying to trick me?"

"If I was the Harpe, old man, you'd already be dog meat. I wouldn't have wasted any time talking to you. Now, I ain't got time for a lot of bull, Stegall. I need your help, but maybe not as much as you need mine. Now what d'ya say?"

With a trace of hesitation, Stegall withdrew the knife from Hawk's throat. "I reckon I will need a little help at that, young feller," he said. "Now finish your tale."

"Well, like I said, this story is gonna sound a little strange. In my dream, the Eagle came to me and told me to find the 'magic blade.' I didn't know what the hell he meant, but my father did. Our ancestor, Dancing Hawk, made a mighty tomahawk that came to belong to the Harpe. The ax held many of the powers of the spirit world, and proved to be one of Harpe's greatest weapons. Harpe used the tomahawk to commit many atrocities, and the animal spirits didn't like that, but there wasn't much they could do. The magic of the weapon was too powerful even for them. When Harpe was finally killed, by that same knife you hold, the men who killed him cut off his head and then just left the body lying there where it fell. For some reason they left the tomahawk where Harpe had dropped it. It was probably several feet from where the body lay, and the men didn't recognize the power it held. It is that tomahawk I have recovered."

As Daniel was now sure he'd found the right man, he walked back to his car and returned with an object wrapped in cloth. He laid the bundle on the porch at Stegall's feet and slowly unwrapped it. When the last of the cloth was removed and the weapon lay revealed, Andrew Stegall let out a long, low whistle. The tomahawk was truly awesome. He could see why the Indians believed such great powers lived in it. And the way things had been happening in the last few days had Stegall believing in things he would have laughed about at one time. With his eyes still on the tomahawk, he realized this just might turn out to be the help he'd be needing.

"First thing we need to do, young feller, is get a handle for that thing. But I'll tell you right now that shore is a hell of a weapon.

That thing and this knife will make a terrible combination. The thing is," Stegall paused while he spit and took another hefty drink of the clear whiskey, then spit again, "the thing is I don't know if even the two of them together will be enough to stand against the Harpe."

Stegall lay the knife down on the cloth beside the tomahawk, and they stared at them for a minute. They were two of the most perfect hand-to-hand killing instruments the world had ever seen, crafted by masters and filled with supernatural powers, and it was easy to see why Harpe had been almost invincible as long as he held the two of them. Yet powerful as the weapons were, both men knew the Harpe might prove to be more than equal to the power contained in both.

Both also knew it wouldn't take Harpe long to feel the spiritual vibrations emanating from the weapons and come looking for them. They just hoped to God they could come up with a way to stop him by the time he arrived. God help the entire countryside if Harpe managed to get his hands on the weapons.

I'll be a son-of-a-bitch, Daniel thought, when the old man leaned out of his rocker to lay the knife on the cloth. He was close enough for Daniel to smell his breath, and the smell of the white whiskey was overpowering.

He ain't exactly what'd I hoped to find, that's for sure, Daniel thought.

As they began to compare notes, it was apparent there would be two or three problems with the plan the Eagle had spelled out for Daniel Hawk.

For one thing, exploring the Nickajack cave was pretty much out of the question. They'd have to find answers somewhere else.

"Look at this," Daniel said, pointing to a map of the Chattanooga area. "When they built the Nickajack Dam, they flooded the cave, and now it's partially underwater. The only way into the cave is by boat, or by swimming. We won't be getting much help there."

119

"You got a point there, Danny boy," Stegall agreed. "So what's our backup plan?"

"Well, I know we don't have time to explore a damn underwater cave. We'll just have to get by with what information we've already got, which ain't a hell of a lot. I've got a feeling things are gonna be happening in a damn big hurry from now on, and chances are Harpe is gonna find us before we find him anyway. When he does, we're gonna have to do whatever it takes to stop him."

Although Daniel didn't say so, he didn't put much stock in the two of them stopping the Harpe. With another sideways glance at Stegall, the feeling of dread worsened.

Stegall looked Daniel directly in the eyes, took another pull on the fruit jar, and said; "Well, I'll tell you what kind of chance I think we've got. I don't think we've got the chance of a plastic fly in hell of stopping that crazy sumbitch, that's what I think."

Daniel laughed at the old man in spite of himself.

"I was thinking the same thing, you old fart, but I didn't want to discourage you before we even got started."

"Boy, you discouraged mw the minute you pulled into my driveway and said you were looking for Micajah Harpe. I knew I was gonna need some help, but to tell the truth I was kinda hopin' fer some super hero to come flyin' in. No disrespect intended, young feller, but even though you're painted up some, and have an earring, I don't see no damned cape on you." He paused for a moment, then grinned at Daniel and said; "And don't call me an old fart, you little red butthole."

In spite of himself, Daniel laughed again.

"You got it, Chief," he replied.

The two of them were truly an odd couple, and would have been out of place almost anywhere, unless it was at a Sunday afternoon chicken fight, or at one of the local trade days.

Stegall was tall and thin, not weighing over one hundred and fifty pounds soaking wet. He was half as old as dirt, and he was slow. Other than when he'd put the knife to Daniel's throat, so far the fastest speed he'd exhibited was little more than a crawl. His shock of white hair was almost hidden by the old brown felt hat he wore, and a long ponytail touched his shoulders in the back. His bib overalls were clean but they were ancient, and he wore a long sleeved khaki work shirt even in the August heat. Both sleeves were rolled up a couple of turns, and the top two buttons were undone. He had piercing green eyes and good even features, and even with his thin nose and cruel mouth, he had probably been a handsome man in his youth. The only thing out of place with the old mans outfit was the well- worn Reebok sneakers on his feet. A couple of years ago one of his neighbors had given him an old pair of the high topped shoes, and when they'd worn out he'd bought another pair. He'd said he'd rather wear them ten to one than the heavy work shoes he'd worn all his life. Of course he never strayed far from his fruit jar of mountain whiskey.

Daniel Hawk, on the other hand, was young and strong and filled with energy. He was constantly moving, almost as if he couldn't stand still. Being a full-blooded Cherokee, he had black eyes and course black hair, and very little hair anywhere else. He was athletic and muscular, and had extremely quick reflexes. He was almost six feet tall, and just shy of one hundred ninety pounds. He wore faded Levi jeans and a clean white T-shirt, and preferred low top sneakers to the high topped ones Stegall wore. Like Stegall, Hawk also wore his hair in a long ponytail, although his was braided, and it was held up with a small band that looked to be turquoise. Daniel had studied karate for about three years, but didn't consider himself as a highly skilled martial artist. Daniel had grown up in the woods, and guns and knives and hunting was almost second nature to him.

But Daniel's greatest asset was his strength.

He was much stronger than he should have been, considering his size, and had worked out with weights for years. When he grew

121

angry, he grew stronger, and would tackle anyone or anything when his temper got the best of him. More often than not, he beat whatever or whoever he was fighting.

But Daniel wasn't fooling himself.

He knew he was strong, and he knew he was good in a fight, and he could tell the old man was meaner than a rattlesnake, but the man they were going after wasn't like anyone they'd ever known before. He was stronger by about five times than Daniel, and would walk through a whole bed of rattlesnakes without even looking down. Harpe was a demon, a living son of the wild DarkWolf, and they might well be hunting him with a willow switch. Still, neither of them had a choice. They had been chosen for this fight, and were the only ones with even a remote chance of stopping Harpe. They had to fight, it was that simple. There was no chance Harpe would let them just walk away.

As Hawk waited for Stegall to finish packing the small bag he was preparing, he heard on television about two fishermen that had been found brutally murdered. He didn't really pay attention until they mentioned the name of the small town where they had been killed.

Cave-In-Rock, Illinois.

The men looked at each other with the same thought.

Too much coincidence.

Stegall threw one more identical khaki shirt into the bag, picked up a brown sack that held three more quart fruit jars, and headed for the door.

They knew Harpe had been in Cave-In-Rock, and they knew he wouldn't hang around there very long. If they hurried, they might be able to pick up his trail. It wasn't much, but it was the only lead they had, and as good a starting place as any.

BETHANY

When Bethany's shift ended, she wasted no time leaving the factory.

She was tired.

She was tired of the factory, she was tired of that souovabitch Jeffery Hankins screwing with her, and she was tired of always having to work overtime; struggling to make ends meet. She was tired of little Mikey having nightmares and crying and her losing so much sleep. She was tired of just about everything, and getting more tired every day. She needed a little time off, and she needed it pretty soon.

She had two weeks vacation time coming, and she thought it was about time she took it. She couldn't afford to go anywhere, but she had to do something.

The hell with it, she thought. If I can get Aunt Emily in Bowling Green to watch Mike for a few days, I'm driving down to Panama City. I could use a little Florida sunshine right now. I'll tell Jeffery first thing Monday morning, and he'd better let me off.

After the hard crying spell that afternoon, Mike suddenly got in a much better mood. Beth wasn't sure why, but she intended to take advantage of it while it lasted. She dialed Josh's number, and when he got on the line she asked if he'd like to take in a movie

"We've got a few things we need to talk about, Josh, if you know what I mean?"

Josh was silent for a minute, and then whispered to Beth that he'd call her back in a few minutes. That was another thing that bothered her. All this sneaking around all the time.

She was tired of that too.

Sitting by the phone waiting for Josh to call back, Bethany made up her mind about a couple of things. She decided tonight was the night. If Josh wanted to tell everyone the baby was his, and start helping her out now and then, that was fine with her. If he didn't, then screw him. She would go to Florida by herself, and who knows, she just might meet a good looking hunk on the beach who could make her forget all about Josh. She glanced at her reflection in the mirror in the hall and stood up. She turned around a couple of times, checking out her body, and after a few moments decided she still had quite a lot to offer some lucky guy. The thought brought a small laugh to her lips, the first one in quite some time.

And it sure won't be Jeffery Hankins, she thought.

Betty hummed a few bars of the little song again as she brushed her hair, and she was still smiling to herself when the phone rang.

"Beth, it's me," Josh was still whispering. "I can't talk right now, and I can't make it to the movie tonight. They think I've been seeing you, and we've been in a really big argument, and you should have heard the hell I caught. I guess we're not gonna be able to tell anyone for a while yet. You understand, don't you honey. I don't like it either, but there just ain't nothing else we can do."

Bethany couldn't hold it back any longer.

"Yeah, there is something else we can do, Josh. We can tell the truth and take our chances, or we can call everything off right here and right now. I can't take living like this anymore. You just do what you think you have to do, and by God I'll do the same. But don't call me tomorrow thinking I'll change my mind. Changing my mind is what I just got through doing, and I ain't changing it back. From now on, I'm only looking out for me and my baby. I'll be seein' you around, maybe."

When Beth hung the phone up, she was surprised to find she was in a pretty good frame of mind. She wasn't heartbroken, or sad, or anything like that. She was still mad as hell, but more than that she was convinced she had made the right decision.

She'd drive up to Bowling Green tomorrow to visit Aunt Emily, and if her Aunt could watch the baby, then Monday would find little ole Bethany Suzanne Roberts headed south for a few days of fun in the sun.

She took one more long look in the mirror and thought; There are a lot more fish in the sea, and you know what, I've got some pretty good-looking bait.

Bethany had no way of knowing her Sunday trip to visit her Aunt in Bowling Green would put her and her baby on a collision course with the DarkWolf, and her life would never again be the same. If she thought her life was rough now, she had another think coming.

MISSISSIPPI

NOT FAR FROM OLD GREENVILLE

Deputy Larry Dodd was so damned tired he could hardly move. He'd had one hell of night and was ready to head for home. He'd worked the car wreck yesterday out by Peanut's place, and then had had to go out and look at what some psycho had done to Miss Mattie Hastings. Dodd was in the need of a good meal, a hot bath, and at least ten hours of interrupted sleep.

Yesterday may have been the worst day Dodd had ever had.

Only one of the three kids Peanut had pulled from the wreck was still alive, and she was in critical condition. Miss Mattie was stone cold dead, and so was Dave Cooper.

For the hundredth time, he went over some of the events in his head.

After the wreck yesterday, Peanut had intended to go fishing with Cooper and Jacob Trabue. They were going down to the river to try and snag some big cats, or so Peanut had said. They took Coop's old pick up, the same as usual, stopped at a local watering

125

hole for a few drinks and a couple of six packs to go, and then hit the highway toward the river.

For some reason, they had pulled the truck off on the shoulder of the highway.

Probably to get fresh beers from the cooler in the back of the truck, or maybe just to take a piss. The truck had gotten mired up in the deep mud. They had tried to get the truck out, but it was mired up almost to the axle, and no matter how hard they pushed and pulled, it wouldn't budge. Jake and Peanut decided to walk down the road to a friends house about two miles away and see if they could talk him into helping them get the truck unstuck. Coop was to stay with the truck, in case someone came along while the others were gone.

"Someone came along, all right." Dodd was talking aloud to himself, as he often did when he was trying to sort something out.

"Whoever he was he must have been some kind of crazy psycho fool. I've been a lawman for twelve years, and I ain't never seen nobody cut up like old Coop was. He was just plain cut all to pieces. Must've been stabbed twenty times. Ain't no wonder Peanut was almost hysterical, what with seeing Coop's head cut completely off. It had to be a whacko, for damn sure. It just don't make no sense at all. Why in the name of God would the killer put Coop's head up on a fence post and hammer a tire iron through it like that? I'll have nightmares about that for years. Hellfire, his eyes were wide open, and them big old front buckteeth of his was just a'shining. Son, it gives me the willies just thinking about it."

Larry Dodd had no way of knowing the killer was already on his way out of the county, and that one of the men who'd met him would soon be hot on his heels.

He as glad when he was able to leave the crime scene to the Sheriff and get started toward home.

Maybe Deputy Larry Dodd was headed home, but High Sheriff Wallace Rice was standing in the mud beside a fence out on highway Eighty-two, staring at the damnedest thing he'd ever seen.

"Boys, if I wasn't seeing this with my own eyes, I don't know as how I'd believe it," he said to the small group of people who had gathered at the scene.

Turning and looking once again at the mangled head of Dave Cooper, the Sheriff added. "You folks be on your way now, we've got police business to attend to. Make sure your doors are locked good and tight, and for God's sake don't panic. Just be careful till we get the guy who done this. Now go on home, ain't nothing else to see here."

Sheriff Rice walked over to where Jake and Peanut were leaning against his patrol car. Peanut was chain smoking Camel cigarettes, lighting one off the butt of another. Rice could see Peanut was scared out of his mind, but Jake seemed to be in much better shape.

"I know you boys have been over the story once or twice already, and I know you've been through a lot tonight, but I got to hear the details one more time. I want you to start at the top, and try not to leave anything out. We've got to get a handle on this son-of-a-bitch, and we've got to do it fast. This is probably the same nut case that murdered Miss Mattie, and if it is, chances are he's already looking for another victim."

The Sheriff took Peanut by the arm and lightly shook him, trying to make his point clear.

"Peanut, stop your sniveling for a minute and pull yourself together. Tell me one more time what happened, and don't leave a damn thing out, y'hear?"

"Yes sir, Sheriff, I hear you, you're coming through loud and clear," Peanut said, his voice sounding like it might break at any minute. The truth was Peanut was scared to death, and didn't really care who knew it.

"It's just that we, uh, me and Jake, didn't see much of what happened. The guy was gone when we got back to the truck."

"Well, just start at the beginning Peanut," the Sheriff replied, "what time today did you boys get together, where'd ya go, and what'd ya do? Just tell the story right up to the time you got back to the truck and found Coop."

"Let's see," Peanut started. "Jake called me yesterday to tell me we were going fishing. That was right before that damn wreck out in the field by the house. I told Jake to call Cooper and get him to stop by and pick me up. Uh, OK, when I hung up, I went out to the garage and got my poles together. Well, Jake called me back about four thirty and said he'd found Dave over at Sissy's house, and they they'd be by after me about ten o'clock. I asked him if Sissy was fixing to go fishing with us, and he said no, it was the wrong time of the month for her and she was going to stay at home. I told him that was fine with me, and he said..."

"Dammit, Peanut," the Sheriff interrupted him, "I don't care about Sissy's period, or how you was getting your poles together, or none of that crap. I want to know what happened after you got together, where you were half the night, and how in the hell you ended up way the hell out here, with Dave Cooper's head stuck up on a fence post with a rusty tire tool stuck through it. Now forget all that other crap, and get on with what you know about what the hell happened out here."

"I'm trying to tell you what happened, Sheriff, I'm trying. But there was something mighty funny going on around my house all day yesterday, and I thought you might like to hear about it."

Peanut lit another cigarette, his hands still trembling almost too much to put the lighter to the butt.

"I'll listen to that later, Peanut. Right now just tell me what happened out here."

"Yes sir, Sheriff," Peanut said, but he'd already decided he was going to tell somebody about all the crap that had happened to him yesterday.

"The best I can recall, Jake and Dave came over and picked me up about five till ten and we headed for the river. You know it was hotter than hell yesterday, so we thought we'd stop and have a few cold beers before we left town. Well, you might say we had more than a few, and before we knew it, it was almost midnight. Dave was about three sheets in the wind and I wasn't very far behind, but you know old Jake don't drink much, and he was still just as sober as a judge. Anyway, me 'n Coop wasn't in no shape to drive, but Jake was fine, so we finally decided to head for the river. But when we got to the parking lot, the damn truck wouldn't start. The battery was deader'n a doornail. Me 'n Coop, being drunk an' all, thought it was pretty damn funny, but Jake didn't think it was funny a bit. He got madder'n hell and went back inside to see if he could rustle up some jumper cables. Well, old Coop, he just wiggled the battery cables around a little, and the truck started just as pretty as you please. Coop went in to get Jake, and I stayed in the truck with my foot on the gas, so it wouldn't die."

"Damn it, Peanut," Sheriff Rice interrupted, "you're doing it again. I'm beginning to get a little bit upset with you, boy. Just tell your story, and cut out all the extras."

The Sheriff was irritated at the rambling way Peanut was going on, and was about ready to continue this story downtown, just to see if it would calm Peanut down.

"Well, Sheriff, I just thought you ought to know about the fight," Peanut countered.

"What fight, Peanut? You ain't said nothing about no fight."

"I forgot about it Sheriff, till just now. I really did. It didn't seem like it was very important anyhow. You know how Coop gets when he's had a couple of beers. He almost always starts a fight, and he'll fight a buzz saw. That's about what happened last night, only, well, Coop started a fight with the wrong feller this time. That feller knocked Cooper flat on his butt, then picked him up and knocked him down again. Then dared me and Jake to do anything about it. Well, hell, Sheriff, you know we don't mind fighting, and Jake was already madder'n hell, but when I looked in the eyes of that big sumbitch, I almost peed in my britches."

"Who was the feller, Peanut?" the Sheriff asked.

"None of us didn't know him Sheriff, but he was a mean sumbitch, and that's a fact. He snatched old Coop up by the hair and slapped him silly, so quick Coop didn't know what hit him. Like I said, knocked him flat on his butt. Jake picked Coop up, but before I could grab him, he hit Coop again. Hit him while Jake was holding him. Knocked him down again. I got hold of his arm, but when he turned around and looked at me and I saw his eyes, I got to tell you, Sheriff, I turned that old boy loose. His eyes was so cold they looked like he'd been dead a hundred years. I tell you Sheriff, he stared right down into my soul, and it plumb scared the hell out of me."

"You say Cooper started the fight?" the Sheriff asked.

"Shore did, Sheriff," Peanut said. "He thought the feller was making fun of his truck. And then, and then, aw, hell, Jake, why don't you tell the Sheriff what happened?"

"Yeah, Peanut, O.K., I'll tell him," Jacob Trabue replied.

Jake Trabue was a good-looking man, tall and tanned with sandy hair, a little over two hundred pounds, and maybe twenty-six or seven years old. He could have passed for the boy next door in almost any small town in the south. He liked pick-up trucks, country music, TV wrestling, and pretty girls, although not necessarily in that order.

Jake worked full time for John Peters, driving a cement truck, and had the muscles to show for the hours of hard work. He didn't smoke, and drank very little, but he did have one habit he couldn't break. It wasn't necessarily a bad habit, but it had gotten him into more than one scrape in the past few years. His one bad habit was hanging around with Peanut and Cooper. That and fishing. Peanut and Coop drank hard, fought hard, and made love to every pretty girl they could sweet talk out of her pants. And both men had a way with words. Cooper had been going steady with Sissy Taylor for a couple of months, and so there hadn't been a lot of girls lately, but they still hung out at a little local joint called the Wagon Wheel, and they still got in a lot of fishing time.

Jake saw the big guy sitting at the bar when he went in to try and borrow some booster cables. Just the look of the guy sent the hackles rising on the back of Jake's neck, but he wasn't particularly worried. Jake could hold his own in a fight, and anyway, Peanut and Coop were right outside. Jake knew this was a good time of night for a lot of people to be looking for a fight, and the guy on the stool was a mean looking customer, so Jake intended to avoid him if there was any way at all he could.

Jake saw Eddie Pickett sitting at the bar, three stools down from where the big stranger sat, and he walked over to talk to him.

With his eyes half closed, Jake was trying to remember as many details of the incident as possible.

"I walked over to Eddie Pickett, Sheriff, and asked him if he had any jumper cables. Eddie's still driving that old Ford he's had for twenty years, so I figured he might have some cables. Eddie made some smart crack about Coop's truck, and I said something about his old Ford, and we went to laughing about it. Hell, you know how Eddie is, he don't take nothing seriously. Well, I accidentally bumped the stranger's arm and caused him to spill his drink. You know, it's funny, but he was drinking water. That's strange. Anyway, I apologized, and he said it was OK, and I turned around to see if Eddie was ready to go get the cables. Well, Eddie said if Coop was still as drunk as he'd been a little while ago, then we might have to jumpstart Coop himself, and not just the truck. Then the stranger said, 'Hell, if that truck's in as bad a shape as the old boy was in, then maybe you oughta just shoot 'em both.' And he started laughing real hard. I thought it was kinda funny myself, but when I turned around to go, I saw Coop standing in the door. He'd heard what the big guy had said, and he was madder'n hell about it. I walked over and told him to let's go, but he said aw naw, he was going to knock that big dude's lights out for making fun of his truck. I grabbed his arm and told him it didn't make no difference, but he shook loose from me and walked over and began calling the stranger as many kinds of names as he could think of. To tell the truth, it really didn't seem to bother the guy all that much. He just looked at Coop, and took another sip of water. Well, that really got under Coop's skin, and he grabbed the guy and spun him around on his stool. I reckon grabbing the feller was his big mistake. He took hold of Coop's hand and pulled it loose from his arm, and damn near broke Coop's fingers when he did it. He stood up from the stool, looked at me and Coop, and his voice was damn near as cold as his eyes. 'Boys,' he said, 'I'll not allow anyone in this world to lay a hand on me. And I'll only tell you the one time.'

"Sheriff," Jake went on, "I'm kind of like Peanut in this. That big guy gave me goose bumps. But you know Coop, he never could leave well enough alone. When he swings at a man, he most generally hits him, and when he hits a man, they most generally go down. Coop is fast, he's strong, and he's a good fighter. He took his best shot at the stranger. I know. I've seen him fight a lot a lot of men. But Sheriff, I ain't never seen nothing like that guy. He caught Coop's fist in mid swing with his right hand, then grabbed Coop's hair with his left hand. Faster than you could follow, he turned loose of Coop's fist, then reached out and slapped him across the face so hard it glazed Coop's eyes. I ain't never seen nobody hit that hard with just a slap. He knocked Coop smack down on his rear end, and I ain't never seen nobody do that before either." Jake paused for a breath, and shook his head as if he still couldn't believe what he'd just said.

"And you ain't never seen that guy before last night, is that right Jake?" the Sheriff asked.

"No sir. I'd remember if I had, and that's a fact."

"Well, what happened then?" the Sheriff said.

"About that time, Peanut came running across the floor, and I knew he was fixing to get in on the action. But before he could jump in, the big dude hit Coop again. I had picked Coop up off the floor and was holding him, when, bam, the guy hit him so hard it knocked him out of my hands and halfway cross the floor. Have to say it rattled me up pretty good too, Sheriff. Up till then, I didn't know a man could hit that hard. Then Peanut jumped in between us, and I thought he was going to get his head pounded in too, but he took a long look in the strangers face, and didn't do one damn thing. He just stood there. Peanut ain't afraid of nobody or nothing, Sheriff, but that guy was just plain downright spooky. Like Peanut said, you could tell just by looking at him he wasn't a man to fool with."

"Sounds to me like he was the worst hardcase you boys ever ran into," the Sheriff said, as Jake paused again to gather his thoughts.

"You got that right Sheriff," Jake continued. "Anyway, me and Peanut half carried old Coop out to the truck, and finally got him sittin' down in the seat. The truck was still running, but we sat there for a good while anyway. We got Coop awake, and then had to talk him out of going back inside to fight the guy again. Me and Peanut, we knew we didn't have no business fighting that guy. We weren't scared, Sheriff, it's just we ain't never seen nobody like him before. Anyway, we finally talked Coop out of going back inside, and we pulled the truck over to the door and Peanut went in and got four six packs to take with us to the river. You know, come to think of it, it did feel like maybe somebody jumped into the bed of the truck just as we took off."

"Damn it Jake, you're right," Peanut exclaimed. "I remember feeling something too. It could have been somebody jumping in the truck."

"Well, did somebody get in the back of the truck or not?" the Sheriff said.

"I think maybe they did, Sheriff," Jake said.

"Me too, Sheriff," Peanut confirmed.

"OK, go on with the story Jake. You're making a hell of a lot more sense than Peanut was."

"Yes sir," Jake replied, and picked up where he'd left off.

"We had been driving about ten minutes when Coop started going on about needing to take a leak. I pulled the truck off the highway, and it was just our luck I stopped in the middle of the biggest mudhole in the whole county. The truck got stuck and we couldn't get it to move an inch in any which a direction. It wouldn't go forward and it wouldn't go backward, so we just sat there cussin' for a good long time. Then we got out and tried to push it, but it wouldn't move a lick. Me and Peanut decided to walk up the road to Ricky Wooden's house and get him to come down and pull us out. Ricky's daddy has got a tow truck, you know, and we knew he wouldn't mind helping us out, even if it was after two o'clock in the morning. Coop was gonna stay with the truck, in case somebody came along that might could help. Well damn, Sheriff, we was nearly a half mile up the road and even from there we heard the screamin'. We didn't know where it was coming from at first, so we spent maybe three or four minutes looking around, and then Peanut, he said he thought it sounded like Coop. Whoever it was, he was really carryin' on. Hell fire, he was hollerin' as loud as he could. It's a wonder you didn't hear it all the way back in town. Damn, it sounded awful. Put goosebumps all over me. Anyway, we got back to the truck as fast as we could, but it was all over. We didn't see anybody at all. There wasn't anybody at the truck, and we hadn't met anybody on the road. We couldn't find old Coop at first, it was so dark, but then Peanut stumbled over his body. It was laying about twenty feet from the truck, up here on the bank just where you found it. But his head wasn't even there, Sheriff. It was just gone. I can't believe it, not even now. Coop's head had been cut off. Then me and Peanut got sick, Sheriff. Couldn't help it. We'd never seen anything like that before. We was throwin' up, and gaggin' and cryin' and stuff, and then I looked up and saw Coop's head, up there on that fence post. Damn Sheriff, I almost messed in my pants. It scared the hell out of me. Why would somebody want to do a thing like that? I don't understand it, Sheriff, I just don't understand it."

Sheriff Wallace Rice took another long look at Dave Cooper's head skewered to the fence post. In the half-light of dawn, it was like a scene out of hell. He turned to Jake and Peanut, spat in the muddy water they were standing in, and said, "I don't understand it either, boys, but let's hope like hell it ends right here, right now."

JAKE TRABUE

Jake Trabue was at home by eight o'clock. He brewed a pot of coffee, poured a cup and sat down on the couch to go over everything that had happened yesterday and last night. Almost as an afterthought, he switched on the police scanner that was sitting on the table. Jake sometimes worked for the local fire department, and the scanner came in handy now and again.

Jake wasn't inclined to believe a hell of a lot of Peanut's wild stories. In fact, he didn't believe very many of them. Peanut could come up with some of the craziest things he'd ever heard, especially when he'd had a couple of drinks. But the strange thing about the story of the wreck, aside from the fact that Peanut had been cold sober when it happened, was there was absolutely no reason for those people to have driven down that old dirt road. It wasn't really open to traffic, although it wasn't exactly closed off either. It was overgrown and filled with deep ruts, and dead ended in a thick patch of pine trees at the other end of the field. So what in the hell were they doing driving their car there in the first place?

Jake couldn't understand why Peanut kept on insisting there had been four people in the car. The cops and the rescue workers had only found three people, and they had walked all over the field a half dozen times since the accident had occurred. At first Jake thought Peanut had just imagined the fourth person, or maybe he'd been hit on the head when the car exploded, but the more he listened to Peanut talk, the more he wondered about what really happened. Peanut was holding strong to his story, right down the line.

He swore at first he couldn't open the right hand door of the car, but when he went back around the car after he'd pulled the driver out, the door was open and it looked as if someone had walked or crawled off into the woods. Course, other than Peanut's word, there was no evidence of the fourth passenger.

The girl who'd survived the crash was still in critical care, and heavily sedated, and it would be a while before she was up to being questioned about the wreck. It had only been a little over twenty hours since all this crap started, and a lot of things had gone down in that time. Jake had a hell of a lot more questions than he did answers.

He couldn't believe Coop was dead, that someone had killed Miss Mattie, and he sure didn't know how much of Peanut's story to take for gospel. If there had been a fourth passenger in the car, it was just like he had disappeared off the face of the earth. The same went for the guy Coop had fought with. There was no trace of him either. It was getting wilder and wilder, and Jake was getting a little more upset all the time.

Jake sat there for a couple of hours, going over and over what had happened, and at the same time listening to the police scanner. He was really interested in the details of Peanut's story. Something just didn't make sense. If the mysterious fourth passenger in the car was somehow tied in with Coop's death, Jake wanted to know how. He'd give a hundred dollars to get his hands on the dirty son-of-a-bitch that killed Coop. The law wouldn't have to worry about bringing him in, or about him murdering anybody else, that was for damn sure. Thirty minutes alone with him, that's all he wanted. Just thirty minutes.

Suddenly the police scanner came alive with a crackle.

"Deputy Batey, you hear me? Car ten, come in."

More crackle, but no answer.

"You hear me, J.W., this is Sheriff Rice. Come in."

"Yeah Sheriff, this is J.W. come back."

"J.W. where the hell are you?" the Sheriff responded.

"Hell, Wallace, I just now got out here, and I've been standing by the side of the road where old Coop got killed, and I just can't hardly believe it. I seen it with my own eyes, and I still can't hardly believe it." The deputy was clearly in a state of distress over the murder.

"Well, J.W. it's true enough all right. But right now I need for you to go back over to the field where that car wrecked yesterday and take another look around. The girl woke up long enough to tell us a few things, and guess what? Peanut was right, there was another guy in the car. Since we ain't found him, he's got to be laying out there somewhere, or else wandering around the woods in some kind of daze. Anyway, get on back out there and see what you can round up."

Deputy Batey could hear the tension and tiredness in the Sheriff's voice.

"Check, Wallace," Batey replied, "I'm on my way."

Jake was out of his house before the crackle of the scanner died away.

Son-of-a-bitch, Jake thought. *Peanut was right. For once in his life, he actually knows what he's talking about.*

Jake checked his watch as he started his car. If he hurried, he could get over to the field before the Deputy. He roared out of his drive, hung a sharp left, and headed for Peanut's place as fast as his car would go.

He was wrong.

When he got to the field, Deputy Batey was already there, walking around with his eyes glued to the ground.

Walking out into the field, Jake yelled at the Deputy.

"Hey, J.W., you care if I take another look around?"

"Help yourself, Jake," J.W. answered, "but if you find anything, you sure as hell better turn it over to me."

"Don't worry bout that, J.W." Jake replied. "I ain't planning on withholding no evidence. I'm just trying to be of some help."

Jake walked over to where the burned hulk of the car still lay. The Sheriff hadn't let the garage move the wreck yet, and wouldn't until he was finished with his investigation. Jake bent down and peered around inside the charred automobile. It was only a couple of minutes until something shiny caught his eye. There was a round object wedged between what was left of the rear seat and the side panel, and Jake thought it might be clue to the identity of the man who had been sitting there. He carefully leaned into the car and picked the object up, but closer examination revealed it was only a quarter.

He straightened up and flipped the quarter into the air, reaching out to catch it with his right hand. He watched the quarter spin in the air, catching the early morning sunlight with every turn, and suddenly there was an awful pounding sound in his head, and he became a little dizzy. He squeezed his eyes shut and shook his head a few times to clear it, and somehow failed to catch the quarter as it spun down and hit the ground.

The quarter bounced a couple of times and came to rest not far from the car. Jake's head was still pounding and when he bent over to pick up the quarter he found the dizziness was also still there. In a half crouched position, Jake braced himself against the car with his left hand, once again squeezing his eyes tightly closed, trying to shut out the insistent sound that was tearing through his skull.

thud. thud. thud. thud.

Dull and low and steady the pounding came.

Jake blinked his eyes and just for a second he imagined he saw the car disappear. He was almost sure of it. The car disappeared and a six or seven foot high weather beaten post took its place. But then he blinked again, and as suddenly as it had disappeared, the car was back.

What the hell is going on? Jake thought. What's happening to me?

He looked around, saw the quarter lying by his leg, and reached for it. As Jake's hand closed about the quarter, the pounding was suddenly back. This time it was stronger, until in a few seconds it was the only thing in his mind.

THUD. THUD. THUD. THUD.

The sound had such force Jake sank to his knees and clutched his head with both hands. Tears filled his eyes as the pounding became too much to bear.

THUD. THUD. THUD. THUD.

Jake opened his eyes and once again saw the field flicker and the scene change.

Once again the car was gone, and the tall pole was there. Jake wiped the tears from his eyes, shook his head from side to side and then opened his eyes fully. What he saw was unbelievable.

The field was bustling with activity.

Over at the far side some men were busy putting the finishing touches on what appeared to be a scaffold of some sort. As Jake watched, several other men rode by on horses, headed in the direction of a small cluster of log cabins standing where Peanut's house should be.

Close beside Jake a small fire was burning. It looked like a cooking fire. At least, there was a large pot suspended over the fire, and it sure smelled like someone was cooking something. Soup. Some kind of soup or stew. Four women stood by the fire, each wearing a long dress and a wide brimmed bonnet. Most of the men Jake could see were dressed in buckskins, and all of them were carrying weapons. Jake didn't see even one man who didn't have a knife at his belt, and many of the men also had one or more pistols strapped to their sides. There were several dogs running about, and Jake could have sworn he saw two Indians standing at the edge of the field talking to a short man with red hair.

This is crazy, Jake thought, Now what the hell's going on?

He rubbed his eyes and shook his head, hoping somehow to bring things back to normal. But when he opened his eyes again, he was still looking at a scene straight out of a history book. He leaned back and felt his shoulders come in contact with something. Slowly reaching behind him, he felt a large, rough post of some kind, set into the ground. The top of the post was higher than he had first thought, standing about nine feet off the ground, and it was solid and sturdy, like whoever set it intended for it to be there for a while.

Jake tried to get to his feet but found he couldn't rise. Frantically he called out to the women at the cooking fire, but they seemed not to hear him. Waving his arms, he tried to attract the attention of one of the men standing by the gallows, but again got no response.

Damn, Jake thought. This is like a dream. These people can't hear me, they can't see me, or anything, and yet I can see and hear them just fine. I can move my hands and legs, but I can't stand up and walk around. A dream. Hell yeah, it's just a dream. Now all I have to do is wake up.

Waking up was proving to be impossible. Jake had about decided to pinch his arm for the third or fourth time, when all at once he heard a wild commotion from one of the cabins. Looking in that direction, he saw ten or twelve men emerge from the cabin and begin walking toward the now completed gallows. Taking a closer look, Jake could see two heavy ropes suspended from a cross member, and a man testing its strength by yanking repeatedly on it. The scaffold was crude, but it looked as if it would serve the purpose it was intended for. Bringing his attention back to the men walking toward the gallows, he could see they were escorting two prisoners, and it was obvious they were preparing to hang them.

As Jake watched, the five or six men who were actually holding one of the prisoners moved apart just a little, and Jake got his first good look at the man.

Suddenly the dream turned into a nightmare.

It was the stranger from the bar, the man who'd fought with Coop, and he was staring directly at Jake.

That's impossible, Jake thought, no one here can see me.

Jake waved his arms over his head again, just to prove the point in his own mind, and once again got no response. The men continued talking, the women watched the pot boil, even the dogs just kept on running around.

But when Jake looked at the stranger again, he found the man was still staring directly at him. His wild blue eyes were glowing as if they were on fire, and the man was smiling.

"Don't laugh at me, damn you," Jake shouted, and tried unsuccessfully to jump to his feet.

It was no use, he still couldn't stand, and after a superhuman effort he sank back to the ground, letting his shoulders come to rest once again against the post.

The group of men passed within six feet of where Jake sat leaning against the post, and when they were closest to Jake, for some reason they stopped.

Jake found himself six feet away from hell, staring into the eyes of the devils best friend. Jake felt his soul shudder, and the acrid taste of fear rose up in his throat, hot and vile. Jake spat at the man, and the demon smiled back at him. He cursed, and the demon smiled again. With a mighty effort, Jake lurched to his feet and managed to grab the evil stranger by the arm. The demon spoke.

"I don't allow anyone in the world to lay their hands on me, boy, and like my brother used to say, I'll only tell you the one time."

With those words the demon smiled again, and shook off Jake's grip as easily as if Jake were a child.

Then the men resumed their slow walk to the gallows, dancing the stranger along between them, using all their strength to keep him moving.

Jake fell back against the post and lay there trembling. With each breath he thought his lungs would explode, and there was a warm wetness at his crotch. Once again he felt his eyes fill with tears, and helplessly he beat his fists against the ground.

"Why don't you tell them guys holding you that 'only tell you one time' crap, huh. They're gonna hang you, and that'll be the end of you. You're a dead man, mister, a dead man." Jake was screaming at the top of his lungs, but no one except the stranger noticed.

The only response the man made was to take one more look at Jake and smile that same little secretive smile. His look was one of utter disdain, as if nothing that had happened or was going to happen made a hell of a lot of difference.

Helpless and weak as a kitten, Jake could only lean against the post and watch as the men placed the rough homespun rope around the stranger's neck. End even as the trapdoor dropped, the man once again smiled at Jake, and winked one of his cold blue eyes.

In a few moments he was swinging at the end of the rope, doing a grotesque dance as the life and breath left him.

The second man was hanged with the same efficiency, and both men were soon dead, their limp bodies twisting and turning at the whim of what little wind was blowing.

Jake saw the men slap each other on the back, and the women were smiling as they saw the bodies swinging gently to and fro at the end of the rope.

One by one the people passed by the bodies of the two outlaws. They paid scant attention to one of the hanged men, but all spent some time looking at the man with the strange eyes. They stared at the body as if they couldn't believe it was really hanging there. Some spat on it, and others cursed at it, and even the two Indians seemed happy the man was dead. Jake didn't even want to know what horrible crimes the man must have committed for the people to hate and fear him so, but they must have been awfully bad to get this kind of reaction. Anyway, Jake was glad the whole ordeal was over.

Or was it?

Time seemed to speed up, night came and then another day, and Jake watched as some men came to the gallows.

One of the men began to untie the rope, as three others caught hold of the body. Jake watched as they laid the body on the ground and couldn't believe his eyes when one of the men took a small axe and began to chop at the dead man's neck. Jake turned his head away from the spectacle, but the heavy sound of the striking axe came to him over and over.

When the chopping sounds ended, Jake once again looked up, only to see the men walking toward where he sat leaning against the post. One of the men carried the head in his right hand, swinging it from side, flinging drops of blood about as he walked. As they came closer, Jake could see the eyes on the head were still wide open, and they still seemed to be looking at him.

Not wanting to see any more of the gruesome scene, Jake closed his eyes and placed his hands over his face. All at once, he felt the post shake, and suddenly all of the fears were back.

THUD. THUD. THUD. THUD.

The pounding came again, louder and more insistent than before.

Not wanting to look, but unable to help himself, Jake forced his eyes to open and to look upward. The men were nailing the head to the top of the post with a long, rusty iron spike.

THUD. THUD. THUD. THUD. went the hammer.

THUD. THUD. THUD. THUD. went Jake's brain.

In horror, Jake felt something dripping on him and realized it was blood from the head, forced out as the nail was driven deeper and deeper.

Jake looked at the back of his left hand and watched as four drops of blood spattered there. He stared in amazement as the blood began to form into a shape. As he watched, the blood formed a perfect, four pointed star on the back of his hand.

The star was the last thing Jake saw before his tortured mind slipped back into unconsciousness.

The last thing he heard was the dull *THUD. THUD. THUD. THUD.*

Jake opened his eyes to find Deputy Batey roughly shaking him by the shoulder.

"Where the hell am I? What happened?" Jake frantically asked the officer.

"You're laying out here in the middle of this damn field, Jake. Where'n the hell do you think you are?"

"I ain't none too sure, J.W., right at the moment," Jake answered. "But I'll tell you one damn thing, I ain't gonna be out here in the middle of this damn field much longer, and that's a natural fact. How long was I out? Long time, huh?"

"Well, I saw you fall, and I come runnin'. Then I shook till you woke up. Two or three minutes seems about right."

"Damn it J.W., I had to be out longer than that. I had the damnedest nightmare I ever had in my life. I ain't never been that scared before. You don't know how happy I was when I opened my eyes and saw your ugly kisser staring at me. I'm sure glad stuff like that only happens in dreams. Uh, you don't believe in dreams coming true, do you J.W.?"

"Why hell naw, Jake, I don't believe dreams come true. If they did, I'd spend all my time screwin' one of them lifeguard gals on television. You know that old show where all the girls run around in them little bitty skimpy bikinis all the time. Hell, that's all I ever dream about, and ain't never a damn one come true yet." J.W. laughed as Jake sat there shaking his head.

"You old horny son-of-a-bitch," Jake said, and laughed in spite of himself.

Reaching out his hand he said, "Here, help me up and I'll be headed for home. I've had enough of this field foe one day."

J.W. reached down and took Jake's hand to help him to his feet. "Maybe you ought to have the Doc look you over, Jake, and see if he can figure out why you passed out like that. Say, I never noticed your tattoo before. When did you have that done?"

"Hell J.W., I ain't got no tattoo..." Jake started, and then looked at the back of his hand in horror.

On the back of his left hand was a blood red, nearly perfect four-pointed star.

Jake looked at the star for a moment. "J.W., you might as well go on home too. I don't think anybody is going to find another damn thing in this field." Without another word, Jake began his slow walk back to his car.

Jake lived about three miles from Peanuts house, and in the short time it took him to drive home he re-lived the scene in the field.

None of it made the least bit of sense.

Like Deputy Batey, Jake didn't really believe dreams came true, but on the other hand, he wasn't really sure what he had experienced had actually been a dream. He'd never had a dream that had seemed this real, and he sure as hell hadn't dreamed up that damned pounding in his head. Even if there was some reasonable explanation for everything else, how could he explain the star that had appeared on his hand? No, right now there were just too many questions, and not enough answers.

Hell, there aren't any answers at all, Jake thought. But there will be, and soon. I know he's out there, and I'll find him if it's the last thing I do.

The first thing Jake did when he got home was to climb into a hot shower. Not only did he have dried blood on the back of his hand that needed washing off, his jeans were still a little damp at the crotch.

"I can't believe he scared me so bad I peed on myself," he said, talking to his reflection in the bathroom mirror.

He managed a weak smile as he discarded his clothes, and his thoughts went back to the eyes of the stranger. They were a shade of blue that Jake had seen somewhere before, and he had just remembered where.

It was in a picture, he mused, a picture of a glacier.

The frozen ice had had the same cold blue frigidness he'd seen in the eyes of the big stranger. Just thinking about the way the man had looked at him was enough to send fresh shivers down his spine, and he reached over and turned the hot water on again, letting his bath warm up just a little.

Turning his attention to the star on the back of his hand, he began to gently rub it with his thumb. When it resisted his efforts to rub it off, he picked up the soap and a fresh washcloth. Soaping the cloth, he tried vigorously to wash away the damned mark, but the scrubbing had no visible effect on it.

"God," he said aloud. "What in the hell is going on? This thing has got to come off."

But it didn't.

No amount of washing and rubbing had any effect on the star, and Jake finally gave up, realizing all at once it was there to stay. After a few moments, Jake managed to relax a little and let the hot water begin to soothe away some of his physical aches and pains. At least he knew for certain the bruises and scrapes were for real.

Finishing his shower, Jake pulled on clean jeans and a white tee shirt and sat down on the couch to give some more thought to what the hell he was going to do now. With a weary hand, he reached over and flicked the scanner off. The static made it hard to think, and Jake didn't think the police were going to find out anything else for a while.

With no better plan in mind, Jake decided to go down to the public library and look up the early history of Old Greenville. There just might be something in the books about the old field. He knew the town had had its share of outlaws. He'd heard many stories of the wild days on the Old Natchez Trace.

What the hell, he thought, I sure as hell ain't got no other clues.

To his surprise, Jake struck pay dirt at the library almost immediately.

Not wanting to appear dumb, and certainly not wanting to tell anyone what had happened to him, Jake asked the librarian if she had ever heard of any hangings or anything like that back in the early days of Greenville.

"Why, certainly young man," she said. "There were many public hangings around here. That used to be the best way they had of handling things. Killers were brought to a swift punishment back in those days, not like today at all. And that's what they should do when they catch the man who killed Miss Mattie. They should hang him to a high tree with a new rope. Did you hear about that?"

"Yes ma'am, I did," Jake said. "And I feel the same way. Where could I find a book about the hangings?"

The librarian suggested e begin with an old book that told the history of the Natchez Trace. There were several colorful outlaws, and all of the stories were interesting. Jake took her advice and carried the book to a table.

It was only a matter of minutes before he came upon the story of an outlaw named Mason, who raised pure hell along the trace back around 1800. Supposed by many to be the meanest outlaw the trace had ever seen, Mason was a robber baron of the first order. He was so mean, in fact, that in 1804 there was a nine hundred dollar reward placed on his head, dead of alive.

Mason's right hand man for the last four years had been a man named Setton, who had drifted down to the trace from Kentucky or Tennessee. Setton was a close mouthed man, content to let Mason lead the gang and take all the glory for the crimes, preferring to keep to himself most of the time. That changed, however, when the reward was placed on Mason's head.

After Setton learned of the huge reward, the meanest man on the trace met someone a hell of a lot meaner. It only took Setton a matter of hours to bash in Mason's head, then cut it off and take off for the nearest magistrate to try and collect the reward.

Mason's head was identified by the size of his front teeth, which were extra long and fang like, and the incident would have ended there, had not the man who called himself John Setton been recognized as being none other than Wiley Harpe.

Joshua Wiley Harpe, known in Kentucky, Tennessee and on the Ohio River as "Little Harpe," was one of the notorious Harpe brothers who had terrorized people for several years in the late 1700's. Wiley was the brother of Micajah Harpe, the murderer they called Big Harpe, and they were said to be the most savage and ruthless killers the territory had ever known.

According to the account in the book Jake was reading, the Harpes killed without regard to sex, age, or race, and from all reports killed much of the time simply because they found pleasure in killing. Both were large men, and cruel beyond imagining. They were vicious, homicidal maniacs, unafraid of either man not Devil. Wild wolves they were, roaming the countryside, preying on innocents and outlaws alike. No one was safe when the Harpes were about. White man or red, young or old, man or woman, to meet the Harpes in the open was a nightmare all wished to avoid. They were like demons, more animal than human, and perhaps the most vicious, bloodthirsty pair of men that ever drew breath.

"The Harpes are coming," were four words that struck terror into the bravest heart, and were the most dreaded words known along the frontier.

Jesus H. Christ, Jake thought as he read the Harpe's story. I'd sure as hell hate to run into one of them in the dark. Wolves, huh?

A little light came on in Jake's mind.

Jake grew even more excited as he read the story of what happened to Little Harpe after the swift trial.

A gallows was hastily erected in a field on the edge of town, and the very next day a group of townsmen escorted Wiley Harpe to the gallows and hung him by the neck until he was dead, dead, dead.

After letting the body hang until the next day to be sure all life had left his body, they proceeded to lower the body and chop off the outlaw's head. The head was then nailed to a large post in the middle of the field, and left there as a warning to others that the people of Greenville would not tolerate murderers in their town. It was said Harpe's wild blue eyes remained open, staring at travelers as they passed.

Jake was about to close the book, when one other line caught his attention. Wiley Harpe's rifle had a perfect, four pointed silver star inlaid in both sides of it's stock, and the rifle had mysteriously disappeared soon after his death.

Jake looked down at the star on the back of his hand, and lightly rubbed it.

This just gets crazier and crazier, he thought. I never heard of this Harpe feller until just a few minutes ago, and I feel like I've known him all my life. And I don't understand why this star on my hand won't come off. What the hell is going on?

Jake suddenly realized he had spoken the last sentence out loud, and guiltily looked around to see if anyone had heard. He found the librarian, Mrs. Jenkins, staring at him. Jake looked at her with a sheepish grin and said "I'm sorry bout that ma'am. It just slipped out."

Jake read a little more, and left the library knowing he had found exactly what he had been looking for.

Sitting in his car, Jake closed his eyes and tried to picture the face of the man in his dream. He jumped, startled, as the bloody head of the man vividly appeared in his mind. The eyes were still open and staring at him.

THUD. THUD. THUD. THUD.

Jake sprang forward in the drivers seat, opening his eyes and forcing the image from his mind. The star on his hand was throbbing, and the wild blue eyes of the stranger seemed to dance in the air directly in front of his windshield.

"Stop it," he cried, "get the hell away from me."

Jake cranked the engine to roaring life and angrily raced out of the library's parking lot, determined to outrun the images that threatened to swallow him.

Jake was five miles out on Highway 52 before he brought his emotions under control. Not even realizing it, he had driven back to the scene of last night's murder. Of course, Coop's body and the old pick-up were gone, but when Jake looked around, he found a trace of blood on top of the fence post. He knew the Sheriff and his men had searched the scene without finding much of anything, but he decided to look for himself anyway. After all, he seemed to have been experiencing things no one else had, so maybe he'd spot some kind of clue.

Suddenly, an idea formed in Jake's mind. He walked over and sat down and leaned back against the fence post. Closing his eyes, he gently began to rub the star on his hand. It was only a few minutes before the pounding started.

thud. thud. thud. thud.

It started low and distant and began to grow until it thundered in his brain.

THUD. THUD. THUD. THUD.

Once again it seemed as if his brain would explode from the pressure. His body shook, the fence post rocked violently, and the star on his hand seemed to come to raging life, searing his hand like a brand. With a harsh intake of breath, Jake raised up and opened his eyes.

And was back in the nightmare again.

Standing not ten feet from where Jake sat stood the man called Harpe. Although Jake had never seen even a picture of the man, he knew immediately who the man was. It was Wiley Harpe, it could be no one else. Harpe's icy blue eyes were on fire, and his gaze laid bare Jake's soul, sending terror coursing throughout every fiber of his being. Harpe looked at Jake and spoke;

"Yore marked, boy, marked by the sign of the Wolf. Ye have my star upon ye, and thet makes ye mine. Follow the Wolf, boy, follow the Wolf if ye dare. And I'll only tell ye the one time."

Then the apparition turned and headed north. Jake watched as it slowly paled, and then disappeared altogether. It was at that moment Jake became certain Little Harpe had somehow returned to life, and had already begun a new reign of terror to the countryside. He was headed north, up the Natchez Trace, toward Tennessee and Kentucky.

"God help us all," Jake whispered to the wind, "the Wolf is loose."

Worse than anything else, Jake recognized Harpe as the man who'd fought with Dave Cooper at the Wagon Wheel last night.

Jake was right.

The Wolf was loose, it was hungry, and this time it was smarter than it had ever been. Not only did it possess the natural savagery and cunning of Wiley Harpe, it also had all the abilities of the man whose body and mind it now inhabited. No longer a simple woodsman, the man called Harpe now knew how to drive a car, operate a computer, and was accustomed to riding around the country in airplanes. And a smarter enemy is a more dangerous enemy.

It took Jake several minutes to regroup, and then he headed home. He knew he didn't have a lot of time to decide on a course of action. Harpe was on the hunt, and every minute lost meant a minute that brought the man closer to his next kill.

On the way home, Jake made up his mind he would head for Tupelo. That was north along the old Trace, and seemed as good a place to start as any. He'd drive slow, and keep his eyes peeled for any sign of Harpe.

At home, Jake threw a couple of pair of socks into a bag, and packed his last two pairs of clean levis. He threw in a change of shirts, some underwear and T's, a toothbrush and paste, and a spare pair of sneakers. As he closed the bag he looked at the gun rack on the wall.

It would be pretty stupid to go after this guy without a gun, he thought, as he picked up his old lever action 30-30 deer rifle and a box of shells. Jake had hunted all his life, and was a good shot, and he knew he'd need all his skills when he caught up with Harpe. Opening a drawer, he removed his favorite pistol, a Smith and Wesson Model 19 .357. It was a big powerful pistol, but he knew he'd need all the stopping power he could lay his hands on. He was taking no chances at all with Harpe.

Funny, he thought, I'm thinking of this guy as Wiley Harpe, a man who's been dead for over two hundred years. If someone had told me this crap, I'd think he was crazy as a bed bug. But by God, I really do believe it's Harpe. I don't know how, but I think the bastard has come back to life.

Jake sat the rifle down crossways in the front floorboard on the rider's side of the car, then loaded the .357 with six hollow point shells and laid it on the seat close to his right hand. If he needed it at all, he wanted to be able to get to it as quickly as possible. He tossed his bag in the back seat, got behind the wheel, and cranked the engine. For a moment he rested his head against the steering wheel, and let his mind think about what he was about to do. He was tired, and he was afraid of Harpe, but he also felt a sense of responsibility. He knew somehow he had to catch up with Harpe, and he had to kill him. He wouldn't be able to rest as long as the man was on the loose. If he had any doubts at all, the burning star on the back of his hand served as a constant reminder.

WILEY

Leland, Mississippi, is only a hop skip and jump up the road from Greenville, and it was there Harpe decided to make his first stop.

If Jake had any doubts about where Wiley was headed, Wiley himself sure as hell didn't.

When he spotted the small drive-in market with only three cars out front, he immediately pulled his car into the parking lot.

He needed to change cars, and he needed another kill. He could satisfy both needs with one stop.

Wiley pulled the nose of his car in toward the building and cut the engine.

He waited five minutes, letting two of the customers leave, then got out of the car and entered the store. The clerk was a pretty girl in her early twenties, with dark eyes and medium length light brown hair. She wore faded blue jeans and a low cut white top, and seemed to be a little bored. She noticed Wiley when he walked in, but her attention was on ringing up the sale for the customer who stood at her check out counter.

"That's two six packs of Bud and a pack of Winston lights," she said, as she lightly tapped the keys on an old fashioned cash register. "That'll be $13.92, sir. Will there be anything else tonight?"

As quick as the girl was in ringing up the sale, Wiley was quicker.

Between the time she had started ringing it up and the time she finished, the killer had struck.

When the girl looked up and spoke to the customer, the man was already slumping to the floor, his throat slashed from ear to ear, and blood was spurting all over the place. With horrified eyes, the girl opened her mouth to scream, and never saw Harpe's hand as it buried itself in her hair. She felt his hand touch her hair, but never knew when the sharp point of Miss Mattie Hasting's butcher knife drove into her left ear, and pierced her brain. She dropped without a sound, dead before she even hit the floor.

Without even glancing at the cash resister, Wiley stepped from behind the counter and took his time walking over to the big cooler in the back of the store and taking out two four packs of bottled water. He liked the word "spring" that was printed on the bottle for some reason.

As he left the store, he paused for a moment beside the body of the customer the girl was waiting on. As he reached down and took the car keys from the dead fingers he noticed the beer and cigarettes. He pushed the glass door open and as he stepped over the body he shook his head and said,

"Smokin' and drinkin' is bad for your health, feller. Never touch either one myself. Nowadays you just can't be too careful. But don't worry, I'll be glad to be your designated driver tonight."

Looking up, Wiley noticed a video camera was mounted on the wall behind the cash register. He looked directly into the camera and smiled, then turned and walked out the door.

Wiley left Miss Mattie's car where it sat and climbed into the old Cougar that had belonged to the dead man. As he pulled out of the parking lot, he opened one of the bottles of water and took a long drink. He had a feeling he was going to like this new life, and he knew for damn sure Micajah was somewhere out there waiting for him.

"I'm on my way, brother, I'm on my way," he spoke aloud into the night.

JAKE

From the highway, Jake could see the blue lights flashing, and without even thinking he swerved into the parking lot and jumped from his car. Trying not to attract attention, Jake walked over to a bystander.

"What the hell happened, feller? Must have every cop in town out here."

"I ain't sure mister," the man replied, "I just got here. They said there's two people dead in the store. Somebody killed Kathy Turner and a customer. I heard one of the police say they was cut all to pieces, but I dunno. They won't let anybody in there yet."

"Guess it must've been a robbery, huh?" Jake asked.

"I don't think so," the man replied, "that one cop said the cash register was shut up tight."

"Well, I'll be damned," Jake said, then turned around and walked back to his car. According to the books he'd read at the library, Wiley Harpe didn't always rob the people he killed, and Jake was sure the man had been here. The only thing he didn't know was why he'd stopped so soon. He hadn't been on the road over twenty minutes.

He sure does like to use that knife, Jake thought, not realizing he didn't even begin to know how much Wiley liked to use the big butcher knife.

As Jake drove away from the parking lot, he spotted Miss Mattie's car parked at the end of the building. Now there was no doubt in his mind Wiley Harpe had been the man in the store.

When he reached the city limits sign, Jake picked up a little speed and once again headed north on the Natchez Trace Parkway.

Jake passed through the small towns of Indianola and Greenwood with no further signs of the killer, but as he entered the small town of Winona, it was just like he had driven back into Leland. Another small drive-in market, a lot of police cars with their blue lights flashing, and a large crowd milling around out front.

As Jake walked to the edge of the crowd, the first thing he saw was the body of a man lying crumpled on the concrete, and one of the large plate glass window's in the front of the store had been shattered. On closer examination, Jake saw it looked as if the dead man had been thrown out of the store through the window, with enough force to land him six feet out in the parking lot. The inside of the store was well lit, and even from the parking lot Jake could see at least three more bodies lying about.

There was a large, bald man standing beside him, who seemed to almost be in a state of shock.

"What happened?" Jake asked.

"Some big sumbitch come in about twenty minutes ago and started killing everybody in sight, that's what the hell happened," the man said. "Didn't leave nobody at all alive inside the store. Throwed old Ray Dean clean through the winder, and almost cut little Markie

Johnson's head off. It's the worst thing I've ever seen, man. They's seven people dead in there, and one is a little boy, not over eight years old."

The man was close to being hysterical, and the words came rushing out of him in spurts.

"I saw a car taking off just as I got here, but I didn't pay no attention to it at all. Then I walked around in front of the store and saw Ray Dean, laying there just like he is now. I run inside, and they was dead bodies and blood all over the place. I got so damn sick I almost couldn't stand it, but I grabbed the phone and called 911. I knew Ray Dean pretty well, and I know he'll shoot a man, so I checked to see about his pistol. It's gone. I guess the guy took it. Damn it, why didn't I look a little closer at that car."

"You say there's a gun missing, feller? Know what kind it is?" Jake asked.

"Shore do. It's a Taurus Bulldog .44 mag. I sold it to Ray Dean myself, a couple of years back. He got robbed twice, in less than thutty days, back in the summer of 97, and he said he wanted to buy a gun so he could shoot the next sumbitch that tried to stick him up. And he done it, too. Shot and killed Buster Davis. In 1999, it was. Buster come in on him, thinkin' he was going to rob the store, and old Ray Dean shot him deadder'n hell. Well, he didn't have much trouble after that. Until tonight, that is. Damn it, anyway. Why'd anybody want to do something like this?" The man was almost in tears as he finished speaking.

"I don't know feller, I just plain don't know," Jake said. And that was the truth. Jake knew who the killer was, but still didn't know why he was killing so many people.

Course, if it really is Wiley Harpe that's come back, I don't guess he needs a damned reason, Jake thought.

And now he had a gun, as well as that damned knife.

"That's just great," Jake said aloud. "That's just damn great."

WILEY

Wiley hadn't even meant to stop in Winona, but he'd finished three bottles of water, and his bladder was about to burst. He had to piss in the worst way. He was about to pull over to the side of the road and relieve himself, when he spotted the market. His eyes began to glow with the blue flame, as he remembered the other store, not so many miles behind him.

It's just so easy, Wiley thought. So damned easy. These people don't hardly put up a fight, and ain't a damn one of 'em got a gun. I might as well let the Wolf feed tonight. I can sleep the next time I'm dead. I've got a lot of catching up to do.

This time he didn't wait for any of the customers to leave the store. He left the engine running on the car and picked up the long butcher knife. Without haste, he stepped out of the car and walked inside the store. He pushed the knife inside his belt as he walked.

A middle-aged man was behind the counter, picking his teeth and watching two women and a little boy as they begin to empty the contents of their shopping cart on the counter. They had gotten out several items of canned food, and were discussing whether they had a coupon for a box of cereal one of the women held.

"Pardon me Chief, but do you mind if I borrow your bathroom," Wiley asked.

"Ain't got no public bathroom in here feller," the man answered with a snarl. "You'll have to head on down to the 66 station if you got to go."

The blue eyes flamed as Wiley eased the knife from his belt.

"Naw, here'll do just fine, feller," he said.

With a savage slash, he ripped apart first one woman and then the other, and without hesitation the knife found the neck of the boy. Without slowing down, he dropped the knife on the counter, took a quick step to the side and broke the neck of a man standing there browsing through the magazine rack. He dimly heard someone yelling and turned in time to see the man behind the counter bring a pistol into view. With a movement too swift to follow, Wiley reached the counter in two jumps. Without hesitation, he grabbed the clerk by the front of his shirt with both hands. In an incredible display of raw strength, Wiley lifted the large man and shook him about as if he were a rag doll. The pistol dropped from the man's hand as Wiley twirled him around and tossed him through the plate glass window at the front of the store. There was a woman standing by the bread shelves, paralyzed with fear, who was trying with all her might to scream. Wiley scooped up a 14 ounce can of vegetable soup that was sitting on the counter and hurled it at the woman with such force it half buried itself in her forehead. Suddenly, from the rear of the store, two men bolted toward the door as fast as they could run. Wiley quickly grabbed the pistol the clerk had dropped and fired without even seeming to aim.

Two shots, two hits, two deaths.

Bits of bone and meat were plastered all over the front of the store, and tiny droplets of blood fell like crimson rain. Wiley allowed himself a smile as he saw the two men he'd shot were dead. Even after all this time, he hadn't lost his shooting eye.

Wiley took a quick moment to be sure there was no one else in the store. Finally satisfied he was alone, he retrieved the butcher knife from where it had fallen and then walked to the back of the store where he could see a door marked;

NO PUBLIC RESTROOM. SORRY.

"Well," he said aloud, "sorry ain't good enough. Reckon I'll just have to piss where the employees piss. Damn, these people ain't very hospitable."

As he walked back to the front of the store, Wiley looked at the body of the woman with the can of soup embedded in her brain, then calmly stooped down and wiped the blood from the blade of the knife on her blouse. Stepping over her body, he paused long enough to exclaim;

"Let this be some kind of lesson to you, lady. Remember all that crap your Mama told you about vegetable soup being good for you? Well, it ain't necessarily true."

Once again, he spotted the video camera and smiled openly into it.

Still on an adrenilin high, Wiley left the store and roared out of the parking lot without looking back. Another car pulled into the lot as he was leaving, but it didn't bother him. He knew most people didn't pay much attention to cars, so he wasn't too worried about being recognized.

He was glad he'd stopped here. Not only had he let the Wolf have a regular feast, he'd also managed to get his hands on a gun.

Business should really pick up now.

RUSSELLVILLE, KENTUCKY

JESSICA BUTLER

Jessica Butler was born in Russellville, Kentucky, she had lived there all of her eighty-one years, and she knew she'd die there. She had already cashed in her burial insurance and paid for a lot in the old cemetery where most of her family had been laid to rest. Her father was buried there, and her mother, as well as her eight brothers and sisters. So was Morgan, her beloved husband, and Baby James, their only child.

Jessica was the only one of her family still living, and she was tired, very tired. Most days now it seemed as if things were just too much to face, especially when she had to face everything alone.

Six months earlier, she'd lost Morgan to a sudden heart attack.

They'd been married fifty-nine years, and it wouldn't bother her if she went to join him today. Jessica believed in a better life after death, and there had been a lot of times lately she was sure she'd heard Morgan calling to her.

She'd taken to awakening in the middle of the night, with her hand touching a cold empty pillow, and the tears would start again. Jessica had never been one for crying, but that bed without Morgan in it was just more than she could bear. Lately she'd taken to sleeping on the couch downstairs three or four nights a week, and that was when she'd begun to hear Morgan calling her name.

It always happened just before midnight. Jessica would doze off and the first thing she knew she'd hear him calling, soft and low.

Jesssssie... Jesssssie... almost too soft to hear.

The first few times it happened, it had scared her so badly she'd lain on the couch trembling, afraid to open her eyes. More than once she'd covered her head with her blanket, hoping the voice would go away.

Then one night, just a little over a week ago, she'd heard the voice calling, and it seemed like the most natural thing in the world for her to answer.

Jesssssie... Jesssssie... it called, and in a weak and fluttering voice, Jessica had replied.

"Morgan? Morgan Butler, is that you?"

Jesssssie... Jesssssie... she heard the voice call again.

"Morgan, what do you want?" she'd cried.

But there was no answer.

It was strange but after the first time she'd answered the voice, she'd lost her fear of it. She came to anticipate the nightly visits, and though the voice never said anything more than her name, she had begun to talk to it, telling it how her day had gone, and all the other little things she used to tell her husband every evening.

Jessica truly believed the voice was real, that it was her Morgan, come to take her with him, to live in the better world they had often spoken of. Well, if he was coming for her, Jessica was ready to go.

All afternoon, Jessica had been preparing for tonight's visit.

She felt sure tonight would be the night when she'd once again feel Morgan's arms around her, and she'd walk beside him to a land beyond the clouds.

MICAJAH

Big Harpe had to find the Amulet.

Only when the Amulet was back around his neck would he be at peace in this new world. He could feel faint vibrations from both the Amulet and the knife, so he knew he was on the right track. Also, for the past hour or so, he'd begun to feel other, even stranger vibrations, from some source he couldn't identify.

The knife and whatever was causing the new vibrations were closer than the Amulet, but for the moment he disregarded those two things. He'd rather recover the Amulet first if there were any way at all to do it.

Then there had been the several times when he was certain he'd heard a Harpe child crying. He knew from past experience that if the crying should become stronger, there was the chance he'd lose control of the Wolf. The Wolf simply could not stand to hear the sound of a crying Harpe child. It turned him even more savage than usual.

There was no way Micajah wanted the Wolf in control.

With a grim smile, he brought his left hand to his throat. No, he remembered all too well the last time the Wolf had taken over, and he didn't want history to repeat itself. If he could find the Amulet, he felt sure this time around he'd be able to hold the reins on the Wolf a little tighter.

162

Of course, it was the knife that had taken his life once before, and he was none too sure how much power it held. He'd rather have the Amulet around his neck first, if it were possible.

The source of the other vibrations were still a puzzle. They seemed to be neither good nor bad, but they were becoming stronger, and it was only a matter of time before he'd have to find out where they were coming from.

He stopped the bike for a moment on the side of the road and tried to open his mind a little more to the Amulet's vibrations.

There. West. The Amulet was west of where he sat, he was sure of it.

From the bike's saddlebags, he took a road map of Kentucky, and saw he could take I-24 down to Highway 68, and then over through Hopkinsville and Russellville straight to Bowling Green.

As his fingers traced his route, the closer they got to Bowling Green the stronger the vibrations became. He felt sure he'd find at least one of the things he was searching for in that city. Anyway, that was as good a place as any to start looking.

There was also something strange in the way he felt as he read the name Russellville on the map. He'd also stop there, he decided, as he pushed the starter and felt the powerful engine roar to life.

There was a gathering sense of urgency as he neared I-24, and Micajah was sure he was drawing closer to the knife with each passing mile.

So be it. If he must confront whoever had the knife before he found the Amulet, then that was just the way it was. He hoped the knife was in the hands of one of Moses Stegall's descendants. He still remembered the promise he'd made to Moses, and he would surely like to see the promise fulfilled. He'd said he'd return, and even though he wasn't sure exactly how it had happened, here he was, and revenge would be sweet.

High above the man on the motorcycle, other eyes watched every move made by those on the ground. Silently riding the upper wind currents, circling among the lower clouds, flew the mighty spirit Eagle. Keeping watch not only on Harpe, but also on the car that held Daniel Hawk and Andrew Stegall as it merged into the traffic pattern, approximately one and a half miles behind the man on the speeding bike.

The Eagle screeched a cry of warning to the unsuspecting men in the car, but it was carried away on the winds long before it reached the ground. When Hawk and Stegall caught up with Harpe, the hunters stood a good chance of becoming the hunted. Neither party knew the exact location of the other, but as the car crept up towards seventy miles an hour, they began to close the gap on the slower moving motorcycle. It was now only a matter of time.

Micajah felt the vibrations from the knife grow stronger and stronger, but couldn't tell where they were coming from.

He slowed the bike still more, and almost at once the two men were upon him. He checked each car as it passed, and scanned his rear view mirror. Suddenly, out of nowhere came a small green car, and Harpe recognized the old man riding on the passenger side.

It was Stegall.

The vibrations became so strong that Harpe's hands were shaking, and the bike began to weave in and out of traffic. Micajah didn't know who the driver of the car was, but there was no way he could mistake Stegall, he'd seen those features in his restless slumber for the better part of two hundred years.

He slowly regained control of the bike and pulled it into the lane directly behind the two men. He was sure they were still unaware of him, and that gave him the advantage of choosing the time and place for their confrontation. But for the time being he'd just hang back and follow them. They were going in the same direction as he, so there was really no hurry. A smile played at the corners of his mouth, as the blue flame flickered into life deep in his eyes.

The Wolf smelled blood.

Foooood Harrrrpe, Steggaaal isssss frooooood...

HAWK AND STEGALL

Daniel Hawk was pissed off at Stegall.

They had agreed to head directly to Cave-in-Rock once they left Stegall's house, but they weren't even out of the driveway when Stegall changed his mind. Daniel stopped at the end of the drive and was beginning to turn the wheel to the left when Stegall spoke.

"Boy, we got to head East, not West. I got the dangedest feelin' I ever had. This knife is a'twichin' and a jerkin' like it was alive, and it's pullin' us East. Harpe ain't very far away. I don't know how I know, but I'd sure as hell bet on it."

"But we agreed the logical thing was to head for Cave-in-Rock, Stegall, and see if we could pick up Harpe's trail there. Are you sure about this?"

"Since when has any of this crap been logical, boy," Stegall answered. "I got a two hundred year old knife and a bad feelin' in my bones, and you drove a couple of hundred miles on the strength of a dream, found a chunk of old rock you believe is Harpe's tommyhawk, and now here we are chasin' a ghost across the country. Not only that but we're both scared to death of a man that's been dead for two centuries. Now is any of that logical?"

"Well, I guess not," Hawk admitted.

"You're danged right it ain't. Now head East you red peckerwood. We're on the right track, I can feel it in my bones."

Without another word Daniel hit the Interstate and rolled East toward Hopkinsville at about seventy-five miles an hour. He had a real sense of urgency and he'd have liked to drive even faster, but he sure as hell didn't want a speeding ticket. There were only a few cars on this stretch of highway, and up ahead Daniel could make out a guy on a motorcycle.

As they drew closer, the motorcycle slowed and began to weave back and forth across the highway. Daniel pulled into the left hand land and carefully passed the bike. The way the rider was weaving, Daniel wanted to make damn sure there was no chance of colliding. As Daniel passed, the rider looked over at the car and smiled. Daniel was relieved when the motorcycle stopped weaving about, and noticed the bike had pulled up fairly close to the back of his car.

The two vehicles stayed in that position as they headed West.

FIRST CONFRONTATION

Harpe saw the sign that said Highway 68 was the next exit, one mile up ahead. He made up his mind quickly, and pulled the bike into the left lane and alongside the car. As he drew close to the car, the old man on the passenger side looked at him and his eyes grew wide with recognition. Harpe smiled as the driver almost ran the car into the ditch as the old man shouted something at him. Harpe gunned the powerful engine and roared off the Interstate at the exit. The car was right behind him, and gaining.

Yessss...Foooood...Haarppe...Fooood.

"That's him," Stegall shouted. "That's Harpe. Run him off the road. Run over him. Damnit Injun, run over that murderin' rascal."

Hawk pulled the wheel hard right to avoid the speeding motorcycle and almost ran off the road. "Damnit, Stegall, you old fart, you almost made me wreck the car. Stop that damn shouting. What do you mean, that's him? Where?"

"On the motorcycle, you dumb redskin. Run over him."

166

"The hell I will. How do you know that's Harpe? What if we run over some innocent biker?" But Daniel swung the car off the Interstate and onto the exit in pursuit of the motorcycle. If it really was Micajah Harpe, maybe they could end the whole damn thing right here and now, with no one else getting hurt.

"I'm telling you, I know that's Harpe." Stegall was still shouting. "I've seen his face and them blue eyes in my nightmares all my life. That's the Wolf, for damn sure."

Stegall turned and grabbed the wooden box off the back seat and began trying to fit the key into the small lock. But between the bouncing of the car and the way his hands were shaking, he was having trouble getting the key into the keyhole.

"Hang on, Stegall, I'm gaining him," Daniel shouted as he gave the car more gas. "You better hurry and get out that damned knife. While you're at it, unwrap the tomahawk. If that really is Harpe, we're gonna need all the weapons we can get our hands on."

Stegall succeeded in opening the box and removing the knife, and then turned again and grabbed the tomahawk. He laid the axe on the seat beside Hawk. "Ain't you got a damn gun, Injun?" he asked.

Daniel risked a quick look at Stegall.

"Hell no, I ain't got a gun. Ain't you?"

"Yeah, I got one, and I knew damn well I should have brought it with me."

"If you're talking about that old World War II relic you showed me, it's probably a good thing you didn't bring it. It would have blown up in our faces the first time you pulled the trigger. Probably killed the hell out of us instead of Harpe. I told you I intended to buy a 30.06 rifle just as soon as I could, I just didn't know we'd be needing it this soon."

"Well, we need a gun, and we need it right now. Unless you want to fight that big mother bare handed? I sure as hell don't."

167

"Hell, I don't want to fight him at all, but it don't look as if we got a lot of choice, does it?" Daniel pointed about halfway up the off ramp to where the motorcycle was sitting parked in the middle of the road. The big man was standing beside the bike, waiting for the car to approach.

Harpe turned the bike across the road and stood on the other side of it. He wasn't sure if the men would stop or not, and he was ready to jump out of the way if they tried to run him over. He needn't have worried. The driver of the car locked the brakes and slid to a stop just inches short of the motorcycle. The two men sat in the car looking at Harpe for a couple of minutes, and Harpe just stood there and stared back. Finally the older man leaned half out the window and shouted at Micajah.

"That is you, ain't it Harpe?"

"It's me alright, old man, and I know who you are too. I can smell the stink of Stegall blood all the way over here. You got my knife with you?"

Stegall started scrambling to open the door. "Yeah, I got the knife. Want to try and take if from me?" Stegall brandished the knife in his right hand, and the blade gleamed in the bright sunshine.

"This blade cut off your ugly head once, and I'm bettin' it can do it again."

"Stakes are pretty high, old man, you sure you want to make that bet?"

Stegall looked at Micajah for a moment, but he still didn't climb out of the car.

"Who'd gonna hold me down this time, Stegall? That little guy with you? Last time it took six men hold me, and I was bad wounded then. I don't see nobody except the two of you, and I sure as hell ain't wounded."

Harpe turned his attention to Daniel Hawk. "What's your name, feller, and what's your stake in this fight? There's still a chance you can get away, you know. Just shove the old man out of the car and drive off. You'll be long gone before I get through killing him. I plan on taking my time sending him to hell."

Daniel found speaking to Harpe face to face was the hardest thing he'd ever done, but he knew if he didn't get in his two cents worth, he might never have another chance. He stepped out of the car and stood looking at Harpe.

"I reckon I'll be hanging around, Harpe. I ain't got a lot of use for this old fart myself, but all the same it'll be two of us fighting you today. Tell the truth, I'm a little surprised you don't also know who I am."

Harpe had focused all his attention on Stegall, but now he took a closer look at Daniel. The boy shuddered under the full intensity of the blue flame that burned in the man's eyes, and he knew he was face to face with a demon, and the demon was hungry.

"Ha ha ha ha," Harpe laughed. "I see you now. You're a Cherokee boy, ain't you? Damn, boy, you're fighting on the wrong side. Did your people happen to live in Nickajack?"

"Yeah, I reckon they did. My name is Daniel Hawk, my ancestor was Dancing Hawk. What do you mean, I'm on the wrong side?" The man's friendly tone of voice had taken him by surprise.

"I fought with Dancing Hawk, not against him," Harpe said. "I'm a brother to the Cherokee, and your ancestor was my friend. I have not made this offer many times in my life boy, so consider it well before you answer. I am in an unfriendly land, with every hand against me, and the days to come will be filled with death and destruction. I seek revenge for what happened to my family, and I want my knife and one other thing I have lost. No one will stand between me and regaining these things. I was brought back for a reason, and I must determine what it is. Now hear me well. Out of respect for your family, If you wish I will let you join me. Or I will let you drive away and even take Stegall with you. Leave the knife and go. Or join me. It's your decision. But know this also. Should you side with my old enemy, the DarkWolf will drink your blood as readily as it does Stegall's. And I'll only tell you the one time."

Daniel Hawk didn't know what to say. Harpe was asking him to join him, and he was actually considering it. His hand, almost as if it were moving by itself, moved to the medicine bag at his neck and closed around it. Daniel needed to re-confirm his commitment, and he desperately needed to find strength somewhere. His father's medicine was all he had to rely on.

"I am honored by your offer, Harpe. But I also know of the DarkWolf, and something of his hold on you, so I must oppose you. Also, I have spoken with the spirits, and they have chosen me to stop you. Once before, you used the power given to you for evil, and the spirits do not wish that to happen again." Daniel wasn't sure whether he could bluff Harpe or not, but it seemed like it was the only chance he and Stegall had of living through this encounter. He decided to take his best shot, and see what happened.

"But know this, Wolf Spirit," Daniel said, calling Harpe by his Cherokee name, "I too have a mighty weapon. A mighty weapon that once belonged to you. The Eagle spirit took me to its resting place, and I reclaimed it to use in my fight against the DarkWolf."

Daniel walked around the car and laid the wrapped object on the hood. He looked at Harpe, and without taking his eyes off the man, he slowly began to unwrap the object.

"Hold, Daniel Hawk," Harpe commanded. "I know what it is you carry. I've felt its presence for a few hours now, but didn't recognize it until this very moment. Once Dancing Hawk stood before me, even as you do now, and proceeded to unwrap that same object. The power within the tomahawk is something you know little of, and something you will not be able to control once it is opened in my presence. Its power was neither good nor evil till I made it my own, and then it became as one with me. In my hand the tomahawk was mighty indeed, and when I held it my strength increased by tenfold. You cannot wield the power, young Hawk, only I can. Unwrap it if you will, but remember, once unshielded the tomahawk must drink innocent blood. In my hand it drank deeply indeed. Even as the DarkWolf forever hungers, the tomahawk forever thirsts. Give me the tomahawk, lay down the knife, and the two of you can leave this place alive. We will settle our differences later."

In the sky the Eagle circled. He could no longer exert any control over them, not even Daniel Hawk. With one last fleeting notion, he sent a thought directly at the mind of the young warrior. Perhaps Daniel Hawk would hear and understand.

Daniel looked at Harpe as he stood with his hand outstretched, waiting for the tomahawk, and suddenly, for some reason, he realized a small portion of truth.

"You cannot take the tomahawk, can you, Harpe? For you to use its power, it must be given to you freely, even as Dancing Hawk once did. Dancing Hawk made a mistake, and it cost the world dearly. Don't expect the same of me."

Without warning, Daniel whipped the cloth from the great tomahawk and held it overhead. As his eyes turned skyward, he saw the mighty bird as it spiraled higher. Suddenly he realized the Eagle had been with him from the beginning.

"Look up, Harpe. See the Eagle? You and the DarkWolf aren't the only spirit beings here today." Daniel wasn't sure what effect the presence of the Eagle would have on Harpe, but he knew Harpe couldn't take the tomahawk from him. Not and use its power anyway. And he sure as hell knew he wasn't about to hand the weapon over freely.

"The Wolf could eat the Eagle for dinner, young fool," Harpe growled, "and I could take the tomahawk from your lifeless fingers. It would kill as easily as before, and although you have it now, it still belongs to me. Once given, always kept. If you have spoken with the spirits, as you say, then you know the blade has no power over me in this world. The magic is mine, and mine alone. Used by you, the tomahawk will soon drink friendly blood. If you keep it, young Hawk, it will become your master. But now the time for talking is passed. Old man, lay down the knife or I will bring you so much pain you will beg me to take your worthless life. You both know the truth is that even with the knife and the axe, there is no way the two of you can stand against me."

With these words, the Harpe started walking around the bike. The flame in his eyes was now a raging furnace, and suddenly Daniel Hawk and Andrew Stegall realized they'd made a grave mistake. They weren't anywhere near being ready to fight Harpe, and to do so now would mean their death.

For Harpe was human in form only. The man was truly the personification of the DarkWolf, and ten men such as Hawk and Stegall could not stand against him.

Daniel Hawk took a few tentative backward steps, but saw Stegall was standing his ground. "Lay down the knife, Stegall," Hawk said in a hoarse whisper. "And maybe we'll live to fight another day."

"I won't give it up, Injun, I'll die first." Stegall was trembling, and his voice was rasping from between lips suddenly gone dry.

"Lay down the knife, old man," Hawk repeated, "we have no choice."

Daniel knew he spoke the truth, and could only hope Stegall would come to his senses before it was too late. Better to live now and take the Harpe on a time when it was more to their advantage, than to fight the man here and die without a chance. Daniel knew Harpe wouldn't make them another offer such as the one he'd made today.

Daniel looked again at Stegall and saw a flicker of realization come across the man's face. For the first time, it seemed as if Stegall understood.

Stegall did understand, for he himself had now stared directly into Harpe's flaming blue eyes, and saw his own death reflected there.

Stegall shook his head slightly from side to side as if he were awakening from a bad dream. He had indeed looked into the eyes of the demon, and saw there what his ancestor Moses Stegall had seen more than once. The blue flames raged, but they were cold, and Andrew knew they would devour his soul if he chose to fight Harpe right now. Stegall had never felt such cold, and it turned his hastily formed plan into meaningless random thoughts.

He had intended to let Hawk make a move on Harpe, and once the two were fighting, Stegall would jump in and try to slash Harpe's throat with the big knife. But it was now plain Hawk was not going to fight Harpe at this time.

Stegall spat on the ground and turned the fury of his gaze on the young Indian.

"What the hell's the matter with you, boy? We got to fight Harpe, and we got to do it here and now." He was trying to work himself into a state of mind that would send him against the big Harpe, regardless of the consequences.

"We can't fight him, old man, you know that. Look at his eyes, for God's sake, and use what little brain you've got left."

Stegall was using his brain, and his brain told him if he could kill Harpe by sacrificing Hawk, then the end would justify the means. But for some reason he did as the boy said, and took another look into the eye's of the man standing by the bike, and this time he felt the coldness running through his own veins, and he shuddered as the raw emotion gripped him.

This time, when he stared into the blue flames again, what was left of his courage deserted him. Stegall was an old man, and had faced death more than once in his life. But not death at the hands of this demon. His head was pounding, and it felt as if his heart would burst from his chest at any moment. He'd never seen such power in anyone before in his life.

Stegall slowly laid the knife on the ground in front of the car, and watched as Daniel picked up the cloth and re-wrapped the tomahawk. Silently, and with nothing more than a glowering look, the two men climbed into the car and carefully backed back down to the interstate. Harpe stood by the bike and watched as they drove away, and a little smile played around the corners of his lips.

As Daniel accelerated back to cruising speed, Stegall vowed to himself that he wouldn't make this mistake again. He knew it was only a matter of time before they faced Harpe again, and the next time, they'd fight. Scared or not, kill or be killed, devil be damned, next time Andrew Stegall was fighting the big son-of-a-bitch.

MICAJAH

Micajah picked up the knife and ran his thumb across the edge of the blade. It was as sharp as it had been the day he took it and its twin from the old smittie in Knoxville. Harpe remembered the old man well. There were few who had been his equal in the art of knife making. The twin blades were works of art, and not just simple tools. Long and heavy, with handles made of white stag bone and the ends wound with supple leather, the blades had been forged for one purpose and one purpose only. They were perfect killing weapons. Harpe could almost sever a man's head with one mighty swipe, and rip out half a man's insides with a single upward thrust. The blades would cut off a hand as quickly as an axe would, and were much easier to wield. With one of these knives in each hand, Harpe could face ten men, and live to brag about it.

He placed the knife he had recovered from Stegall in the pocket of the saddlebags alongside the one he'd found in the cave. They gave him a great feeling of comfort as he once again rode down the highway. He would rather have gotten back the knife than to have killed Stegall, at least at this point. The old man would be easy to find, in fact he would probably find Harpe, and the un-blooded Cherokee boy would present no problem.

Harpe would have liked to have gotten his hands on the tomahawk.

He could well remember the feel of the axe as it crushed through flesh and bone and splattered blood. It was indeed a mighty weapon, but it was indeed a fact that only Harpe could use its mystical power. He'd told Daniel Hawk the truth about that. But perhaps the young Indian was partly right. After all this time, perhaps the tomahawk would have to be freely given again in order for Harpe to use its power fully.

Perhaps. Then again, perhaps not.

The magic in the axe came from the spirit world, and no one knew at any given time how the spirits would choose to act. After all, the tomahawk had already once been given to Micajah, and that may be sufficient for him to use its power for all time. It had not known an owner since Harpe, and the ties between the man and the blade may be as strong as ever. The power of the spirit world was not to be taken lightly. The mighty animal spirits only bestowed their magic once in a great while, and then only to someone they considered worthy. If they had once decided Harpe was worthy of their power, they may still consider him so.

When Dancing Hawk had given the axe to Harpe, its power was needed to help drive the white eyes from the homeland of the People. That the white eyes could not be driven away was no fault of the tomahawk, nor of Harpes. He had used the weapon as it had been intended, following the guidance of the spirits in every way. And so long as he had not violated their trust, then perhaps the tomahawk would still lend its powers to Harpe, once it was back in his possession.

There was no doubt the battle axe would be a formidable weapon here in this day and age, whether or not its awesome magical powers were still intact. And should it ever find its way back into the spirit world itself, its power would be dreadful indeed. The spirits themselves would have little or no means of controlling whoever wielded the tomahawk, and it may be the only weapon in either world that had the power to stop the Wolf.

Micajah tore his thoughts from the tomahawk and the knives as he saw a sign that signaled the exit to Hopkinsville. He had begun to feel hungry, and decided a stop was in order. He could get a bite to eat, and have a little time to think about his next move.

He had been feeling the vibrations from the Amulet grow stronger and stronger as the motorcycle ate up the miles across Kentucky, and he knew it was only a matter of time before the star was once again around his neck. Time enough then to deal with Stegall and his red friend.

He knew they were still following him.

Several times he had noticed the small green car, and even if he hadn't seen them, he could feel their presence, as they pressed hard to keep him in sight.

Micajah anticipated very little trouble in recovering the Amulet.

He knew beyond a doubt no one was wearing it, for the vibrations were much too weak. Had it been around the neck of a Harpe child, the power would be singing and shouting, and its call would be thundering through his head like a runaway stallion. No, the Amulet was still resting, as it had since he so long ago gave it to Susan. Micajah knew its power was his to reclaim. The Wolf was waiting for Micajah to once again drape the Star around his neck, and then the world would tremble.

He was riding along a tree lined street, in a neat clean sub-division filled with nice, almost new brick homes. His mind was on the Amulet, and finding a cafe, and resting undisturbed for a few minutes.

Suddenly, cutting like a blade through his mind and instantly wiping away all other thoughts, came the cry of the baby.

The Harpe child.

Its cry echoed into his mind and rang and rang and rang, until he could think of nothing else.

He lost control of the motorcycle, and it careened off the street and into a private drive, and only stopped when it violently slammed into a car parked in the drive.

Harpe lay stunned on the ground, too shocked to move. He knew he wasn't even close to the child, and yet, as he had back at the cave, he heard it's crying. He covered his ears, but the cry was inside his head, and still as clear as ever.

Then, as suddenly as it had begun, the crying stopped.

The Harpe raised himself on one elbow and opened his eyes. The wild blue Wolf flame was raging, brought on by the crying, and was now more out of control than it had been since he'd first awakened back in the cave. The Wolf had heard the crying also, and was furious in his desire for Harpe to turn him loose.

The world swam before Harpe's eyes as he sat on the ground. The only sound now in his head was the distant echo of the infant's whimpers, and the hissing urging of the Wolf as it called on him to free it.

He was still not exactly sure what was happening when the owner of the car he had crashed into came rushing up and grabbed him by the arm. It was obvious the man wanted to see if he could be of any help. Harpe's hand was trembling, and he instinctively reached for the saddlebags that lay nearby. His numbed fingers fumbled as he tried desperately to open the saddlebags.

As the leather bag finally opened and his hand closed around the handle of the knife, the trembling ceased. The air seemed to almost crackle energy as Harpe brought the knife into view and turned first time to look at the man who knelt beside him. Almost by itself, the knife struck.

The blade penetrated the man's right ear and exited through his left, burying itself in the twisted metal of the car's wrecked door. Harpe lurched to his feet and savagely wrenched the knife from the man's head. In the corner of his vision, Harpe saw a pretty young woman standing nearby, a scream frozen on her lips, trying without success to force its way out. With a roundhouse backhand swing of his hand, he buried the heavy blade in her throat, ripping across and upward. Blood rushed out in a wild torrent and began to flow down the slight incline of the drive.

Still reeling from the sound of the baby crying and the insistent calling of the Wolf, Micajah hardly knew where he was, and was aware of nothing save the bodies of the two victims lying haphazard on the ground.

As his vision cleared, he became aware there were three more people standing on the other side of the car, staring at him in horror.

They were in shock at seeing their neighbors killed, but were still too stunned to cry out. Harpe might have left them as they stood, had not the baby chose that time to once again start its crying. The flame glazed his eyes, and with a wild cry of his own, Micajah bounded across the car and landed in the middle of the others, giving them no time at all to recover their wits.

His feet barely touched the hood of the car as he leaped, and as he descended upon the three people, he drove the point of the long knife directly into the top of the head of the old woman, burying its great blade to the hilt. His body struck the other two, knocking them to the ground, and as they landed he smashed his knee into the throat of the larger of the two men, instantly breaking his neck and crushing his windpipe. The last man rolled with the force of Harpe's blow, letting the momentum carry him into a backward roll that ended with him on his feet and facing Harpe.

Without hesitation the man launched a quick right hand at Harpe, landing it on the point of Harpe's jaw. Micajah shook his head, and the man struck again, this time to Harpe's ribcage. The man was obviously a better than average street fighter, and wasted no time in sending a blistering left fist crashing to Harpe's sternum, actually sending Harpe reeling to his knees.

But however good a street fighter the man might have been, he had never fought anyone like the Harpe. Micajah came to his feet in a motion almost too fast to follow, and easily dodged the hurried right hand the man threw at him next.

Harpe was beginning to come to his senses, and a smile crossed his face as he watched the other man drop into a fighting crouch. He didn't understand what the man intended to do, not recognizing the karate stance the man had assumed. The part of his mind that was controlling him during the fight was not familiar with fighting methods used by martial artists, having never seen them in the old days, and Micajah studied the man for a moment.

He watched as the man began moving in a slow circle, waving his hands in front of his face and making small unintelligible noises.

The boy who had been Billy Harp would have known what the karate stance meant, and might have been a little wary, as it was obvious the man was well trained in the martial arts.

Not so the monster that Billy had become. This was the Demon DarkWolf, and the DarkWolf had no knowledge of karate.

He cared even less.

The man rocked back a step and began a lightning fast spinning kick, intended to land on the side of Harpe's head with killing force. He thought he now had the fight under control as his foot streaked towards his opponents face. And if the kick had landed, perhaps the fight may have lasted a few moments longer.

But it didn't land.

The Harpe saw the move as if it were in slow motion.

With a mighty right hand, he almost casually caught the man's ankle as it neared his face. In one move he lifted the man's leg and raised him high in the air, using the man's own momentum against him. As the man became perpendicular over Harpe's head, he jerked

179

on the leg with a sharp whipping motion, stopping the upward motion and violently bringing the body down and forward. At the last moment, he sat his shoulders and jerked backward on the man's leg. It was just like cracking a bullwhip. Many times he had snapped the head off a snake in the same manner.

The man's body stopped as Harpe jerked backward, but the force kept his head moving forward until his neck snapped with a sickening crack. Blood veins ruptured and scarlet rain burst from the man's ears, nose, and mouth. His eyes popped from their sockets, and there was a loud 'plop' as Harpe turned the body loose and it flew through the air and struck the trunk of a large nearby tree.

In a few moments, Harpe's eyes were almost clear of the flame, and he was back in control of his senses as he stood over the body for a second.

"To tell the truth," he said to the dead man, "I was kind of enjoyin' your little dance, right up till the time when you tried to sneak in that kick. I don't remember nobody doin' that step at none of the hoe downs I was ever at."

He heard what sounded like dozens of police sirens and figured he had a couple of minutes at most to get out of there. He picked up his bike and saw the only damage was a bent front fender. The tire wasn't even flat, so he wrapped his hands around the fender and exerted enough strength to get it straight enough for the wheel to roll. With a last glance around, he cranked the engine and roared out of the drive and down the street, not paying attention to the several people gathered along the way.

He was already thinking about the crying baby.

He knew the baby wasn't close, and yet he sensed it wasn't really very far away. He also knew one way or another, he had to find the baby and stop the crying. The Wolf was impossible to control when the child cried, and Harpe didn't want another incident like the one he's just been through. It was just too time consuming.

Harpe wanted to finish his business as quickly as possible, preferably with no more killing other than his old enemy Stegall.

And another thing. He never had gotten anything to eat, and he was still hungry as hell.

RUSSELLVILLE

JESSICA BUTLER

Jessica felt better this afternoon than she had in a long time.

She had always liked to look good for Morgan on Saturday nights, and so today she had put on her prettiest summer dress, the one with the roses on it Morgan had always liked, and brushed her long hair until it shone. She was sure Morgan was coming for her tonight, and it was a great relief. She so looked forward to being with him again, and to seeing Mama and Daddy and all her loved ones.

She danced around the kitchen like a schoolgirl waiting on her prom date.

The kitchen was spotless, and there was a fresh pot of coffee on the counter.

On the windowsill lay three large, sun-ripened tomatoes, and she had sliced up a pint of juicy strawberries for dessert. Morgan dearly loved fresh strawberries, and always liked a cup of hot coffee.

There had never been any doubt in Jessica's mind that one day she would join her husband. As she looked around the familiar kitchen at all of the things Morgan had loved so much, she knew she was right in picking tonight to go with him. She couldn't stand even one more day in this house alone.

She was humming as she poured the coffee, the same little tune she had learned so long ago from her mother. It was a family tune, and she usually found herself humming it when she was particularly emotional, either very sad, or very happy. The tune always seemed to gladden her heart, and this afternoon, Jessica's heart was light, and her mind was clear. She was going to be with Morgan tonight, and so she hummed the tune in anticipation.

When Jessica turned from the counter to put down the hot cup of coffee, she was startled to discover there was a big man standing just inside her kitchen door.

Jessica had grown up in the country, and had never turned anyone away from her door, and she wasn't about to start now.

"Come in, young man," she said, "would you care for a cup of coffee?"

Micajah Harpe had intended to steal a car as soon as he got to Russellville.

He knew the police would be checking every motorcycle rider they came across, after the incident in Hopkinsville.

There was an outside chance he might have been seen by someone, and there was no use taking unnecessary risks. He'd ditch the bike, find a car, and be on his way before the people in Russellville knew he'd even been in their town.

He rode around for awhile, looking for a car that would be easy to steal. One he wouldn't have to kill to get.

He had other business to take care of, and he knew if by some chance the Wolf got loose in this town, he would waste even more time before he found the Amulet.

He was on Highway 431 about two miles south of town when the felt the vibrations begin once again.

There was a difference this time, but he couldn't tell exactly what it was. The vibrations were perhaps even stronger than before, and once again he found himself pulling the bike off the road.

He let the vibrations lead him along an unpaved drive to an old farmhouse, with a weathered, half gone barn sitting to one side. The yard was overgrown, and there were no crops of any kind, save a small garden in the back of the house, where a lot of beautiful flowers could be seen. The garden and the flowers seemed to be well tended, as though they were all the owner really cared about.

He was off the bike and walking toward the house when the strongest vibrations of all caught him full force.

He grabbed his head and held it in both hands, trying to stop the pounding that threatened to tear his brain apart.

He didn't understand this, but he knew there was something about this place that was driving him crazy.

For several minutes he stumbled about in the yard like a man who'd had too much to drink.

More than once he lost his balance and fell to his knees in the grass.

The falls didn't hurt him, if anything they gave him a few minutes to think.

Something really strange was going on here.

For some reason this time the Wolf didn't seem to be paying attention to what was happening. Harpe hadn't felt the presence of the Wolf at any time since he'd left the road.

He had to find out what was happening to him, and he had to find out quickly. If the authorities were indeed looking for him in Russellville, he couldn't allow himself to remain in this condition. They'd capture him for sure.

There was no way he could put up a fight until he got himself under control.

In one of his clearer moments, he decided the old farmhouse was where the answers lay, and he headed in that direction as fast as he could. Still, it took him several minutes to get close enough to the house to tell anything about it.

Even in his strange state of mind, he was cautious. He was aware there might be a trap waiting for him inside the house, and he approached it with that in mind.

It was an older, white frame farmhouse, very much like many others in the quiet little town. Once it had been a beautiful home, with a large front porch and blue shutters on every window, but now it was growing old. The paint was peeling, and two of the shutters hung sideways. The house, like the farmland itself, was in sad need of repair.

As he approached the house from the rear, he noticed an open window. From inside the house came the sound of someone softly humming a haunting melody.

Harpe stopped dead in his tracks.

It was a song he knew, but one he hadn't heard for over two hundred years.

He carefully looked through a window and saw an elderly lady pouring a cup of steaming coffee. The coffee smelled good, and Micajah knew he had to find out where the woman had learned the melody she was humming, so he quietly opened the door and slipped into the kitchen. He stood by the table and watched as she finished pouring her coffee, waiting for her to turn around.

When she did, she seemed neither shocked to see him there, nor afraid of him. She smiled at him, pointed vaguely at the counter, and asked if he wanted a cup of coffee.

"Yes Ma'am," he said, "If you don't mind. That coffee does smell mighty good. Do you mind if I sit down?"

Jessica got another cup from the cabinet and filled it with coffee.

"Cream or sugar," she asked.

"No Ma'am, I'll just take it black," he answered. "Tell me, do you live here all alone?"

"Just me and my husband Morgan, young man," she replied. "My name is Jessica Butler, and I've lived on this farm all my life. It's been in my husband's family for generations."

"That's nice, Ma'am," Micajah said. "Where might your husband be? I didn't see anyone about when I came up."

"Oh, I expect him most any time," Jessica smiled, "I'm sure he'll be here soon."

"Tell me, Ma'am, where did you learn the tune you were humming when I came in? I remember hearing long ago."

"My husband's Grandma taught me that little song, young man," Jessica said, and there was a look of remembrance somewhere way in the back of her eyes.

"I've been knowing it for close to eighty years. It was an old melody she learned from her own Grandma, I believe. You know, she was the granddaughter of Katie White herself."

"Katie White, Ma'am? I don't believe I know the name."

"It's a long story, young man, but an interesting one. Part of it isn't very pretty, and some say it isn't even true, but I know what our families have always believed, and what they passed down to us."

It was plain the old lady liked to tell the story, and if it would explain where she learned the melody, Micajah was more than willing to listen.

"If you've got the time before your husband comes home, Ma'am, I sure would like to hear the story."

"I told you a little fib, young man, a little white lie about my husband."

Jessica's eyes fluttered and glanced around the kitchen, almost as if she expected to see someone else there with them.

"You seem like you were raised right, and you're a very polite young man, so I guess I'll tell you how it really is."

"Yes Ma'am," Micajah replied.

For the first time he could see the sadness in her eyes, and hear the sorrow in her voice as she spoke. He knew what she was about to say, even before the words left her mouth.

"My Morgan died, about six months ago," she began. "He won't be coming home today. We were married most of sixty years, Morgan and me, and for some reason I always believed I'd be the first to go. Morgan was so strong and healthy. He never had to see the doctor. I was the one who wasn't well."

She moved about as she spoke, touching first one item, then another. It was clear she was very distressed.

"Morgan always got up early," she continued, "earlier than I did, and he always had the coffee ready when I came down. Well, one morning back in March, I got up and started downstairs and didn't smell the coffee. That seemed strange to me, and when I came into the kitchen he was lying on the floor.

The doctor said it was a heart attack, and he didn't suffer any, and I'm glad of that. But to tell the truth, young man, I need him a lot. I miss him more today than I did yesterday. But he is coming for me, and I truly believe it will be tonight."

Micajah looked at Miss Jessica and saw her eyes were filling with tears. He suspected she didn't have many people to talk to, and had a lot of things she needed to get out.

"Miss Jessica, Ma'am," he said, "I've got plenty of time if there's something you need to talk about."

"Thank you young man," she said. "I could tell you were a good boy from the way you talked."

Micajah took a sip of the coffee as she continued.

"Morgan comes to visit me, you know. Almost every night. He comes in and calls my name, and I talk to him. He always said he wouldn't leave me alone, so that's why I think I'm going to join him soon. In fact, like I said, I think tonight will be the night. I'm sure he'll come for me. You don't think I'm just a crazy old woman, do you? I mean, what with me talking to my husband and all?"

"No Ma'am. I don't think you're a crazy old woman. And it doesn't surprise me that Morgan comes to visit. Love as strong as yours and Morgan's doesn't die, and I should know. Strange things happen in this old world, and I should know that as well. But tell me about the song. I really do want to know the story."

"Well, young man, as I recall it, many years ago there were some pretty bad people around these parts, and they went on a killing spree and killed a bunch of folks. There were two men and three women and a passel of children. They were finally caught and the men were executed, but the women got put on trial and all three of 'em got off scott free. Well, two of the women moved on down to Tennessee, but the other one, she stayed right here in Russellville. They said she always aimed to follow the others down to Tennessee, but one thing led to another, and her health got bad, and she just never got to go. But they say she never quit wanting to leave. The old stories say even when she was on her death bed, the last thing she said was that she'd promised someone she'd be waiting in Tennessee, no matter how long it took for him to get there. She swore that even if it took a hundred years, he'd come looking for her, for he had said he would, and he was a man true to his word. Any way, the people in town never let her forget the days when she was an outlaw, and they made it pretty hard on her I guess. Callin' her names and shunnin' her in public and such as that. And she never done a thing to a single one of 'em either. They took to tearin' up her garden, and killin' her chickens, and just makin' life a livin' hell for the poor woman. If finally got so bad Old Colonel Butler, that'd be my Morgan's ancestor, he took her in and gave her a place to live on his farm. This very farm, in fact. And they say she changed her name and told everybody she'd gone to Tennessee, but truth is she lived right here till her dying day. She took the name Katie White, and Colonel Butler built her a cabin down by the spring, and for years and years this little valley was known as Katie White's Bottom. She had a daughter that stayed with her, Katie did, named

Lovie, who married Colonel Butler's youngest son, Anthony. Anthony was in the Army or something, and went off to Texas. Lovie went with him but hardly a year had passed before she came back. She moved back in with her Mama and stayed there till Miss Katie's dying day. For some reason, Lovie took on the name Roberts, and I think she finally did move to Tennessee after Miss Katie died. Anyway, they buried Miss Katie down by the spring, close to where her cabin used to stand. It was Miss Katie that first sang the little song you heard me humming, young man, and it's been passed down through the family since then. Now I don't want to dispute your word, but I believe you're mistaken about hearing that song before. It's a kind of a private song, one we've always kept to ourselves. Out of respect for Miss Katie, of course. Cause, regardless of what the folks hereabouts said about her or did to her, the fact is Katie was a good woman, and didn't deserve to be treated the way she was treated by the folks in Russellville."

"Lordy, Lordy young man, I didn't mean to talk your ear off. I just get carried away sometimes."

"Miss Jessica, you've told me just exactly what I needed to know. But you're wrong about me not knowing the song. Would you hum it one more time for me? Please?"

Jessica looked at the big man sitting so calmly at her kitchen table, and for the first time noticed his beautiful soft blue eyes.

Such a nice boy, she thought, and began to softly hum the song.

Micajah was lost in a world he remembered as if it were yesterday. He closed his eyes and began to hum along with Jessica, singing a few words now and then.

Jessica heard the man singing and realized he did indeed know the song, perhaps even better than she. And when she reached the end, he sang two short lines that even she didn't know.

"Tell me young man, what is your name? And how do you come to know the song?"

Micajah opened his eyes and took one last sip of the still hot coffee.

"My name is Micajah Harpe, Ma'am," he answered after a moment's pause. "I learned the song from my mother many years ago. And my wife used to hum it all the time, much as you do."

Jessica gasped when she heard the name.

She got up from the table and moved over to the door.

"Would you like to take a walk with me, Mister Harpe?" she asked.

Without a word he stood up and opened the door for Jessica, and they slowly walked down across the back yard.

Jessica stopped by a small, white marker at one end of the little meadow, and stood looking at it in silence for a moment.

It was worn smooth by time and the ravages of weather, but it was clear it had stood guard over a grave that had been well tended over the years.

If there had ever been an inscription, it had long since vanished.

Jessica turned away after a minute and looked deeply into the blue eyes of her visitor.

"This is the resting place of Katie White, Mister Harpe. For some reason, I don't believe I have to tell you her real name."

Micajah looked at the smooth marker for several more long silent moments.

Still not speaking, he knelt on one knee by the headstone, and gently placed his right hand on the ground.

"Susan," he whispered. "Susan, I've come for you. I promised I would, and I have. They cannot keep us apart."

For only the third time in his life, William Micajah Harpe shed a single tear.

He didn't know how long he knelt by the grave, but the sun was low in the west when he finally arose. At some point Miss Jessica had gone back to the house, and he hadn't even realized it. With one last look at the stone, he turned and walked back to the house himself.

For treating Susan the way they had, this town deserved whatever fate the Wolf visited upon it. Gone was his intention of moving quickly through Russellville.

"I make another promise to you, Susan. The people who hurt you will be repaid in kind. The Wolf will feed in Russellville, and feed well. And I'll only tell you the one time."

When he reached the house, Jessica had supper on the table.

Fresh green beans, cooked with new potatoes and small ears of corn on the cob, and baby squash with onions, and some of the best smelling pork chops he'd ever smelled. There was a big pan of large, flaky home made biscuits, and without asking he knew they were made from scratch.

They had fresh iced tea, and when he had eaten enough to stuff a horse, Jessica brought out a hot apple pie for dessert. They were having another cup of fresh coffee when Jessica spoke again.

"Mister Harpe, it's almost dark and my Morgan will be here most any time now. I have a favor to ask of you, and I don't quite know to ask it."

"Just tell me what it is you want, Miss Jessica, and if it's within my power, you'll have it."

"I want to go with Morgan tonight, Mister Harpe. This may sound foolish, and be a bit hard for you to understand, but that's what I want. I don't want to face another day by myself. We were together for almost sixty years, and I don't want to live another day in a world he isn't in. Can you forgive a foolish old woman for feeling this way?"

"There's nothing for me to forgive, Miss Jessica. I'll sit beside you through the night, and when you hear Morgan calling, you just squeeze my hand. You're a fine lady, Miss Jessica, and your Morgan was a lucky man."

Jessica lay down on the couch and closed her eyes, and for the first time since Morgan died, she felt at peace. Micajah Harpe, true to his word, sat in a chair beside her and held her hand.

About eleven o'clock she roused a bit, and heard Morgan calling.

Jessie...Jessie...he softly called.

Jessica smiled and very gently squeezed the hand of the big man who sat with her.

Micajah's right hand rested softly as a feather on the back of Miss Jessica's neck.

When he felt the light pressure as she squeezed his hand, he applied just enough force to cut off the flow of blood to her brain, and she quickly and peacefully slipped away to join Morgan. Her eyelids softly fluttered once. A tiny smile played around the corners of her mouth, and her hand reached out in the air as though to touch someone.

Micajah leaned over and very tenderly kissed Jessica on the forehead. "I know you're with your beloved Morgan now, Miss Jessica," he whispered. "Would you please tell Susan my thoughts are on her, and I came for her as I promised?"

SUNDAY NIGHT

RUSSELLVILLE, KY - MICAJAH

Micajah had little trouble falling asleep that night. He lay on the floor beside the couch upon which lay the body of Miss Jessica. Micajah slept soundly, without even so much as a dream to disturb him.

He awoke the next morning and sat for awhile in Jessica's kitchen, before deciding to carry out his plan and ride into Russellville. He wanted the Amulet very badly, but after learning what had befallen his beloved Susan as the hands of the people of this town, he knew he had a debt to repay.

Micajah cranked the motorcycle and felt the engine roar to life beneath him. In a cloud of dust and gravel, he thundered out of Miss Jessica's drive and sped toward town. He was almost sure he'd be recognized, but now he really didn't give a damn. The Wolf was hungry, and Micajah meant to see he fed well.

WILEY

TOMBIGBEE NATIONAL FOREST

MISSISSIPPI

Tupelo was to be spared this night.

Wiley had at first thought he would head directly for Tupelo, but decided to take to the back roads once he left Winona, and soon found himself in the small town of Steadman.

He slowed down, but didn't stop as he passed through town, feeling he needed to put a few more miles between himself and the authorities in Winona.

He passed through Bellefontaine and Woodland and then came to the little town of Houston.

He was roughly following the northward route of the trace, on a more or less parallel course with the new parkway.

He stopped in Houston for a quick bite to eat, and it was only by a strange quirk of fate he avoided an incident there. A few miles outside Houston, several miles south of Tupelo, Wiley came to the Tombigbee National Forest. As soon as he saw the first stand of trees, he pulled off the road and parked the car.

He spent the night in an environment in which he felt much more at home. Since he had awakened in this body, he had seen only towns, houses, and too many damned people. His host body might be used to this overcrowding, but Wiley sure wasn't. He craved a few minutes alone, away from the sights and sounds of civilization.

As far as he was concerned, he could spend the rest of his life here, at peace with himself. If he didn't have to meet up with Micajah, that's what he'd do. Of course, as long as Micajah waited for him, Wiley knew tonight was the only night he'd have to spend in a place such as this.

He walked well over a mile into the forest, and then spent the night curled up at the base of a big oak tree, with soft moss as his mattress and the sky as his ceiling.

While police all over the state looked for him, one of the most ruthless killers that ever set foot in Mississippi lay sleeping soundly on Mother Earth, as if he hadn't a care in the world.

DANIEL HAWK AND ANDREW STEGALL

RUSSELLVILLE, KY

Daniel Hawk and Andrew Stegall spent the night on the side of the road just outside Russellville.

They'd lost Harpe somewhere yesterday afternoon, despite their best efforts to keep the man in sight. They knew he had passed through Hopkinsville, and from the news they also knew Harpe was the man the police were looking for in connection with the brutal murders that had taken place there.

The next morning found them slowly cruising the streets of Russellville, hoping to catch a glimpse of Harpe, and determined to stop him before he killed again.

JAKE

TUPELO, MISSISSIPPI

Jake rolled into Tupelo about ten o'clock, sure he was still behind Wiley. He didn't have a plan, and had no idea what he intended to do.

He knew he couldn't tell the police his story. If he tried, they'd be sure to detain him with a hundred questions, and Wiley would be long gone before Jake would be able to get away. He couldn't risk that, there was too much at stake.

But he also didn't have any idea how to go about finding Wiley tonight. He'd tried to make the star on his arm lead the way, just as it had back in Greenville, but for some reason now the damned thing didn't work. Maybe Harpe wasn't even in Tupelo, for all Jake knew.

He finally decided he needed to get at least a little rest, so he pulled into the parking lot of a small shopping plaza and parked the car on the side of the lot. He turned off the engine, made sure the pistol was handy, and settled down in the front seat. He was asleep in minutes.

But it wasn't a very long sleep.

Jake didn't know how long he'd slept when he became aware of someone watching him. Very carefully he opened one eye in a thin slit. He could see out of the side window and part of the windshield without moving, but he couldn't tell if there really was someone out there, or if his overworked mind was just playing tricks on him. He slowly opened the other eye, and began to turn his head a little at a time. He caught movement out of the corner of his left eye through the driver's side window, and carefully closed his hand around the butt of the .357. Whoever was out there was in for a hell of a surprise.

The star mark on his hand still wasn't throbbing as it had been, so Jake didn't think it was Wiley who was outside the car. Actually, he kind of hoped it wasn't him. He'd seen what Harpe had done to more than one person, and if he had to fight him, Jake wanted the fight to be a little more to his own advantage. Although he wasn't sure exactly what that might be.

The best way to fight Harpe, Jake thought, would for me to be twenty-five or thirty feet away from the bastard, shooting at him with every gun I can get my hands on.

Jake grinned at the thought.

Making no sudden movements, Jake twisted his body until he could see clearly through the window. To his relief, the face he saw peeking into the car was not that of Harpe.

He was big and mean looking, but he wasn't Wiley Harpe.

Jake still wasn't sure how he'd react when he finally came face to face with the man he was chasing, and he wasn't sure if he was ready to confront him at all, but there was one thing he was damned sure of.

The guys the car might be a bad man, but there was no way he could be in the same class as the man Jake was looking for.

Wiley Harpe was among the killer elite. A homicidal maniac in the purest sense of the meaning. He killed for pleasure, and had no pattern that Jake could find. Somehow Harpe had stepped out of the pages of history, and directly into the path of Jacob Trabue. The only thing Jake was sure of was he and Harpe were on a collision course, and there was going to be one hell of fight when they met.

Anyway, knowing it wasn't Harpe that was trying to break into his car, Jake raised up in the seat and opened the door.

"What d'ya want, pal?" he asked, stepping out of the car and keeping his right hand hidden.

"Whatever you got, buddy, will be fine with us," the big ugly guy responded.

For the first time, Jake noticed there were three men standing outside the car.

"Somehow, I seriously doubt you want everything I've got," Jake said.

The big guy looked at his companions. "We got us a joker here, boys. Think we ought to teach him a few new punch lines." He laughed out loud at his own play on words.

"I think so, Pete," one of the other men said.

"Yeah, me too." This from the third one.

"Well, Joker, you've been outvoted, three to one," the one called Pete said to Jake. "It ain't nothin' personal, don't get us wrong. It's just that you're in the wrong place at the wrong time. We're thirsty, and it looks like you're gonna have to spring for us a couple of six packs. Of course, we're gonna beat the hell out of you too, but that's just the way we roll."

By now all of them were laughing.

Pete was laughing so hard he didn't even notice the .357 until it was about two inches from his nose. The laughter had already brought tears to Pete's eyes, and he had them closed while he wiped the tears away with the back of his hand. He opened them to find himself staring directly into the barrel of the large pistol. Even in the dark, the bore of the gun looked enormous, and Pete thought he could see the lead in the end of the bullet.

"This joker's a wild card, boys," Jake said. "Open your mouth, Pete, I've got something funny to show you. That's it, just a little wider. Good, that's good."

When Pete had his mouth open as wide as he could get it, Jake shoved the barrel between his lips.

"Don't make any sudden moves, Pete, or the jokes on you. You two other assholes, sit on the ground. In fact, why don't you sit on your hands? That's good. Now Pete, you fools woke me up, and the first thing I got to do when I wake up is take a leak. That's what I'm gonna do right now, and, Bubba, if you move, even the tiniest little bit, part of your brain is gonna be all over that coke machine over by the Dollar Store. You got that?"

Jake watched as the would be hold up man's eyes grew larger and larger. He tried to keep them focused on the gun, and at the same time he tried to see what Jake was doing.

What Jake was doing was simple. He unzipped his jeans and took a leak all over Pete's right leg, all the time holding the pistol rock steady in Pete's mouth. Looking across the lot, Jake saw a jet black Pontiac Trans Am, about a 1978, with the Firebird on the hood. None too gently, Jake yanked the pistol out of Pete's mouth.

"You boys rob a lot of people out here, do you?" he asked' "Oh yeah. And you beat them up too, cause that's just the way you roll. That right?"

"When we feel like it feller," Pete said. "When we feel like it we do. And you ain't out of this crap yet. Just because you got a gun don't mean you're no Rambo. You lay that pistol down, and I'll kick the holy hell out of you. Besides, I don't think you got the balls to fire that damn thing here in the parkin..."

Kaboom. Kaboom.

Jake rapidly fired the big pistol two times. The shells seared the air close enough to Pete's ear that he felt the heat from them. A drop of blood appeared and oozed out of his ear, shining wetly in the scant light of the parking lot.

Kaboom.

Jake fired again, and Pete dropped to his knees on the asphalt.

"Say what," Jake asked.

"Wait a minute, man, wait just a minute," Pete shouted. "You don't have to kill us. We wasn't going to hurt you. Really we wasn't. We were just trying to get a little beer money, and maybe scare you some."

"Well, you didn't scare me," Jake replied, "not even a little bit, and you ain't gonna get any beer money from me. And if I'd been trying to kill you, you'd be dead. I wouldn't have missed you, especially not three times. Naw, it wasn't you I was killing. You guys ever seen what a .357 will do to a radiator and an engine? Well, boys, take a look. I just killed your car."

The three of them looked at the Trans Am, and saw three large holes had been punched through the right front fender, and steam was rising from under the hood.

"Now I've got three shots left in here without re-loading. You know I don't mind shooting in this parking lot, and I'd just as soon kill you as let you go. But, I'll tell you what I'm gonna do."

"You," he motioned to one of the men. "Are there any guns in that car? Lie to me and it'll be the last time you lie to anybody."

"Naw, man, we ain't got no guns. Hell, we wouldn't have walked over here empty handed if we'd had a pistol or two. I ain't lying, mister, there ain't no guns in the car."

"Ok," Jake said. "I'm gonna let you boys walk over to your car and get in it, and sit there while I leave. One other thing. If you two let this idiot so much as say one more word, I'm gonna shoot off your peckers. I don't care if you knock him out, choke him, or stuff something in his mouth, just as long as you shut him up. I'm tired, and I don't want to listen to any more of his crap tonight. You got it? Tell me you got it."

"We got it, man, we got it," they said together. "Don't worry bout Pete talking no more. If he opens his mouth, we'll stomp a mudhole in his butt. You hear that Pete. Don't you say a Damned word."

The one closest to Pete held a big fist in Pete's face, and the other one took him by the arm. They walked across the parking lot and looked for a minute at the car, then got inside.

Jake sat back down in his car and decided he'd handled this pretty well. He hoped he could handle Wiley Harpe even half as well, when the time came.

He started the car and drove out of the parking lot, knowing the gunshots would bring the police any minute.

Jake wasn't the only one who thought Tupelo might be the killer's next stop. So did half the police in the state. To most of them, Tupelo seemed like a logical place for the killer to strike again.

First there had been the two murders in Greenville, then the two in Leland, and then the massacre of the seven people in the market in Winona. It was plain that whoever was doing this was headed up the Trace.

Officer Jack Tandy and Sergeant Doyle Henry had been on duty all night, but hadn't seen a thing. The whole town was quiet as a tomb. People were locking themselves inside their houses, and not opening the door for anyone they didn't know.

Jack and Doyle had driven past every all night market in town at least four times, and so had all the other patrol cars. They had checked out every suspicious car they saw, and stopped and questioned anyone they found walking on the streets. But there was nothing going on.

"Damn it all, Doyle," Jack said, for perhaps the tenth time, "I wish that old boy would show up around here. I'd sure like to unload this twelve gauge on his butt."

"Don't wish too hard, Jack," Doyle replied. "From all of the reports we've gotten, that twelve gauge might not be enough to stop this feller. He got seven people in that market in Winona, including Ray Dean White. And you know yourself Ray Dean wasn't a man to screw around with. He'd shoot your ass so fast it'd make your head swim. That's what he did a few years ago, remember?"

"Damn straight, I remember. I used to run with Ray Dean, back before I joined the force. That's one of the reasons I want a shot at this sumbitch."

All at once the radio came crackling to life.

"SHOTS FIRED - repeat - SHOTS FIRED - repeat, SHOTS FIRED, in the GiantMart parking lot. Who's close? Repeat, who is close?"

Doyle grabbed the mike and shouted, "This is Doyle, we're rolling."

Jack whipped the car around in a tight U-turn and tromped down on the gas pedal as Doyle held on to the door handle. The powerful police cruiser gathered speed quickly. They were only five blocks from the shopping center, and two streets over. They'd be there in a flash.

Jack slid the cruiser into the nearly empty parking lot less than two minutes after they'd received the call, and even as they roared up to the sole car in the lot, they saw another black and white come around the building from the other direction.

"That's Joe and Wayne," Doyle said, and keyed the microphone again.

"Hey guys, we'll check 'em out, you back us up. Roger?"

"Roger that, Doyle. Be careful. If that's the guy we're looking for, he's more than a dangerous."

"Roger that 'be careful'," Doyle replied, "hang on boys, we're goin' in."

Jack slipped out of the car on the driver's side, the big riot shotgun ready in his hands, while Doyle exited the car on the other side, his service revolver drawn and cocked.

Behind the protection of the car door, Doyle called out to the people in the other car.

"This is the police. Throw down your weapons and get out of the car."

Doyle's voice was tense, and his tone left absolutely no doubt in anyone's mind he intended to fire if he had to.

"Hold on, damnit," came a voice from inside the other car. "We're gettin' out. We ain't got no weapons. Don't shoot."

Both car doors opened, and three men slowly crawled out, their hands in the air.

"We ain't done nothin'," one of them called. "What you hasselin' us for?"

Neither policeman moved from his cover behind the car's doors.

"Turn around, place your hands on top of your heads, and spread your legs. Move it, damnit, I ain't playin' with you."

Doyle still was taking no chances with these men. He and Jack very carefully advanced over to the men, who were standing quietly by the car.

"Now, let's see what we've got here," Sergeant Doyle said.

He touched the closest man and commanded. "Turn around, buddy, and do it very carefully. Don't make any funny moves."

"I ain't goin' to, Sergeant Doyle," the man said, as he turned to face the officers.

"Well, damn," Doyle said, as he got his first look at the man. "It's Pete Grant. I guess them other two are Harold and Lonnie?"

The men were no strangers to the Tupelo police force. Each had been arrested several times before, mostly for public drunkenness and fighting, but Pete had pulled eleven twenty-nine in the county jail a couple of years ago for aggravated assault. All three were considered borderline dangerous, so the officers didn't relax their guard. But neither of the policemen thought these three were the persons responsible for the night's murders.

"What goin' on out here, Pete? Why are you shootin' up the place?" Jack didn't like any of the three men, and didn't intend to listen to any crap from them.

"It wasn't us, Tandy," Pete said. "They was a crazy man out here shootin' at us, not the other way round. Man, we ain't even got a gun."

"If you ain't packin', it's the first time. What happened?" Doyle asked, looking the three men over carefully. "What the hell is your pants leg doin' wet, Pete? It smells like pee. You didn't pee on yourself, did you?"

"Hell naw, I didn't pee on myself. The guy who shot at us peed on me." Pete was madder than hell. "And he shot our car. We worked hard on that car, Deputy, and that sumbitch had no right to shoot it."

"You boys been tryin' to rob somebody here tonight? Is that it?"

Doyle knew it wouldn't be the first they had caught someone out alone and beat and robbed them. Usually they scared their victims so badly they wouldn't press charges against them. It looked as if they had bit off more than they could chew tonight though.

"Hell naw, we wasn't tryin' to rob nobody. We was sittin' in our car, mindin' our own damn business, when this guy pulled into the parking lot and started poppin' caps at us. For no reason at all. Bang, bang, bang, just like that. He shot our car. I wish I could get hold of the sumbitch, I'd wring his neck."

"Shut up Pete," Lonnie said, joining the conversation. "If that sumbitch hears you runnin' your mouth, he's liable to come back. He told me and Harold to keep you quiet, and by God, that's what we're fixin' to do. You keep talkin', and me and Harold is goin' to stuff an oil rag in your mouth. Now just shut up." Lonnie was plainly upset, and he was looking anxiously about the parking lot as he spoke to Pete.

"All right Lonnie," Sergeant Doyle said. "Suppose you tell me what the hell's goin' on."

Lonnie looked at the other two men before he answered Doyle, but it was plain he didn't care what they thought, he was going to tell the law what really happened.

"They was a feller parked out here in the lot gettin' a little sleep," he started. "We seen him and decided to see if he would loan us a few dollars to buy some beer with. We knocked on his car window, polite as could be, and woke him up. Well, I guess that was a bad move. He got out of the car and told us if we would leave him alone, he wouldn't hurt us. Guess you know how that went over, 'specially with Pete. Pete laughed and told the feller we was goin' to kick his butt, and I guess we would have too, ceptin' he had this giant pistol in his hand. Anyway, he poked the pistol in Pete's mouth, just as calm as you please, then told me and Harold to sit on our hands in the parking lot. Then he peed all over Pete's leg. I ain't never seen nothin' like it. Fact is, now that I think about it, it was pretty funny. Pete was just standin' there, scared half out of his mind, with drops of yeller runnin' down his leg. Hell, maybe part of it was his, for all I know." By this time Lonnie had a huge grin on his face, and Harold was looking at Pete and laughing.

The only one who didn't think it was funny was Pete. He stood there with a scowl on his face, looking daggers at Lonnie.

"What about it Sarge," Jack asked, "you think they're tellin' the truth?" Jack Tandy was also grinning. He's been wanting to see someone cut Pete Grant down to size for years. "You think maybe it was the guy we've been looking for?"

"Yeah, I think most of it's true. I still think they were trying to rob the guy, and it looks like it backfired big time. Besides, I don't think Lonnie has got enough sense to make up a story like this. But to answer your other question. It's pretty much certain they didn't have a run in with the crazy guy we're huntin'."

"Why do you say that, Sarge?" Jack asked.

"Because they're still alive. If they'd crossed paths with the feller we're lookin' for, they'd be deader than high noon in Mamie's cat house. Our boy wouldn't have peed on Pete if he'd been on fire. And it sure wouldn't have been their car he shot. Nah, our boy would've left 'em scattered all over the parking lot. He ain't left nobody alive yet, has he?"

Doyle turned and started back to the police cruiser, motioning Jack to follow. He flung one last remark over his shoulder at the three would be robbers. "Boys, you can go on home now, we ain't holdin' you. We got a lot more going on tonight than three fools like you. By the way, you can thank your lucky stars you didn't meet up with the guy we're lookin' for. Sometimes gettin' peed on ain't all that bad, considering what might have happened. Let's roll, Jack, we're through here. We've wasted enough time on these dipsticks."

They waved at the other patrol car and watched as it drove away.

As they pulled their own car out of the parking lot, Doyle said to Jack. "I don't know who the feller they ran into was, but he did us a big favor. It'll be a long time before those boys try anything like that again."

Some people never learn. Pete Grant was one of them.

WILEY

TUPELO. MS

Pete, Lonnie and Harold watched as the two police cars drove away, then walked back over to their own car and stood looking at it.

One of the .357 slugs had ripped through the fender and totally destroyed the carburetor, and another had taken out the radiator and pretty much ruined the distributor. The third bullet had penetrated the firewall of the car, completely blowing away the expensive radio. That made Pete even madder. He'd only stolen that unit a little over two weeks ago.

Pete looked at the other two.

"So you're goin' to stuff an oil rag in my mouth, huh? I'll kick both your tails all the way to the Mississippi river if I ever hear you talkin' like that again. Come on, we might as well start walking. Maybe somebody will come along that will let us borrow a car for awhile. I hope so. We ain't had no luck at all tonight, and I'm so damn mad I'm goin' to kick the livin' crap out of the first person we come across."

Pete had suffered more tonight than his pride could stand, and he had to do something about it or he just might burst wide open.

It was a little after five A.M. and just barely daylight when the trio left the parking lot of the shopping center. They cut across two blocks to the nearest all night market, hoping they could find some early riser, and, in Pete's words, borrow his car. And maybe his wallet as well.

They were in luck. A new model white Cougar had stopped at the corner traffic light, and there was no one in it except the driver.

"Here we go, boys," Pete said. "When I hit the chump, y'all jump in the car and we'll get the hell out of here."

Pete was looking forward to this. He needed to take his frustration out on someone, and the guy in the Cougar just happened to be available.

"He sure is an un-lucky sumbitch," Pete whispered under his breath to the other two as they ran toward the car.

Pete stepped up to the driver's door and pecked on the window. "Hey feller," he called, "let me talk to you for a minute."

The driver obliged by rolling down his window.

"What can I do for you?" he asked.

As soon as the window was down far enough, Pete hit the driver with a short powerful punch.

"Get in the car," he yelled at Lonnie and Harold, as he quickly jerked open the driver's door. Harold jumped into the back seat, and Lonnie leaned over, grabbed the driver and pulled him out of the driver's position. Pete slid into the car and grabbed the wheel.

As the big car kicked up dust from its wheels, Pete glanced at the car's owner. "Guess this just ain't your lucky day, feller," he grinned.

The driver of the car tasted the blood on his mouth with his tongue and looked at Pete, and his strange blue eyes seemed to glow. "Oh, I don't know," he said, the words barely grating out from between his teeth, "it seems to be starting off pretty good." He leaned back in the seat between Pete and Lonnie.

Pete and his buddies didn't know they had jumped out of the frying pan and into the hottest fires of hell.

Jake Trabue was a mean man, but comparing him to the man whose car they had taken was like comparing a Doberman to a Wolf. Jake was the Doberman. This man was the Wolf, and after getting a good night's sleep in the forest, he was ravenous.

Pete drove the car to the edge of town at a leisurely pace. He wanted to enjoy the torment of the driver as long as he could. He wished this was the old boy that had pissed on his leg, but if he couldn't get him, then this guy would have to do. He thought about what he was going to do to the man. He needed to do something really big time, so he could show Lonnie and Harold he hadn't lost his nerve.

Pete stopped the car on a little used side road and slid out, then motioned for the driver to get out too.

"Come on out on this side," he said, and leaned into the car to grab the driver and pull him out.

As soon as he leaned into the car, Pete saw the flame burning in the man's eyes. He hesitated for a moment, beginning to understand he may have screwed up for the second time tonight.

It was too late.

In a motion too fast for Pete to follow, or to stop, the man grabbed him by the hair at the back of his head. The last thought Pete Grant ever had was; Oh God, now I really am peeing on myself.

The man jerked on Pete's head, slamming it into the steering column hard enough that the turning indicator lever pierced Pete's left eye and embedded itself in his brain. He was dead instantly. Without even looking the driver shot his right elbow backward and into the face of Lonnie, who had reached for him as soon as he saw him grab Pete. His elbow struck Lonnie directly in the nose, splintering it and sending bone fragments upward and into Lonnie's brain. He was dead just as quickly as Pete. Then the man turned to Harold, who was sitting frozen in the back seat.

As soon as Harold saw the man grab Pete, he started trying to get his knife out of his pocket. He didn't see the elbow that took out Lonnie, all he knew was the car suddenly got very quiet. The knife got hung up on a hole in Harold's pocket, and he couldn't get it loose, but all at once it dawned on him it didn't make any difference. He raised his eyes to look at the man in the front seat, and stared death straight in the face. The man's eyes weren't even human. They were filled with blue flame that sent chills down his spine, and Harold gave up on getting the knife out of his pocked, choosing instead to put his hands over his eyes. He couldn't stand to look at the man for another second. Harold never saw the butcher knife that swept across his neck from right to left, nearly decapitating him.

Officer Jack Tandy and Sergeant Doyle Henry were still on duty at seven-thirty that morning when the call came in. They drove out of town with blue lights flashing and siren howling, but there was no need for speed.

Ruth Pirtle had been taking a short cut to her daughter's new house when she saw the bodies.

Ruth's daughter had a brand new baby girl, and this was Ruth's first grandchild. All she was thinking about was that she was much too young to be a Grandmother.

She saw a man sitting by the fence on the side of the road, but didn't think anything about it until she saw the other two men lying on the ground. She slowed down to get a better look, and what she saw made her jerk the wheel hard left and stomp on the brakes as hard as she could. The car slid to a stop by the side of the road, and Ruth spent five minutes being violently ill in the ditch. Then she called 911 on her cell phone as fast as she could.

When the two seasoned officers arrived at the scene, for the first time in the career of either officer, both of them also got very sick, and both left their breakfast in the ditch along with Ruth's.

It wasn't a pretty sight, to say the least.

Each of the three men had their head cut off. Pete's body was leaning against a fence post, but both Lonnie and Harold's bodies had fallen over on the ground. Their heads were resting on top of the fence posts, held there by knives that had been driven down through the skull. Later the police found out the knives had belonged to the victims, and this was not the first time they had drawn blood. But it was the first time the knives had drawn the blood of their owners.

There was blood, tons of blood, all over everything.

Sergeant Henry stood slowly shaking his head and looking at the bodies. "Look's like Pete's luck finally ran out." He looked at Jack. "I'll guarantee you they ran into our boy this time."

"I'd have to agree with you on that, Doyle," Jack said. "But look on the bright side."

Doyle cut his eyes toward Jack.

"At least we won't have to worry about these three tryin' to rob anybody else in the K-Mart parking lot."

JAKE

DECATUR, ALABAMA

Jacob Trabue didn't see the bodies of the three men who had accosted him last night. He had already eaten breakfast and was rolling northward when the men were discovered. He had no way of knowing he had passed Wiley Harpe during the night. He assumed the killer was still in front of him, and was desperately trying to figure out where he might strike next.

Jake had been listening to the news ever since he'd left the parking lot, and that's how he found out about the three murders in Tupelo. About eight o'clock that morning, he was turning the button across the dial when he got his first shock of the day.

"...decapitated. All three men were well known by local authorities. Each had been in and out of trouble in the Tupelo area for years. During the night they were reportedly involved in a shooting incident in the GiantMart parking lot, but no details are known at this time whether the police have a suspect in that incident. Funeral arrangements are incomplete at this time, pending notification of next of kin. Repeating our lead story, three local men were found early this morning on the outskirts of Tupelo. They had been brutally murdered, and first reports say each man was decapitated. Police have released no statements, but have said it is possible drugs were involved. We will interrupt our programming as more information becomes available. And now back to our regularly scheduled program."

Drugs my butt, Jake thought. Those guys met up with Wiley Harpe, just as sure as hell is hot.

Jake pulled into a small drive in market. He needed some cigarettes and a cup of hot coffee. He also needed to take a few minutes to study his map.

Jake still believed Harpe was headed up the Trace, but trying to second guess the man was getting him nowhere. He didn't know how he'd missed him in Tupelo, but somehow he had. And Harpe had struck again. Three men this time. And if they were the three men Jake thought they were, they would have already been pissed off enough to put up a hell of a fight before they got killed. Once again Jake wondered just what the hell he was going to do when he finally confronted Harpe.

Jake sat in his car until he finished his coffee, but even as he started his engine, he still wasn't sure where his next stop should be. The Tupelo murders were on all the local radio stations now, but they had happened hours ago. Harpe was almost certainly long gone.

Jake had just heard the account of the three murders for the fourth time, when suddenly he heard the DJ say;

"...and now, in an unrelated incident, police have found the body of eleven year old Melissa Danton, missing from her home in Decatur, Alabama since early last night. The body was found alongside Highway 24 about seven o'clock this morning. It appears the girl is a victim of foul play, but no details are being released at this time. Stay tuned..."

With a quick glance at his map, Jake wheeled his car into the morning traffic and headed for Decatur. With Harpe in the vicinity, the chances of this being an un-related incident were very small.

Jake reached Decatur in a little over two hours and found he was undecided about where to start looking. He didn't like the idea of going to the police. They would ask too many questions, it would take too much time, and they might very well suspect Jake himself if he appeared too curious.

Finally, he decided to stop at one of the truck stops along the highway. The truckers knew everything that happened on the road, and there was a chance he could get some information from a waitress.

"I'd like a cup of coffee, and one of those honey buns, honey," he said, and smiled at the pretty girl who took his order. When she left the booth, Jake looked around at the other customers. Most were men, truckers; Jake supposed, but there were a few women scattered about the room. Jake noticed most of them seemed upset about something.

"Here ya go, Hon," the waitress said, sitting his order on the table. "Enjoy."

"If the coffee tastes as good as it smells, I'll enjoy it just fine," Jake said. "Say, what's got everybody in such an uproar?"

Jake was trying to remain calm, but in the back of his mind there was a small thud...thud...thud, and the star on his hand was itching like crazy.

"They're all madder than hell about the little Danton girl they found this morning. If the truckers could get their hands on the guy who did it, there wouldn't be enough left for the state to execute. They'd skin the son-of-a-bitch and leave his body for the buzzards to pick over. Oops, sorry bout that, Hon. I forgot you were trying to eat. But I just so damn mad..."

"That's alright Darlin'," Jake said softly. "What happened to the girl?"

When the waitress started talking, Jake could see she had been crying not very long ago. "Some low life cut her all to pieces, that's what happened. And left her little body in a ditch by the road." Fresh tears pooled up in her eyes as she told the story again.

"She was just a baby. Her Mama sent her to the store about five-thirty yesterday afternoon and she didn't come back. It's only a couple of blocks from her house to the store, and when she wasn't back in half an hour, her Daddy went out to look for her. Well, of course he didn't find her. The family and the cops looked all night long, and then this morning they found her out by the highway."

The waitress was crying openly now.

"Anyway, she'd been stabbed a lot of times, and cut up real bad. How can anybody do that to a kid, mister?"

"I don't know, Hon, I really don't," Jake said, and he meant it.

He may not know why the little girl was killed, but he had a good idea who'd done the killing.

Damnit, he thought, if I thought the cops would believe me, I'd just go in and tell 'em what I know. But they'd throw me in jail for sure. Jake knew he couldn't go to the police with a story about a man who had been dead for two hundred years and make them believe him.

He also knew he couldn't stop looking for Harpe.

"I'm headed up toward Nashville today," he told the waitress. "I'll keep my eyes open. If I see anybody who looks the least bit suspicious, I'll call the police. And, Hon, if I run into the sadistic psycho who killed the girl, and I know it's him, I'll blow him away myself. And you can take that to the bank."

As Jake paid his check and left the truck stop, the waitress was till drying her tears.

WILEY

NEAR DECATUR, ALABAMA

Jake wasn't the only one listening to the radio. Wiley was also twisting the dial up and down the scale and listening to the news reports.

He smiled every time he heard the report about the three punks in Tupelo. Hell, he'd done the good people of town a favor, they just didn't know it. Well, screw 'em. Next time he was through Tupelo, he'd just keep right on going.

But the little girl was another story.

It was after daylight when he came upon her walking down the side of Highway 24. She had accepted a ride without any questions, and had finally told him she was running away. She'd been walking most of the night, and hiding from cars that came along the road. She was afraid the police would take her home, and she didn't want to go back.

"They been abusin' you, girl?" Wiley had asked.

"Yes sir, kind of, I guess," she had replied.

"Your Dad?" Wiley asked.

"No sir, my step Dad," she answered.

"That why you runnin' away?" he asked.

"I guess. I just don't think I can go on like that. He gets worse all the time, especially when Mom's not at home. So I'm runnin' away. You won't take me back, will you mister?"

"No child, I won't take you back," Wiley had said.

It was then that the Wolf took over.

Before he could stop, he'd slashed the girl until she was dead. He didn't even know how many times he had stabbed her, just that there was a lot of blood all over everything.

He'd thrown her body into the ditch, and cleaned the car the best he could, and by the time he was five miles down the road, he'd mostly forgotten about her.

But not about her step-father.

Wiley would like to run into that gentleman, just for a few minutes. It would be the last time he ever abused a little girl.

But right now he had other things on his mind. He had to find another car. This one still had a lot of blood in it, and besides, it was almost out of gas.

Wiley snapped back to attention a minute later though. He reached down to turn off the radio, and just as his fingers touched the button, he heard the account of another killing. Five men had been murdered in a little town in Illinois, three local bad guys, and two fishermen. A waitress had tried to describe a man she believed had had a run in with the three toughs, but there wasn't much to go on. Certainly not enough to identify anybody. When he heard the DJ say Cave-In-Rock, Wiley slapped his leg and laughed.

It had to be Micajah.

Wiley let out a shout of joy, and gunned the engine. He had to get another car, and he had to figure out where to meet his brother. That wouldn't be hard to do. There was a bond between them, and he'd know when his brother was close. He'd been feeling the vibrations since yesterday, and they were growing stronger the farther North he went.

Micajah was somewhere in Kentucky, headed for Tennessee. Just like he'd promised so many years ago.

The Wolf was loose, and he and Wolf Brother were soon to be re-united.

And let the whole damned world beware.

MICAJAH

RUSSELLVILLE, KY

Micajah slowed down when he hit the city limits of Russellville. He was determined the town would pay for what had happened to Susan so many years ago. He just wasn't sure how to go about it. There was no way he could spend enough time in town to seek out descendants of the ones responsible. He finally decided the only way to proceed was to find a few city officials and let them pay the price.

He pulled into a drive-in market that had a small sign that read 'Sausage and Biscuits.'

Just what I need, he thought.

The sausage turned out to be a pre-packaged sandwich the girl at the cash register stuck in a small microwave and heated. Surprisingly, it didn't taste bad, and he bought three more. There was salt, pepper and napkins on the counter, and the coffee was scalding hot. Just the way he liked it.

As he ate, he sat at a small counter in the front of the store where he could see the parking lot. He noticed a black and white police car pull into one corner of the lot, but the officer didn't get out of the car. About two minutes later another police car, this one an unmarked Ford, pulled into the other corner of the lot. This cop also remained in the car.

The girl at the check out counter looked out the window.

"Wonder what they're looking for?" she said. "Must be something pretty big. That unmarked car belongs to the Sheriff himself. He usually stays in his office, especially on days as hot as today."

"No telling what they're doin', little girl. You ain't done nothin' wrong, Have you?"

"Not me mister. How about you?"

With a wink, Micajah looked the girl. "They'd have to see me lookin' at a girl as pretty as you, darlin' and then be able to read my mind. Course, I ain't sure what I'm thinkin' is wrong, least ways not wrong enough to bring the Sheriff himself out of his air conditioning."

The girl looked at Harpe and giggled.

"I bet I know what you're thinkin, and maybe it don't seem so wrong to me either. Hold on, he's gettin' out of the car."

She was right.

The driver's door on the Sheriff's car had opened, and the sheriff was now standing beside the car. Harpe checked out the other car, and saw the cop was also outside his car. They both began walking toward the store, and Micajah noticed they kept their hands close to the butts of their pistols.

The girl was standing close to Micajah as she looked out the window, and he knew he could use her as a shield if push came to shove. There weren't any other customers in the market right now, but there was an old man in the back room putting up stock. Harpe had noticed him when he first came in.

The Sheriff walked into the store as if nothing were wrong, and stopped at the cash register.

"Howdy Gail," he said. "I'll have a pack of Camels, thank you."

He casually looked around the store, letting his eyes come to rest on Harpe as if by accident.

"Howdy to you too, feller," he nodded. "Hot enough for you?"

"Plenty hot enough for me Sheriff, how bout yourself?"

The Sheriff was a good sixty or seventy pounds overweight and although he had only been out of his air-conditioned car for a few minutes, he was already sweating heavily. He looked to be fifty years old, give or take a couple of years, and was almost bald. His face was flushed with the heat, or something, and every so often he wiped the sweat from his face with a white handkerchief he held in his left hand. His right hand was still staying close to the pistol on his hip.

"It ain't the heat so much as it is the dang humidity. That's what gets you round here, the humidity. You just passing through, are you boy? I don't reckon as how I've seen you before."

"Yeah, Sheriff, just passing through. On my way to Bowling Green. Stopped in here for a quick bite. Pretty little town you got here Sheriff."

Micajah was being polite to the Sheriff. Maybe it would turn out to be nothing more than a false alarm.

"We think so, son. Say, you wouldn't have happened to have been over in Hoptown yestidday, now would you?"

"Yes sir, I was. Rode right through there. Is there anything wrong?"

His eyes were on the Sheriff's face as he spoke, and deep inside them a tiny blue flame burst into life.

"Ah, not much. Had a little disturbance over there, and some people seen a motorcycle leaving the scene. You wouldn't have happened to have seen anything yourself, would you?"

"Not me Sheriff. Didn't see a thing. I didn't even stop. I came on over here to visit with a relative of mine, before gettin' on to Bowling Green today."

"A relative? Who might that be, son?"

"My great aunt, Miss Jessica Butler, Sheriff. Lives a couple miles outside town. She ain't been doin' none too good since Morgan passed, y'know."

"Jessica Butler's your great aunt? I don't recall her and Morgan having any kin. Passing through, huh? Tell me, son, what kind of business you got in Bowling Green, son, if you don't mind me askin'?"

"Hell naw, Sheriff, I don't mind you asking. Long as you don't mind me tellin' you that my business ain't none of your business.

You got something you want to say, you'd best be sayin' it. I'm bout ready to get the hell out of Dodge."

"Boy, you ain't gettin' the hell out of nowhere till I say you can. And I ain't sayin' you can, not just yet. Now, what kind of business you got in Bowling Green?"

The Sheriff's hand moved a tiny bit closer to his pistol. It was plain he was getting nervous. He didn't like playing these cat and mouse games, and the calmness of the big man at the counter was beginning to get to him.

Micajah knew the Sheriff was suspicious. And the deputy was much too close to Micajah's motorcycle for his liking. He knew he could handle the situation, but he'd like to get by without killing anyone just yet. He wanted revenge on the town, but he wanted it on his own terms.

But the Sheriff wasn't letting up.

"If I have to do this the hard way, boy, I will. But it'll be harder on you than on me."

"I wouldn't say that, Sheriff," Harpe responded.

He was off the stool and had his hand closed around the Sheriff's gun hand before the Sheriff could move. The Sheriff couldn't draw his weapon, and Harpe's other arm was around his neck, cutting off his air, and not letting him yell for help. Before the Sheriff even knew what happened, Micajah spun him around and grabbed his chin with his right hand. All it took was a single wrenching twist, and the Sheriff was dead, his neck broken and his head hanging at an odd angle as Micajah let his body slump to the floor.

Micajah moved to the counter just as the girl's hand was touching the pistol hidden under the cash register.

She was fast, Harpe was faster.

Another violent twist of his huge hands, and the girl joined the Sheriff on the floor.

"You just thought you knew what I was thinkin', darlin," he whispered as he stepped over her and headed for the stock room.

A quick glance told him the deputy was still checking out the bike, so he had at least another minute or two.

The old man in the stock room had heard the commotion and had seen the big stranger grab Gail. When he saw him heading toward the stock room, he was ready.

James Earl Taylor had been in World War II, and in Korea, and damned if he was scared of this big old boy. He quietly opened his large Barlow knife and held it ready. He'd cut that big sumbitch from collarbone to appetite.

As Harpe stepped through the door, James Earl leaped out from behind a stack of boxes and swung the knife through the air. It made a keen whistling sound as it parted the air close to Harpe's left ear.

But close, as they say, only counts in horseshoes and hand grenades.

Micajah took a quick side step and as the old man's swing got close enough, he reached out and caught the fist, knife and all. It was like catching a baseball. Harpe caught the fist in his right hand, rocked back on his left foot, and let the motion of the old man's swing continue. Its momentum, together with the force of Harpe's right arm, carried the fist and knife around until it came to an abrupt halt as the blade entered James Earl's open mouth. Micajah gave a last savage shove on the old man's fist, and felt the knife drive through the man's throat and exit out the back of his neck. James Earl's teeth gave way, and his fist was wedged inside his mouth.

The point of the knife pierced a cardboard case of dishwashing detergent James Earl had been putting away, slicing through several bottles as the body slid to the floor.

Harpe took a minute to look at the old man. He shook his head in disgust.

"You got to be more careful how you open boxes, feller," Harpe said to the dying man. "If you cut 'em below that line, sometimes you waste a lot of detergent. That's a good way to lose your job. Inventory shrinkage, and all that crap. You know?"

As he started out of the stock room, Micajah noticed the detergent seemed to be thinning down the blood pretty well. He leaned down and noted the brand name of the detergent. "I know they say you can't believe many TV ads, but I guess maybe this stuff really works. Got to try and remember that."

Then he wasted very little time in returning to the front door.

"Hey, Deputy, the Sheriff wants you," he called.

Killing the deputy wasn't nearly as much trouble as killing James Earl had been.

One well placed palm of the hand to the deputy's nose sent bone fragments splintering into the man's brain, and he was dead before he even got inside the store.

Harpe took a quick look around and headed out the door for his bike. Just as he climbed aboard, an old brown and white van with Kentucky plates pulled up to the gas tank. There were three men inside, and it was their bad luck that they saw him before he had a chance to ride away. He couldn't leave any witness' behind, not just yet anyway. Besides, they could be related to the people in this town who had treated Susan so badly those many years ago.

The hell with this town. No quarter asked, none given. They deserved to have the Wolf loose among them.

Harpe stepped back off his bike and began to walk over toward the van, smiling at the three men as he walked. All three got out of the van and headed for the store. But Harpe was between them and the front door.

When the first one was close enough, Micajah's fist shot out and the single, unexpected blow knocked the man down. The other two reacted fast, but not fast enough. The razor sharp long knife sang its deadly song as it whistled toward the first man, catching him just above the belt buckle and ripping upwards, cutting his breast bone as neatly as a surgeons scalpel. The last man turned to run, but he too was too slow. Harpe jerked the knife loose from the first man's chest and with the same motion plunged it into the third man's broad back.

Almost as if it had a mind of its own, the knife found the man's heart, and stopped its beating for good. Harpe quickly stooped down and slit the throat of the man he'd hit first.

Quickly, Micajah grabbed the gasoline pump and locked it wide open. He doused the van, then tossed the hose on the ground.

This time he didn't bother with the bodies. He ran to his bake, jumped on and roared back over to the van, where the gasoline hose was still pumping furiously. He pulled a book of matches from the pack on the bike, struck one and used it to light the rest.

A small streak of gasoline had made its way to the front of the van, and Micajah dropped the matches in it. He didn't even look as the gasoline quickly ignited and flames began to lick their way back to the streaming hose. He gunned the big bike and roared away from the market, leaving the parking lot looking like a blazing slaughter yard.

He didn't slow or look back when he heard the explosion that meant the flames had found the streaming nozzle of the gas pump.

He hadn't gotten a block from the market when he met a third police car headed directly toward him. Driving at high speed, lights flashing and siren howling, there was no doubt he was headed for the market. As the policeman drew abreast of the bike rider, he slammed on his brakes and slid the car around in a vicious spin.

Micajah cursed under his breath and whipped the bike into a side street, and then cursed again, this time out loud.

He'd turned onto a dead end street, and when he slid to a stop and looked behind him, there were now two police cars in pursuit.

Both cars screeched to a stop, and one of the cops yelled something. The other cop merely started firing at Harpe as soon as he could take aim. Although he wasn't hit, the bullets caused Micajah to let the bike fall to the street. He ran around the corner of a building, with the cops chasing and yelling at him, and crashed through a closed door. He was inside the building before the cops turned the corner.

He found himself in a dark room, occupied by a couple of old desks and a rusting filing cabinet. It was obvious he was in some kind of un-used old office, but there was light coming from under the door on the opposite wall. He headed that way.

Knowing he had very little time before the cops were inside the building, he slammed through the door and into the next office.

He was the front office of a used car lot, and he wasn't alone.

A sign on the desk said "SALES MANAGER" and there were four people talking to the man who sat behind the desk.

The man looked up as Harpe burst into the room.

"Hold your horses, feller, I'll be with you in a minute," he said.

The knife screamed through the air as Harpe slashed the throat of the nearest man, who also looked like he might be a salesman.

Two girls, who might have been in their early twenties, and were probably the ones trying to buy a car, were next. Harpe caught them both by the back of their necks, one in each hand, and lifted them from their chairs. With hardly any effort, but with great force, he smashed their heads together as if they were dolls. The skulls made a horrible sound as they ruptured, and Harpe dropped them to the floor as he reached for the last man.

The sales manager was scooting his chair backward and hastily trying to get his middle desk drawer open as Micajah grabbed the last man by the back of his shirt. The material tore and the man ran toward the door as fast as he could. Harpe's knife buried itself in his back just as his hand touched the doorknob.

By this time, the man behind the desk had pulled a little .25 caliber automatic from his desk drawer. He ducked down in his chair and had time to get off one shot before Harpe turned his attention back to him.

The bullet took Harpe low in the left side, and he bent forward with the impact. Other than that, it hardly slowed him down at all.

He kicked the front of the desk with his right foot, slamming it into the sales managers chest. Harpe kept pushing on the desk until the man's chair toppled over backward and he slid to the floor. His chin was resting on the desk as he tried to get to his feet and get off another shot.

Neither happened.

Harpe leaped high into the air and brought both feet slamming down into the front of the metal desk. With one last effort, he shoved the desk and the man behind it into the wall. The front edge of the desk sliced into the sales managers chin, and when his head met the wall, the desk pinched its way completely through the neck. One eye was closed in a grotesque wink as the head rolled into the middle of the desk. Harpe winked back and then turned to retrieve his knife from the other man's back.

The flame in his eyes was out of control. It raged higher and flared brighter by the second, The Wolf was in full hunting mode, and there was no way Micajah could stop him until he had satisfied his cravings.

The Harpe tore off his shirt and looked at the bullet wound, which had already stopped bleeding. He saw the small bullet had passed completely through his side, and already he could feel the power of the Wolf as it coursed through his body, and the wound closed itself even as he watched. For another second he stood there, nothing showing on his face except the wildness of the demon that raged within him.

He crossed the room and looked out through the plate glass window.

As of yet, the parking lot was empty.

The cops weren't sure which building he was in, but he knew the sound of the gun would bring them running. He looked down at the wound again and saw it was completely healed, leaving only a thin puckered spot on his side. The Wolf was running wild now, and couldn't be bothered by being wounded. The Harpe threw back his head and laughed.

Outside, the policemen had heard the shot and come running. Now they heard the wild laughter, and stopped dead in their tracks. The sound was enough to send shivers up the spine of the bravest of them.

The Harpe needed the saddlebags from his bike, The other knife was in them, and so was his money. And he'd like to remove the license tags. He didn't think they had a make on the bike yet, and the longer before they found out his identity better.

It was hard for Harpe to keep the Wolf from leaping out the front door and among the policemen, but he knew that wouldn't do. There were seven or eight out there now, and while he might take them all out, there was always the chance they might overpower him. After all, he didn't have the Amulet, and his strength was not all it could be.

He eased back through the office, picking up the little. 25 automatic as he passed the desk. He winked again at the severed head on the desk.

"Sorry I cost you a sale today, feller," he said. "But there wasn't any reason to lose your head over it. Keep an eye on the place, huh?"

He walked back through the building the way he had come, and peeked out through a crack in the opened door. A cop was across the street behind a trashcan, but that was the only one he could see.

He took careful aim at the cop and fired the little gun. The bullet struck the trash can with a twang, and ricocheted down the street. The cop jumped to his feet and hastily fired off a volley in

Harpe's direction. He was reaching for a new clip when Harpe's second shot caught him high in the forehead. The little bullet twisted and turned as it entered the policeman's skull, finally lodging itself in his brain. He died without knowing it was a bullet from his brother's gun that killed him, or that his brother's head was keeping a one eyed silent vigil over the bodies in the sales office.

The Harpe ran across the street and scooped up the pistol from where the cop had dropped it, and took the time to grab a fresh clip from the man's belt. The pistol was a Beretta .9-millimeter, but Harpe didn't have time just now to wonder why a small town deputy was carrying such a heavy duty weapon as this.

He ran to the bike and grabbed the saddlebags. With no time to find tools to remove the license tag, he merely grabbed it with his right hand and ripped it off. He was almost a block away when the other cops got around to the back of the building.

RUSSELLVILLE, KY

Frank and Bobby Johnson were brothers and had been playing golf together for years. They tried to play at least once a week, usually on Sunday, and most of the time they played the municipal golf course at Russellville. Their opponents were usually Cotton Grogan and Carl Lee Farmer, and that's whom they were playing today. All four had been hitting the ball pretty well off the tee all day, but Carl Lee and Bobby had been having a lot of trouble with their irons, especially the long shots.

In fact, Carl Lee was madder than hell right now. He was already laying two and stood looking at a long 230 yards to the pin. He knew he'd have to hit a five wood or a two iron to get home, and he couldn't hit either of them worth a damn. Bobby was ten yards closer to the green, but faced with the same situation.

Carl Lee gritted his teeth, and against his better judgment pulled out his two iron. He smiled as he remembered the old golfer's joke about this club being the only safe one to play in a lightning storm, because even God can't hit a two iron. But he decided to try it one more time.

He should have known better.

He lined up the shot carefully, set his feet, wiggled his butt and swung the club.

"Damnit, Damnit, Damnit." Carl Lee threw the two iron as hard as he could at a nearby tree as he watched his ball start toward the green and then about a hundred yards out start a wide, lazy looping banana slice to the right. The last time Carl Lee saw the ball it was headed deep into the woods that bordered the hole.

"That was a brand new ball," Carl Lee said to Cotton, who was still sitting on the cart. "I'm going after that sumbitch."

"Well, take me to my ball first, and I'll hit while you look." Cotton's ball was about thirty yards closer to the pin, and he figured a three iron would get him home from there. He stepped off the cart, got out his three, and laughed as he heard Carl Lee cursing out loud as he drove toward the woods.

MICAJAH

RUSSELLVILLE, KY

Harpe crossed two or three streets at a dead run before slowing to a walk. He took a minute to get his bearings, and suddenly realized he was in someone's backyard.

An old man came running out of the house, waving a shotgun at him and shouting something, but Harpe couldn't make out the words.

The Wolf was in a feeding frenzy, and the blues flames were raging wildly through his blood.

The old man leveled the shotgun but before he could squeeze the trigger the .9-millimeter in Harpe's hand spoke. The shotgun went off with a roar, but was directed straight up as the man was blown backward from the force of the heavy pistol slug as it hit him in the chest. A second shot took out a face that had appeared in the window of the house, and a third hit a little boy who was standing in the yard of the house next door.

Harpe spun around, searching for targets, and found plenty. The gunshots had brought neighbors out to see what was happening, and Harpe fired without discrimination. Hardly slowing down, he ejected the clip and jammed in the second one. Four more people fell as he ran across the yard and jumped a low fence. Without stopping he sped through the back yards of the subdivision, firing whenever he found a target, and only stopping when the clip was empty. In one backyard a middle-aged woman was watering her flowers, and Harpe left the empty pistol buried butt first in her head as he leaped over the flowerbed, being extra careful not to step on any blossoms. Back in Knoxville, Susan would have called him to task if had stepped on her flowers.

Old habits die hard, and that goes double for two hundred year old habits, Micajah thought as he speeded up again.

He rounded the corner of a two-story brick house, and found himself on a patio in the middle of seven or eight people. A gas grill was smoking, and he saw three or four large steaks sizzling. Two or three women were in lounge chairs, and a man was at the grill, turning the steaks with a long shiny grill fork. Without any hesitation, Harpe snatched the fork from the man's hand and drove the prongs upward into the bottom of his chin. A second man jumped at Harpe, and found himself caught by the head and rammed face first into the hot grill, which turned over on one of the women. In frustration, Micajah looked at the steaks, now lying on the screaming woman's bare stomach. He hadn't intended to ruin their food. Less than a minute had passed from the time he had rounded the corner, till the time when he was running down the drive to the front of the house.

He looked inside each car as he passed them, looking for one that had the keys in the ignition. Sure enough, he got lucky when he reached the third car in the drive.

He jumped into the car, a late model Honda, cranked the engine to life, and backed into the street. He roared out of the drive, and then cut across two more streets, finally coming to the main highway through town. He felt Russellville had more than paid for everything that had happened to Susan, and he was ready to put the town in his rear view mirror. He turned left and headed south on Highway 431.

He knew he couldn't keep the Honda very long, and was looking for a place to ditch it when he spotted the hospital parking lot.

He quickly turned around and drove about a half mile back toward town. He had spotted an old barn on the side of the road that looked like a good place to hide the car. He didn't see anyone around, so he drove the car off the highway and slid to a stop behind the barn.

He ran back to the road, crossed it, and headed into the woods, not far from the hospital. It was only a short walk to the hospital parking lot, and he'd seen plenty of cars sitting there.

He had been walking through the trees about ten minutes, when suddenly something hit him in the back with enough force to actually shake him up a little. He quickly stepped behind a tree and looked around, but for several minutes he saw no one.

He glanced at the ground around the tree hoping to find out what it was that had hit him. It only took a minute for him to spot the bright white golf ball lying on the grass. He picked it up, noted it was a "Proshot 2" and wondered how in the hell anyone could hit a ball this far into the woods.

Suddenly the Wolf was gone, and Micajah heard the boy that had been Billy Harp as he whispered silently in his brain.

Some ignoramus trying to hit a two iron.

For the first time in days, Harpe laughed at something that was funny, and not because the Wolf was showing his teeth.

Suddenly he heard someone coming through the trees. Without a sound he stepped back behind the big tree and waited.

"Where the hell could that sumbitch be," Carl Lee said aloud, as he clumped through the trees. "It has to be somewhere right around here. Damn two iron. I ought to wrap the sumbitch around that tree."

He was holding the two iron in his hand as he walked through the trees, and the more he thought about it, the better he liked the idea. Picking out a large oak tree, he gripped the two iron like a baseball bat and took it back over his shoulder. Just as he began his swing, a deep voice said;

"Reckon you can even hit the tree with that thing, feller?"

Carl Lee almost jumped out of his skin. He didn't see anybody, and he was sure he was alone in the woods. He lowered the club and looked around just as a large man stepped from behind the very tree he had intended to hit with the golf club.

"Where the hell did you come from?" Carl Lee said. "Damnit, you almost scared me to death."

"Just takin' a short cut to the hospital, feller, that's all. Don't get excited. This what you're lookin' for?" He held the ball out to Carl Lee.

"Yeah, I think so. Is it a Proshot?"

"Sure is," Micajah grinned, "a Proshot 2, damn near brand new."

"You play golf, mister?" Carl Lee asked.

"Not really," Micajah said, then reconsidered. "Well, maybe I do. I'm not sure. Seems like I remember bout half way playin'."

"Yeah, well, that's all I been doing lately. Half way playing. Got a bad case of yips, and can't hit my irons worth a damn anymore."

"I can't help you there feller. But if you'll point me in the direction of the hospital, I'll get out of your way while you keep tryin' to beat down that oak tree with your two iron."

Carl Lee laughed, a little self-consciously, and pointed in the direction of the hospital.

Micajah tossed the ball to the frustrated golfer, then turned and walked off through the trees. Carl Lee was still muttering to himself, and Micajah hadn't gotten out of sight before he heard a loud whack as the two iron met the trunk of the big oak tree.

Harpe had violated one of his own cardinal rules. He had let someone who had seen his face live. It wasn't like him to do something like that. But once again he heard the small voice of Billy Harp inside his mind.

"Leave the guy alone. He's in deep enough crap trying to hit that damned two iron."

About then Harpe heard the loud whack again.

"Guess you're right about that," he laughed, and kept walking.

Annie Dowlen had been a nurse in Russellville for twenty years, and had transferred from the old hospital when the new one was completed. She'd been on duty since early this morning, in fact every nurse they had was on duty. With some crazy man running round killing people they needed all the doctors and nurses they had. But it had been a long day, and she was more than ready to get home.

She began digging in her purse for her keys when she was still ten or fifteen feet from her car. A woman couldn't be too careful these days.

She had just unlocked her car and when a big man stepped out of the shadows at the edge of the parking lot, and Annie didn't hear him until he was close enough to grab her around the neck. By then it was too late. Much too late.

Annie never felt the bite of the blade as Harpe drew it across her throat, and she was dead by the time he laid her in the bed of a near-by pick-up truck.

Harpe had stayed hidden in the woods till dark, and most of the people at the hospital had left. He'd then slipped over to the parking lot just in time to see Annie headed for her car. He watched as she fumbled in her purse for her keys, and then moved almost soundlessly up behind her.

Annie was driving a late model Chevvy, and Harpe wasted no time in starting the engine and backing out into the parking lot.

He still had the car in reverse when all at once there was the sound of tires peeling rubber in the parking lot, and before Harpe knew it, someone had crashed into his car with a hell of an impact.

He turned, and even in the pale glare of the overhead lights, he recognized the little green car that held Stegall and the Indian boy.

He grinned to himself as he felt the Wolf stir. Maybe he could take care of a little unfinished business before he left this town after all.

JAKE

TENNESSEE

Jake knew he had to catch up with Little Harpe soon.

The man was a homicidal maniac, and could no more stop killing than Jake could stop breathing. Every hour that passed with Little Harpe on the loose meant danger to everyone along the route they were traveling. He made most of his kills for no reason at all, and there seemed to be no way to predict where he might strike next.

The death of the little Danton girl had almost been more than Jake could stand. He had to stop this monster, and the only way to stop him was to kill him. Jake hoped he got the chance to try soon, and also hoped when the opportunity presented itself, he would be able to do the job. He had enough firepower, he was sure of that, and he sure as hell wasn't afraid to use it. But with a man like Harpe, just shooting at him wasn't enough. In fact, shooting at him and actually hitting him might not be enough. Jake had to be sure he hit Harpe in a vital spot, a spot that would either kill him instantly, or stop him long enough for Jake to shoot him again. Maybe even a lot of times. If he could get real close to Harpe, maybe one shot would be all it would take. A direct hit in the head, or the heart, might be sufficient to kill him.

Of course, Jake wasn't even sure of that. From all indications, Harpe seemed to have come back from the dead already, and Jake didn't even know if the man could be killed again.

But he knew he had to try.

Jake thought about the story he'd read and the scene in the old field. He remembered Harpe had been killed the first time by hanging. Maybe a rope around the neck would work again.

Jake saw a sign that said he would be coming into the town of Franklin, Tennessee in about twenty minutes and just for the hell of it he decided to stop at a hardware store and buy a good, heavy rope. You never could tell, maybe he'd get a chance to slip it around Harpe's neck.

He pulled off at the first Franklin exit he came to, and drove around for a few minutes till he found a hardware store in a small shopping mall. He parked the car and went in.

While he was in the hardware store, a display by the garden center gave him another idea. He bought a large can of charcoal lighter fluid and a box of big kitchen matches. Maybe he could set the son-of-a-bitch on fire. Jake was getting desperate, and was about ready to try anything at all to stop Harpe.

As he drove around Franklin, Jake hoped the pretty town wouldn't be the scene of another of Harpe's savage killings. The Sunday morning sunshine was just too peaceful here for anything to happen.

He should have known better.

The man he was looking for was at a Frosty Queen not a half-mile from the hardware store where Jake had stopped.

WILEY

FRANKLIN, TENNESSEE

Wiley had ditched the Cougar behind an empty service station just after he crossed the Tennessee state line. Against his better judgment, and from the lack of a different car being handy, he'd stolen a 1988 Buick, which had broken down about a hundred yards from the Franklin exit. He'd left the Buick on the Interstate off ramp, and walked the rest of the way into town.

Right now he was enjoying one of the Frosty Queen's famous hit chocolate double dipped ice cream cones. There hadn't been anything like this around in 1799, and Wiley found it very much to his liking.

But as much as he liked the ice cream, he knew he had to find another car quickly. He had to meet his brother as soon as possible. But this time he wouldn't settle for another damned old clunker. He'd find something a hell of a lot better.

He was just finishing the ice cream cone when a young, good-looking couple walked in. The girl wore white short shorts and a tiny black halter-top, and was beautifully tanned on every part of her body that showed, and that was quite a lot. The boy also had on shorts, and was also very tanned. He was trim and athletic looking, and had that smug, self-satisfied look that some kids have. He acted like everyone in the Frosty Queen should be happy to kiss his butt, and that was an attitude Wiley had never liked.

Wiley stepped out into the parking lot and stood at the corner of the building studying the cars. He was trying to decide if any of them would suit his needs. There were several that looked promising, but before he could make up his mind, the young couple came out of the ice cream parlor. They walked over to a brand new, solid white Mustang convertible. The top was down, and Wiley knew that would make it even easier for him.

"Just what I need," Wiley said, under his breath.

He started walking across the parking lot, and when the boy started the engine, Wiley leaped into the back seat.

"Son," he said, "if you don't start no crap, there won't be none." He showed the boy the big .44 magnum he had tucked in his belt. "Now drive this thing somewhere out in the country."

Wiley was wearing a baseball cap he had found in the Buick, and had it pulled down low over his eyes. He doubted if anyone in the Frosty Queen had paid much attention to him, at least not enough to give a good description. If anyone had seen him jump into the car, they'd more than likely think it was just another kid playing around, and wouldn't report anything strange. All in all, he felt reasonably safe as the boy turned the car out into the highway.

Wiley was in a hurry to get to Kentucky, and he didn't have a lot of time to waste taking care of two kids. But they had seen his face, so he knew he couldn't leave them alive.

As soon as the boy turned the car off the highway and onto the old country road, Wiley started looking for a place to stop. They had only driven about half a mile when he spotted just the place he was looking for. The road was narrow, and there was a ditch on the right side that was fifteen or twenty feet deep, with water at the bottom and a lot of thick undergrowth.

Wiley tapped the boy on the shoulder with the pistol and motioned for him to pull over. Before the car was completely stopped, Wiley had already climbed up on the back of the seat, out of the boy's reach should he decide to try and be a hero. The girl started to say something, but Wiley put his finger to his lips in a 'hush' gesture, and winked his right eye at her. She gave him a little smile and stood waiting for her boy friend to walk around the car to join her.

The boy took the girl's hand and turned to face the side of the road, expecting to hear the car roar away. Instead, he heard the roar of the big pistol as Wiley shot the girl in the back of the head. The boy didn't hear the sound of the second bullet as it took him just below his right ear.

Little Harpe climbed into the drivers seat and eased the gearshift in drive. He knew it would be a matter of hours, if not days before the bodies were found. He would be in Kentucky and with Micajah long before that.

He was back on the Interstate less than twenty minutes after he had jumped into the car at the Frosty Queen.

JAKE

TENNESSEE

Jake had turned off the radio, but the fingers of his right hand tapped a steady beat on the steering wheel as he drove, keeping time with the thoughts racing through his mind. He knew Wiley Harpe was a supernatural being, strong, ruthless and fearless. He also knew Wiley would not blink an eye it he had the opportunity to kill Jake. The only way Jake had a chance against would be if he were as cold blooded as Harpe himself. He couldn't make the mistake of trying to talk to Wiley, or trying to capture him alive. He had to strike first, and he had to strike fast. The hell with all the old fair play stuff. He had to kill the son-of-bitch the instant he laid eyes on him.

While it was true Jacob Trabue had a pretty good idea of what he was up against in Wiley Harpe, the fact was he had no idea at all what was waiting in Kentucky.

He didn't know Wiley was like a Sunday school teacher when compared to Micajah.

Perhaps if Jake had known what he would have to face in reality, he would have changed his mind about seeking help from the authorities.

The police in Mississippi and Alabama were stumped. There was a barbaric killer on a rampage, and neither state had any significant clues to either his identity or his motive. He wasn't killing for money, and his victims didn't fit any pattern at all. It looked as if he were traveling northward, and randomly stopping and killing everyone he came into contact with.

At two of the markets where he had stopped, the security cameras had been on and had recorded the killer from the time he entered the stores until the time he left. All the gruesome details were caught on film, except for one.

Every single time the camera had touched upon the killer himself, for some reason the picture had blurred. It was almost as if there were something about the man, some electrical energy or something, that was causing a powerful interference in the video surveillance system. But of course, that didn't make any sense at all.

All they could tell was the killer was a man, and he was big. From the audio portion of the tape, they also knew he showed no emotion when he killed. Men, women and children were all the same to him. They knew he used several different weapons. His hands, a knife, a gun, even a large can of soup, had all been used to take a life. The recorder had picked up the last words he had spoken to the woman about the can of soup, and even the toughest of officers had trouble believing what they heard.

They didn't know there were already two more victims lying at the bottom of a ditch beside a country road just outside Franklin, Tennessee.

Neither did they know the killings in Illinois and Kentucky had a direct relationship to the murders in Mississippi and Alabama. But even if they could have tied them all together, the end result would have been the same. They had no clues, no description, no idea what the killer was driving now, and no idea where he was headed.

Most agreed he was headed North, but roadblocks and helicopters had had no luck finding him either.

And every law officer in the South was thinking the same thing.

"Let me get a crack at this sumbitch."

WILEY

NASHVILLE, TENNESSEE

Officer John B. "Shooter" Bollinger of the Metropolitan Davidson County Police Department of Nashville, Tennessee was sure as hell hoping he got a shot at taking the son-of-a-bitch out.

Bollinger had heard the story at the station as he was getting ready to go on duty and had found out as much as he could about it later in the briefing room. His duty officer believed the killer was headed in the direction of Nashville, and told all the men to be especially watchful. Whoever the killer was, he was one of the most dangerous men most of them had ever run into. Although it was strictly against departmental procedure, many of the men made sure they had their back-up weapons where they could get to them easily if they had to.

Some of the men still carried standard .38 caliber pistols, the famous "Police Special," but most of them had begun using bigger weapons, such as .40 caliber or 9 millimeter automatics.

John Bollinger carried a Glock 9MM as his primary weapon, and a smaller snub-nosed .38 as his back-up. John had earned the nickname "Shooter" while in 'Nam, and was considered one of the best marksman on the force. He'd served two hitches with Uncle

238

Sam, and had joined the Nashville police department soon after he'd received his discharge.

Shooter Bollinger had fired his weapon three times in the line of duty since he'd become a policeman, resulting in two dead men and a third who'd never walk again. All three times he'd held his fire until fired upon, and had then responded with a cool head and deadly precision. The Shooter was definitely not a man to screw with.

But Shooter had another ace in the hold. For seven months he'd been assigned to the K-9 patrol, and was currently working with one of the meanest damned German Shepard Police dogs he'd ever seen.

The big dog's name was "Rawhide," and he was a perfectly trained killing animal. He was in his prime, and Bollinger had never seen him scared of a living thing, animal nor human. Needless to say, Shooter Bollinger would like nothing better than to turn the hundred plus pounds of fury loose on the man responsible for all these damned killings.

Bollinger was patrolling South Nashville in the vicinity of Franklin Pike when he spotted the white Mustang convertible. The driver was driving like he'd never seen a city before, weaving and swerving, changing lanes without signaling, his eyes everywhere except on the road.

Bollinger, like all Nashville patrolmen, was used to a lot of sightseers. After all, Nashville is Music City, and everyone knows you can never tell who you might see walking down the street. You might run into one of your favorite Opry stars anywhere at all, at any time. Country music stars, and country music star watchers are nothing out of the ordinary, and at first Bollinger thought the man in the Mustang was just another country music fan, come to town to try to catch a glimpse of his favorite signer.

Shooter followed the car for several blocks before deciding to pull him over, and then intended to only warn him. Hell, tourism was not something they liked to discourage in this town. But the guy was driving just a little too erratically, and it made Bollinger suspicious. There was a good chance the man was drinking, and Metro officers are pure hell on DUI offenders.

Bollinger hit the lights and siren at the same time and pulled up close to the rear bumper of the Mustang. He ran the plates as the guy pulled over to the curb, and they came back clean, registered to a Brandon A. King of Williamson County, with no outstanding wants or warrants. Bollinger picked up his ticket pad, and before he got out of the small K-9 police truck, he checked his weapon. Pure force of habit. You never knew what you were walking into when you pulled someone over, and Bollinger knew from experience it paid to be ready for anything.

As John opened the truck door, Rawhide began to really raise hell. He was barking and growling and seemed as if he would like to break down the door to the cage in the back of the truck and eat the driver of the Mustang alive.

"That's enough boy," Bollinger softly spoke to the big dog, but with little effect. Rawhide was more upset than Bollinger had ever seen him. With a strange premonition, Bollinger unlatched the gate and reached back and patted the dog on the head.

"Stay, Rawhide. Stay."

The dog was among the best trained animals John had ever worked with, and he knew he would obey the command. But with the gate unlatched, the dog would respond immediately if he was called.

Shooter got out of the truck and began walking to the Mustang. He saw the driver watching him in his rear view mirror as he approached the car, and once again checked his weapon. He felt the hackles rise on the back of his neck as his eyes locked with the eyes in the mirror. He hadn't felt this way since the jungles in 'Nam, and it wasn't a feeling he enjoyed.

"Could I see your license, please?" Bollinger asked as he stopped by the driver's door. He stood slightly sideways and just a little to the rear of the driver, another couple of habits he'd picked up over the years. Made him less a target, he figured.

"Sure thing, officer," the driver responded, "why'd you stop me?"

"Way you were weaving, Sir, I thought maybe you'd had a few too many. Decided to stop you and have a look see. You don't mind answering a few questions for me, do you?" Bollinger took the driver's license from the man with his left hand and glanced down at it to see what the mans name was.

The name on the license matched the make on the car, but the picture wasn't even close. Bollinger raised his eyes to take another look at the driver, and found himself staring into the business end of a huge .44 magnum. The man had brought the gun up from the seat in the split second it had taken John to glance at the picture for identification.

"Sorry officer, I ain't a drinkin' man," the driver said with a grin. "And I purely hate gettin' stopped when I'm just ridin' along, mindin' my own business. You plumb screwed up my whole day, and I don't like it a damned bit. Oh, and I might as well tell you right off, if you as much as twitch a muscle, I'm gonna send your butt to police heaven, if there is such a thing. And I'll only tell you the one time."

Bollinger had had a gun pulled on him before, and he knew better than to argue with the man. He looked at the driver and said; "I ain't twitching, feller, but I think you should know I got back-up on the way. The smartest thing you could do is to give me the gun right now, before things really get out of hand."

"Son, it was out of hand the minute you turned on them purty blue lights and hit yore sireen. And you ain't got no back-up coming, not for a routine drunk driver stop, you don't. And they ain't much of a chance I'll be givin' you my gun. Now they is a chance I'll give you some of my bullets. Probably one at a time."

"Why in the hell would you want to shoot me feller?" Bollinger asked.

The driver looked down at the name tag on John's shirt and said; "Now that's a fair question Officer...Bollinger. Huh. Used to be a feller named Ballinger chased after me and my brother all the time. You ain't kin are ye?" Without waiting for an answer he went on with what he was saying. "Like I was about to say, that's a fair question, and it deserves a fair answer. The answer is, I don't really care if I shoot you or not. Rather not, really. It's just that I don't think you'll leave me alone if I let you go. I wasn't doing anything illegal, and then you pulled me over, and now we got us this little problem. What I'd like to do is turn you loose, get back in my car and drive off, and then you'd drive off in the other direction, and that'd be the end of it. But you wouldn't do that, now would you? You'd jump back into that little truck, call a bunch of your buddies, and then the whole lot of you would try to blow me away. Now ain't I right, Bollinger? Ain't that the way it would go?"

"I guess you're right, feller. But it's already too late. Even if you kill me, my 'buddies' are gonna get you anyway, you oughta know that."

Wiley grinned. "Tell you what chief, why don't you back up bout three steps and stand still. I wanta get out of the car, and then we'll talk about it."

They were still in the same position as when Bollinger had first approached the car. Bollinger was still standing beside the door, and the man was sitting in the car, leaning slightly over the window, not even trying to hide the gun in his hand.

Bollinger stepped back three steps, as he'd been told to do, and waited. He was hoping for a chance to make a play as the driver got out of the car.

No such luck.

The driver didn't even open the door. Instead he turned about half way round in the seat, never taking his eyes or his gun off

242

Bollinger, and quickly scooted backward across the seat until he was out from under the steering wheel. He then stood straight up in the car, still holding the gun steady, and said to Bollinger.

"OK, lean over into the back seat and stick both hands down beside the seat, like you're lookin' for loose change or something. You know what I mean."

As soon as Bollinger crammed both hands into the space between the seat and the seat back, the man leaped lightly out of the car, landing on the pavement directly behind Bollinger. "Just hold still a minute now will you?" he asked.

John felt the man remove the Glock from its holster, but there was nothing he could do. Hell, the position he was in, if the big guy decided to pull down his pants and poke him in the butt there wouldn't be much he could do about that either.

Just like the man was reading his mind, Bollinger felt his belt loosened and his pants and shorts dropped to his ankles, leaving him half naked and bending over the car, his hands still wedged down into the seat.

"What the hell are you doing?" Bollinger yelled, and started to yank his hands loose from the seat.

"Don't do it feller. I've done told you the one time, and that's the only time I'll say it. Ah, what's this," he said. He'd found the hide-out gun strapped to the inside of John's left calf. He removed the little gun and suddenly noticed a few cars had slowed down to look.

"Pull up your pants, Officer. I hate to see a grown man embarrassed in public. Now, where were we?"

John didn't know if the man was crazy, on drugs, or what the hell was the matter with him, but he knew he had to make some kind of move pretty soon if he wanted to live.

Bollinger was thinking about the big dog in the back of the truck. True to his training, Rawhide had lain still and quiet, waiting a call to go into action. It was a call Bollinger was on the verge of making.

"Can I ask you a question, Officer Bollinger, before I do anything else," the man asked.

"Sure thing feller, don't look like I got much choice."

"None a'tall, Bollinger, none a'tall. My question is, what you waitin' on to sic that big dog on me? I figured you'd already have him out here by now."

"You know about the dog?" Bollinger was a little surprised.

"Of course I know about the dog. Hell, I smelled him a long time before I did you."

Without another word Bollinger loudly spoke the dog's name.

"Rawhide. Attack, Rawhide."

Even as the big dog came roaring out of the truck, the man brought across a huge fist and swiped John along side his right ear, knocking him to the ground. Although the blow hardly struck him, its force was sufficient to cloud his senses and dull his eyesight.

Bollinger hit the rough asphalt on his knees, and through blurred eyes he watched as Rawhide bounded across the short distance between the two of them. The dog was silent, and his large teeth flashed in the sun as he snarled at the man. Then the strangest thing of all happened.

Later, John Bollinger thought he must have imagined the next few moments.

Rawhide launched himself into a full power jump, straight at the chest of the big man who stood before him, and then the impossible happened.

The man reached out with one hand and caught the dog by the throat, then stood holding him suspended in midair. The dog suddenly uttered a low whimper. Raising his eyes, Bollinger saw the look on the face of the man and understood a little of what must be going through the mind of the dog.

The man's lips were curled back in a ferocious snarl that was more savage than the dog could ever be. His wild, fierce features were those of a natural predator, and the dog recognized in the man the full force of the Wolf. It was a force that was more than the animal could deal with. The man's eyes were wild and ruthless, and the dog turned away from the gaze quickly. The man set the dog down on the pavement, never once looking away. Rawhide tucked his tail between his legs and slunk back into the truck, as the big man stood up and softly laughed.

He grabbed Bollinger roughly by the collar of his shirt and jerked him to his feet.

"Now where were we?" he asked.

Bollinger shook the cobwebs from his brain, still unable to believe what he'd just witnessed. Who was this guy, anyway? Or what was he?

"You said your buddies would get me anyway. How they gonna do that? Who they gonna be lookin' for? You couldn't have radioed in my description, cause you didn't see me till you walked up to the car. I stole the car, so it won't do any good lookin' for the man the plates are registered to, besides which, even if they find him he won't be doin' a of a lot of talking. Naw, here's the way it's got to go down. I kill you, leave the Mustang where it's sittin', take yer truck, and I'll be long gone by the time anybody else gets here to check up on you."

The hell of it was, Bollinger knew the guy was right. He looked around and figured he only had one chance to stay alive even for a few more seconds.

"There's an awfully lot of traffic out here today," he said. "Lot of people around. You think they won't know what's going on as soon as you start shooting? And they will report it, you know that. And they won't take long doing it."

The man took a look at the busy street. "You got a point there, I reckon. Tell you what. We'll be takin' your truck, but the dog's gonna have to stay here. And you're gonna have to drive. I got too much to do to take a chance on another cop pulling me over. And feller, let me make it plain that I've done had too much trouble with you. Won't be standin' fer much more. Catch my meanin'?"

It took a few minutes for John to get Rawhide to come out of the back of the truck. The animal was scared to death of the big man and didn't want to leave the safety of the vehicle. When he finally had the dog in the Mustang, John gave him another order to stay, and they got into the truck and pulled away from the curb.

John checked his watch and couldn't believe his eyes. The entire incidence had taken less than five minutes, but had seemed more like five hours.

Pulling into traffic, Bollinger had one more thought about getting away. "Let's see him shoot me when we're going eighty miles an hour."

Once again, it was like the man was reading his mind.

"Pull around that corner and stop," he said to Bollinger before they'd gone half a block.

Bollinger pulled the truck into a narrow alley between two old buildings and stopped it.

"Step out of the truck and pull off all your clothes, except for your shirt and hat, and don't get any cute ideas or I'll shoot off your privates. Assuming I can hit the little rascals that is." The man laughed at his own joke.

When Bollinger was almost naked, the man quit laughing and spoke again. "Throw the clothes in the trash can, shoes and all, and get back in the car."

"Now, when we leave this alley, I want you to head for I-65 the closest way you know. The first time you get too fast, I'll shoot you. The first time you break a traffic law, I'll shoot you. You got one chance of getting out of this alive, and that's to do as you're told. If you try to screw with me the least little bit, somebody will be collecting your insurance, cause you'll be a dead Nashville cop. Understand, Officer Bollinger? And like I said, I'll only tell you the one time."

"I understand all right," Bollinger replied, "but you better understand something too." Bollinger was more angry now than he was afraid, and was about to get mad enough that he didn't care what the guy thought. "If I get half a chance, I'm gonna screw with you all right. I'm gonna blow your crazy butt into the next county."

"Well, by God, Bollinger, that's good to know. I like a man that speaks his mind. You real sure you ain't kin to old Joe Ballenger himself?"

Something about that name struck a chord inside John Bollinger's mind. Joe Ballenger? Joseph Ballenger? By God, he did know that name. An elderly Aunt of his Dad's that lived in some little town up in Kentucky had once told him a story about a man named Joseph Ballenger, and had said she thought they had once spelled their name with an "A and an E" instead of the current "O and I." If this guy didn't kill him first, maybe John could find out who the hell Joe Ballenger was, and how he tied in to all of this.

"You know what else I like, feller?" the man spoke again.

Thinking to humor him, Bollinger asked the obvious question. "No, what else do you like, feller?"

"I like them damn Frosty Queen ice cream cones. You know, the ones dipped in that chocolate stuff. Them damn things are delicious."

"Yeah, they are, ain't they?" Bollinger said, trying to keep the man in a good mood.

But to himself, Bollinger thought; This guy is a full fledged looney tune, completely fruitcake city. He don't know if he wants to kill me or eat damned ice cream cones. Probably wants to do both.

"Tell you what Bollinger. When we see a Frosty Queen, pull over. I'll get us both one, and try my damnedest not to kill anybody doing it."

The funny thing, Bollinger thought, is this feller don't even act like he's mad or nothing. He acts like this is just a regular Sunday afternoon. Like he was sitting round the house, watching the game, decides to go out for pizza. While he's out, he has some ice cream, kills a few people, kidnaps a Metro cop, scares the hell out of my dog, looks for more ice cream. What the hell is wrong with this picture? This feller is seriously crazy. Like he's two different people. I've got to take him out, one way or another. Or he'll kill me for sure, and no telling how many more.

By this time, John had no doubts at all he'd found the man every cop in the South was looking for."

Bollinger was closer to the truth than he realized. There were two minds inside the big killers head, and although Wiley Harpe was the dominant one, the other mind was still active. Harpe was the homicidal maniac, the killer, the wild Wolf. The other mind was the boy who knew his way around today's world. He was the one who could drive cars, operate a computer, and knew how to get places and where things were. Every now and then, Harpe's mind would completely take over, and he really was "seriously crazy" as Bollinger put it. He had no idea about things like cars, and cities, and ice cream cones. Harpe reacted to things the same way he always had. If he felt threatened, of if he needed something, he resorted to violence. When he found something he liked, like the ice cream, or his first time in a big city, he reacted like a child. Filled with awe and happiness, determined to discover all he could about the new thing he'd found.

Either way, with Harpe completely in control, or partially sharing control, he was the most dangerous man Shooter Bollinger would ever come in contact with.

Unless of course, he survived long enough to meet Micajah.

"What's your name, feller, if you don't mind me asking?"

"Don't mind a'tall, Officer Bollinger. Name's Wiley Harpe. They call me Little Harpe."

Bollinger looked at the man who stood well over six feet three and weighed two thirty or so; "Damn, man, if you're 'Little Harpe' I'd sure as hell hate to run into whoever they call 'Big Harpe'."

"Well, that's where we're headed, Chief. They call my brother Micajah the Big Harpe, and he's the real Wolf in the family. Hell, I'm just the baby. But don't worry, I think he'll like you, if I manage to get you there without killing you that is. Try to act right for a few more hours, OK? I'd kinda like for you to meet my big brother."

If anyone had asked John Bollinger if he knew the meaning of the words "Homicidal Maniac," he'd have looked at Wiley and answered "Of course I do."

But he didn't. Not yet, anyway.

JAKE

SOMEWHERE ON I-65 NORTH

Jacob Trabue had driven through Nashville without stopping, and was headed North on I-65, not really sure where he was headed. Other than the same old stories on the news, he'd heard nothing he could connect to Wiley Harpe. The star on his wrist was staying silent, and no help at all. He kept changing stations on the radio, hoping for some kind of clue, but so far he'd had no luck at all.

He was almost to the Kentucky state line, and he'd just twisted the dial to local station when he heard the disc jockey say;

"...stay tuned for the latest development in the multiple murders in Russellville this afternoon. So far all we know is a person or persons has seemingly been running wild in the streets of the city, randomly killing people. It has now been confirmed Sheriff Hugh Wrenn was one of the first to fall. We do not have any additional details at this time, and no other names to report. Please, I repeat, please do not call the station. We will update you as soon as we receive any information at all. This is Smilin' Jack McCall in Tuckasee, sayin' stay tuned..."

Jake immediately pulled the car to the side of the interstate and checked his road map. He wanted the quickest route to Russellville, Kentucky. There was no doubt in his mind Wiley Harpe had somehow beat him to Kentucky, and was raging war in the little town of Russellville. There was also no doubt in his mind that Harpe was winning.

HAWK AND STEGALL

RUSSELVILLE, KY

Daniel Hawk and Andrew Stegall were arguing.

Stegall hadn't wanted to give up the knife under any circumstances, and especially not to the Harpe. He'd rather have given it to the Devil himself.

Hawk could see the wisdom in the action they had taken when they had confronted Harpe, and knew for a certainty if Stegall hadn't laid down the knife, both of them would be stone cold dead. The knife was the only reason Harpe had let them live, and Daniel knew they didn't have another damn thing to bargain with. But he was having a hell of a time making Stegall understand that.

"I'm telling you old man, we got off damn lucky. Harpe would have killed us for sure if you hadn't given him that damned knife. It ain't nothing to be ashamed of, Stegall, you really didn't have much of a choicc."

"Like hell I didn't. I should have cut his head off. And you should have helped me. If you hadn't been peeing your pants we could have kicked his butt, and ended it right then."

"I wasn't peeing my pants, old man, and it would have taken a hell of a lot more than the two of us to kick his butt. That man is pure death on two legs, and we never had a chance." Daniel knew for sure he was right about this.

"Death? Ha," Stegall snorted, "the blade would have killed him as sure as I'm standing here talking to you. It killed the big sumbitch two hundred years ago, and it would have killed him today. We should have stood our ground and fought him."

"That's a bunch of crap, Stegall, and if you had any sense you'd know it. Anyway, we aren't far behind him. I think we'll have another chance at the Harpe. He wants you as bad as you want him. Check the map and see what town we're coming to next."

Stegall studied the map for a second, then answered. "Near as I can tell, we'll be in Russellville in about ten minutes. You think he'll stop there?"

"Hell, I don't know. But I know I've got to have a bite to eat pretty soon, and Russellville is as good a place to eat as anywhere else. We'll stop, and hope he does too."

They were hanging several hundred yards behind the speeding motorcycle Harpe was riding, barely keeping him in sight on the highway. If the man was aware they were behind him, he sure didn't seem to be too concerned about it.

Sure enough, the motorcycle turned off the highway and headed toward a small market. Daniel slowed and watched as Harpe pulled the bike over and parked it. He then pulled his car into a similar market across the street. They had to get something to eat, and Daniel didn't want to lose track of Harpe. He decided it would be best if Stegall went into the market alone, while he watched to see what Harpe did.

"Hurry up Stegall, he won't be in there very long. Grab a package of baloney and some bread, and maybe a sixpack of cola. I'll keep an eye on Harpe."

"Cola my rusty old butt," Stegall replied, half under his breath. "I'm picking up a couple of sixpacks of cold beer."

Daniel heard the remark, and even though he knew the old man didn't need anything else to drink, if beer would keep him happy, then beer was what he'd get.

Stegall had gotten back to the car and the two of them were eating a bologna sandwich when Daniel noticed a police cruiser pull into the parking lot across the street, and then was joined buy a second cruiser in a few moments.

"Heads up Stegall." Daniel was whispering as if he thought the people in the other store could hear him. "Something's going down across the street. I'll bet he's started again."

"Yeah, I see the law dogs," Stegall answered. "Think we ought to go on over there?"

"Not just yet. Let's watch for a few minutes and see what happens."

They saw one of the officers go inside the store, and it was only a couple of minutes later that Harpe stuck his head out the door and called to the deputy who was still outside. The deputy also went inside, and in not more than another minute, Harpe hurried out and started his bike. As Harpe started his engine, Daniel saw a van pull in to the gas pump and watched as three men jumped out. What happened next was so quick Daniel couldn't believe his eyes. He watched in horror as Harpe brutally killed the three men, torched the station, and then roared away from the market. Daniel was only a hundred yards behind the bike as it flew down the narrow street. He saw the third police car skid around in the road and begin pursuit, and Daniel was still following when Harpe and the police car turned into an alley between two buildings.

Daniel parked his car and waited. There was nothing he and Stegall could do right now. Best to let the police handle Harpe, now that they were on the scene. Actually it was a relief. Surely the law could capture the man.

They had been parked there for about ten minutes when they heard three gunshots, and then saw Harpe come running out from between the buildings and cut across to another back street. He had a pistol in his hand, and wasn't moving as if he been on the receiving end of any of the shots they'd heard.

Daniel started the car, and tried to keep the man in sight as he raced down street after street. They lost him for minutes at a time, and had to stop and listen for any sound of a chase.

They were sitting in the middle of the block, trying to decide which direction they should take, when suddenly they heard the boom of shotgun. Daniel headed the car toward the sound. In only a few seconds they caught a glimpse of Harpe running through the back yards of the quiet little neighborhood. Daniel turned the car hard to the right and gunned the motor, trying to keep Harpe in sight. Now it was easy to keep track of the man just by listening to the sound of the rapid gunshots.

All at once a silver gray Honda came flying backward out of a paved driveway, and Daniel recognized Harpe behind the wheel.

Daniel slowed down. He didn't want Harpe to know he was this close to him. Not just yet, anyway. It would be better to follow the man for awhile, and try to take the battle outside the city, and away from innocent people.

Daniel followed the Honda out of town and was just barley keeping it in sight when all of sudden Harpe pulled the car to the side of the road and made a quick U-turn. All Daniel could do was turn his face away and hope Harpe didn't recognize him. He got lucky. Harpe was preoccupied with the events of the last hour or so and didn't notice Hawk and Stegall in the other car. As soon as he saw Harpe's car was out of sight, Hawk made a U-turn of his own and caught sight of Harpe's car just in time to see it pull off the road and disappear behind a run down old barn at the side of the road. Daniel slowed and watched as Harpe ran across the road and into the trees on the other side.

Hawk and Stegall both realized they couldn't follow Harpe into the woods. It would be sure death for both of them if the confronted the man in his own element. Daniel brought the car to a complete stop on the shoulder of the highway and turned in the seat for a conference with Stegall.

"He'll have to find another car, that's for damn sure. The only question is where," Hawk said.

"Well, I don't see many houses around here, so he'll probably head for the nearest little community. Or maybe there's a shopping center somewhere around. Anything like that. Someplace where there are a lot of cars. Hell, let's just drive around and see if we can find a place like that."

"I don't think he'll head back toward town. There are just too many cops prowling around back there. He'll most likely keep on headed south. Let's drive on down the road a piece and see what we find."

"Son, that sounds like a plan to me." Stegall said, as tossed an empty beer can out the open window and popped the top on another one. Without another word he leaned back in the seat and took a big drink of the cold beer. "Might as well get some rest while I can young feller," he said, "looks like we're gonna be in a hell of a mess before we get through."

"Whatever gave you that idea?" Hawk answered with a little smile.

They had driven barely a mile when they found exactly the place they were looking for.

The hospital, with its rows of parked cars, adjoined the municipal golf course, and there were still several cars parked at the golf course as well.

"Looks like we've struck pay dirt, old man," Hawk said, as he pulled the car onto the side of the road so they could watch both the cars in the hospital lot as well as the golf club lot. "We might as well watch for Harpe here as anywhere."

"I hate to admit it but you're probably right" Stegall answered, and then pitched another empty can out the window.

As the afternoon wore on, more and more golfers finished their rounds and left the club. When it was almost dark, and there were only two cars left in the parking lot of the golf club, Hawk decided to move the car so they could see the hospital lot a little better. There were a lot more cars there for Harpe to choose from, if he showed up here at all.

It was becoming obvious Harpe had been detained somewhere. He'd had more than enough time to walk the short distance from where they last saw him to the hospital, if he was headed in this direction.

The hospital was busy. There had been police cars and emergency vehicles all over the place all afternoon. Several patients had been airlifted out by helicopter to hospitals in nearby Clarksville, and several more had been carried away by local funeral directors. The emergency room and out patient areas were crowded by family and friends of the victims, and there were curious people standing around everywhere. This was the closest thing to a disaster that had ever happened in this little rural town, and the police had their hands full with not only the crowd, but also with the media people from the radio and television stations in the area. Each of the three big television stations in Nashville already had reporters broadcasting live from the scene, and cameras and equipment was scattered all around.

When Daniel Hawk and Andrew Stegall decided to get a little closer, they were turned around by the police and told they'd have to park at the back of the lot. Hawk drove the car all the way to the back and parked as close as he could get to the tree line. Once again they settled down to wait for Harpe, but they knew the chance he'd come was slim. Still, this was the only chance they had.

Stegall had been asleep for a couple of hours, and Daniel was dozing when suddenly he heard a sound in the parking lot.

Someone was walking through the lot.

Hawk raised his head, and slowly reached over and nudged Stegall awake. In the rearview mirror Daniel saw a woman walking down between the rows of parked cars, fumbling in her purse for her car keys as she walked. With a sigh Daniel started to settle back down in his seat, and pulled his hand away from Stegall, who was still mostly asleep. He took one more short look in his mirror, and to his surprise he saw a large figure step out of the deeper shadows and with a swift lunge grab the woman around the neck. Before Daniel could react, the man laid the body of the woman in the back of a nearby pick up truck and jumped into the car the woman had just unlocked.

Without thinking Hawk started the engine and threw the shift lever into reverse. He pushed the gas pedal to the floorboard and roared backwards, crashing into the car Harpe was in just as the man backed out of the parking space.

The force of the crash threw Hawk's head at first backward and then sent it plummeting violently into the steering wheel. He was dazed, although not unconscious, and blood was flowing from his forehead as he turned to see if he'd managed to stop the killer. Daniel wiped the blood from his eyes with one hand and grabbed the door handle with the other. The door was stuck, and before he could get it open he heard the other door slam and turned to see Stegall rushing toward the other car as fast as he could run.

"Damn it, Stegall, wait for me," he yelled, but Stegall didn't slow at all.

Andrew Stegall ran up to the side of the other car and peered inside. Sure enough, it was Harpe that sat behind the steering wheel. The big outlaw was dazed from the force of the crash but his eyes were wide open, and Stegall saw he was already beginning to regain his senses. Stegall looked inside the car and saw the motorcycle saddle bags on the front seat beside Harpe. The knife, still wet and shiny from the woman's blood, lay on the seat beside the bags.

Without stopping to think, Stegall jerked the car door open and grabbed the knife.

"You're a dead man, Harpe," Stegall shouted.

With the knife back in his hand, Stegall truly realized the awesome responsibility the weapon carried. It had the power to stop this monster right here, to bring an end to the senseless slaughter for once and for all. Killing the Harpe was what Stegall had waited his entire life to do. Even as his ancestor had done before him, Andrew must now stand and fight, and pray both he and the knife were equal to the task.

Leaning across the seat with a quickness that surprised even himself, Stegall took a vicious swipe with the blade, and grunted as it made contact with Harpe's right arm, high on the biceps.

"That'll teach you not to mess with me," he shouted, and took a second swing with the blade, this time connecting with only the padding in the front seat and ripping a long gash in it.

With a sudden moment of clear thought, Stegall realized his only chance to win this fight was to end it quickly, and to do that he'd have to get inside the car. If Harpe ever got out of the car his strength and speed would make it impossible for Stegall to kill him. With a savage snarl, Stegall threw himself across the front seat of the car directly at Harpe, bringing the knife around with all his might. This time the blade caught the dazed Harpe full in the right side and a torrent of blood rushed out, flooding the seat and splashing on the dash.

Andrew Stegall shouted. Not words, for mere words couldn't express the emotions raging inside him when he saw the knife had actually struck Harpe. Generations of Stegall men had waited for this moment, when the long knife would once again drink the blood of the Harpe.

Whispers and screams came rushing down across the years, and filled Stegall's mind, and he knew what old Moses Stegall must have felt back in 1799, when he sat astride the Harpe's body and stabbed, and stabbed, and stabbed.

Stegall threw his head back and laughed. Wild laughter that echoed across the parking lot, and resounded through the trees. Laughter that valiantly tried, but failed, in its attempt to disguise the fear that still raced through Stegall. As the laughter died away, Stegall looked into the face of his ages old enemy for the first time.

And saw the same thing Moses Stegall had seen as he hacked at the head of the Harpe.

There was no fear in Harpe's eyes.

Instead, there was the blue Wolf fire, raging wild and uncontrolled. Flickering tongues of flame engulfed the man and licked away the pain from the knife wounds. Cold flame that filled the car and washed across Andrew Stegall's soul.

For the first time, Andrew Stegall was looking full into the eyes of the Wolf, a gaze that took his mind straight into the hottest fires of Hell.

With a snarl, Harpe's huge hand grasped the handle of the knife and slowly withdrew it from his side. He stared across the car at the man who had stabbed him, and his voice was soft and even, and cold as ice when he spoke.

"I knew you'd come back, Stegall. You're just like old Moses was. Not smart enough to leave well enough alone. You and the Indian kid should have turned around and gone home, while you still could. I let you walk away once, I'm not apt to do it again."

"You ain't got no way of stopping me, you big sumbitch. I'm gonna kill you if it's the last thing I do. If it takes me and the Indian both, so be it. He's got your magic tomahawk, and I've already stuck you once. Your life blood is running out, and pretty soon you'll be too damn weak from the bleeding to keep us from killing you."

"Bleeding? Who's bleeding, old man?" Harpe moved his arm out of the way so Stegall could get a good look at his wound.

Stegall couldn't believe his eyes.

The bleeding had already completely stopped. The stab wounds, both on his arm and in his side were already closing. Instead of being torn and bloody cuts, they were already little more than scratches. Slowly, Harpe reached down and wiped the blood away from the wound in his side, and Stegall could see it healing as he watched.

"What kind of fiend from Hell are you?" he whispered. "I stabbed you a good 'un, I know I did. Right in the side. Why in the hell ain't it bleeding? And why ain't it hurtin' you? You're a monster, Harpe, some kind of psycho monster." Stegall was frantic.

"Perhaps, Stegall, perhaps I am a monster." Harpe's voice was still soft. "Or maybe it's just that a monster lives in me. I call him the Wolf, Stegall, and he's your worst nightmare. Old Moses knew the Wolf, and knew him well. We rode together, Moses and me, and my brother. Damnation, old man, Moses didn't cut off my head because of his family, or because of justice. Moses was a traitor. A friend who betrayed me and my family to save his own worthless hide. And he was afraid of me, old man, just like you are. It took ten or twelve of his buddies to hold me while Moses hacked away. He sure as hell couldn't have done it alone. And you can't either. Not even with the help of the Indian. I don't care if he does have my tomahawk, it won't work any better than the knife did."

Harpe paused for a moment and sat looking at Stegall as if his mind was somewhere in the past, and not even on the man who sat in the car with him. With no change in his voice, he continued.

"You're right about one thing though old man. This is the same knife Moses used. But at least Moses had a reason for what he did, not like you and the boy. Moses was a killer as much as me and my brother were, and I knew him as well as he knew me. He killed me that day because he was afraid if I lived I'd tell the others about him, and then they'd want him dead as much as they did me. Well, they killed me all right, but with my dying breath I told them it wasn't over. And I meant it. One thing you'll learn, old man, if you live long enough, is the Harpe never goes back on his word. I didn't back then, and I won't now. I told them I'd be back, and here I am. Here I am Stegall, the Wolf has returned from the dead. I am your death and destruction, old man, make no mistake about it. And I'll only tell you the one time."

Stegall looked at Harpe for one last moment, and then half scooted, half fell out of the car. He struck hard against the asphalt of the parking lot, almost breaking his tailbone, barely managing to catch on his elbow and keeping his head from slamming into the hard pavement. Again he scooted backward, intent on putting as much distance as he could between himself and Harpe. With a quick look at the other car, he saw Daniel Hawk finally manage to pry the door open and stumble out. Daniel was holding something in his hand, and Stegall prayed it was the tomahawk. He didn't know how effective the ax would be against Harpe, but it was the only weapon they had left.

He half heard, half saw Harpe emerge from the car, and another quick look told him Harpe had the knife in his hand. Andrew couldn't break his gaze away from Harpe's face. The man's eyes were still burning, the blue flame brighter even than the pale moonlight. With one last final effort, Stegall lurched to his feet and ran into the woods, leaving Daniel Hawk to face Harpe alone.

Daniel Hawk didn't know what to think when he finally got the door open and managed to get out of the car. He saw Stegall on the pavement, first scooting backward on the asphalt, and then jumping up and running toward the trees. Then he saw Harpe climb out of the wrecked car. Daniel Hawk gasped as he looked at the huge killer. Harpe had looked formidable when Hawk had seen him standing by the motorcycle in the daylight, but here in the shadows, with the great long knife in his hand, the man was totally awesome. He was much bigger than Hawk had originally thought, and was covered with what looked like blood. There appeared to be blood dripping from the blade of the knife also, and Hawk wondered if Harpe had injured Stegall. Then Harpe turned and looked at Daniel Hawk, and for the first time, Hawk saw the man's eyes.

They were the eyes of the creature that had appeared in Daniel's vision. The DarkWolf, his father had called him. His eyes were fairly crackling with the energy of a raging blue flame, and now Hawk knew why his father had been so upset. This man would upset the Devil himself.

With more than a little apprehension, Daniel Hawk raised the magic tomahawk and started around the car and toward Harpe. He had never been more afraid, but he knew he might as well go ahead and get this crap over with.

Harpe watched the young Indian come around the car, and stood waiting for him. The boy had the tomahawk, and Harpe wanted it. With a final glance, he watched as Stegall disappeared into the trees, and decided he could catch up with the old man anytime he wished too. Right now he'd give the Indian his full attention.

Hawk advanced around the car, the tomahawk raised over his head. His lips were pulled back from his teeth, and his breath came in short, raspy gasps. His heart was beating so hard he thought it might burst from his chest at any minute. His palms were hot and sweaty, but for some strange reason his mouth was dry as cotton. He was taking slow, careful steps, trying to figure out the best way to begin his attack on Harpe, knowing there wasn't much chance he'd survive the fight, but determined to go down hard. At least he'd give the son-of-a-bitch a fight.

Suddenly, when Daniel was still several feet away, Harpe raised his head to the moon and sounded a blood curdling dry, almost a howl. It echoed across the parking lot, and bounced off the brick walls of the hospital, sending waves through the trees of the golf course. Even as the cry faded in the night, it was replaced by the sound of several police sirens, whooping at high speed toward the hospital, growing closer by the second.

For the first time, both men seemed to realize where they were. The parking lot was rapidly becoming filled with people, most drawn by the sound of the crash.

Many of the people had seen Stegall run into the woods, and all had heard Harpe's wild cry as he vented his fury into the night. They gathered closer, not knowing whether or not to try and come between the two men.

Harpe looked once again at Daniel Hawk, and without a word or any trace of fear, he turned back to the car, gathered his saddlebags, and slowly began walking toward the tree line where Stegall had disappeared.

As Hawk watched Harpe fade into the darkness that enveloped the trees, he didn't know whether to laugh or cry. He was ashamed to admit it, but in his heart he was relieved he hadn't had to fight the Harpe. Even though Daniel had the tomahawk, Harpe would have killed him, and Daniel knew it. He also knew they'd meet again. They were destined to do battle. Hawk's life was entwined with the Harpe just as surely as was Andrew Stegall's.

Andrew Stegall scrambled through the trees as fast as he could, not paying attention to see if anyone was pursuing him or not. He could still feel Harpe's sticky blood on his hands and shirt, but couldn't take the time to try to get it off just yet. He was surprised to find he was making pretty good time through the dark woods, and his legs didn't seem as tired as they should be feeling by now.

He decided to risk a short pause to catch his breath, and as he stopped he shouted into the night. "We'll meet again, and when we do it'll be a different story."

Micajah ran into the trees scarcely two or three minutes after Stegall, hoping to be able to follow the old man in the dark, but soon found that for some reason he couldn't pick up his trail. He didn't understand that, but he didn't have time to dwell on it.

He was disappointed he hadn't recovered the tomahawk, but knew the Indian boy wouldn't stop the chase at this point. He'd have another opportunity to get the axe, and soon.

After a few minutes had passed and Micajah hadn't caught Stegall, he decided to go back to his original plan. He needed a car, and he needed to find the Amulet.

The vibrations from the Amulet were the strongest they had been, so Harpe knew he was still headed in the right direction, and was only a few hours away from regaining the full power of the Wolf. Stegall and the Indian boy could wait. They'd both try again, they had no choice. When they did, the battle that had started almost two hundred years ago would finally be finished. It was a fight none of them could walk away from.

Suddenly he felt another presence in the woods and a minute later heard a voice shout at him from the darkness. He decided to deal with this new party rather than just getting away from him. He was frustrated over losing Stegall, and the man shouting at him would be one way of partially venting that frustration.

Jack Fowler lived within shouting distance of the hospital and the golf course, and had heard the commotion when it first began. At the sound of the crash, Jack headed toward the hospital as fast as he could run.

Jack was twenty-eight years old, a big strong country boy who had quite a reputation around the Kentucky/Tennessee border counties as a wild brawler, and a hard man to beat in a fight. He was known in every honky tonk in a thirty mile radius of Russellville as being quick tempered and uncontrollable once he got excited and a little drunk. Which was almost every weekend.

Jack got to the parking lot just in time to see Harpe as he walked into the woods after Stegall.

He ran into the darkened trees and it was only a matter of minutes before he caught up with the man he'd seen enter the woods. The man wasn't particularly trying to be quiet as he walked through the trees and Jack had no trouble getting close to him.

When he got close enough, Jack shouted at him;

"I saw what you did, and you ain't gettin' away with it."

Harpe stopped for a moment and looked at Fowler, the blue eyes twin beacons of flame in the darkness.

"Feller," Harpe said, in that same soft, deadly voice, "I used to try to tell people, at least one time, to quit screwing with me."

"What do you mean, used..."

Fowler started, but never finished the sentence.

For even as he finished speaking, Harpe had plunged the gleaming blade of the long knife into Jack Fowler's right ear, driving the point a good two inches out the other side of the mans head. The knife was very effective in cutting off Fowlers last words in mid-sentence.

"Used to means I don't do it anymore, sometimes," Harpe replied, jerking the knife from Fowlers head as the man slumped to the ground.

JAKE

RUSSELVILLE, KY

Jacob Trabue was sitting in a small country cafe in Russellville trying to finish the plate of mashed potatoes and meat loaf. It was pretty good, but Jake's mind just wasn't on eating. He'd only been in Russellville for about half an hour, just long enough to order his food, and already he was trying to figure out his next move. He hoped he could pick up Wiley's trail here in the small town, but didn't really know where to start. As he'd driven into town he'd noticed a hell of a lot of excitement for such a little country, but still didn't know what was going on.

It was already dark, and Jake knew he needed to find a place where he could get a few hours sleep. He was dead tired, and needed rest pretty badly.

Two cops had come into the cafe about ten minutes ago, and were now having coffee and doughnuts. They had looked Jake over pretty well before they say down. Apparently they had decided he wasn't whoever they were looking for, so they didn't say anything to him.

Jake had decided he was going to ask the cops a couple of questions and see if they'd tell him what was going on, but as he started across the floor there suddenly came the sound of many sirens, racing somewhere in the darkness. The cops jumped up and ran out of the cafe, and Jake was hot on their heels. He followed as closely as he dared as the raced south along Highway 431, headed toward the hospital.

What they found in the hospital parking lot wasn't pretty.

An angry crowd had gathered, and a few were standing looking into the back of a pick-up truck. Before they could stop him, Jake walked over and too a look. A woman lay there, obviously dead. Someone had slit her throat from ear to ear, and then dumped her in the back of the pick-up truck. It was a gruesome sight, but one Jake was becoming used to.

There were two wrecked cars, and the police were already on the scene, busily questioning a young man standing beside one of the cars. Many of the men in the crowd were brandishing shotguns, and from their shouted exchanges it was plain whoever had killed the woman had run into the woods and the men were intent on chasing him down. The police were just as intent on not letting that happen. Ten or twelve armed men had already broken away and gotten into the woods, and could be heard yelling and shouting and occasionally firing one of the shotguns. It would be a miracle if none of them killed themselves before the night was over.

Trying to appear as just another concerned citizen, Jake eased over and stood as close as he could to where the police were doing their questioning. He was close enough to hear their conversation with the young man they were talking to.

"What the hell are you doing out here feller?" one of the cops asked the man.

"I told you officer. Me and my friend were looking for a place to sleep for awhile. We don't have much money so we decided to sleep in the car in the hospital parking lot. We didn't think anyone would care. We were just dozing off when we heard a commotion and looked up just in time to see this big guy jump out between the cars and attack that woman."

"OK, tell me one more time just exactly what happened then."

Jake listened as the young man vividly retold the events of the night. It sounded more like Harpe with every word. Jake didn't know how in the hell Wiley had gotten so far ahead of him, but this sure looked like his handiwork. Damn, Jake didn't think Wiley had been two hours ahead of him. In fact, he would have bet Wiley was behind him, not ahead at all. But now he wasn't so sure.

Jake had been listening for about fifteen minutes when all at once there came a loud commotion from the forest. Three or four men came running out at the same time, all of them out of breath and as excited as hell.

As they ran, one of the men shouted to the police and the crowd.

"We found another one. We found another dead body in the woods. Come on, damnit, hurry up. You won't believe this unless you see it. His damn head is up in a tree. Come on, people, hurry up." The man was approaching hysteria.

All of the police, including the cops who were doing the questioning, took off in a dead run for the trees, and so did most the crowd. The young man the cops had been questioning was running in that direction also, and Jake found himself running along beside him. He had to get in a few questions of his own as soon as he could.

Several of the police had bright flashlights, and were already standing by the body when Jake and the young man got there. The man had been stabbed savagely through his upper body, and sure enough, he had been decapitated. One of the policemen shined his light up in the tree, letting it come to rest on the grisly object lodged in one of the lower forks. It was the head of the dead man. Eyes wide open and blood still dripping, the look on the face was one of terror. The eyes stared into the darkness as if they were searching for something, or someone.

"Stegall. It's not Stegall. Thank God," the young man standing next to Jake whispered. It was the man's next words that caused a shudder to run across Jake's soul, and the hair to stand up on the back of his neck.

The man was talking to himself, and was barely audible as he spoke under his breath, and Jake had to strain and move closer to make out the words.

"Stegall, you crazy old son-of-a-bitch, at least you had the good sense not to fight Harpe here in these dark woods, all by yourself."

The Harpe. Jake distinctly heard the man say "Harpe." He took another look at the head in the forks of the tree. Yeah, it was the Harpe all right, both Jake and the other man knew it.

Jake moved still closer to the man and whispered;

"I need to talk to you about the Harpe, feller. I'm trying to catch him myself."

Daniel turned and noticed the other man for the first time.

"You know about the Harpe?" he asked incredulously.

WILEY

KENTUCKY

"...update you as further information is made available to us. This is Radio Station KFOX, the Fox, in Tuckasee, stay tuned..."

"You know where that town is, Bollinger," Wiley asked. "If you do, head for it, if you don't, pull over and I'll find me a driver who does."

"Of course I know where Russellville is," John Bollinger replied, "and I'll get us there. But I've got to have some clothes. First time somebody looks in this car and sees my dick dragging, they'll call the law, and they'll be on us like white on rice."

"Reckon you're right about that. Tell you what, the next little community we come to, we'll stop and pick you up a few things to wear, and we'll get us another car while we're at it. I imagine they're already looking for this black and white. We need to stop anyway, Bollinger, I'm beginning to crave another of them little ice cream cones pretty bad. Yep, the next little town'll be fine. Long as they got a Frosty Queen, that is."

John Bollinger would have shot him right between the eyes if he could have gotten hold of a gun. Hell, he'd stab him, or beat him to death with a stick, or run over him in a car, or on a bicycle, or anything he could get his hands on. Bollinger wanted to kill this guy more than he'd ever wanted to do anything in his life. It was driving Bollinger out of his mind. He had to do something.

Bollinger cut his eyes at the man sitting next to him, and saw he was watching him.

He knows. This fool knows I want to kill him, and he's thinking about ice cream.

John was thinking to himself. Even in Nam, and in all my years on the force, I ain't never seen nobody like this. I've seen some crazies, but not like this.

Once again, almost as if he were answering John's unspoken words, the big killer spoke.

"I reckon you'd like to get your hands on me, now wouldn't you? Least ways, you think you would. Truth is, and I ain't braggin' feller, and I ain't tryin' to scare you, the plain truth is, if you got your hands on me, I'd kill you. I'd kill you dead as a doornail, and I'd do it so fast it'd make your head swim. You're big, and you're tough, and I'll bet you're a ring tailed doozy in a fight, but you don't know what you're up against. I'm a Wolf, Bollinger, and to me you're a sheep. If you screw with me, I'll shear you and make a winter coat out of your wool. You'd best keep that in mind, Mister Nashville Policeman. If you screw with me, you're gonna be the deadest cop in seven states. And as my brother says, I'll only tell you the one time."

Then, like so many other people had done in the past, Officer John Bollinger got a look into the eyes of the killer. And knew fear for the first time in his life. It dawned on him that this time he might not get out in one piece. The man might be crazy, but he was the most deadly person John Bollinger had ever seen.

"Where are you from, guy?" Bollinger asked. "And how'd you get mixed up in this deal?" He might as well try to find out something about the man who was likely to be his killer.

"You wouldn't believe me if I told you," the man answered.

"Try me," Bollinger said, "what d'ya got to lose?"

"Not much, that's for sure," was the answer. The man looked at Bollinger again and continued; "In fact, if I tell you what's been happening to me, maybe it'll help me make some sense out of it. I ain't so sure I know myself what's going on."

Bollinger waited without speaking, his interest kindled just a little by the man's words.

"Like I said before, my name is Harpe, Wiley Harpe. Me and my brother Micajah, we killed a few people, hell, we killed a lot of people, some years ago not too far from here. They caught my brother and killed him and I drifted down South. A few years later, I got caught too, and here's where I get kind of mixed up on the story. You see, they killed me too. Caught me and strung me up, and if that wasn't enough they cut off my head and nailed it to a post. Actually, feller, I don't even know how I know that, I just do."

The man's eyes came back to Bollinger, and stared at him, expecting him to say something. When the officer didn't speak, the man continued.

"That was in Greenville, Mississippi, it was, where they hung me. The year was 1804."

When Bollinger heard the date, he heard himself release his pent up breath. He hadn't even known he'd been holding it.

270

Sometimes at night, even after all this time, John still had occasional flashbacks of Vietnam, and the terrible things he'd endured in his two tours of that hellhole. And now, hearing this man speak the name of Greenville, Mississippi and the year 1804, for some reason brought about a flashback of it's own to Bollinger.

In his mind Bollinger could see vast forests, and men in deer skin trousers, and there was a feeling of urgency and violence about the picture, as if Bollinger were chasing someone, or someone were chasing him. He shook his head from side to side several times, trying to gather his wits about him, as he listened to the man called Harpe continue.

"Next thing I knew," Wiley went on, "I heard this loud screaming. It was everywhere, and then I got this awful pounding in my head. It didn't matter if I wanted to or not, I woke up. I woke up and found myself inside a body that ain't mine, in a world I don't know a thing about, and with a feeling there was business left to finish, business I'd been called back for. Whoever this body belongs to is still in here, but so am I. I can hear him now and then. He's the one who knows about cities and planes and how to drive cars and all that stuff. Not me. I don't even know his name. All I know is I'm looking for my brother, and that's why we're going to Russellville. That had to be Micajah that raised all that hell there. Ain't nobody else can raise hell like Micajah. But you'll find out for yourself, now won't you?"

John Bollinger looked at Harpe and didn't know what to think about his crazy story. People didn't come back from the dead, Bollinger knew that, but there was something about this guy that made Bollinger almost believe him. Almost. Maybe it had something to do with the weird flashback he himself had experienced just a few moments ago. That and the fact he'd had a hell of a pounding in his head for the past few days also. It was getting stranger and stranger.

"1804, huh? That's when they hung you? What makes you think I'm gonna believe any of this crazy story?"

271

"I don't care if you believe it or not," the man answered. "I ain't told you one word that ain't the gospel truth. And I ain't got nothin' to gain from lying about it. I don't know what the hell is going on myself, and I was hoping maybe you could shed a little light on it. You've got to see a bunch of strange stuff in your line of work."

"Yeah," Bollinger slowly replied, "I guess I do. But I don't know if I've ever seen anything like this before."

"Well," Harpe said, "If you can explain any of it, start explaining. If you can't, shut up and drive."

Bollinger shut up and drove.

It was well after dark when they got to Russellville, just in time to see two helicopters take off from the hospital. Most of the excitement was over for now, and all that was left was the cleaning up.

Wiley and Bollinger rode around for another hour, but other than what gossip they could pick up at a few markets and cafes, they didn't learn very much of anything. Harpe managed to steal some clothes for Bollinger from a clothesline in somebody's backyard, and Bollinger was thankful for that. He was afraid the man was going to kill somebody for a pair of pants, and he sure as hell wasn't ready for that.

The man Wiley took their next car from wasn't so lucky, however. They were turning around from their second drive by of the hospital when they saw a car pull away from the parking lot at the golf course.

Harpe walked out in the middle of the road and flagged the car down.

It was Carl Lee Farmer.

Carl Lee was still mad about the missed two iron shot.

After he'd met the big guy out in the woods, he had broken the two iron. Wrapped the thing around the trunk of the big tree and left it there. And he never did get his game together. He went from bad to worse. Ended up shooting a 102, and even at that he'd fudged a couple of strokes. And he'd lost over a hundred dollars. Then he'd heard the ruckus at the hospital, and he'd gone over there. The hospital was adjacent to the golf course, and it only took a minute for Carl Lee to get there. Seeing Mrs. Dowlen with her throat slashed and what somebody had done to Jack Fowler hadn't helped his disposition a hell of a lot. So he was in no mood to be stopped by some big guy standing in the middle of the street.

The big guy walked over to the door and started to speak to Carl, but before he could open his mouth, Carl shoved the door open as hard as he could and jumped out of the car.

"What are you trying to do buddy? It's a wonder I didn't run over you the way you walked out in the road like that. I ought to kick your big butt all the way back to wherever you came from. What d'ya think about that?"

The big man didn't answer. His eyes had a strange glow about them, and Carl noticed it a few seconds too late. The man's right fist flashed out and landed on the point of Carl's jaw with enough force to break four teeth even as it knocked Carl Lee unconscious.

Carl Lee never woke up. He was found the next morning on the eighteenth green by the grounds keeper who was turning on the sprinkler system. Carl had a sand wedge driven through his head and its twisted shaft was pinning him to the neatly mown grass. It was ironic at the least, the grounds keeper thought, when he saw Carl was only about a foot from the hole.

One thing was for sure, Carl Lee had broken his last golf club.

BOWLING GREEN, KENTUCKY

When Beth's ten-year old Oldsmobile pulled into the drive, Emily ran out to meet it. She opened the back door, un-buckled the baby's seat belt harness from his car seat and took him out of the car.

As Beth slid out from under the wheel, Emily was already holding Josh and dancing around in the front yard with him.

Beth looked at Emily and grinned. "Ain't you even gonna say hello to me, Aunt Em?" she teased.

"Of course I am honey, but you got to wait a minute or two while I see my baby. This child is growing like a weed. I always knew you'd have beautiful kids, Bethany Suzanne Roberts, but even I never thought you'd have one as perfect as this little guy."

"Well, I think he's pretty special, but I might be a just a teeny little bit prejudiced. Course, the last couple of months he's been a handful. That's one of the reasons I'm here. I'm just about at my wits end, and I want you to watch him for me for about a week while I take a little time off. I'm about to go crazy."

Emily could see there was something really big wrong with her niece, but it was too soon to start asking questions. Beth would tell her all about it in her own time. "Come on in the house and let's have something cold to drink. Then we'll load the car and head over to the park for awhile, if that's OK with you?"

"I can't wait," was all Beth could manage to say, she was so relieved to be here at last.

The park was crowded.

As hot as the weather had been every swimming pool in the city was packed with people trying to find a little relief. There were people scattered all around the park, all trying to find a spot under a shade tree where they could sit and feel the light breeze that blew off the beautiful Barren River that bordered the park.

Over on the other side of the park, the regular Sunday afternoon drag races were getting ready to start, and the roar of the engines could be heard in every corner of the entire park ground. Beth loved this park, as did countless other people from all around the area. It was an old park, and had brought summer fun and relaxation to kids and adults for over a hundred years.

Bethany and Emily found a nice spot under one of the old beech trees that grew all over the park, and spread their blanket on the ground. Beth got the playpen out of the trunk of the car and set it up as Emily took Josh down to show him the creek. By the time Emily returned, Beth had the crib set up, and had opened each of them a bottle of pop. Beth had on tight white shorts, and already a couple of guys had whistled at her. She sat down on the blanket, leaned back and rested on her elbows.

Might as well enjoy the attention while I can, she thought.

Emily placed the baby in the playpen and sat down beside Beth. She took a bottle of cola from Beth, took a long drink, and then said, "O.K. punkin', tell your old auntie all about it."

Bethany couldn't hold it back any longer. She started to softly cry, and as the tears fell, the words began to rush out of her. She had been upset for so long, and had been trying to handle everything all alone, that it had finally become more than she could deal with. Emily was the only one she could talk to, and it was a relief to finally have someone she could confide in.

The baby slept peacefully in the crib, blissfully oblivious to the roar of the powerful dragsters so close as hand. For some reason, he seemed to be more at ease than he'd been for several months.

Once Bethany started talking, the words gushed out in a torrent of emotion, filled with anger, fear, and a sizable helping of frustration. After a while, Mike woke up and they walked around the park, taking turns carrying him across their shoulder. All the while, Bethany continued to talk, laying all her troubles at Emily's feet. Seeking advice, and finding that just letting everything out seemed to help more than anything.

Beth felt so much better after an hour or so, she decided to call in sick at work the next day and spend a couple more days here in Bowling Green with Emily. Hell, Florida could wait. The beach would still be there when she decided to go. She'd much rather spend a little time with Emily, trying to get her head back together.

Of course, Emily didn't mind Beth and the baby staying with her for a few days, but she couldn't shake the feeling that a storm was brewing, and the three of them were going to be caught up in the middle of it.

They returned to where they'd spread the blanket and had a sandwich and some potato chips, and sat there while Beth kept talking to Emily about her problems. They were pretty much alone now that most of the people were watching the races, and the peacefulness of the shade trees they passed the afternoon away.

It was late in the afternoon when Beth looked up and saw the two men standing over the crib, looking down at the baby.

Emily noticed the two men about the same time as Bethany. "Hey," she shouted, "what are you doing over there?"

"Nothin', ma'am, not a thing. Just admiring the child," one of the men replied. "He sure is a pretty little feller. What's his name?"

"That ain't none of your business, boys, and you'd best be moving along before we call the park cop."

"We ain't done nothin' ma'am. No reason to call the cops when nothin's happened. Like I said, we're just admiring the child. Ain't no law against that, is there?"

"No, there's no law against that," Emily replied, "but you've admired him long enough. Now get out of here."

The man never took his eyes from the child as he asked his next question. "This here baby is a Harpe child, ain't it ma'am?" He slowly turned his gaze toward Bethany. His voice had an edge to it that hadn't been there when he first spoke, a hint of harshness that sounded cold and strained.

Bethany looked up with frightened eyes at the mention of the name, and the concern on her face was plain for everyone to see.

"What makes you say that, Mister?" Beth asked the man.

"Just a hunch, girl, that's all, just a hunch. I got a strong feeling this is a Harpe child, and if it is, well, it might shed a little light on my situation."

"Well, the baby ain't no Harpe, that's for sure," Emily almost shouted at the man. "You can bet on that, Mister. Tell him how silly that idea is, Beth." Turning her eyes back toward the stranger, she said. "If you knew who this girl was, Mister, you'd know there ain't no way the child can possibly be a Harpe."

"I do know who the girl is, lady. Maybe not just exactly, but pretty damn close. She's a Roberts. That's for sure. Ain't no way I could miss that smile. Not even after this long a time. In fact, I'd say I know her better than you do. Maybe even better than she knows herself. I ain't wrong about this, am I girl. You are a Roberts, and this is a Harpe child."

"How do you know she's a Roberts? You been following us? We're not scared of you mister, you or your friend. Don't think we are. There's a law against stalking people, you know."

"I ain't been followin' you at all, lady. I don't reckon as how I ever set eyes on either of you till just now. But I know she's a Roberts, cause I been a friend of the family for years."

"I don't recall ever seeing you before, and I've been in the family all my life," Emily said. "Just who are you a friend of?"

"I'm a friend of hers, lady, and of Ms. Roberts and the child as well. They just don't know it yet." Without another word, the man leaned down into the playpen and scooped the child up in one big hand.

"Put the baby down. Do it now," the second man spoke for the first time.

The first man turned on the second man with an unconcealed ferocity in his eyes. "You got two things you can do to keep me from killin' you feller," he said, and there was a ring of truth in his words.

"The first thing you can do is shut up, and the other is to shut up a damn sight quicker. Now that should be clear, even to you. Don't ever tell me what to do. The only one who can do that is Kiga."

John Bollinger was on very thin ice, and he knew it, but he didn't know if Harpe would hurt the baby or not. After the incident with the golf club, he knew the man was insane, and capable of just about anything. He also knew he'd have to try and stop him if he started to harm the baby.

"Don't worry, Bollinger, I ain't gonna hurt this child," Wiley said. "I told you this is a Harpe child, and I think he's a first born son. I've been feelin' his presence ever since we left Russellville. That's how I knew where to come." He turned back toward the two women and took a few steps closer, still holding the child.

"Girl, I'm askin' you for the last time. Are you a Roberts, and is this a Harpe child? I'll know if you lie, girl, and I'll only tell you the one time."

Bethany looked deep into the eyes of the big stranger, and for a fleeting instant thought she recognized him. Yet that was impossible. She'd never seen this man before in her life. How could he know she was a Roberts? More importantly, how could he know Mike was a true Harp? No one knew that for sure, except for herself and Josh. They'd never told a soul.

She tried to tear her eyes from the man, but found she couldn't. The longer she looked at him, the more familiar he became. For some reason, this big man seemed to be calming her and filling her with a sense of safety and belonging. It was almost as if she had known him forever.

Casting a sideways glance at Emily, Beth said. "It's true, I am a Roberts, although I don't know how you knew that." Then, for some strange reason even she didn't understand, she looked straight into the strangers deep blue eyes and said, in a voice that was almost a whisper, "and the baby is a Harp."

Emily gasped. She couldn't believe what she'd heard. It couldn't be true. Roberts and Harps didn't have kids, it just wasn't done. Everyone in the family knew that.

Sensing Emily feelings, Beth quickly tried to explain.

"Josh and me were in love, Aunt Emily, that's how it happened. We wanted to get married, but we knew it was impossible. Then I got pregnant. We even thought about an abortion, but I wanted the baby so bad. We couldn't tell anybody, you know that. Ain't no telling what would have happened if folks had found out the truth. But it's over now. That's why I came up here to visit you. I had to talk to somebody."

The words were rushing out even faster than they had this afternoon, not that the truth was out in the open. Emily just stood there, not wanting to accept the story, but knowing it was true. Little Mike was a Harp. Bethany wasn't lying, Emily could see that now, and the big stranger knew it too.

Maybe he was telling the truth too, when he said he knew Bethany better than Emily did. The man was probably right about that. Emily gritted her teeth together, and closed her fists so tightly her nails dug into her palms. She was getting madder by the minute.

"Just who are you mister?" Emily asked. "Now that you know all about us, it's time we learned a little about you."

Wiley shot Bollinger a sideways look, and decided it wouldn't do any more damage if he heard the rest of the story. The Nashville cop had made up his mind to kill Wiley, first chance he got, and Wiley knew it. Wiley also knew it wouldn't be too much longer before Bollinger was history. That's just the way it was. Wiley didn't know why he'd brought him along in the first place. Just for someone to talk to, and someone to drive for awhile. That's all. Hell, he hadn't had anyone to talk to for a long time.

With a short sigh, Wiley decided to tell the women as much of the story as he knew, and let the officer listen. Maybe they'd be able to help him figure out just what the hell was going on.

"My name is Wiley Harpe, ma'am," he began, and saw a flicker of something flash across the eyes of both women. "And I've been knowing the Roberts women for over two hundred years."

HAWK AND TRABUE

Daniel Hawk was relieved to find Stegall wasn't dead. The man was contrary as hell, but in the few short hours they'd been together, Hawk had come to like him. One thing for sure, old Stegall was dedicated in his fight against Harpe. He'd carried on the family tradition as well as he could. He was just no match for the monster. But then again, neither was Hawk.

Daniel turned to the man beside him and said. "My name is Daniel Hawk, Mister, I don't think I caught yours?"

"Trabue, Jacob Trabue. From Mississippi. I've been trying to catch up with Harpe for two days now. Looks like this is as close as I've been yet."

"Two days? That's how long I've been after him. He's been coming down through Kentucky like a hot knife through soft butter."

"Like hell he's coming down through Kentucky," Jake replied. "I followed him up the Natchez Trace from Mississippi yesterday and today. He left a string of bodies behind him that's hard to believe."

"What makes you think you're following Micajah Harpe anyway, Trabue? I know damn well that's who I'm after. Hell, I've been face to face with him twice already."

"Micajah Harpe? Hell, I ain't following nobody named Micajah. I'm after Wiley Harpe. Don't tell me there's more than one of them? I don't know if I could handle any news like that." Jake knew damn well he didn't want to hear any news like that anyway.

"Well, handle it or not, I'm afraid it's true. At least, if you know for sure you're after Wiley, then there's two of them. I know for sure which one I'm after, and it ain't Wiley. The Big Harpe turned up in Kentucky and me and Stegall have been trying to stop him."

"Stegall? Is that the feller whose head is up in the tree?" Jake was curious.

"Nah. I thought it was as first, but it's not him. I guess Stegall had enough sense not to try to fight him alone. Harpe ain't a man to screw with, but I guess you know that."

"I know Wiley Harpe ain't nobody to screw with, that's for damn sure. He's the meanest sumbitch I ever ran across. Human life don't mean a damn thing to him. He's been killing people just for the hell of it part of the time. Ten or fifteen already, I think. If Micajah is anything like Wiley, you don't want to mess around with either of them."

"Well, hoss, I don't want bust your bubble, but Wiley is the one they call 'Little Harpe.' I've been chasing his big brother. They called Micajah The Big Harpe. He's bigger than Wiley, he's badder than Wiley, and from all I can learn about the two, Micajah makes Wiley look like a Sunday school teacher."

"He'd have to teach Sunday school in Hell, then." Jake said. "I've seen what this man is capable of, and if his big brother is worse than Wiley is, we'd better call in the Marines and let them handle it."

"The Marines won't believe us, hoss, and neither will the police. Hell, I wouldn't believe a story like this either, would you?"

"Probably not. But if no one will believe us, you know what that means?" Jake wished he didn't know what it meant.

"I think it means we've got to catch 'em by ourselves. And it means we've got our work cut out for us. I told you I faced Micajah twice, and for some reason I don't think the third time will be the charm."

"Well, maybe not, but I guess we got to do it. If you can't handle the fightin' Injun, hop back in your car and head home. I'll fight both of 'em by myself. That sumbitch killed one of my best friends and a little girl, and I know he has to be stopped. Seeing as how there ain't no one but you and me that know what's going on, it don't look like we've got a hell of a choice. What's it gonna be, red man? You gonna fight or what?"

"I ain't got no choice either," Hawk said. "This fight has been brewing in my family for two hundred years. OK, you got any guns. Old Stegall thought that damn knife he had would be enough to stop Harpe, but Harpe made him eat it. My Dad sent me to find some kind of magical tomahawk, and that's the only weapon I've got. I think we need some guns."

"Well, I've got a .357 pistol and a hunting rifle. You know how to shoot?"

"Damn, Trabue, I'm a full blooded Cherokee Indian. What do you think? I've been handling guns since I was four. Let's get out of here."

Daniel and Jake took one last look at the grinning head in the tree, still illuminated by several flashlights. "You didn't have much of a chance, feller," Hawk said, "but maybe you'll be glad to know I'm gonna give it one more try."

MICAJAH

Micajah felt better than he had since he'd awakened and found himself in this body, and in this lifetime. The first part of the hunt was over. He'd found Susan, and he'd had his revenge against the town that had treated her so cruelly. He had fought Stegall and recovered his knife, and even though he hadn't killed his old enemy, he knew he'd have another chance. Stegall would come back. It wasn't in him to give up. The next time they met, he'd keep the promise he made to the man two hundred years ago.

Micajah knew it was time to leave Russellville. Too many people had seen him, and if he stayed, it was just a matter of time until they caught him. He had other business to attend to, and he'd already taken a harsh toll on the people of this little Kentucky town. It was time to leave. He had to find the Amulet, and he had to stop the baby from crying, one way or another.

Micajah was out of the woods and into another vehicle before they found the man's head in the tree. He had killed the first man that came into the woods in pursuit of Stegall and himself, and had placed the head in a tree knowing it would slow down the other men hunting him. While they were standing in the woods shining their lights at the head in the tree, Micajah was already headed for Bowling Green, where he thought he could feel the presence of the Amulet. And the baby as well, if his senses were right.

Something else very strange had been happening for the last couple of hours as well. He was feeling another presence, this one much stronger than the others. It was one he hadn't felt for almost two hundred years. Unless he was wrong, he was feeling the presence of his brother Wiley.

One thing was for damn sure, he'd know in a few hours.

BOWLING GREEN

"That's the story. At least, that's all I know about what the hell's going on."

Wiley had told John Bollinger and the two women everything he knew, from the time he found himself in this body, right up to the minute he had been drawn to this park by the energy emanating from both the Amulet and the baby.

"I don't know why or how this is happening, but I suspect the Wolf is behind it all. And I know is Micajah is in Kentucky and headed this way. I know my brother, and he'll be wantin' the Amulet back as fast as he can get it. He'll be wantin' to find this baby, too. He'll know where to come, just like I did."

"Just what do you think will happen when your brother gets here," Bollinger wanted to know? He'd been riding in the car with Wiley and knew the man was the most dangerous killer he'd ever seen. If his brother was even more dangerous, the people of Bowling Green were about to have their worst nightmares come true.

"Hell, Bollinger, I don't know what Micajah might do. He's the true Wolf, not me. He'll be wantin' to see Miss Roberts and the child, and he'll be lookin' to feed the Wolf. If the Wolf is awake, he'll be hungry. And Micajah won't waste any time in findin' a few tasty morsels. I'll guarantee you that was him we heard about on the radio raisin' hell in Russellville today. And that was just a start."

Emily looked at Wiley and in a voice almost too soft to hear she asked. "Do you think you'll be able to stop him, Wiley? Your brother, I mean. Can you keep him from killing people here in Bowling Green the way he did in Russellville?"

It was John Bollinger who answered her question.

"Stop him? Wiley's not going to try to stop his brother, ma'am. He's going to join him. Ain't that right, you big son-of-a-bitch?"

For a moment, there was no answer from Wiley. He just stood and looked at the Nashville cop, a puzzled expression in his eyes. Then in the coldest voice John Bollinger had ever heard, Wiley spoke;

"Yeah, Bollinger, I plan to join my brother. That's why I returned, and it's not something I'm ashamed of. I'm a Harpe. There's no way you can understand what that means. I'm a Wolf, and we don't live by the same rules you do. But the girl understands. Look at her eyes, Bollinger, she knows exactly what I'm talking about. She'll follow Kiga the same way as I will. I'll join my brother, and the

Wolf will feast. And your soul will be one of the first it devours." Wiley's eyes burned into the eyes of John Bollinger, and the cop shivered.

But Bollinger didn't back down, not this time. If Harpe was going to kill him, let him get it over with. He knew the man was a psychopath and if he wasn't stopped there was no telling how many innocent people might suffer. Bollinger wasn't sure if he could beat Harpe, but he had to try. He knew for damn sure if Wiley managed to join up with Micajah the two of them would be almost unstoppable. If a miracle happened and Bollinger did stop Wiley, the danger would be cut in half. But it sure as hell wasn't much of a chance. If John could get Wiley mad, he might make a mistake. If he made a mistake then Bollinger could possibly take him down. No, it wasn't much of a chance, but right now it was the only game in town.

Bollinger took a gamble he might be able to get Wiley mad, and live through it.

"Don't give me that 'Wolf' crap. I can understand a murdering psycho like you better than you think. You get off on killing, damnit, and that's why you do it. You like to kill, and you'll keep on doing it until somebody stops you. Well, that somebody is gonna be me, and it's gonna be right now." John Bollinger was saying everything he could think of, trying to make Harpe mad.

"If you're trying to make me mad, Bollinger, it ain't working. I ain't never said I didn't like to kill people. You ever hear me say that? I told you I was a Harpe, didn't I? Well, Harpes kill people. That's what we do best. And make no mistake Bollinger, we're damned good at it. Maybe the best there ever was. As far as trying to get under my skin, I know you think if you can make me really mad, I might get a little careless, and you can jump me. That what you had in mind, Bollinger?"

"Got to admit it is, Harpe, but what's the difference? One way or another, I've got to try and stop you."

"Yeah, I guess you have at that. Damn shame too, you remind me of a feller I used to know, back in the old days. He was a lawman too. The same man I asked you about before. Joseph Ballenger, himself. Caught me and Kiga once. Only man that ever managed to shackle us. Couldn't hold us though. But he was a decent man, and treated us right while we were in his jail. You do remind me of him in a lot of ways. Bollinger, I'd just as soon not kill you, to tell the truth. But if you won't just walk away and let it go, that's the way it's gotta be. You won't just walk away, will you?"

"You know me better than that, Wiley. I got to try and stop you and your brother, that's my job."

"Well, they don't pay you enough, that's for damn sure." Wiley replied, almost sadly, as the blue flame began to kindle in his eyes.

Bollinger hadn't tried to jump Harpe before because the big killer had at least two guns, and maybe more, and Bollinger knew he'd use them. The policeman training in Bollinger told him if shots were fired in a park such as this, there would probably be innocent people hurt. He'd wanted to avoid that, but now it looked as if he had little choice. He had to fight the man, and he had to fight him now.

"You talk a good fight, Harpe, but that's easy for a man with two or three guns. Why don't you lay down the weapons and at least give me a sporting chance?"

"I ain't never been much of a gambler, Bollinger. I think I'll keep the guns. Hell, you might get lucky and actually get in a good punch or two. Naw, I'll fight you for a while, then I'll shoot you. Don't take it personally, though, I'd do the same for anyone."

Suddenly Harpe hit Bollinger so quickly the cop didn't even see it coming. Bollinger had never been hit that fast, or that hard. The blow slammed him back against a tree and lights went off inside his eyelids. It wasn't bells he heard either, it was a damned freight train roaring through his head. For a long minute he sat leaning against the tree trunk, trying to clear the cobwebs from his brain. He thought about not getting back up. John Bollinger wasn't afraid, but he'd never seen anyone like Harpe before, and now he knew damn well he didn't stand a chance. The man would kill him whenever he wanted too. But he lurched to his feet anyway. No matter what happened, he had to keep trying.

He was surprised to find Harpe wasn't even looking at him. He was looking at the Roberts girl, a little smile on his face.

Damn, thought Bollinger, *this guy is trying to impress the girl. Well, one thing's for sure, he's impressing the hell out of me.*

He took a running leap at Harpe's back.

Leaving his feet when he was still five or six feet from the man, Bollinger hit Harpe high in the back with both feet. The blow drove the killer forward, and Bollinger heard the air rush out of his lungs in a loud gasp. As quickly as he could, he launched a savage left fist straight into Harpes midsection and was satisfied to see a flash of pain cross Harpe's face as his blow landed hard into his ribcage.

Without letting up even a little bit, John pressed his advantage. As Harpe's head came forward with the blow, Bollinger laced both fists together and drove them as hard as he could down on the back of his neck. Again he drove his fists downward, and was again satisfied to hear a grunt escape the killer's mouth. Bollinger reached forward and locked his fingers in Harpe's hair, forcing his head up. "Look at me, you son-of-a-bitch," he yelled. "Look at me. I told you my time would com..."

Suddenly John Bollinger was staring directly into the raging blue inferno of the Wolf's eyes. Instead of pain, he saw fury. Instead of fear, Bollinger saw the wild, unbridled rage that lived within the man. When John Bollinger saw how the flame danced and flared in Harpes eyes, he knew the fight was over.

With a savage cry that was more animal than human, Wiley threw back his head, shook Bollinger off, and leaped to his feet. With dizzying speed, he grabbed Bollinger by the throat and lifted him off the ground as if he were a small child. For a moment Harpe stood there holding John off the ground, shaking him in the air. Then with a mighty heave, Harpe threw Bollinger to the ground with enough force to stun him. Once again the light show started inside the policeman's head, and for a second, he thought he was going to lose consciousness.

When he finally managed to get his eyes to focus again, he found himself staring upward at the sole of Harpes boot, as it was swiftly descending. John Bollinger saw Harpe's foot start down towards his head. Exerting all his speed and strength, he brought both hands up and managed to grab Harpe's boot and slow it down. Although he couldn't quite stop it, he did deflect the foot. Instead of crushing his head, the boot hit him a glancing blow just above the ear, and again he heard the explosion in his head.

Bollinger twisted his body hard to the right, and pulled downward on Harpe's foot at the same time. Wiley lost his balance and stumbled backward, falling hard against the same tree that Bollinger had hit earlier. As Bollinger rolled over and groggily regained his feet, he saw the tree hadn't slowed down Harpe at all. The big killer was standing, glaring at Bollinger, and both men knew Harpe intended to kill the Nashville policeman this time. It was all over but the shouting, and John Bollinger knew it.

Suddenly the baby began to cry.

Time seemed to come to an abrupt stop.

Wiley stood where he was, not moving a muscle, as though he were waiting for something.

Bethany Roberts started to move toward the crib, but she too stopped dead in her tracks, unsure of what to do.

Emily stood as if she were a statue, unmoving and silent, almost not even breathing.

John Bollinger stared at Wiley, and knew something strange was going on. The man had been ready to kill him, and had stopped without a word.

The only sound Bollinger could hear was his own ragged breathing, and the sound of his heart as it tried to tear itself out of his chest.

Above it all was the sound of the crying infant.

Suddenly, he was there.

Bollinger didn't see or hear the man approach; he just seemed to appear out of nowhere. For a moment he stood at the edge of the trees, silently staring at the crying baby, and then he began to slowly walk in their direction.

The stranger walked over to the crib and looked at the child.

"Hush, little one, you have nothing to fear."

As suddenly as he started crying, the baby stopped.

Turning to Bethany, the man continued.

"Pick up the child, girl, and gather your things. We'll be leaving here shortly." His words weren't in the form of a question, but were a direct statement and meant to be obeyed.

Without a word, and without question, Beth did as the man said, as though it were the most natural thing in the world to follow his orders.

Then, for the first time, the man turned his gaze towards Wiley, and their eyes met across the few feet that separated them. The wild blue flame in Wiley's eyes met by an even more intense flame flowing from the eyes of the other man. The energy in the clearing crackled and flared about them, and the air itself seemed charged with supernatural forces, almost powerful enough to be seen. For another moment, there in the middle of a park in Bowling Green, Kentucky, time stood still.

Today, for the first time in almost two hundred years, the Harpe brothers were together again.

The Wolf was loose, and terrible would be the price of anyone unlucky enough to cross into his hunting grounds.

"Hot damn, Kiga, but you're a sight for sore eyes." Wiley said, with just the slightest trace of a catch in his voice.

"So are you, little brother, and so are you," Micajah said, and then stepped forward and embraced his brother.

"We have much to talk about, Wiley, much to catch up on, but it can wait until we're in a slightly less public place. Right now, tell me what's going on with this feller." He pointed a big finger in John Bollinger's direction.

"This here's a friend of mine, Micajah, one I met down in Nashville. He's a policeman, name's John Bollinger. Bollinger, say hello to my big brother, Micajah Harpe."

Bollinger didn't trust himself to speak, and so he remained silent, preferring to see what else happened.

"Don't guess he wants to talk right now, Micajah. Probably because me and him was having a little disagreement when you showed up."

"Must have been a hell of a disagreement, Wiley. It looked to me as if you were fixing to kill him. That's a good way to end a friendship."

"Well, I might have killed him, I can't say for sure. Probably would have, to tell the truth. He's done made me mad, and you know how I get sometimes."

"Yeah, I reckon I do know how you get sometimes," Micajah replied, with a hint of a laugh in his voice.

Micajah walked over to get a better look at the man Wiley had been fighting with.

John Bollinger had always said that as long as you were breathing, you stood a chance of winning every battle. No matter what the odds, you still had a chance as long as you stayed cool, didn't lose your head, and believed in yourself. He took one close-up look at Micajah Harpe, and quit believing all of that crap. Bollinger was still breathing, and was in pretty good shape, in spite of the fight he'd just had. He was a tough, mean man in his own right, but this time, without a doubt, he knew he had about as much chance against this man as a little gold fish in room full of hungry tomcats. Bollinger had thought Wiley was the baddest man he'd ever met, but this damned guy standing here was absolutely the most awesome flesh and blood person he'd ever seen.

The man was big, six-five or six-six and about three hundred pounds, but that wasn't all of it. He didn't look as if he had an ounce of fat anywhere on his body. He had coal black hair, was clean-shaven, except for a light stubble, and was deeply tanned. But what sent chill after chill running down John Bollinger's backbone was the energy of the man. The power seemed to ripple off his body in waves, and as the waves washed across Bollinger he realized the power was more than any normal human man could control. When Bollinger at last found his eyes caught up in the icy stare of Harpe, he knew the man was no normal human. John Bollinger knew that here before him stood the most dangerous man in the world. Wiley was a killer, Bollinger knew that, and capable of cold-blooded murder at the drop of a hat, but Bollinger had confronted killers before.

Micajah was something else entirely.

Not only a killer, but a destroyer as well.

The power that lived in the man was un-natural and evil, and hungered for innocent blood, and it was that hunger Bollinger felt most of all, and feared most of all. For one of the few times in his life, John Bollinger admitted he was indeed afraid. Not only for himself, but for everyone in this part of the country. Hell, maybe for everyone in the entire country. He for sure as hell didn't know how this monster could be stopped.

Then the monster spoke to John Bollinger.

"Well, Mister Nashville Policeman, from what little I saw of the fight, it looked like you might of been a little angry yourself. Course, you'd have to be pretty angry, or a little bit crazy, or both, to get into a fight with Wiley. That ain't the smartest thing in the world to do. You're lucky he thinks of you as a friend."

"Yeah, I was pretty damn mad, that's for sure. And I ain't no friend to him. I'm gonna kill him if I get half a chance, and he knows it. And I'll kill you too, for that matter."

Bollinger knew he was talking too much, but he was dangerously close to panicking, and once the words started, there was no way he could hold them in. He was mad as hell too. Screw Wiley, and screw his big brother too. If they were gonna kill him, there wasn't a damn thing he could do to stop it, so what the hell. Feed 'em fish heads and screw 'em.

"I can see why Wiley likes you so much, feller. We've always been a little partial to a man that speaks his mind." Micajah stopped for a moment and motioned to Wiley. "C'mon over here a minute, brother, and let me show you something. Look at this old boy's eyes. He might call himself Bollinger, but this feller's real name is Ballenger. Old Joe Ballenger was an ancestor of his, less I miss my guess."

Turning his attention back to Bollinger, Micajah went on. "Like I said, I hate a man that speaks out of both sides of his mouth at the same time. I hate to have somebody tell me he's a friend, then stab me in the back first chance he gets. I'd rather know a man is against me, like you are, than to wonder where he stands." This was as close as Micajah ever came to paying anyone a compliment.

He once again turned and spoke to Wiley.

"Wiley, what do you think?" he asked. "Turn him loose or kill him? It's all the same to me." He turned back to Bollinger before Wiley answered.

"Like I said, Mister Bollinger, you're a likeable man. The problem is, you're our enemy. Just because we know you want to blow our heads off, or cut out our hearts, or whatever, don't mean we're likely to let you do it. I respect you, as a man of character and spirit, and I respect your honesty, and for those reasons, I'd like to let you go. But I got a feelin' that would be a big mistake. Wiley, you think if we turn him loose, he'll just go on home and let us be?"

"Naw, brother, I don't. Bollinger is too good a cop for that. If we let him go, he'll try to hunt us down and kill us. It just ain't in him to quit."

"That's about the way I read him too, brother. No hard feelings, Bollinger, but we think you'd just be too big a problem for us if we let you go. Shoot him, Wiley, but try not to make him suffer too much. I kinda like him too."

John Bollinger looked straight at Wiley Harpe, determined to meet his death the same way he'd lived his life, and was as surprised as the others when a loud voice rang out.

"It's about time you got that kid to shut up," the voice said, and then continued, "I was about ready to do it myself."

Wiley had reached into his belt for the pistol that was concealed there when the words were first spoken, and both he and Micajah turned to look at the men who had just walked up.

There were nine of them, and they looked like they were as bad as you can get. Dressed in black jeans and cut off tee shirts, the men were members of the "Low Riders," one of the motorcycle clubs that regularly visited the park. These were the kind of guys that gave motorcycle clubs a bad name.

The Low Riders liked to think they were the toughest bikers this side of the Mississippi, and maybe they were. But even as bad as they were, for the most they just got drunk and fought among themselves. Of course, every now and then, when they'd had a little too much to drink or gotten a little too high, they liked to show off by beating up picnickers in the park. Today, when they'd heard the baby crying, and when they saw there were only three men in the party, they decided to have a little fun.

The problem was, the fun was about to have them.

"What'd you say, feller?" Micajah asked, his quiet voice masking the danger in his words.

"I said it was about time you shut that kid up. Whatsamatter, you deef or somethin'? Maybe I need to slap the wax out of your ears so you can hear."

The guy was almost as big as Micajah, and it was a safe bet he knew how to handle himself. He'd probably be hell on wheels in a free for all.

Micajah looked at the big biker, and the flame began to dance in the back of his eyes.

Deep in the spirit world, the Wolf sensed the impending trouble, and also opened his eyes. The men standing in front of Harpe were nothing more than wildly flaring energy patterns to the eyes of the Wolf, but they smelled of food.

Thiss isss foood, Harrrpe, I feeel itt. Goood. Hungrry.

Micajah shot Wiley a quick glance, and saw the fire mirrored in his eyes.

Another look was directed towards John Bollinger, to see if the man looked as if he might join the bikers when the fight started.

"How 'bout it Bollinger, you gonna join the dance, or sit this one out?"

"Think I'll sit this one out boys," Bollinger replied, "my dance card's full, and I don't like the song they playing anyway. I think I'll just watch, and maybe find out if you're as tough as I think you are."

"Your decision feller. But if you change your mind later and decide to take their part, forget that crap I told Wiley about not making you suffer. He'll blow you away a piece at a time. And I'll only tell you the one time."

"What the hell are you doing?" the big biker shouted at Micajah. "You'd better be worried about me, not him."

Micajah gave the biker a slow, sideways look, and then silently spoke inwardly to the Wolf.

Yeah, Wolf, this is food, for damn sure.

Suddenly, as if by magic, the big knife appeared in Micajah's hand, and before the biker had stopped speaking the blade parted the air with an evil hiss as Micajah thrust it forward with a speed too fast for the eye to follow.

The swift, savage thrust caught the man low in the belly and with hardly a grunt Micajah ripped the blade upwards, disemboweling him with a single stroke. The man on the bikers right tried to react, but it was almost as if he were in slow motion. Before he could move, the knife finished its killing work on the first man, left his body, and continued traveling upwards until it buried itself in the left temple of the second man.

Turning loose of the blade, Micajah leaped sideways and brought his foot around in a mighty kick. The heavy boot came up and into the jaw of the third biker. He flew backward from the force of the blow like a leaf in a tornado, and was dead before he hit the ground. From the way his head hung loosely to one side, it was plain his neck was broken. Harpe came to a stop in front of the fourth man, and by now the flame was a hotbed of raging blue fire.

Bollinger looked at Harpe, his mouth hanging open in shock and disbelief. He couldn't believe what he'd just witnessed. Not ten seconds had passed, and already three men were dead, and the damned Big Harpe wasn't even breathing hard.

The man wasn't as bad as Bollinger had thought he might be, he was fifty times as bad as anything Bollinger had ever even had a nightmare about.

The remaining bikers knew by this time they had screwed up, and screwed up really bad. But they couldn't stop now. Somehow, they didn't think this guy would let them quit.

They were right.

Harpe grasped the closet man by the face with his right hand and began to squeeze. Two of the other bikers took this opportunity to grab Harpe, but they couldn't make him turn loose of the man he held.

Slowly the veins in Harpe's arms began to stand out. The muscles began to bulge in his forearms as he exerted more and more pressure on the man's head. Under the tightening fingers, the skin of the man's face began to turn white, as the blood flow was restricted. His eyes became distended, and his breathing grew more and more labored. Suddenly his ears ruptured and blood burst from them in a torrent, and a moment later his eyes gave up the fight and popped from his head in a watery spray of blood and tears.

The men holding Harpe tried desperately to turn loose, but by then it was too late. The Wolf was out of control and in a feeding frenzy, and Harpe couldn't have stopped then even if he'd wanted to.

With a hand dripping with blood, he delivered a backhand blow to the man on his right, and without even watching as the man fell, Harpe turned to the assailant on the left. The man stared into Harpe's eyes and stood deathly still, almost as if he were hypnotized by the raging blue flame he saw burning there.

Harpe took a second to look around, almost as if he didn't really know what had happened. Four of the bikers were dead, and a fifth lay on the ground, the side of his head caved in. One man stood directly in front of Harpe, unable to move, and the last three were also standing still, staring at the big killer as if they couldn't understand what to do.

The speed with which he had attacked was uncanny, almost supernatural, and the force of his blows was unbelievable. But the most awesome thing about the man was the uncivilized ferocity of his attack. He was more like a wild animal than a man, showing absolutely no compassion, and giving no quarter whatsoever. The bikers were used to violence and fighting, and they weren't afraid, but they had never met anyone like Harpe. As Micajah reached for the man closest to him, one of the remaining two came to his senses. He decided if he didn't make his move now, he'd probably never get another chance.

Reaching under his shirt in the back, he clawed around until his hand closed around the butt of the little .380 pistol wedged in his belt. He brought the pistol around as fast as he could and took quick aim on Micajah. But even as his finger tightened on the trigger, Harpe's hand tightened in the hair of the man he had reached for. With a quick, powerful sling, he threw the man at the biker with the pistol. The man managed to fire one quick, hastily aimed shot at Harpe, only to see it plow deeply into the side of his friend's jaw as he sailed through the air straight toward him. The body hit the two men sideways with enough force to knock them down, and the last thing the gunman saw was the underside of Harpe's boot as it descended towards his face.

When Micajah turned away from the last of the bikers, Bollinger saw for himself the full fury of the Wolf. Unbridled, unleashed, and out of control.

The blue flame was roaring, a blast furnace of energy totally consuming the man inside which it burned. John had never seen such rage in a man before, and he sat for several long minutes and stared into Harpe's face as the flame began to die down.

Throughout the fight, Wiley had remained calm, almost unconcerned, and at first Bollinger had thought that was strange, when the man's brother was fighting for his life.

But now he understood.

Micajah didn't need Wiley's help, and Wiley knew it. The Big Harpe wasn't fighting for his life. There was never any danger for the big man at all. It was like turning nine lambs loose on a hungry lion, except Micajah was meaner than most hungry lions. Not only that, Bollinger realized, Micajah didn't even want Wiley's help in this fight. The demon inside the man needed to feed on the bikers, and that's exactly what had happened.

Well, one thing's for sure, anyway, Bollinger thought, as he once again surveyed the scattered bodies. These dipsticks won't be getting their kicks by beating up innocent picnickers anymore.

Bethany and Emily gathered up the blankets and put the playpen in the car. Emily was worried about Beth. She didn't usually take up with strangers like she had with these two men.

Beth hurriedly put the baby's toys in the trunk of the car and then said to Micajah. "We're ready when you are, Kiga." The name rolled off her tongue as if she'd spoken it all her life.

For some reason, completely out of character, Micajah had decided to let John Bollinger live.

"Tie him up, Wiley," he said. "He didn't try to kill me when he had the chance just now, and he could have tried if he'd had a notion to. He's a man of his word, so I reckon we'll let him live."

Micajah took a last look at the Nashville cop as Wiley was looping a short length of rope he found in the trunk of the car about his wrists. "Feller, the smartest thing I could do in this situation would be to kill you. I don't like to leave any witness' behind. I want you to know the only reason I'm letting you live is because you kept your word and stayed out of the fight just now. And besides, I don't think anyone will believe yer story anyway. Don't push your luck. If we cross paths again, you'll be just as dead as any one of these fools lying here. I don't give much advice, Bollinger, and even fewer second chances. You'd be well advised to heed my words. And I'll only tell you the one time."

He turned around and walked away, without a backward glance.

With Wiley, the baby and Emily in the back seat and Bethany driving, Micajah seemed to relax for an instant.

Bethany took advantage of the lull to say; "Let's head for Emily's house, if you don't mind. We need to talk, and I really need to know just what the hell is going on here."

Emily couldn't even speak. She was still in shock from seeing Harpe fight and kill the bikers, and it wasn't even real to her that she was in the car with men such at these two. Not only that, but she still couldn't understand what in the hell was happening to Bethany. She'd never seen her like this. Somehow, someway, Emily had to break away for a minute and get to a phone.

HAWK AND TRABUE

Daniel Hawk and Jacob Trabue were headed for Bowling Green as fast as the law allowed, and most of the time a little faster.

The star on the back of Jake's hand had been giving him hell, and he knew he was getting closer and closer to Wiley. He still wasn't sure exactly who the Indian was chasing, but if it really were Big Harpe, then the two of them were in for a world of hurt. All Jake knew for sure was Wiley had somehow come back from being dead two hundred years, and was killing people just like he had back then. If Wiley had come back, then it stood to reason his brother probably had too. So it could be that Hawk was right. If Wiley got together with his big brother, how the hell would they stop them? For that matter, how the hell would anybody stop them? Jake wasn't sure at all about stopping Wiley, let alone Micajah.

Jake had his doubts about Daniel Hawk. The Indian had said himself he'd faced Harpe twice, and didn't even slow him down. Also, Jake didn't know a damn thing about this Stegall character

Hawk had been talking about. There was no telling where the hell he'd run off to, and when he might show up again. Not that he'd be a hell of a lot of help, assuming he even showed up at all.

Jake decided to go along with Hawk for now, but at the first sign something was up, he'd ditch the Indian and try to take out both of the Harpes by himself. He'd made it this far alone, and if push came to shove, he'd fight them with his bare hands. With or without the help of Daniel Hawk. Or Andrew Stegall.

Daniel Hawk didn't know how Jacob Trabue had found out about the Harpes, and he didn't care. All he knew was he needed all the help he could get, and Jake seemed willing to fight the brothers. Daniel also didn't know anything about Wiley Harpe. He hadn't read much about Wiley, concentrating all of his attention on Micajah. He had no idea Wiley had also returned. If Jake was right, and both Harpes were back, this part of the country would run ankle deep in blood if they couldn't stop them. And the animal spirits sure as hell hadn't been much help. They'd told him to find the damn tomahawk, when they should have led him to a fifty-caliber machine gun. Jake had a couple of guns, and some ammunition, and Daniel had the tomahawk, and for right now that would have to do.

What the hell, Daniel thought, The chance's are they'll kill us so damn fast it won't matter if we've got two guns or two hundred.

They were almost to Bowling Green when Jake felt the star on his hand began to throb. Looking down, he noticed a drop of blood had fallen from his hand to his leg. Unbelieving, he touched the back of his hand and found it was bleeding.

"Look at this Hawk," he said, hardly able to control the excitement in his voice. "Look, the crazy star on my hand is bleeding. So far, I've found that means I'm getting closer to Harpe. Or that he's killed someone else. Or both. I'll bet a dollar to a doughnut he's in Bowling Green, and maybe the one you're looking for is there too."

"Yeah," Daniel answered, "and there's no telling what they're doing. One thing's for sure though, you can also bet your butt somebody is catching hell."

Hawk also thought they were getting closer, and he knew they were in for the fight of their lives. Damn, he wished Stegall hadn't ran off. They could use all the help they could get.

BOWLING GREEN

The police were quick to answer the call about the fight in the park, but not quick enough to catch the killers. The Harpes and the women met the Sheriff's car going into the park, as they were leaving.

It was only a little after five when they pulled into the drive at Emily's house. Beth cut the engine and climbed out of the car, as Micajah opened the door on the other side. Micajah unfastened the seat belt holding the baby's car seat, than lifted the baby out, seat and all, and started towards the house.

Wiley also walked toward the house, leaving the two women to follow behind.

When they got inside, Micajah un-strapped the baby from the car seat and stood holding the child and looking at him intently.

"He's a first born son," Micajah said, without taking his eyes away from the baby's face. "I can tell. That's why the crying has bothered me so much. You're a Roberts girl. And this is a Harpe baby." Again, it wasn't a question as much as a statement.

"Yes," was all Bethany could say, and found she didn't need to say anything else. The big man understood completely. Now if only Emily would. But that was probably impossible.

"You know who we are girl?" Micajah asked.

"Kind of. I don't really know much about you, just what Wiley told us in the park, and the stories I remember my Mama telling me when I was a kid. Emily, you remember any of those old stories?"

Suddenly it dawned on Emily exactly who these men were.

"But that's impossible," she exclaimed, "people don't come back from the dead. Especially after two hundred years."

She remembered all right. She'd heard all the old tales herself, when she was a child. She remembered bad dreams, and nightmares, and lying awake scared of the dark. She remembered crying herself to sleep after hearing what all these men had done. Most of all, she remembered being afraid. Afraid of the Terrible Harpes. These two men. She was afraid of them then, and she was afraid of them now.

"Wiley told us his story, suppose you tell us yours? Not that I believe any of this crap, not for a minute, but I'm willing to listen." Emily was trying to buy time. She wanted to call the law, and she thought if she could get the man distracted by talking, she might find a way to slip out and use the phone.

She had no such luck as that. Micajah told his story, but he never once let his attention wander.

"There's not really all that much to tell, ma'am," Micajah began. But for the next few hours the women, and Wiley as well, sat and listened as he told of his last fight, back in 1799, and then told what had happened since he had suddenly found himself alive once again.

He told them about the knife and how Stegall had used it, and how he had gotten it back again just yesterday. He told them of the spirit world, and what he had seen when he'd followed the Wolf that night in the cave at Nickajack. He told of living with the Cherokee, and he and Wiley laughed as they remembered things that had happened almost two hundred years ago, yet were still as fresh in their memories as if they had happened last week. Even Emily was spellbound as the big man talked.

It was plain from listening to him there was more than one side to the man known as Big Harpe. Not that he was a gentle man, far from it. He was a born killer, cruel and almost completely without compassion. But throughout all of his tales, the dark sinister control the Wolf had over the man was evident. It also became plain he had served the evil desires of the spirit Wolf, and had clearly paid a great price for the power of the Amulet.

The Wolf was his inheritance, and with the Wolf in control, the man was capable of little more than carrying out the wishes of the power that lived within his soul.

At the same time, even though the women felt the immense peril that seemed to dwell all too closely about the man, they also felt safe with him. The enormous energy of the Harpe seemed to wrap itself around them, and give them a sense of protection from all danger.

Somehow, they knew nothing could harm them as long as they were in the keeping of this man.

Emily felt the power just as strongly as did Bethany, but still she knew that however much she felt drawn to this big man, she couldn't turn her back on the things he'd done. There was no way she could stay with these men. She had to somehow get away and call the authorities.

Bethany Suzanne felt the power of Micajah Harpe in an entirely different way from her aunt. Beth knew from this day forward, wherever this man went, she'd follow. To Heaven or to Hell, her destiny was to be beside Micajah Harpe, and for some reason, it seemed as if it had always been that way.

EMILY

MONDAY - THE LAST DAY

It was a little after two A.M. when Micajah finally decided to lay down and get some sleep. Emily tried to get him to go into the bedroom, but he refused, stretching out instead on the couch in the living room. Wiley found his way to the second bedroom, and was asleep almost as soon as his head touched the pillow. Micajah lay on the couch for a few moments, staring at the ceiling.

"Conscious bothering you, Harpe," Emily asked, somehow sensing he was still awake.

She could feel his eyes turn in her direction in the darkness, and there was a trace of ice in his reply.

"No, ma'am" he said. "It's not my conscious at all. A conscious can't bother a man if he don't think he's done anything wrong. And I don't think I have. The people I've killed were trying to kill me, or standing in the way of my escape from other people who were trying to kill me. And the people in that damned little town treated Susan wrong. They deserved what they got. So to answer your question again, no it's not my conscious that's on my mind. I'm looking for something, and I know it's real close. In fact, it's here in Bowling Green. I can feel it. That's all I was thinking about. Now if you don't mind, I think I'll get some sleep. Goodnight."

Emily leaned back in her recliner and closed her eyes. She had a plan, but she knew she must be damned sure Harpe was asleep before she tried anything.

It was almost four in the morning before Emily was sure everyone was asleep. She stole over to the couch to check on Micajah, and was surprised to find that in sleep he looked quite innocent. Almost like any other average, clean cut, young man, and not anything at all like the monster she knew he was. She didn't know the face she was looking at in the pale light actually belonged to a barely grown boy named Billy Harp, a boy whose body was only being used by the Wolf as a vessel to hold the spirit power.

Making no more noise than a mouse, Emily silently and very slowly slipped by the couch and made her way to the door. Her hand touched something, and she saw Micajah had laid one of the long knives on the floor, where it would be close at hand should he need it in a hurry. Just for a moment if crossed her mind to try and use the knife on Harpe. One quick slash and it would all be over. All she had to do was quietly pick up the knife, lay it against the skin of his throat, and then cut as hard as she could. But she also knew if she missed, she wouldn't get a second chance. She decided to take the knife with her, and stick with her original plan. Get out of the house and call the damn police, and let them take care of this mess.

After what seemed like an eternity, she made it to the front door and slowly opened it, hoping the hinges wouldn't squeel. God, she'd meant to oil those hinges for months. This would be a hell of a time for them to start squealing. But her luck held, and the hinges barely made any noise at all. She allowed herself a small sigh of relief as she finally crawled out on the front porch into the cool night air.

All the way to the street she remained on her knees, not wanting to take a chance anyone seeing her. She'd have to walk to the market two blocks over and use the phone there. She sure didn't want to wake up any of her neighbors and get them involved with the Harpes. Harpe would kill any of the men she knew and not even break a sweat. Hell no, let the police handle him.

She noticed that Tom Slaughter, her next door neighbor, had his eighteen wheeler cranked up. He was an independent trucker, running from Bowling Green to L.A. once a week, and he often left early in the morning. Tom was a big man himself, and pretty good at taking care of himself, and for a moment she thought about calling on him to help her. She knew Tom would take on Harpe, but she also knew he was no match for the man who was asleep on her couch.

Emily was breathing a little easier by the time she reached the market. She hadn't been able to grab her cell phone as she left the house, but it was still early, and no one was using the pay phone at the market. She fumbled around in her pocket as she walked up the to phone, and found three quarters and two nickels. Her hand was trembling as she dropped two of the quarters in the slot, and she was holding Harpe's big knife with the same hand with which she held the receiver.

She brought the phone to her ear and was calm as she punched the "Nine" with the point of the knife.

She never expected anything at all as she touched the knife to the first "One" and pushed down, but just then, a hand came from behind her and closed over her mouth, and she was roughly jerked away from the phone. She struggled, but it was no use, she couldn't break the hold of whoever had grabbed her. Whoever it was just too damn strong. She felt the knife jerked from her hand, and heard a course voice whisper in her ear; "If you make a sound, you'll eat this blade. One sound, that's all it'll take. Be very, very quiet, and you'll live."

Then she felt herself being guided back down the street, back toward her own house.

HAWK AND TRAUBE

THE LAST DAY

Daniel Hawk and Jake Trabue didn't know a damn thing about Bowling Green, Kentucky. Neither of them had ever been in the city before, and neither knew anyone who lived there. It was late afternoon when they pulled into a McDonalds for a quick bite to eat. As they finished the last of the French fries, Jake broke a little more bad news to Hawk.

"You know, Hawk, the only thing this star on my hand will do is tell us when we're close to Wiley, not exactly where he is. And in case you ain't noticed, this ain't exactly a small town. There ain't no way the star can lead us straight to the son-of-a-bitch. If you got any ideas on how we're gonna find the Harpes, you'd best be lettin' me in on 'em."

"Hell, Jake, I don't know how to find 'em. It was pure luck the last time I ran into Harpe, and the first time was when old Stegall recognized the man out on the Interstate. We sure as hell can't just waltz into the police station and tell 'em what we're doing in town. Damn, son, they'd lock us up, just on general principals."

"Well, we do know they're close," Jake answered, and then paused for a moment, as a silly little grin curled up the corners of his mouth. "Maybe you've got a good idea, at that. Why can't we ask the cops? Or at least, one cop. If we've heard one siren in the last twenty minutes, we must have heard a hundred. Look, let's just stop and ask a city cop what the hell is going on. All they can do is tell us it ain't none of our business."

"That's a fact," Daniel Hawk agreed. "What the hell, it's worth a chance. Let's do it."

They didn't have far to go to find a cop. The city was literally crawling with them. They saw four patrol cars and two unmarked cruisers before they'd driven a mile. In a matter of minutes they spotted two cops in a car parked in front of a boarded up gas station.

"Might as well ask those two," Jake said, and Daniel pulled the car into the lot beside the idling black and white police car.

"Say, officer," Jake began, "what the hell's going on? I ain't never seen this much commotion about anything before."

"What's your name, Buddy," one of the cops asked, looking at Jake first and then moving a bit to get a better view of Daniel.

"My name's Jake Trabue, Officer, of Greenville, Mississippi, and this here's Daniel Hawk. We were just passing through and heard all this commotion and was wonderin' what was happenin'. Didn't mean nothin' by askin'."

"Want to step out of the car, boys," the officer said. Jake saw the second cop had already got out of the patrol car and was coming around in their direction.

"Sure officer, no problem. But we ain't done a damn thing."

The first cop took a good look at Jake and Hawk as they climbed out of their car, and the turned to the second officer who was already most of the way around the car.

"Aw damn, Keith, they ain't nowhere near big enough to be the guys we're looking for. And we ain't got time tonight to screw around with nobody except the guys we've been told about."

Turning back to Jake and Hawk, he said. "You boys can get back in the car. And I'd watch myself it I was you. Lot of trouble coming down around here tonight."

"Sure officer. Like I said, no problem. But what the hell is going on anyway? You've sure as hell have my curiosity stirred up."

"Well, there was a big fight down in the park a while ago, left a bunch of bikers dead. We've got a fair description of the guys that did it, and you're plumb lucky you don't look nothin' like 'em."

"Sounds like a fight between two gangs to me," Daniel said.

"Yeah, we thought so too, at first. But a couple of eyewitness' swear it was just one man fightin' all the bikers, with one or two other guys watching. I been to the park, and I know it's the damnedest thing I ever seen. Look, like I said, you boys be careful tonight. I wouldn't want your first visit to our city to be your last."

"Yes, sir, officer, we surely will. Thanks for the advice," Jake said, and climbed back into the car just as the radio in the police car began to crackle. In another moment, the powerful car sped off with its tires screaming and its siren howling.

Once the cops had gotten out of the parking lot, Jake turned to Daniel and said. "Take us to the park, my good man. Perhaps we'll get lucky again."

"We're on the way," Daniel replied, and threw the car into gear. "It had to be the Harpes, didn't it?"

"I'd say so. It sure sounds like them. Which one do you think was doing the fighting?"

"Hard to say. It could have been either one. Probably Micajah, though. Best I can tell he's overdue for a kill."

When they got to the park, there were still cops all over the place. The bodies had been zipped up in body bags, but were still lying all over the ground. The area had been roped off, and the cops weren't letting anyone cross the line.

There were three policemen standing by a huge tree questioning a man and a woman. The two had on jogging clothes and had probably been running in the park when they had witnessed the fight break out. Jake edged over as close as he could, but couldn't hear much of anything.

"Damnit, I don't know what to do," Jake growled. "There has to be a way to find them." Absent mindedly he scratched the back of his hand, and noticed the star had begun to bleed again. This time there were tiny needles of pain shooting through his hand. This was the first time it had done that since he'd left Mississippi.

"Hawk, I think I might have been wrong," Jake said excitedly. "Maybe the star will lead us to 'em after all. We're as close as I've been to Wiley in a good while, and the star is beginning to hurt like hell. Let's ride around and see what happens. I think I'll know when we find the right place."

He was right.

They had driven out of the park and started riding up and down the streets in each residential area they came to. When they turned down Oak Street, the needle-like pain became a steady ache, running halfway up his arm. They passed by a parked tractor-trailer, and as they pulled even with the next house, the pain grew even more intense.

"I think that's the house, Hawk," Jake said, pointing to the large old-fashioned white frame house. "Pull on down a little way and park. We'll see what we can find out."

Daniel drove about half a block down the street and pulled over to the curb. They were near enough to see anyone that came out of the house, but far enough away so they wouldn't be noticed. Unless they sat there too long, of course, and then someone on the street would surely be wondering what they were doing.

Jake thought for a moment and then got out and raised the car hood. If anyone asked, they'd say the car had overheated and they had to wait until it cooled off before it would start again.

As soon as it was full dark, Hawk started the car and drove around the block, this time stopping closer to the parked transfer truck. Both men got out and walked past the house, hoping to catch a glimpse of someone inside, but every window had mini-blinds and they were all lowered and closed.

"We're gonna have to sneak up on the house, Jake," Hawk said. "We can't see a thing from the street."

"Yeah, but we've got to be careful. If this is the wrong house we'll find our butts in jail."

"Son, if it turns out to be the right house, we'll probably wish we were in jail."

Jake laughed. "That's for sure," he said. "But I'm ready to get this whole thing over with. I just want to kill that sumbitch and get my tired self back to Mississippi. If I manage to get out of this in one piece, I'll be as happy as a catfish in a mudhole. Look, when we get to that hedge on the side of the house, drop to your knees and start crawling. Try to stay in the darker shadows. We've got to get a look in the window one way or another."

Hawk dropped to his knees and scooted down along the hedge as fast as he could, and Jake was quick to follow his lead. They got lucky.

The hedge led all the way to the house, and as long as they stayed low, they couldn't be seen from the house or from the street.

Hawk slipped over to the house, squatted beneath a window, and motioned for Jake to move to the next window. The room Hawk peeked into was dark, and he couldn't make out anything at all, but there was a night light on in the room where Jake stopped to look, and he could see a baby asleep on the bed.

"I don't know Hawk. There's a baby in there. We may have the wrong house after all."

"Not a chance, Jake, not a chance. Slip over here and take a look at what I see." Hawk was whispering, but there was no mistaking the excitement in his voice.

When Jake looked in the window, he let out a gasp that sounded loud enough to be heard in the next county.

"Hot damn, Hawk, it's them," he said in a course voice. "That's Wiley sitting in the recliner."

"Yeah, and that's Big Harpe, kicked back on the couch. Ain't no way to mistake him."

"Son, you were right, that's for damned sure. Compared to him, Wiley does almost look like a Sunday school teacher. How are we gonna fight that monster. He'll eat our lunch like we were baloney and crackers."

"Well, like you told me a while ago, Son, if you don't want to fight, take your redneck, peckerwood butt back to Mississippi. I'll fight both of 'em by myself."

"Nah, I guess I'll stick around, Injun. It might be fun to watch old Big Harpe scalp the hell out of you."

"Yeah, well, just hide and watch, son, just hide and watch."

In spite of their levity, both men knew they had a hell of a fight on their hands, and they both knew that neither of them would back down.

When they got back to the car, they decided now that they had found their quarry, they had better come with some kind of a plan to catch them. Right now, they had no idea at all what they were going to do, and any kind of plan beat no plan at all.

Daniel had the tomahawk, and he hoped when the fight started he'd get a little help from it's magic. And maybe a little help from the spirit world as well. But he knew he couldn't count on that.

Jake had the .357 magnum and the 30.06 hunting rifle, and for some reason he'd brought along the rope and the lighter fluid. He had a rough plan in mind he thought might work, if they could only set it up right. As he sat there thinking, suddenly the big tractor trailer came into focus, and another segment of the plan presented itself.

"That's it," he exclaimed. "I got it Hawk. I know how to beat that sumbitch. Listen to this."

He started talking low and quick, explaining the details of his plan to the incredulous Daniel Hawk.

After Jake finished his explanation, Hawk looked at him as though he were crazy.

"That's as stupid as anything I've ever heard. That won't work."

"You got a better idea, Injun," Jake answered.

Hawk considered for a moment.

"Naw, can't say as I have," Hawk admitted.

"Well, you just figure out a way to get that damn truck running and keep it running," Jake said.

"I'll get the truck running, alright, but don't expect me to drive the damn thing very far away. I'm gonna be right here when this fight gets finished."

"You won't have to drive very far. It'll just take a couple of blocks and he'll be dead. It'll work, dammnit, I know it will."

"I hope so, Kemosabe, I hope so. It'll be the only chance we have." Hawk was not quite as sure as Jake about the plan.

"Do I look like the damn Lone Ranger to you, you ignorant red savage? Don't give me that 'Kemosabe' crap."

Hawk studied Jake for a long second before he answered. "All white eyes look alike to Injun, you dumb peckerwood. Don't you know that?"

Both men had another short laugh before they settled down to wait for the right time. It might be the last time either of them had a chance to joke about anything.

JOHN BOLLINGER

THE LAST DAY

The hours slipped by, and Hawk and Jake took turns getting a little sleep. They'd need to be as fresh and rested as they could be when the crap hit the fan later that night.

At twenty-five after two, Jake nudged Hawk awake. "We got company," he whispered in a strained voice.

"What? Where? What do you mean, we got company?" Hawk asked.

"Look over by the truck. A guy just crawled under the truck. You can just barely see him from here."

Hawk strained his eyes, but it was several moments before he could make out the figure of the person lying in the shadows under the front wheels of the big truck.

"I see him. Who do you think it is? One of the Harpes?"

"No way it's one of them. First, no one came out of the house, and second, what the hell would one of them be doing crawling under the truck. It's us that's trying to keep from being seen, not them."

"Yeah, well, you got a point there. And it couldn't be the cops either."

"Naw, it's not the cops. It's somebody else. When I say go, we'll open both doors. I'll pretend to take a leak, while you sneak around the truck and grab the sumbitch. But don't make any more noise than you have to, we don't want to wake up anybody, especially the Harpes."

"1...2...3...Go."

Both car doors opened at the same time and as Jake got out on one side, Hawk slipped out the other. Jake stood by the side of the car and pretended to unzip his jeans, as Hawk slid into the darkness beside the truck. It only took a couple of seconds before Jake heard Daniel struggling with someone. As quietly as he could, Jake ran over to the truck to help out.

"Shhh...be quiet, damnit," he whispered, but Hawk was too busy trying to hold on to the stranger to make a reply.

Jake quickly flopped down and rolled under the truck. In the darkness he couldn't tell which man to grab, so he wrapped his arms around both men and hung on for dear life.

"Hold on a minute, damn it, just hold on one damned minute," the stranger whispered. "What the hell do you think you're trying to do?"

"That's what we want to know about you, feller," Jake whispered back. "Exactly what do you think you're doing?"

"Well, it ain't a lot of your business, but I think there's a couple of men in that house I've been looking for," the stranger replied.

"Then I guess you might as well join the crowd. Mind telling me just who the people you're looking for might be?" Jake was starting to suspect he and Hawk weren't the only ones looking for the Harpes.

"If you two rambos will let me up, we might talk about it. Unless, of course, you enjoy laying in the dirt under a damned transfer truck, feeling of my cute little butt."

"OK, get up Bubba, but do it real slow. If you try anything, anything at all, you're gonna have a hole in you big enough to drive this Freightliner through. We ain't playing no games here, and we ain't got time for anybody that is. The guys in that house are more than likely the two most dangerous murderers that ever walked the face of the earth, and if you're looking for them, then you're as crazy as we are."

Somehow Jake knew the man was telling the truth.

The three of them rolled out from under the truck and stood up, careful to keep in the deeper shadows. The only light was from a pale yellow street light half way down the block, and in it's wan amber glow the third man stuck out his hand.

"I'm looking for two murdering psychos that call themselves Harpe," he said. "I'm a cop from Nashville, name's John Bollinger."

At about twenty till four, Tom Slaughter walked out of his house and down the drive to his truck. He had to roll out in about an hour, and the big diesel engine needed to warm up for a while first. He noticed the car parked across the street with three men inside, and started to go over and find out what the hell they were doing, but he still had a lot to do before he pulled out, and the men didn't seem to be hurting anything. They were probably just sleeping off a little too much to drink, or they had had some car trouble. Either way, if they were still there when he left, he'd check it out.

EMILY

THE LAST DAY

Tom hadn't been back inside his house over ten minutes before Emily came creeping out of the side door of her house and began to make her way down the street. It was plain she didn't want anyone to see her from the way she kept to the shadows and looked over her shoulder several times a minute. She disappeared around the corner in a couple of minutes, without stopping for anything. The worst about her leaving was that she was too good at it. She managed to be

315

so secretive that even the three men in the car didn't see her. If they had, it might have saved her life.

HAWK - TRABUE - BOLLINGER

THE LAST DAY

The three men in the car watched as the man walked down to the truck and started the engine.

"Boy, that'll save us some trouble," Hawk remarked, when he heard the big engine come thundering to life. "Now I won't have to hot wire the damn thing."

They had explained the plan to Bollinger, and even though he wasn't sure it would work, he hadn't been able to come up with anything better either.

"Tell me the truth, boys," Bollinger said, "what kind of chance do you think we've got against the Harpes? I've traveled over a hundred miles with Little Harpe, and I know he's mean as hell. I watched Big Harpe, all by his damn lonesome, totally wipe out a handful of the meanest bikers I've ever seen. I don't know about y'all, but if we can't shoot them before they see us coming, I think we've got about as much chance as a plastic fly in hell."

Jake was the first to answer.

"Yeah, well I've also seen firsthand what Wiley can do, and I guess I agree with you, Bollinger. But maybe we can outsmart 'em. I hope so, cause I sure ain't looking forward to going at 'em in hand to hand combat. Damnit guys, if we're hell bent on committing suicide, why don't we just stand out in the middle of I-65 and let a concrete truck run over us. We'd probably get about the same result."

"Well, you two can do whatever you want to, but I'm fighting them," Hawk said. "I'll hit big Harpe so hard with this tomahawk he'll wish he'd never come back from the dead. I'll send him back to whatever hell he came from."

"Yeah, well, if you say so, son, if you say so. We'll be finding out pretty soon, won't we?"

MICAJAH AND WILEY

THE LAST DAY

If Micajah and Wiley hadn't have been so tired, they probably would have sensed the men lurking around outside the house. But as it was, the first they knew of it was when something crashed through the window and hit Micajah on the leg as he lay on the couch. He was fully awake before the broken glass had settled to the floor.

"Wiley, in here," Micajah called, "looks like we've been found."

Wiley was already staring out the window.

"Just one of them, Micajah, standing on the walk. See him?"

"Trying to get one of us to step outside, more than likely. Or both of us. You can bet there are more than just the one we see. Soon as we get close to the door, sure as hell they'll start shooting. Stay low, brother, and go out through the basement door. There's a car parked across the street, and it's good bet it belongs to whoever's after us. You circle around behind the car and stop the shooters. I'll take care of the one on the walk. Ready? Go."

Micajah didn't wait to see if Wiley was moving, he knew he was. Wiley was headed for the basement before Micajah had stopped talking.

Micajah eased over to stand by the front door, and called to the man standing in the drive.

"What do you want, feller," he yelled? He was immediately rewarded by a high powered shot blasting through the door.

I'm not that stupid, he thought to himself, and just then another round plowed directly through the wall, not two inches from his head.

Damn, for a minute there I forgot where I was. I never had a gun in my life that would shoot through a wall.

He dropped to the floor and crawled to the other side of the room just as yet another shot blew a hole in the wall, and blasted a picture of an old man off the opposite wall.

"Come on out, Harpe," a loud voice called. "If you're so big and bad, come on out and fight me. This is Daniel Hawk. Remember me? I've got your damned tomahawk. Why don't you just come on out and get it."

Harpe remembered Daniel Hawk all right, and he wanted the tomahawk.

"I'll be out, Indian, you can bet on it. Just as soon as the shooter runs out of bullets."

"Naw, Harpe, you'll be out before that. It won't be long before the law gets here. Somebody will report the shots, and they'll get here pretty fast. If you want the tomahawk, you'll have to get in a damn hurry."

Harpe knew Daniel Hawk was right. It wouldn't take long for the police to arrive. But then again, it wouldn't take Wiley long to take care of whoever was doing the shooting. And the guys outside didn't know Wiley was already out there.

WILEY

THE LAST DAY

Sure enough, Wiley was already at the car. He had gotten out of the basement door and around the house without anyone seeing him, and he used the shadows of the hedge the same way Jake and Hawk had used them earlier, except he was going in the opposite direction.

He reached the car and saw a man leaning across the hood, a big heavy caliber hunting rifle in his hands.

Without a word, Wiley grabbed the shooter by the neck. With a great heave he threw him backward, forcing him to drop the rifle. Wiley bent to retrieve the gun, and when he straightened up, he felt something fall around his neck. Dropping the gun, he reached up with both hands and discovered it was a rope that had struck him. Before he could slip it off, it began to tighten, catching one hand inside the loop.

Suddenly he heard the powerful engine begin to rev up, and the gears growled as someone let the clutch out. The rope tightened with a jerk, and Wiley was violently pulled from his feet. Wiley found himself being dragged along behind the truck, and as it built up speed, the rough pavement began to shred the skin from his elbows and hands. As he was dragged past the man he had fought with, he saw the widely grinning face of Jake Trabue, and recognized him from the little bar in Mississippi.

Wiley tried to scream something at Jake, but the rope wouldn't let him talk. He was being hung, just as surely as he'd been hung in 1804.

Jake watched as the rope tightened and saw Wiley being dragged down the street, but he was taking no chances. Grabbing the opened can of lighter fluid, he ran along beside the man and squirted the volatile liquid all over him. The truck shifted gears and was gaining speed, and still Jake ran along beside it, shouting oaths at Wiley, and squirting him with more and more lighter fluid, until the big can was completely empty.

The last thing Wiley heard was Jake as he yelled;

"This Zippo lighter belonged to my buddy Cooper, the one you killed. I thought you might like to have it."

Jake struck the flint and then struck it again before the lighter burst into life with a bright red/orange flame. Jake was still running as he threw the lighter and watched it hit the fluid soaked body of Wiley. His clothing and skin instantly ignited, and he was flipped head over heels as the mighty truck gathered even more speed.

Jake had stopped on the sidewalk and stood there, his chest was heaving from the exertion, and hot tears streamed from his eyes. His laughter was wild and maniacal, coming from a mixture of fear and relief. He dropped to his knees and knelt there watching as the truck roared down the street.

From the walk where he stood, Daniel Hawk saw the body burst into flames and knew Jake's plan had worked.

It was simple, really. Daniel shouted at the house from the walk as Jake fired the shots from the hood of the car. Bollinger remained hidden in the darkness beside the truck, expecting one of the Harpes to come out. When Wiley showed and grabbed Jake from behind, Bollinger threw the rope around his neck, then jumped in the truck and took off.

It had worked to perfection.

Jake had placed the open can of lighter fluid alongside the curb, where he could grab it as he passed.

The only thing they had forgotten was that they were dealing with a supernatural being. It was entirely possible the rope would burn faster than the skin of a Wolf-demon. A mis-calculation could spell disaster.

God help them all if Wiley lived.

Hawk turned back to the house and saw Micajah was now standing outside the house on the walk, much too close for comfort. The big Harpe was staring at the truck as it rolled headlong down the street, and at the flaming body of his brother being dragged along behind the rampaging vehicle.

THE FINAL BATTLE

"Wiley..." Micajah screamed. "Wiley..." As he saw the blazing body of his brother being dragged along the asphalt behind the huge truck. "Wiley," he called once again, and then turned his full fury to face Daniel Hawk.

Hawk suddenly found himself looking full in the face of the wild Wolf, and in that instant he knew he could not win.

The blue eyes were raging. The flames were alive and almost hot enough to raise blisters on Hawk's face. From deep in the flames, this time even Hawk could hear the awful voice of the DarkWolf as it spoke to Micajah.

I hunger Harpe, I hunger. Thisssss... isssss... foooooood...

And he heard Harpe answer.

"Food? Yes. But this time Wolf, the Harpe also hungers. This time I will feed first."

With those words Harpe turned the fury of the dancing flames against Daniel Hawk, and now they were a physical thing, as real as any flames Hawk had ever felt. And there was no way Hawk could fight the terrible heat.

No way, except maybe...

Without thinking, Hawk raised the tomahawk before his face and braced himself for the onslaught. To his surprise he found the weapon deflected the worst of the heat. Turning the tomahawk to and fro, he used all of his strength to make a charge at Harpe. With an oath screaming from his dry lips, he swung the weapon of his ancestor around with all his strength, chopping at the breast of Harpe. The suddenness of the blow caught Harpe unaware, and the tomahawk landed squarely in the middle of his chest, cutting through flesh and breaking bone.

Daniel Hawk stood stunned; unable to believe he had actually hit the big man. In shock he watched as Harpe slumped to the ground.

Harpe didn't make a sound. He looked at the wound, and slowly sank to his knees. In a moment he raised his head to the first light of dawn, stretched open his arms, and clenched his fists. After several long moments of silence, finally two words escaped his lips.

"The Amulet."

Barely loud enough to hear were the words spoken.

Daniel Hawk, Jake Trabue, and John Bollinger stood in the yard, thinking the fight was over as they watched Harpe take what they thought would be his last breath. They watched as Bethany ran from the house, the baby in her arms. They saw her run to the fallen Harpe, and they could see an object in her hand, but they had no idea what it was. They should have looked closer.

Bethany knelt beside Micajah and sat the baby down on the grass. She opened her hand and the object she held caught the rays of the morning sun, shining for a moment like the star it was called.

She held the Harpe Amulet. As the rays from the sun bounced from it's silver surface, the dancing light fell upon Harpe's face, and he opened his eyes.

He looked at Bethany.

"Put the Amulet around my neck, Susan," he whispered, and the eyes closed again.

Without a word Bethany did as Harpe had instructed. He had called her Susan, not Suzanne, and somehow the name seemed to fit. Quickly she shook loose the leather thong and looped the cord around Micajah's neck. As soon as the star touched his chest, a smile played across his lips.

It all happened too fast for the three men to stop. One minute Harpe was lying there, eyes closed, obviously dying, and then in an instant, his eyes opened again. The flame that had begun to die suddenly flickered and began to roar back to life, still weaker than before the tomahawk blow, but growing stronger even as the two men watched.

Harpe's big hand came up and touched the gaping wound, pressing the edges together, and the men gasped as they saw the edges stay where he placed them.

The blood stopped flowing, and the crushed chest heaved and filled with air.

Even as they watched, the wound healed itself.

Harpe brought himself to one knee, then the other, and in another second the outlaw was once again on his feet, a little unsteady, but certainly not dying.

The wild blue eyes swept over each person standing there watching him, and each felt the awful intensity as though it were a real thing.

"I am the Harpe."

Not much more than a whisper.

"I am the Harpe."

Louder now.

"I am the Harpe. The DarkWolf. Your Death and Destruction."

These words were flung from his mouth in a shout.

"I am the Harpe."

This time at full strength.

"I am the Harpe."

Suddenly a voice answered.

It was a voice Harpe knew well.

"Yeah you're the Harpe alright, but now you have to fight me," the voice said. It came from the other side of the yard.

Hawk, Trabue, and Bollinger all turned and looked in the direction of the voice. None of them had seen nor heard anyone approach.

Harpe also looked, and he was the only one not taken by surprise.

Andrew Stegall stood in the yard, Emily held in front of his body like a living shield.

His thin, bony hand held the long knife of Harpe to her throat. He stared at Harpe and then without a word or even a threat, Stegall drew the knife across Emily's neck. Blood gushed like a river, washing across Stegall's hands, and running down his forearm.

Bethany screamed. A long, loud scream that pierced the stillness of the dawn.

Hawk, Trabue, and Bollinger stood as if frozen by the act, still unable to move. None of them had ever encountered an act of such terrible ferocity and violence before. They couldn't believe their eyes, especially Daniel Hawk. He had thought he knew the old man, and didn't think him capable of such a thing.

As the others stood staring in disbelief, the Harpe laughed.

"I've waited long for this moment Stegall. There was no call to slaughter the woman, she meant nothing to me. But then, your family was always that way. Killing the helpless and the wounded, and those that could not fight back. Look at me Stegall, look closely. This time I'm not wounded, nor am I held by a dozen men. Look at me, Stegall, I am your death. I am your destruction."

But something was happening to Andrew Stegall.

As Emily's blood flowed across his hands and arms, its touch was causing Stegall's flesh to grow firmer. Where there was sagging skin, muscles were forming. Harpe watched in wonder as the old man's bent back began to straighten, and the thin white hair started turning darker and thicker. The old man grew taller and broader, and the years began to melt away. It wasn't possible, but Stegall was growing younger before their eyes.

The buttons on the shirt popped, and the skin beneath had lost its pallor. His chest was suddenly tanned, showing no signs of age. His mouth was bleeding, and the reason was soon apparent. New teeth were growing where none had been for years. Through the blood he flashed a gleaming white smile at Harpe.

The transformation was complete in less than two minutes, and was so intense that none, not even Harpe, thought to strike at the man as he changed.

When the transformation was complete, only by looking into his eyes could you see his true age. The eyes betrayed him. They left no doubt that the man was ancient, and it was plain they had looked upon scenes not meant for mortal man to see.

Harpe stood still, staring at the man who faced him.

"Moses Stegall. It's really you, isn't it? Good. I had looked forward to killing the old man, but this is better, much better. I will enjoy taking your life even more."

Moses laughed. "It remains to be seen who will kill who, old friend. I still have the blade I once used to cut off your damned head."

"Do you Moses? Are you sure which blade you hold? Even so, on your best day, you were never a match for the Harpe, and you know it."

Harpe's eyes were glowing and there was a trace of a smile on his face as he spoke.

Floating above the silence came the gentle humming of Susan's song.

"We'll see, Micajah, we'll see. I believe you're afraid of the knife. You now what it can do, and you're afraid of it."

"No, Moses, I'm not afraid of the knife. It belongs to me, remember? What's past is past, and besides, the knife you hold is not the knife you used before. I have that knife. The blade in your hand is its twin."

"What? That can't be. This is the knife, I know it." But when he looked as the blade he held, he wasn't sure, and in that moment of indecision Harpe struck.

In his hand, Harpe held the other of the twin blades. Regardless of which one it was, it was still one of the most awesome killing blades ever crafted. With a savage overhand throw, the Harpe loosed the blade, and it arched through the air toward his old friend. The knife whistled slightly as it flashed through the air, and vibrated with a ringing throbbing sound as it buried itself in the breast of Moses Stegall. With a violent effort, Stegall hurled the knife he held, and it turned end over end in the air as it flew toward Harpe. With a motion that looked slow, Harpe deftly reached out his right hand and caught the gleaming blade in mid-air. With a smile, he walked over to where Moses lay on the grass.

But Moses wasn't finished.

To his own surprise, he found that although the knife wound hurt, it wasn't a mortal wound. In fact, the injury didn't affect him the way it should have. The bleeding had already slowed to a mere trickle, and the pain was almost gone. With a twisted sneer on his lips, Stegall gripped the handle of the knife with his right hand, and laughed as he withdrew the blade from his chest.

"What think you now, Big Harpe? Can you now see that Moses Stegall is a man to be reckoned with?" Moses said, courage returning to his voice as he found himself unhurt.

"No Moses. I see a chicken thief and a man that betrayed his only friends to save his own neck. I see a man that sent raiders to burn a cabin, killing a child that was precious to all of us, including yourself. I see a man that stalked a battlefield, killing wounded men who were unable to fight back. Not a man to be reckoned with at all.

I don't even see a man, Stegall, I see a dog. A mad dog that should have been left to hang for eating stolen chickens. It was me who saved you that day, Moses, remember? And it will be me who takes your worthless life today. Today, Stegall, you will feed the DarkWolf."

With the mention of the DarkWolf, the fear returned to Stegall's face. He had seen the Harpes turn the Wolf loose too many times, and had heard the dying screams of dozens of souls as they became victims of the terrible hunger. With an oath, he flung himself across the few feet that separated him and Micajah, and locked both arms around the waist of Harpe, driving him backward into the three men who had stood and watched. With each twist of his body, he brought the knife around, not caring who he cut.

It was this act that brought the others out of the state of shock, and they suddenly realized it was time for them to act, if they intended to act at all.

They all leaped on Harpe.

Jake Trabue grabbed Harpe around the neck, as Daniel Hawk tried to capture his feet. John Bollinger piled on top of the others, and found himself staring into the cold blue flame of the DarkWolf's eyes.

Bollinger turned his head, unable to stand the ferocity of the gaze, and shouted to the others. "Don't turn loose. What ever you do, don't turn loose." But it was advice easier given than carried out.

Harpe tensed the muscles in his right arm, and flung Jacob Trabue head over heels into the street. With a grunt, he grasped Hawk by the hair and pried his head backward, until Hawk was forced to either turn loose of Harpe's ankles, or risk getting his own neck broken. Micajah slammed Hawk's head into the ground face first, and then turned his attention to John Bollinger.

"I let you live back in the park mister. Is this how you repay that kindness?"

"Wiley was right, Harpe, when he said I don't know how to quit. I can't stop as long as you're still loose. You should have killed me when you had the chance." Bollinger was out of breath, and the words came rushing out as he tried to maintain his hold on Harpe.

"It ain't too late for that feller, not yet," Micajah said, and pulled the Nashville cop into the path of Stegall's knife as the man once again brought it around in a savage slash.

The knife struck Bollinger under his right arm and plunged into his shoulder. With a mighty jerk, Stegall wrenched the knife free from Bollinger's body. Bollinger wouldn't die, but he'd feel the sting of the blade in his nightmares for the rest of his life.

Moses rose to his knees and looked at Harpe. The fear was still in his eyes, but now there was a raging fury there as well. With a move as quick as a striking rattlesnake, Moses brought the point of the blade down into Harpe's shoulder. Seeing blood spurt, he raised the knife again, and again stabbed downward. This time the knife struck Harpe in the left side. Stegall pulled the knife sideways, feeling it slice across Harpe's side, and felt the man's warm blood on his hand.

With a snarl, Stegall raised the knife to the back of Harpe's neck, intending to repeat what had happened two hundred years earlier. Suddenly, he found himself face to face not with Micajah Harpe, but with the DarkWolf.

"You're a rough butcher, Stigall, but cut on and be damned." The DarkWolf growled.

This time a reply came from Micajah Harpe himself.

"I told you Wolf, this one is mine. The Harpe also hungers. And he would feed on the soul of Moses Stegall."

In a motion faster than the eye could follow, Harpe rolled sideways and then brought his own blade around and across the neck of Moses Stegall. Blood gushed out and spattered on both men and on the ground, and on the other three men who still lay where they had fallen. Harpe slashed again, back across the neck, cutting deeper and deeper. Rising to his feet, Harpe took Stegall by his hair and held his head backward, and completed his cut around the neck. As Stegall stared up at him, Harpe slowly drew the knife around the neck, feeling it grate on bone. He cut around the base of the neck, and through the large muscles, finally severing the top of the spine.

Harpe laid the blade on the grass, and grasped Moses Stegall's head with both hands. With a hard twisting motion, he tore the head loose from the body as though the man were a fattened pig. He held the head high, and brought himself to his feet. He stood staring in the direction where he had last seen Wiley, and shook the head in the air.

"Wiley." Micajah screamed into the morning air. "Wiley. Stegall is dead. Our betrayer is no more." With these words he flung the head across the yard toward a tree. The little grin found its way to his lips as he saw the head wedge itself into a fork in the tree. The eyes were open and staring, and the mouth was frozen as though it were screaming. Truly, perhaps Moses Stegall was screaming, in whatever hell he was in now.

"It still ain't over Harpe, not yet."

Micajah turned and saw Daniel Hawk was back on his feet. His nose was bloody, and one eye was swelled almost shut, but the boy had the tomahawk in his right hand, and was ready to resume the fight.

"The ax didn't do you a hell of a lot of good a while ago, young Hawk, what makes you think it will serve you any better now?"

"Because now I've got some help, you son-of-a-bitch." Hawk was shouting as he began to tear open the medicine bag that hung around his neck.

Dense smoke and fog began to roll out of the medicine bag. High the smoke rose, and higher still, and slowly began to take form. Harpe stood dumbfounded, unable to believe his eyes.

On giant wings of mist, high in the morning sky the Spirit Eagle soared. Swooping and dipping in the air, dancing on the currents flew the great bird. Then with a shrill cry, he dove toward the ground.

Gathering speed he dropped toward Harpe with the sound of a hundred jet planes, his razor sharp talons fully extended. Faster, ever faster he plunged downward, till suddenly he spread his wings and slowed himself, opening and closing his talons as though he were already ripping and tearing at Harpe's flesh. He dropped closer and closer still, until he was almost upon his mesmerized prey.

Suddenly, in the instant before the Eagle struck, the DarkWolf appeared.

From the time the amulet had been placed around Micajah's neck, the star had been softly glowing, and now from the midst of that glow, a gateway appeared in the yard. The gateway that linked the world of man to the ancient world of the animal spirits.

The DarkWolf stormed and raged through the gate directly into the path of the Eagle, and howled his savage battle cry, causing the world to tremble.

Larger he grew, and larger still, and more savage with each second. The beast braced himself for the Eagle's onslaught, his great fangs snapping at the air. Wild blue flames shot from his eyes, and he leaped high to meet the Eagle among the clouds.

The Eagle's mighty talons closed in the fur of the DarkWolf's chest, and the Eagle beat the air with his wings, and shook the DarkWolf as though he were a lamb.

But this lamb had teeth, large razor sharp teeth, and a mighty hunger for the taste of the Eagle.

The DarkWolf twisted his head, and his fangs ripped at the leg of the Eagle, causing him to partially release his hold upon the DarkWolf's fur.

Again the Eagle beat the air with his wings, and clawed his way skyward. Only in the heavens would he stand a chance of defeating the DarkWolf.

With a roar, the DarkWolf bit at the Eagle's other leg, and feathers became bloody as his teeth grinded against the bone. With a scream, the Eagle ripped his talons loose from the DarkWolf, and once again his wings beat heavenward.

The Eagle circled in the sky, his eyes never leaving the DarkWolf as the DarkWolf dropped to the ground. The DarkWolf roared, and leapt among the humans, once again becoming his true self, and his true size. He snarled as he came to a stop in front of Harpe.

With an oath, the DarkWolf spoke to Micajah.

"We are old, Harpe, you and I," the DarkWolf said. *"Father and son are we. One and the same are we. And we both hunger. I can no longer stay on this world, Harpe, not when you choose to feed yourself first. I must go, and the Eagle shall follow. He cannot live in this world, any more than can I. Farewell to you then, Harpe, for now. Make no mistake, we shall meet again. You will need the DarkWolf, Harpe, you will need me. In spite of everything that has happened between us, when the time comes that you need me by your side, all you have to do is call upon the Amulet."*

The DarkWolf looked around the yard and his blue eyes came to rest upon the child Bethany held in her arms. Frantically she tried to cover him from the DarkWolf's terrible gaze.

"That is a first born Harpe child woman. He belongs to me."

Micajah leaped toward the girl and the child. The DarkWolf must not gain the baby. The power that would be unleashed would be great enough to destroy both worlds.

As fast as Micajah was, the DarkWolf was faster.

The DarkWolf leaped across the yard and stripped the child from Bethany's arms, and then, before any of them could react, he flung himself through the rapidly closing gate that was already beginning to close.

Harpe looked at Daniel Hawk.

"There is another gate to the DarkWolf world in the spirit cave at Nickajack. The tomahawk has much greater powers there than here our world. There are three of you, and I feel that human kind will need every warrior that will fight to do so. The fate of two worlds may well lie in our being able to recover the child from the Wolf. Follow if you will, but I must go now. I will not leave the child unprotected and alone with the DarkWolf. If Wiley is truly dead, and you find his body, give it and the body of Stegall to the police and tell them nothing more. Let it end here. The Harpe is no longer of this world, and it would serve you little to try to explain the truth to anyone who has not seen firsthand what has happened."

Turning to Bethany, the Harpe spoke one last time;

"Do you wish to go with me girl," he said, and extended his hand to her.

Bethany looked at the DarkWolf as he disappeared with her child. Without a word, she took Micajah's hand, and the two of them stepped through the gate, just as the Eagle swooped down and through it himself. The smoke and mist swirled upward and away, and the Harpe and the girl were gone.

A tiny whisper floated out from the gate, and across Daniel Hawk's soul. He heard the haunting melody of Harpe once again, and the final words of the DarkWolf.

I hungerrrr Harrrrpe. Follow if you dare

The answer whispered back.

Well do I know your hunger, DarkWolf, but lest ye forget, I am the Harpe. Cut on and be damned.

ABOUT E. DON HARPE

Award winning author *E. DON HARPE* has had a varied career, from military service in the 60's to years spent as an industrial engineer for a major appliance firm. Harpe is a songwriter who has had many of his songs recorded, and who for years ran his own music publishing company. While in Nashville Harpe was the office manager of a publishing company that had several number one country music hits, and was also the Creative Director for Climbing Country, one of the most successful syndicated radio programs of the early 90's. During this time he won the coveted Silver Pen Award from the Nashville Banner daily newspaper.

Since retiring from public work in 2004, Harpe has concentrated on writing novels, and the next few years will see more of his works published. He also has nearly 40 short stories available on line, including two in an anthology called Twisted Tails II, published by Double Dragon Publishing, which won the EPPIE AWARD for best science fiction anthology of 2007.

His memoir, *THE LAST OF THE SOUTH TOWN RINKY DINKS*, published in September of 2008, was an instant success with friends and readers alike. The stories are touching, down to earth tales of small town America, and will bring tears and laughter to all who can remember when the world was a kinder, simpler place. It's the kind of book that you won't want to put down, and one that you will re-read many times over the years.

Now retired and living in the foothills of the Smoky Mountains in North Georgia, Harpe devotes his time to Helen, his wife of over 50 years, to his children, grandchildren and great grandchildren, and to his writing.

"I'm pretty satisfied in my own skin right now," Harpe says, "and I just want to continue to write things that will entertain and hold the readers interest."

Connect with E. Don Harpe on the Internet at his website, as well as on Facebook and other social media.

My personal websites - http://www.donharpe.com/

And http://www.flintriverpress.com

Facebook - http://www.facebook.com/home.php?

Follow @Harpe on Twitter

ALSO BY E. DON HARPE

DARKWOLF UNLEASHED: BOOK ONE IN THE HARPE TRILOGY
THE LAST OF THE SOUTH TOWN RINKY DINKS
REDNECK UNIVERSE
MUSIC CITY MYTH
UNDER THE INFLUENCE OF A FULL MOON
SUNDOWN TWO with PHIL WHITLEY
JAGGED EDGE OF OTHER WHEN with EUGEN BACON
BOWLING BETTER: HOW TO RAISE YOUR AVERAGE

SHORT STORIES

THE HARPE'S LAST RAMPAGE
FIRE FROM HEAVEN
REDNECK RIVIERA - A REDNECK RIVIERA STORY
TALLEDEGA TWOSTEP - A REDNECK RIVIERA STORY
COTTONDALE CONFIRMATION - A REDNECK RIVIERA STORY
MUSIC CITY MOJO - A REDNECK RIVIERA STORY
STUBIAN SWAMPDEVILS - A REDNECK RIVIERA STORY
FLAMINGO FIASCO - A REDNECK RIVIERA STORY
REDNECK RASSLIN' - A REDNECK RIVIERA STORY
ANGEL IN AMBER
KILLING FROST
THE DEMON REGISTRATION ACT
CYPHONS
THE TROPICAL TABOO CAPER
MILLER'S LUCK
THE EDGE
THE SKY IS FALLING
WHAT GOES AROUND
THE BIG PICTURE
FEBRUARY
THE WEDDING HELMET
SLUGGER
THE FLAT ROCK KID

www.ingramcontent.com/pod-product-compliance
Lightning Source LLC
Chambersburg PA
CBHW050922030726
47503CB00007BB/2416